WARDENS OF THE WORLDS

THE CIRCLE OF VALSTAN

MARK DAVID LINDQUIST

First paperback edition 2021.
Living Pages Press, LLC
Maps by Sarah B. Lindquist

ISBN 978-1-7367165-0-2 (paperback)
ISBN 978-1-7367165-1-9 (ebook)

www.markdavidlindquist.com

CONTENTS

For Kristin, the one who always believed, always cheered, and always encouraged me to finish. For my eight daughters, Rachel, Elizabeth, Catherine, Sarah, Miriam, Susanna, Sophia, and Bethany who have dreamed this book into existence. To all of them, I am forever grateful.

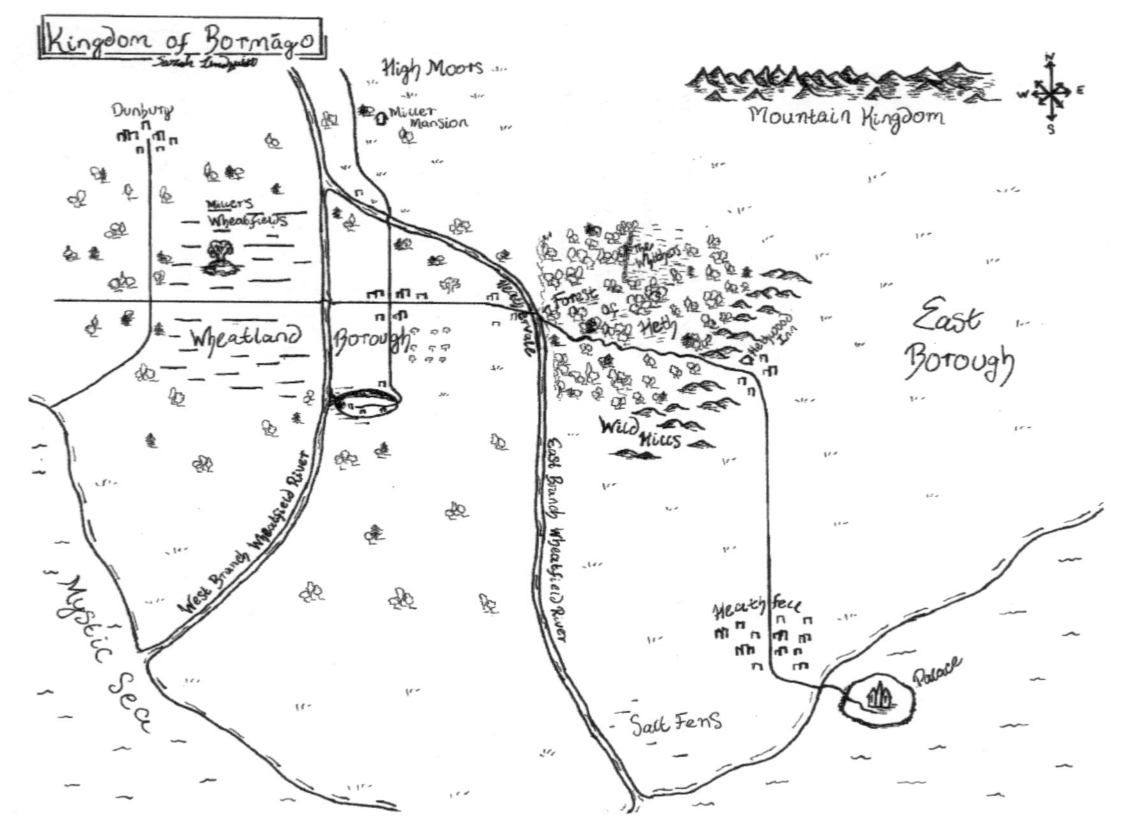

Kingdom of Botmãgo
Sarah Lindquist
High Moors
Dunbury
Miller Mansion
Miller's Wheatfields
Wheatland
Borough
Nethervale
Forest of Neth
The Whispers
Hollywood Inn
Mountain Kingdom
East Borough
Wild Hills
West Branch Wheatfield River
East Branch Wheatfield River
Mystic Sea
Heathfell
Salt Fens
Palace
N W E S

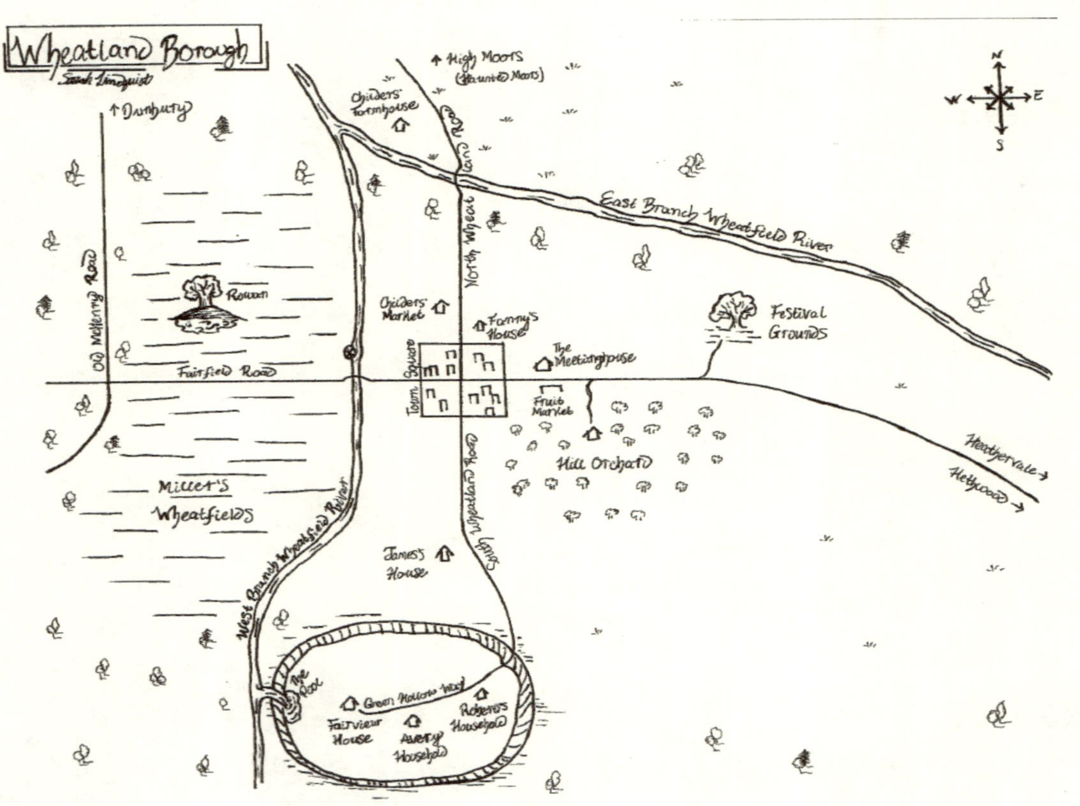

Wheatland Borough
Sarah Lindquist
↑ Danbury
↑ High Moors (Haunted Moors)
Childers' Farmhouse
Childers' Market
North Wheatland Road
East Branch Wheatfield River
Festival Grounds
Fanny's House
The Meetinghouse
Town Square
Fruit Market
Hill Orchard
Old Mettering Road
Rowan
Fairfield Road
Miller's Wheatfields
West Branch Wheatfield River
South Wheatland Road
James's House
Heathervale →
Hetywood →
The Pool
Green Hollow Wood
Fairview House
Avery Household
Rogers's Household
N W E S

CHAPTER 1

WHEN DREAMS BECOME NIGHTMARES

Golden lamplight bathes the back of my home. *No one there.* Mustiness saturates the air, layering gray mist into long sheets. I heard pathetic groans in my nightmare, but when I awoke, real ones whimpered from outside my window. If Mom catches me outdoors at night again, she'll think I'm up to mischief. "Jonathan Conrad Jackson, why do you test me so," she often says through clenched teeth as her gentle eyes flash flame red.

With urgency, I step to where we collect the household waste and hold the lamp over its gate. *Not a soul.* Stars spangle the heavens with a dying moon reaching the rocky brim of our hollow.

Air rushes from my lungs in frustration and I purse my lips. Another practical joke by my neighbor friend, Linus. No doubt he's hiding and laughing at my bedclothes, wanting to scare me enough to jump out of them. A grin crosses my face. This one is passable,

but nothing compares to mine from yesterday. He thinks a skunk died in their barn, but I found the carcass along the road and hid it where he'd never find it. His chores will be unbearable for days, so I congratulate my genius.

Check back by the waterfall pool, I tell myself. If I discover him out there, then I'll have dirt on him. In a war of wits, blackmail comes in handy. He knows it's off-limits to kids—he wouldn't dare. Would he? Long ago, my grandparents' tragic drowning ruined our exploring fun. Plus, it marred the innocence of Wheatland Town, where I live.

Funny, I don't see a soul or hear any strange noises out here, either. I've searched enough for one night, and later I'll have a busy start to the day. For now, back to bed.

I turn toward home. Leaves rustle behind me—a twig snaps and then another. Before I can face the sound, a leathery hand cups my mouth and nose. An arm thick as a tree limb bars my chest. *Not Linus!* I drop the lamp, throw an elbow—then the other—but they do nothing to the beefy mass holding me. I thrust my head backward, but it rebounds off a muscled body. My smothered yells become panicked gasps. I stomp at his enormous feet. *Air . . .* My heartbeat thumps in my eardrums. *Have to . . . hold on.* Darkness edges my vision.

Before I go limp from lack of air, I flail my arms in desperation. My left hand grazes his face.

"It burns," he grunts.

What burns?

A knife pushes into my Adam's apple. "Quiet, I won't kill you," says an accented voice, reeking with the unholy smell of tobacco and old fish.

I relax, so his grip loosens. Brawny limbs turn me around to meet him. A bearded man stares back at me. I've seen his people before, in books and on posters hanging in the town square. From his enormous size and dark features, he descended from the T'Anakim race, our mortal enemies to the south.

He glides a hand across his cheek. "Are you a sorcerer, boy?"

"A what? No."

Deep-set eyes say he knows better. Then his pained gaze drops to his leg. Blood oozes from it, soaking his shredded trousers. My stomach teeters on the verge of retching.

His breathing becomes shallow and rapid, then he glances at the knife. "Forgive me . . . didn't see the cliff into this hollow and fell . . . hit my head, and gashed my leg." Beneath his tangled black hair, blood streaks across his forehead.

Judging by the two wounds, he's lost much blood. No way could my slight frame match his powerful one. Still, a brisk wind could knock him to the ground. He totters, drops the knife, and collapses to a knee. In a desperate fit, he digs through his pocket. *He'll kill me for sure.*

He grabs my sleeve, pushes a coin purse into my hand, and closes my fingers. "Water . . . and medicine. Asylum here . . ."

My jaw clenches, and an angry fire burns in my gut. *The swine pulled a knife on me.* But my wall of icy defense melts. *I'd do the same if I wanted to defect to my enemies.* Conflict battles within me—revulsion or pity. The scale tips. "Okay, I'll help."

He pats my hand. "Wheatlanders are good folk."

I offer a slight smile. *The man doesn't know we've had run-ins with our king.* "Wait here."

Weak, he sprawls on the ground.

I grab the lamp and dash next door to Linus's younger sister Rebecca's bedroom. Moonlight can't break through the thick tree canopy overhead. After fumbling around the dirt for tiny stones, I find a few and toss them at her window. A dim light grows bright. Curtains slide, and the window creaks open. A golden-blonde head with a long braid draped across the shoulder peers outward.

"Locked out again, Linus?" she says through a yawn.

"It's me, Rebecca, Jonathan. Sorry to wake you." *Respectful manners work best with her.*

She rubs her eyes and says, "What's the time?"

"Late. Please get dressed and come with me."

Her eyelids narrow. "This isn't a stupid prank, is it?"

"A wounded man could die if no one helps him. There's blood . . . lots of it." The sick feeling seeps back into my stomach. "You're the finest healer in Wheatland."

"Flattery won't work." Her pale face glows next to the golden lamplight, baby-blue eyes look skeptical.

"Trust me just this once."

She lets out a metered breath, and raising a warning finger, says, "Okay, but I better not regret this." The curtains snap shut.

Within moments, Rebecca slides through her bedroom window in a fluid motion. When she drops to the moist earth, she combs through her satchel. "I need your lamp, please." I give it to her, but she fumbles it. "Ouch, lower the flame!"

I turn back the wick, which dims the light somewhat. "I needed it as bright as possible."

She stares at me, hand shaking out the pain. "How can you hold the handle?"

A witty reply doesn't come to mind. I have no clue why hot things have no effect on me. In the kitchen, I use oven mitts to keep up an appearance, but I don't need them. Otherwise, my twin, David, calls me "weirdo." My hand burned the stranger. *Impossible.*

I shrug, hoping to dodge her question.

Her eyes release mine. She closes the satchel flap and hops to her feet. "Let's go."

We find him in the same place. Slight foot movements tell me he didn't bleed to death. Rebecca gasps and punches me harder than I thought she could.

"You left out that he's a T'Anakim man."

I rub my sore arm. "Would you have come if I did?"

She purses her lips.

"He's injured. Doesn't your conscience say we should help him? Besides, he just wants asylum."

She grabs my shoulder, turns me away from him, and in a hushed voice, says, "What if he's a spy?"

Didn't think of that. "What does your conscience tell you?" I repeat.

Hands on hips, she sticks out her bottom lip, no doubt debating within herself. Linus tells everyone I have a crush on her, but that's hogwash. I notice minor things.

She shakes her head, then kneels beside him. "I will touch these wounds."

He nods. "Sure."

"Hold him still."

I push on his shoulders.

Rebecca presses his leg wound with her hand until the blood stops welling through her fingers. She rummages through her satchel and pulls out a small vial, a large jar, and a flask. She measures a drop from the vial into the flask, adds another drop, and then gives it to him to drink. I hold his head upright, so it goes down his throat. She breaks a wax seal on the jar, dips a finger in the gooey salve, and applies it to his exposed skin. He winces, but a soothing effect takes over his trembling.

When she finishes, I hop to my feet. "We should move him."

"Will you have another roommate? Because I won't," she says, nodding and then shaking her head.

I extend my hands, palms outward, and wag my head. "Sir, you'll find the cave behind the waterfall pool comfortable and private."

"We aren't allowed back there, Jonathan. You know that."

"This is an emergency. My dad will understand. After the sun comes up, I'll bring him there to meet our patient."

She nods. "Sounds good—I hope."

I pull in a tentative breath, letting it out in bursts. "Wait here, sir."

We dash to my front door and ease inside the house. In the linen closet, we grab a blanket and old rags, then in the kitchen, I find bread and water. Rebecca's eyes beam. She must agree we're doing the right thing.

We help him hobble farther into the backyard, where a splinter of the South Wheatland River empties off a twenty-foot-high cliff and collects in the pool. While exploring a few years ago, friends and I found a cave behind the waterfall. My dad banned the neighborhood kids from going near it, but he'd bend the rules for this. I can't bring the stranger into the house, nor can I leave him in the open.

Our weak efforts to help such an immense man must look ridiculous. He steadies himself with a heavy hand on our shoulders, tottering back and forth. Water from the falls mists my face while ripples lap the pool's rocky rim.

I sidle along the path, leading them to the cave mouth. He could kill us now if he wanted. But my trust grows with each honest-sounding "Thank you for your help, Wheatlander" and "I shall not forget your kindness" he utters.

Not much has changed inside the old cavern. Stalagmites reach for the ceiling, and the stalactites do their best to help them. Lamplight glows on streaking orange, yellow, and white mineral deposits. The side extends farther back than I dare to go, so the main chamber will do.

I set the lamp on a flattened stalagmite, and the light fills the cave. "You'll like it here tonight."

He lays his hand on my shoulder. "I didn't introduce myself. They call me Ulgar. If things work out, I'll repay your kindness someday."

"My pleasure, sir. We'll come back later this morning. Then she can change your bandages."

Rebecca nods. "For sure."

He draws up to his full height. "I'm feeling better, my friends, thanks to your powerful medicine."

She pats her satchel. "The strongest I have. Believe me, someday even Death will die."

"You're an ambitious girl." The T'Anakim extends his hand in friendship, and she and I shake it without misgivings. As we venture back to the house, joy bubbles inside because we saved a man's life and did our part to repair relations between T'Anak and Bormágo.

Rebecca eases through her window. I hand her the satchel. When situated, she peers out at me. "Ulgar might have died if you didn't get me. He may lose the leg. But big decisions belong to a seasoned healer. We'll see him later; for now, let's go to sleep."

I press my lips together and say nothing. *Amputation? Gross. Can't blame him for wanting freedom. I'd defect from T'Anak, too.*

As I inch into my home, called Fairview House, nobody stirs in the foyer. Failing moonlight struggles through the hallway to my bedroom. Opposite my door hangs the painting of my grandparents I see every day. A scene of happier times. Their innocent faces beam back at me. Grandma's wedding gown flows like a waterfall around her. My dad says my brother and I inherited her thick raven hair, but nothing else. No one has her piercing aquamarine eyes.

The portrait shows off his features, a strong nose, and a square jaw. His bright green eyes are an odd color here in the Wheatland Borough, even throughout the Kingdom of Bormágo. Others say I resemble him, but David, not so much. Grandpa's coat, necktie, and vest are too formal for my tastes.

Life isn't fair, because my friends have their grandparents, and I don't. Mine never got to take us out for ice cream. What did they do on summer break when they were young? I'll never know. Not ever. Someone stole those years from them. From me.

Every year my dad tells their story, and the next morning, Mom finds him passed out with half a wine bottle sitting on the end table. Bad things happen to good people.

Frightening images from the nightmare that had awoken me flash in my mind. The same one Dad has had. A raised mace slices the air and hits its target. Grandpa and Grandma, dead. But I was there, too, as if floating above the scene.

I clutch my head to drive out these thoughts, and the haunting screams. "Jonathan, pull yourself together," I wheeze. A few measured breaths ease into my lungs, calming me.

In the nightmare, I saw who murdered them—black haired, imposing, and wielding a deadly mace. *If I ever find him . . .* I gawk at and cycle my fingers into fists—my newfound weapons. "I'll kill him."

My dad says Grandpa drowned trying to save Grandma. He's told his story so many times it doesn't paralyze me anymore. But in my nightmare, someone attacked them, and dumped their bodies into the pool. Why would anyone want to hurt them? The image faded, and my dream drifted someplace else, I recall. Ice water filled my veins. A dark door stood in a wide-spreading glade. Stale air reeking of death clung to it. Breathless, I then awoke.

My body shudders.

Did it lead to somewhere dangerous? How can it relate to Grandma and Grandpa's deaths?

CHAPTER 2

THE LONGEST WEEK

"Wake up, we're late," says a voice echoing inside my head. "Jonathan?"

My eyeballs flicker to life, but the bright sun stings. *Not in bed.* I remember now. A drool puddle sticks my cheek to the pages of my favorite story.

"You read out here last night?" my dad says. His face comes into focus as I rub a kink out of my neck. His styled hair and neat outfit suggest he's leaving.

"Couldn't sleep," I say through a yawn. Offering aid and comfort to an enemy had frazzled my nerves. I drifted off after I'd locked the front and back doors.

Dad motions with his hands. "We overslept, let's go. Should've been on the road an hour ago."

I slap my palms on the table. "Dunbury, I forgot. Great, another long day." My apprenticeship to Jonah Winslow, the district's chief

librarian, began last year, but I've only seen him twice since then. How will that prepare me for life? Some future I'll have.

On the book cover, the hero deals a death blow to a dragon, saving his true love. I wish I was slaying it to rescue the princess. How many sixteen-year-olds get to do that? None. I wipe the drool from the pages, close it, and toss it onto the table.

My dad forages for breakfast. "I told you he wanted to see us. Be grateful for this special opportunity."

I sigh. *His* opportunities, not mine. I love to read, but there must be better jobs other than ordering books into neat little rows.

From the kitchen counter, he grabs a cratered and disfigured loaf of bread. It looks as if a shark attacked it. What my siblings do to food should be a crime. He slices it the best he can.

"When will Wheatland have a library again?" I say.

"Up to King Alfonse, or his ministers. Besides, we use the building as the elders' meetinghouse."

"Given up trying?"

The pleasant look on his face sours. "I've accepted our place after the king punished us. He could have judged harsher. Illegal emigration can carry the death penalty. I'd say we're lucky."

"Well, you shouldn't. People who oppress others should get what's coming to them." I tighten my fists. *The one who killed my grandparents will for sure.*

Dad's eyes narrow. "Don't have time for your smart mouth. Get ready, so you can study *hard*. And don't forget, starting tomorrow, you have everyone's chores for the week."

Forgot another one. Parental retribution for a harmless prank threatens to ruin the end of my summer vacation.

As I stand, all muscles in my body stretch alive.

"Honey," my mom says from the living room.

Dad disappears. "Yes?" his muffled voice says.

"Don't be hard on him, dear."

"He won't ride my coattails into the librarian business. Wasn't easy for me after my parents died. He needs a stronger work ethic."

Here we go again.

"William, let them go and hold onto the living. You can't be angry at your son forever."

"I'm not, Elizabeth . . . You're right, I *am* still mad. He's old enough to make better choices. Fool pranks are not funny to anyone. His lie compounded the problem."

My dad is a bulldog when he wants to be.

"In time, he admitted to it."

"You miss the point. A first lie stands upon a slippery slope. No one will believe a thing he says anymore. Why does Goldie look up to him? Besides, he earned this punishment. Your son skirts chores, does the least, and who knows what else. I have a hunch he breaks curfew, too. Someday I'll catch him, or worse, the king's men will arrest him."

I doubt it.

"His prank didn't hurt anyone. We brought the blackened cake remains outside and fanned the smoke from the house. Total damage: one cake, two oven mitts, and Goldie's pride. He's a smart lad. Give change time."

"There's his problem. He's a showoff, too bright for his own good."

"With a heart bigger than life."

Smarts will help me live on my own someday.

"He reads so he can confuse everyone around him. It's a sport for him. Watch how he treats David."

Fun for sure. David's a big boy.

"We want smart kids, equipped to take on the world."

"To him take *on* the world means take *over* the world. Imagine him as an evil overlord."

Silence.

You've gone too far. Mom will rescue my blameless name.

"Don't give me that stare, Eliza."

"He's a good lad."

"Every mother's boy acts 'good.' I'm entitled to my opinion. Why can't he model David—acting sensible and responsible? The only thing they have in common is their black hair."

"And hazel eyes."

"They're not hazel, look again."

"To me, they are, dear."

"But their similarities stop there, as if Fate foreknew their personality differences."

"Oh?"

"Consider the twins and their different birthdays. You can count on David and February 28 to be there for you. Jump forward twenty minutes later when you had irresponsible Jonathan. What benefit is February 29 to anyone? It's an ailment to a healthy month."

She doesn't answer.

"More chores will build respectable character, Eliza, which is what this kid needs."

My dad enters the kitchen as if their conversation was private. He drops a heavy backpack on the table. "Take this, we have a long road ahead."

"Dad?" Feelings from last night come back . . . fear, anger, happiness. My tongue sticks in my dry mouth. How can I start?

My twin traipses by, interrupting.

Dad's eyes spark with life. "Chores done, David?"

With his thick arms, he wipes sweat from his forehead. "Not yet. It's warm, and I forgot my canteen." He gulps a mug of water, dribbling droplets onto his shirt. "Split the whole tree."

Dad pats him on the back. "What a huge elm. Marvelous work." He frowns at me as if I'm an old thing found in the pantry's darkest corner. "Grab the backpack. Time to go."

If anger were steam, I'd have blown the top of my head clean off. But I can't fight with him. Not now. I promised myself I won't get into any more trouble, because a happy end of summer relies on it. "I have something to tell you."

"I forgot. What?"

"Last night, a strange noise outside my window awoke me."

David homes in on my words.

"When I searched the backyard, I discovered an injured T'Anakim man."

Dad chokes on his coffee. When his coughing fit stops, his stare bores into me. "You found what?"

"Must have fallen over the cliff. His leg and head were bloody. Rebecca helped—"

"Why didn't you wake me instead?"

"She can heal."

His eyebrows rise, and he nods. "No argument there."

"Will only take a minute."

His eyes narrow. I've seen his skeptical face many times, but hard proof should convince him.

"Where is he?"

I hesitate before answering. "You realize the best places to hide an enemy of the Bormagian kingdom were few."

Dad's hands slide to his hips. "Jonathan—"

"The cave behind the pool."

A red spasm flashes across his cheeks, but it passes. "What if you fell into the water? You can't swim."

Thunderous noise pounds my eardrums as we walk along the pathway beside the pool. The sun showcases green moss and orange mineral streaks layered in the rock wall. My dad lights a lamp and takes the lead into the cave.

Golden light spreads on the walls but stops at the first turn. Anxious thoughts flood my mind. What if I misjudged Ulgar's gratitude? If it comes to it, will we be strong enough to overcome him?

My dad's heavy feet wear on my nerves. Even the dead could hear us coming.

Around the final bend, the lamplight overtakes the space where Rebecca and I left him last night. I blink in disbelief. No food, no blanket, and no T'Anakim man.

My dad searches the chamber, the lamp held high. When it's clear he isn't here, his face turns toward me, jaw muscles throbbing. "Why? You . . ." He stomps past me. When I catch up to his quick pace, he grabs my shoulder. "What's wrong with you?"

"Believe me, Ulgar was here last night. We left him in the cave, go check the rear chamber."

An amethyst glint sparkles in his flitting brown eyes. "Oh, he has a name now. You know this place well. Have you been back here?"

Time to redirect his questioning. "Rebecca came with me."

A bulging vein throbs in his neck. "Sure, drag in the neighbor girl. Her reputation outshines yours. No point chasing this rabbit into its hole. I give you so many breaks. How can a wounded man disappear?"

I press my finger to my lips, saying nothing. Dad asks a good question. How *could* Ulgar leave? He needed help. And may lose the leg. But who wants to aid him?

"I thought as much. Jonah won't be happy that we're late. I must face his snide comments." He points at me. "Best behavior, okay? While there, don't yell 'fire' or tear out book pages and return them backward, or any such nonsense. Most people find your pranks annoying. The archive room houses ancient books and scrolls from Dunbury's most prominent families. You're there to work, understand?"

"Yes, Dad."

An undulating stone wall borders Green Hollow Way to the distant uphill climb, leaving the hollow. We rush by Rebecca's house. My dad pulls ahead as I search for her on the porch. Each morning, she reads while sipping bergamot tea with her brown dog, Gunnar, at her feet. Not today. *Figures.* She could have corroborated my story.

The last cottage on our road belongs to George and Margaret Roberts, who act as our grandparents, although they had no children. We labor up the shallow cliff face to the end of Green Hollow Way, where Wheatland Road joins ours and follows the western branch of the Wheatland River. Sweet apple scent wafts through the air. Off my right shoulder, the Hill family orchard grows in long ranks and files. I won't see their eldest son, Greene, when the harvest starts.

In less than a mile, we reach town. Impatient farmers zigzag their wagons through the crowds in the square. The king's men patrol the streets, but nobody says a word to them, not even at the tavern where they stay. Here to keep order, as they say, but everyone knows instead to watch us. And to report back. We have a constable, Winston Beasley. Wheatlanders, including my parents, attempted to leave the kingdom thirteen years ago. Why did they defy our supreme monarch's law during tense political times? To live as they want, I heard. Other people don't understand that. Not sure I would have done it. Why trade a warm bed for a hammock on choppy seas? As a result, the top brass in Heathfell appoints new soldiers to rotate every six months. The current set will ship out soon.

In the square, a line stretches from one end to the other. Today is Debt Day—the last Monday of the month where mortgages, taxes, and other debts drain the Wheatland pocketbook. At the head sits a pasty-white guy whose body hangs over the sides of his chair. Rej, short for Reginald. The busy hands of the person we call the Collector scribbles ledger notations.

"Holms III, Herkus Herschel," the next in line says, dropping a small money pouch on the table.

The fat man empties it and fingers through the pile. "Wait a minute, you got it wrong. You missed a payment, so this one's double, plus interest and a finance surcharge. Today you owe two gold royal lions, one silver royal lion, and three silver bits."

"Last month, you said one gold cub and two silver lions."

"No, Herky, you heard me."

"Friends know me as Herky. You may call me Mr. Holms."

"You'll stand here next month and pay us triple plus fees, if you don't come up with it now. And the king should tax you more for calling his royal lions cubs."

He digs deep into his pockets and finds a few more coins. He slaps them on the table. "Thief."

The Collector's muscle, a mountainous brute named Hazo, armed with a crossbow and a sword, takes a step toward him.

"Lucky you had it, dimwit. Next," the Collector barks.

Hazo glowers at me as we pass. I earn his ire whenever I happen across his path. The ruffian points to his eyes and then to mine. My glance darts away. Because of the Fairview inheritance, Wheatlanders consider my family privileged. But on my dad's librarian salary, we can't even afford to replace the horse we sold a few years back.

Fairfield Road heads west from town into the wheat fields, where the covered bridge I dread crossing—the confluence of rustic charm and decrepitude—spans the swift-flowing Wheatland River. As we step onto the floorboards, wagons rattling the structure threaten to dump everyone into the water. To take my mind off the danger, I focus on the millwheel turning a half mile upriver.

"Hey, Jacksons," says a voice behind me. Herky drives his wagon alongside us. "Whoa, whoa." Shaded eyes peep from a straw hat pressed to his ears. His grubby, holey overalls aren't the only thing needing a good washing.

"Hello," my dad says, clearing the air with a discreet hand wave.

The farmer extends his hand to me. "William, Jonathan." He pulls me into his natural perfume. No difference between shaking it or a leather glove.

"Rough time in line?" my dad says.

He jerks his thumb rearward. "Can you believe him? I need grain for my cattle, but now I can't afford enough."

"May not be enough for the town. Brief rain and hungry bugs kill the Golden Archie yields. If Old Man Miller weren't in his grave, his failing seed would put him there."

"What brings you two this way?"

"Heading to the Dunbury library to work on Jonah's project list. Jonathan will learn the ropes, and if he studies hard and does well, someday he'll fill my shoes," he says, tapping my arm with a loose fist.

I manage an awkward smile, hiding my genuine feelings. *Dad knows nothing of my dreams.*

"Tell him I said hi."

"Will do." My dad fidgets, which means he's aware we're late.

"I best let you go. You two have yourselves an agreeable day." The rancher tips his hat, urges his team, and rides away in a puffy dust cloud.

Ahead, a green hillock rises above the flat wheat fields with an ancient tree we call Rowen towering in the middle. With the northern breeze running across the heads of grain, the majestic tree stands king over his bowing servants. At its feet bubbles an artesian pool where the farmers water their animals.

Dunbury's tall poplars, smooth-skinned beeches, and lofty oaks border the western edge of the fields. Before long, we arrive at the Old McHenry Road crossing, where the faded sign tells us our destination remains a mile farther north.

Once reaching Dunbury, we weave in and out of busy merchants, finicky customers, and mothers towing bratty kids. Crowds at the Plow and Sickle Tavern jam the entryway. On the square's farther side, the memorial library dominates the skyline with its high columns and white-stone dome.

A robed granite statue welcomes passersby with water cascading from the book she carries. Her placard reads, "Wisdom and Knowledge."

My dad stops, bothered by something. His eyes flit to mine in a tentative glance. "Jonah called this meeting with no warning."

"Unlike him," I acknowledge.

"Right. Winslow didn't elaborate in the letter, but he always acts mysterious. I sense strange circumstances here, so stay focused."

My strong point, not yours, I think. "Okay, Dad."

The word *strange* describes the past twenty-four hours the best. First, I found a wounded enemy who vanished without a trace. Next, a routine meeting with my master becomes a covert action. What do these things mean? Not the stuff of slaying dragons and rescuing princesses, but if I keep on my dad's good side—more or less—this apprenticeship may be my chance to live on my own. That'll show him I'll make something of myself. Better learn as much as I can from Jonah today.

CHAPTER 3

THE KEEPER OF MYSTERIES

Patrons gather in the antechamber, but the library appears empty. I can't wait to rest my sore feet. As if mice who search for cheese, we wind through a bookstack labyrinth to the back. At last, we rush through a door and hustle downstairs to a dim room filled with parchments and scrolls layered with dust. A librarian shelves a small cart full, but he ignores a few books that drop and sprawl open. He leaves them in a heap.

Lazy.

An old leather scent hangs in the musty air. Jonah studies at a thick-legged table, surrounded by book stacks. He struggles to his feet, tucks a loose pendant into his shirt, and shuffles toward us. More wizened and frail than last year, it looks as if he's lost ten years off his life clock.

Wringing his hands, he says, "You worried me, William, you're two hours late."

"Sorry. Rambunctious kids love to stay up all night." He clears his throat and then thrusts me forward. "You remember Jonathan?"

A wide grin grows on Jonah's face. "I don't forget my apprentices, although I have trouble starting them. Great Scott, boy, you've grown so much in one year."

I smile and shake his hand. "How do you do, sir?"

"Well, when you take into account my age, thank you."

We clear a place to work among the books he had set out. Jonah takes his seat, and Dad and I sit beside each other.

When the door at the top of the stairs clicks shut, Jonah's head snaps upright. "Is he gone?"

My dad's eyes triangulate between the book he opened, the staircase, and him. "The other librarian? I believe so. Must be his first week on the job."

The Chief Librarian rubs his chin. "It's a year since you have been here last."

"Not quite, but Jonathan came with me, too."

"I never see unfamiliar people around here. If I did, I'd watch them, because these days, one can't be too careful with their associations."

Here we go again. My dad hates his conspiracy theories.

A tic twitches the corner of Dad's mouth. He sighs. "Why did you send us a letter?"

"We who guard our past dwindle in numbers every year, even though we offer an essential service. If a people forget their bygone days, they repeat old mistakes. 'History is the prophet to the future,' the saying goes. But who heeds this warning?"

"We do."

"Correct."

I yawn. *We should get on with it.*

Jonah turns to me, saying, "We're the banner bearers, my young student. Within a weak kingdom, the unprincipled stop at nothing to wrest power from those who have it." He draws in closer to my face. "I have another purpose for bringing you in today."

Dad chews his lip but stays silent.

"Strange things always happen now. More than ocean tides flow in and out of Heathfell these days. The prophesied Two Combining may come to pass."

My dad fidgets with a writing quill. "The what?"

"Your private collection won't be enough for this assignment. We need the borough's full resources. My master quoted it years ago, but curators lost the text. As I recall, it says, 'Twain lords their power combined,' in an end-of-the-world sense. History chronicled the prophecy, so you can help me find references."

"Wait a minute, Jonah. Did something happen to you?"

A sheepish look grows on my master's face. "Remember, William, *you* asked me."

My dad spreads his hands in innocence.

"A week ago, I had a dream about this 'Two Combining.' The last time was when I was young. No matter how hard I try, I can't forget it."

I understand how he feels. *Dreams—odd things.*

"Begin here." The Chief Librarian gives him a thick book. "I'm guessing, but I fear this might involve our king, for good or ill. In times past, justice's guardian forgot his role."

"An understatement."

"But I believe he's a helpful ruler."

"If he abdicates the throne."

"I remember what he did to the Wheatlanders years ago." His eyes narrow. "But if King Alfonse seeks to strengthen the kingdom, he'd restore its former glory. His plan might include the western land holdings, whose rich resources and Bormagian naval supremacy would fuel the empire's strength."

Jonah glides a finger along his nose in contemplation, then snaps his fingers. "He and Crown Prince Albert could make a formidable pair if they combined their power. First, they must lay aside their differences, most important, the kingdom's role in the world. The upcoming Council of Lords could spark this change."

My dad folds his arms and leans back in his chair.

Jonah unfolds and holds up a newspaper article. "If reports are accurate, T'Anakim spies have infiltrated our lands, so the king must take action against them."

Now he will believe my story. But then my win turns into a loss in a half second. *Is Ulgar an enemy spy as Rebecca warned and was I played for a fool?*

"You can't always trust the papers, Jonah. Your words, not mine."

My master purses his lips together.

"Thirteen years ago the king, along with then Chief Inquisitor Charles Tarleton—the kingdom's greatest ever legal mind—sought to destroy us. I'll never forget my trial. That peacock strutted around the courtroom. With the thread of truth and of half-truth, the master tailor wove a fine tapestry of accusations against me, which left the jury's verdict a foregone decision."

Shock drains the blood from my master's face.

"The court found the Wheatlanders guilty, 'illegal emigration,' the charge. Crazy. Everyone should be free to leave whenever. As an ultimate insult, he banned us from the capital city forever."

"I understand—"

My dad holds up his hand to halt him. "Further, *he* sent spies to watch the elders. If the balance tipped to 'disobedience,' the 'uncooperative' disappeared. Distrust grew in town as if gangrene and threatened to destroy our way of life."

"Those were tragic days, William, but the T'Anakim threat was a reality then. The king had his reasons, and so he does again."

Dad folds his arms.

My master relaxes into his seat. "I'll travel to Heathfell by this weekend to learn what I can at the Archives. You use the resources within the district libraries. We'll meet in a week and compare notes. More Two Combining commentary must hide out there somewhere."

"Jonah, many Wheatlanders want to leave Bormágo. We can't get ahead as tenant farmers, where the weather, plagues, and indebtedness fight against us."

He remains silent.

With each passing moment, the hostility in my dad's countenance eases. He lets out a deep breath. "Okay, let's start."

"Thank you. You won't regret it."

Book stacks tower on the table. My dad grabs for himself *A Complete History of Bormágo and the Surrounding Kingdoms* by D. A. Heady but hands me *The Olden Days* by Joachim B. Alter.

The first page stirs hope in me that a hint to the Two Combining hides around the corner, but after the first fruitless hour, it drains to empty. How can something important elude the kingdom's historians? Shouldn't every page I flip show a reference?

My eyes flit upward when I sense Dad's gaze on me. "I want a couple books from the reference section. They are *A Military History of Bormágo* by Gilford O'Brien and *Nordlont Military Campaigns* by Onèsimus. If you need any help, ask a librarian."

I stifle a leap from the chair. *Exploring time.*

Long ranks and files crisscross the floor, reminding me of a giant chessboard. They dwarf the half-sized stacks in the reference section. My eyes scan neat rows until they fall upon *A Military History of Bormágo*, but *Nordlont Military Campaigns* isn't in its spot. Figures: lazy patrons.

A sign overhead reads, "Ring bell for assistance." My hand freezes in place above it, because in the antechamber, the basement librarian is speaking with two men. No doubt who: the Collector and his muscle. I drop low, peering through a tiny gap between books. When the parties separate, they lumber in my direction. My mind flies back to the morning when those empty black eyes had bored into mine. They'll recognize me. Time to disappear.

I scuttle along a rank and over a couple files to the rear. Behind the furthermost stack, I hide in a small alcove towered with books.

Labored breathing nears my hideout, and then two sets of feet appear in a space opposite the first shelf.

"Far enough, Hazo; he mentioned no one is back here. Cover the sword, no need to arouse suspicion."

"Rej, what's the plan?"

"Shut up, and I'll explain it in simple terms. He said the old man's in the basement, and the goods hang around his neck. If we steal it, the boss will have his matched set, and we'll be rich. A couple of Wheatland rats joined him, so we must figure out how to separate them."

I chew my lip, my breath shortening with each threat.

"Got it, Rej. I could creep down there and squeeze the life from them. It'd work real good."

"You're never the subtle one, Hazo. We can't commit mass murder willy-nilly in the library. Someone will catch us."

Woozy, I reach for a shelf to steady myself, but the book slips from my hand. The corner of a thousand pages slams into my foot and sprawls onto the floor. My eyes water. I bite my tongue. Too great to hold back, an involuntary shriek blurts from my mouth.

"What was that?" Rej says.

They leave in separate directions. The gap is my one chance to escape. I squeeze through it as each man rounds opposite corners. Book in hand, I spring to my feet and dart away. I round the corner with ease because neither of them thought to stay back. Books tumbling upon cursing men fade when I reach the stairs.

I turn the lock, and it clicks, but this door won't slow Hazo for long. A splintered door will give us an early warning, though. I slide the book under my dad's nose, my jittery hands calmed by its weight. He grunts "thanks," but his eyes continue to track words.

"Dad?"

No response.

"I need to talk to you."

"Mm-hmm . . . what?"

"Over there."

He mumbles something I can't understand. When we step behind a bookstack, I say, "Upstairs, I overheard the Collector and his partner discussing how to kill us. I hid in an alcove surrounded by books, so they didn't see me."

Classic disbelief grows on my dad's face. "Excuse me?"

"It's difficult to imagine, but I'm telling the truth. Go find out for yourself."

His head wags. "This is ridiculous."

"Please, Dad. Check the rear aisle, too."

He sighs and turns his head. "If you say so. Jonah, I'll be back in a few moments."

"Sure, William," he mumbles without lifting his eyes.

Twenty minutes pass, which is too long. Did he search the second floor? Before I investigate, natural light spreads on the stair-case wall with footfalls echoing on the thick marble. Whose? Tension eases when my dad steps into the room. I can't read his expression.

He beckons me to come, so I follow him away from Jonah. When his eyes narrow and he frowns, I'm in trouble for sure. I've seen this face many times.

"For twenty minutes, I searched for two men who don't exist. The back aisle and alcove were empty. In fact, every place in this library is tidy. You sent me traipsing everywhere."

When I object, he holds up his palm to silence me. I've witnessed this on several occasions, too.

"Stop, no more pranks. We'll talk with Mom, because another week with chores may do you good."

Two weeks in the same summer must be against a law.

As I flop onto the high-back chair, Jonah hands me a book. I smear away dust from the cover. *Famous Military Generals* by F. F. McGurk.

While I read, men and women who led powerful armies fade the death threats from my mind. My stomach growls, but nothing distracts me from the story of Valstan, a charismatic general whose exploits passed into legend.

When I realize I'm sitting in a library basement, not out on a battlefield, I notice rhythmic breathing. Hunched over, Jonah's hair hangs in midair. His head dips, and on the upswing, a silver chain twined with gold falls out. A pale-green gem catches the dim light. Rej and Hazo will kill for, and their boss will pay a fortune for, this.

I slap my book shut. His eyes snap open, and the pendant dangles along his chest. Mission accomplished. "Exquisite gemstone," I say, pointing. "I think it's a peridot."

He fumbles for it, seizes it, and tucks it beneath his collar. "No, it isn't."

"Is it an heirloom, sir?"

The Chief Librarian rubs his chin. "A family talisman, lad." Jonah wobbles to his feet, stretches, and yawns. Three joints crack in the meantime. "Time to call it a day."

"Indeed," my dad says, "we need to get home before dark."

I organize books in the backpack. "Master?"

"Yes, son?"

"Can I check out this book?"

He lays a hand on my shoulder and says, "McGurk's volume? Won't be a problem." Dad and he each blow out a lamp, which leaves the room a dreary gray. Our feet echo up the steps we descended hours earlier.

Jonah halts before the door, lamplight casting half his mysterious face in shadow. "Remember, a kingdom's story is a rudder; its leaders, a powerful wind. History uses them to sail into the future. Know your past, know your direction."

Fear deadens my ears to Jonah's wisdom. Hazo could pop out of a dark corner and grab me.

I tap my dad's arm. "Don't forget what I said. They could be hiding."

He casts a dismissive eye roll.

Jonah throws open the door and charges out. *Could he be less discreet?*

We wind through the stacks, snaking between the same ones as this morning.

But my death never comes. I wonder what happened to them.

On the front steps, my master extends his hand in farewell. "Let's meet next week, same day, same time."

"We'll be here," my dad says.

"And don't be late."

When we reach the crossroads, the sun lies beneath the horizon, bathing trees in gray darkness. Aloof, my dad has been no company. I hope he forgets to give me more chores. I whistle as we walk, which helps me think. Nothing could surpass this week. A wounded man turns up in my backyard, enemies infiltrate my kingdom, power plays lurk in the shadows, and men, intent on murder, disappear. What about the Two Combining and Jonah's dreams? Could it relate to mine with the dark door?

"Things are turning more Wheatland-ish," my dad says. "I love coming home after a tiring day, because it gives me a small dose of the Saturday morning feeling."

Nothing beats the no-school-for-the-summer feeling. Ruined by one week of chores for sure, no doubt a second, unless I work the Mom angle. I must practice my sad puppy-dog eyes.

In time, I leave my pity party, because I'm the lone partier.

My dad drones on forever. "I can't wait for my armchair and the ottoman."

I point in the distance. "Miller's fields, Rowen, and the mill."

The orange horizon disappears, and pale green, akin to Jonah's pendant, blends into deep blues and black. Stars poke their heads through the cosmic veil. In the grain fields, horse nickering and oxen bell clanking quieted long ago, because every respectable person is home, eating supper.

"New moon tonight," Dad says.

I point east. "But the Evening Star is shining brighter than I've ever seen."

Perplexity fills my dad's eyes. "Something looks ominous and familiar." He halts, head cocked to one side. "I remember her sing-song voice . . ."

What does that mean?

"After you were born. A lady—" He yanks me behind his back. "She'll come for you again."

What do those last words imply? From the inky sky, brightness plummets to earth and lands before us. I shade my eyes. Over-whelmed, I slump to my knees, and my pack thuds on the ground.

A robed woman emerges from the light. Her eyes blaze with azure fire, silver crowns her golden head, and her noble countenance beams. "Hail, Jonathan, Elect of the eternal Council," she says.

My mouth feels stuffed with cotton. "E-Excuse me?"

"Sophia am I, lady of wisdom. Before you were born and ever was a thought in your mind, we chose you."

My jaw just hangs under my face.

"I name you First Warden, the beginner of new things—first in my heart and mind—firstborn of your kind who shall walk between the light and the dark."

"F-first Warden?"

"You have the mark of the two worlds upon you. And your brother, too. Only you boys can undertake my task which, if fruit-ful, will usher in lasting peace."

"Another chore?" Heat shoots into my face. *I'm an idiot.*

"I am no purveyor of petty labor, Jonathan. In the West, a dark door leads to Eshbanáchbor, the land of gloom and mists. There you must destroy the evil lords before they find the Two Gems, combine their power, and dominate the worlds. Their reign will bring hatred, oppression, and endless war until every life—including yours—comes to ruin. Fear not and take comfort for my words dwell within you, even to the coming end of the age."

Two Gems? Jonah had one?

A yellow streak crosses the southern horizon. Lady Sophia's gaze trains upward, and with a stern countenance, she says, "I must go before he finds me speaking to you. Your life is in grave danger."

"From who?"

"Ishglof."

"Who's he?

"An evil elven lord. One of the two."

"And who's the first?"

"Take these, for I adjudge you a Hôzai knight. Use them well, First Warden."

She hands me a book and a sword hilt, with no blade.

"But—"

"No time to explain now, Jonathan. The seed of my plan germinates within you, and others will water it, even many shall rest in its shade. My eye is upon you, guiding your steps. I planted an idea in your father's mind. Lend this book to him, just for tonight, because I must speak to your elders. They have a part in my plans, too."

"But—"

"Take the door, defeat the evil lords, and then everything will be made new." She streams into the sky with a trail of light and vanishes. The yellow streak follows her, then disappears.

Thoughts drift back to my dream—to the dark door—a door which reeks of death. Whose end? Not mine. I won't go there. Thanks, but not interested, lady. Too much of it in my storied history.

My dad will call for an elder council so I can learn more there. This chance meeting sucks the breath from my lungs. Dizziness clouds my vision . . . My face plants into the dirt.

CHAPTER 4

THE VISITOR'S GIFTS

Blurry vision sharpens to a brown dirt potpourri mixed with straw and pebbles. I spit out grit, grass, and other debris. Luckily, I didn't fall facedown into a pile of horse road apples. Everything happened so fast when Lady Sophia appeared and then Ishglof drove her back into the sky.

I rub my eyes to wipe away bright spots dotting my vision, which fade little by little.

Overpowered by her presence, too, my dad lays sprawled out on the ground nearby. I shake his shoulder and say, "Dad, Dad . . . are you awake?"

He squirms, and after a few seconds, jolts into consciousness. "It's you."

"Are you okay?"

"Think so." He points to the sky. "The light."

"She knows you."

"Hmm, yes, but she never told me her name. Years ago, we left you boys with Aunt Fanny, so we could leave for T'Anak. After we found a place to live, we'd come for you. On a night that resembled this one, we were sneaking through a field heading to the pickup point when she appeared."

"What did she say?"

"Well, she was interested in you two. Uncomfortable with her questions, we ran to the others at the boats. You know the rest of the story—caught, tried, and imprisoned. But we never shared this incident with anyone."

My jaw clenches. "Why did you not tell me?"

"What would you have done if a strange woman asks about your young sons? Now she's back."

I set my hand on his shoulder. "It's okay, I guess you did the right thing."

Two objects lay on the ground, dim in the failing light. I grab the sword hilt and stuff it into the backpack while my dad rubs his eyes. *He won't have it before me.* After hoisting him to his feet, I show him the book. "Look at what she left."

"I only see bright spots," he says, blinking.

As he recovers, I flip through it, curious with what I'll find. Words in spidery, loopy, blocky, or graceful handwriting fill it. I stop at a blank page near the middle. It's pristine and unbent, even resisting a smudge from my grimy fingers.

"Old cover, but new pages. What could it mean?"

He flips them with his finger. "The light's too dim, and my eyes can't focus. Let's peek at it when we get home."

The covered bridge stands against the twinkling Wheatland Town backdrop. Underfoot, the boards rattle my nerves again, the same as this morning when we headed the other direction. When we near the square, the river's clamor fades into lighthearted pipe and violin music.

"Dad, it's the harvest festival band. Can we watch?"

"No—"

Before he finishes his thought, a voice calls to us from a park bench. I recognize the thick-built, narrow-faced man as my friend Clyde's dad. Haven't visited him in a while, even though they live east of town.

"Hello, Bill," my dad says.

Mr. Hoggins points at the musicians. "They have talent this year." He moves over to make room.

Dad taps his foot and nods to the rhythm. "Yes." He glances his way, and says, "It's been a long time since I've seen you. What are you up to these days? Someone told me you left the market."

"Sebastian and I parted ways six months ago, so I work for myself now. Times are better and we don't scrape by any longer."

"Excellent, what do you do?"

He raises his gaze in thought. "Complicated jobs aren't easy to explain, so let's say I'm in the transportation business. And Clare keeps me busy, running here and there."

My dad looks downward. "It holds your interest, so good for you."

"How's the lore-mastering world?" He eyes the stuffed backpack and tests its weight. "What did the old slave driver Jonah give you to study? He'll be your death."

"Sometimes, I wonder the same thing. Our business exhausts me, especially when I travel to Dunbury. I can't complain too much, though. No one will listen, anyway."

"Let me guess, then." He snaps his fingers. "I have it, the borough's lumberjack club wants you to determine which log rolls best: ash, beech, or oak? Or the Wheatland Knitters Guild needs more material to weave into their idle chatter?" A wide smile spreads across his face. "Come on, Willie, my old friend, you've heard my sarcastic humor for years."

"No one called me that in a long time. 'William' is more distinguished, do you agree?"

Bill sighs. "Out with it, what's the mystery with your Dunbury connection?"

The man's desperate. Forget telling him what he wants, I think.

Dad spreads his hands, palms upward. "No secrecy, we have an extra project. Jonathan took an apprenticeship last year, so now he's in the business, too. A slow startup, but Jonah wanted to see him."

He pats me on the back. "Good boy. You must be proud, William."

"Indeed, I am. After his time studying under Winslow comes finishing education. The Mastery School of Heathfell may accept him if he gets exceptional marks, and if they will accept a Wheatlander."

Bill chuckles. "Still haven't answered my question."

My dad points to the band. "The festival will be delightful this year."

"Fine, keep your secrets. Yes, at least, the violin doesn't sound as if a screeching cat is having its fur yanked out."

"Most of the racket comes off Mr. Atwood's bow."

"He's never in tune, but then again, *I* had no music lessons."

Dad rises, extending his hand. "I'll bet the same is true for him. My shadow never darkened the Wheatland conservatory door. Wonderful to see you, but my aging dinner awaits. Except for tonight, it's at five o'clock sharp, so drop in next time."

"I will, thanks. Have a good evening."

Eager to get home, we hustle through the town square and join the road heading south. Bouncy music fades from earshot when Dad glances back. "My dad used to say, 'Beware of employment too complicated to explain.' Shady deals take the same name—the 'transportation business.' I've known Bill for years, and he could never find success until now, but sometimes luck is fickle. You could end up on the unlucky side, having nothing but mischief. When Mrs. Hoggins took a job, at the time I didn't learn what it was."

"Is he jealous? He aimed the logrolling and the Knitters Guild digs at you and Jonah."

"His ire targets anyone who is prosperous. Librarian and market worker jobs were chain links in his lengthy employment history. Years ago, they spread a rumor which damaged his family's reputation, so he hasn't forgiven them. They say, 'Bitterness is a slow-acting poison, but forgiveness is the quick antidote.'"

The South Wheatland Road snakes into sleepy Green Hollow Way. From the brim, our home lies serene. Blackness deepens as the evening turns to nighttime.

I burst through Fairview's front door, tear off my shoes, and, when my dad isn't looking, dash and slide along hardwood floors to my bedroom. I'll go even farther after I coat it with fresh wax. A bright spot in this chore sentence.

Six pairs of eyeballs hurry me to my seat. Piled roast chicken and dumplings dare me to wipe my plate clean. *She didn't disappoint.*

Dad rushes to his place, rubbing his forehead.

The first bite makes my taste buds sing. I'm up to the challenge. I stop inhaling my food when there's a sudden silence, and so I glance upward. Everyone except my little brother, Conrad Junior, stares at Dad.

Mom darts past me, lifts his chin, and says, "William Jackson, your face is white as a sheet, and did you singe your eyebrows?"

He rubs his brow. "Tell you after dinner. For now, stop staring at me and finish eating."

Flatware clangs, plates scrape, but no voice breaks the uncomfortable silence.

After a few moments, Pep (his given name is Joseph), says, "Mom, Thomas and I caught a frog and a turtle. Can we keep them?"

"We won't let them die," Thomas says. "We promise."

"The other ones had a death wish."

Last time, the stench didn't leave the house for a month. Who could forget when she'd found their cooked bodies under the oven?

"Later, boys, your father and I need to talk."

They trade hopeful glances, for it wasn't a flat-out no.

My sister, Goldie, digs into her pocket. She fishes out a wrinkled parchment and hands it to my dad. Her eyes flit between it and him. A grin plays on his face. Transparent from the table lamplight, it shows two figures, one in a dress with cascading hair and the other with a round belly. Both have crooked smiles to the eye dots. The lowercase double *D*'s point the wrong way.

"Sweetheart, I love it." Her gaze fixes on his missing eyebrows until he distracts her with a hug.

Conrad Junior, named out of respect for Grandpa rather than for direct lineage, tugs at Mom's sleeve. "Mama, we gonna have appa pie?"

"Sorry, dear, not tonight."

He wrinkles his pudgy cheeks. "I *h-hungry* . . . yes, I *h-h-hungry*."

"Mama and Daddy need to talk, so if you're finished, you may go play."

Junior's face turns sour, his head slumps, and he sulks out of the kitchen.

After the fastest dinner in our family's history, my brothers and sister scurry away like mice discovered in a cellar. With my last bite, Mom's stare tells me I should vanish, too. No time for seconds.

I dash toward the door.

"Not so fast, mister."

"What?"

Her warm eyes scowl.

"Uh, yes, ma'am?"

"Much better. Trash duty is part of your chores this week. Since we're not doing any science experiments in the house, take it out before it turns into one."

"But, Mom, I'm tired."

"It's called punishment," my dad says, "so get to work."

I don't dare talk back when they're in a mood. No doubt, she wants to learn every detail from our day. Their private business becomes a chance to eavesdrop. I yank the barrel from the pantry, drag it across the tile, and stop when out of sight. I turn my ear toward the kitchen.

"So, the eyebrows," my dad says. "I found a strange gadget in the backpack."

"And . . ."

"A flaming blade shot out, almost taking off my head."

He rummages through my things now?

"Why did Jonah give this to you? And where did he get it?"

"Don't know, to me it makes no sense."

Nope, try the Lady gave it, and the book, to me.

"I'll ask him next time. On our way home . . . at Miller's fields, a dazzling light fell from the sky."

"Oh?"

"A woman dressed in white appeared in it. We met her before, Eliza."

"After the twins were born?"

"Yes. Back then, the cowl hid the woman's face, but now brightness clothed her."

"Maybe she gave Jonathan the fire sword?"

Good question. Why?

A lengthy pause tells me he thinks over her words. "Hard to imagine why."

"Many riddles, but no answers. I fear for them!"

"Calm yourself, dear. She wants to talk to the elders."

"Why?"

"She'll tell us more. I want to learn what the book says. I'll explain to Cornelius, Margaret, and George on the way to the meetinghouse. The runner can summon the rest."

My friend James will join this council and inform me on what he remembers. The chance to eavesdrop is over, so with a final tug, I heft the barrel to the foyer.

Moonless dark settles on the porch with a hint of lamplight peeping through the front door I kept ajar. Overhead, stars spangle the sky, welcoming a cool night. At Rebecca's house, a silhouette stands at the ready. Gunnar's soft whines and taut rope tell me he caught a scent.

Last time I brought out the trash, one of my careless brothers left the corral gate open, which let critters into the barrels. Should check it first before giving them more chance to feast.

I round the corner to the backyard but halt when I hear a rustling sound. Absent-minded Pep took the garbage out last, so I bet they're available to any critter in the neighborhood. Something moved, so I strain my eyes to see. A silhouette, too dark to identify, lurks outside the kitchen window. People inside cause the eavesdropper to back away, toward me.

I step backward, a twig snaps, and the silhouette turns my direction. Petrified, I hope to blend into my surroundings. If my dad lights a lamp when he leaves the house, this person will see me.

The front door shuts, freezing my heart midbeat. Without porch light, the garbage barrel may . . . A thud, crash, and muttering curses punch the air. "What the devil" and "Dratted boy" chase the spy away. Dad throws the loose contents back into it, storms through the courtyard, and slams the gate.

The silhouette vanishes, but in a moment I find him again, hurrying toward the waterfall pool. If I'm discovered outside after dark, I'll earn a beating by the king's men, because of the dumb underage curfew. Indecisive, I wring my hands, for one foot prefers to ease inside the house, the other wants to follow the person spying on my family. But he can't escape. Nerves steeling, I step after him into the yard.

At a far distance, I lose, but then pick up the trail. Thunder from the waterfall grows until fine mist sprays my face. With Ulgar needing shelter, I had an excuse to go into the cave. My parents may kill me if they knew I was here. Or worse than death, ground me with more chores. I inch along the path to the forbidden place where Rebecca and I left him. Was he the person at the window? Without moonlight, who can tell? Around a corner, a flint strike catches a lamp wick aflame and pours light onto the wall.

The cavern mouth opens wide, flickering shadows on stalagmites and stalactites forming hungry jaws. Dim lamplight spills ahead, but not enough to see who I'm chasing. If Ulgar, then Rebecca's healing knowledge runs deep, because he walks without a limp. Heat rushes to my face. Jonah said enemies infiltrated the kingdom. *Jonathan, you fool.*

Light disappears into the back chamber, so my lead feet obey my curiosity. My night vision is excellent, better than most, which helps when I play nighttime games such as Ghost in the Graveyard.

As I round the corner, a lamp with familiar arching handles sits beside a wall-to-wall-spanning pool. The one we gave to Ulgar. The dying glow, soaking up the last oil fumes, glints off tiny ripples. In less than a minute, the cave will become pitch-black. Distant footsteps trail away. Scale the wall to the other side, then continue the chase through the next passageway? If I turn back now, I'll never know who spied on my parents and what he or she wanted to learn from them.

Bubbling water tempts me to play a dangerous game. The reward for crossing? Bragging rights over Linus, David, and James. There's no way I can swim across—no Jackson could, thanks to my dad's hydrophobia. *The wall is my best chance.* My fingertips dig into the mossy face, the hold secure enough. Hand then a foot, the next hand then the next foot, I inch along, the closest to rock I've ever been.

Comfortable with my newfound skill, I hit a slick patch catching me off guard. I throw my left hand out for a new grip to steady my weaker right. Chest heaving, I calm my breathing with a few deep breaths.

In seconds, the dying light ushers in a palpable darkness. Extreme panic sinks its iron talons into my flesh. Before I decide what to do next, push on or go back, my grasp slips.

The retry misses.

I fall into the water.

Cork-like, I bob to the surface, but the undertow claws me downward. Mouth an inch above the waterline, I suck in my last breath. How many summer days did I wish I could dive into the pool? The grand idea vanishes in a single terrible moment. Heavy clothes drag me underwater.

Currents whisk me along their labyrinthine path. Ahead, a green light pierces the darkness, an outlined rectangle with glowing edges etched in stone. I leave it behind, entering deep blackness. Nothing else matters, but one question: How long can I hold my breath? I tumble past a boulder but hit a rock column jutting from the floor. Air bubbles jet out of my mouth and nose in a violent instant. My lungs burn. Why didn't I listen to my parents? In another minute or less . . . I'll die. Can't hold it any longer.

This is it.

Will anyone find my body?

Water rushes into my stomach and lungs, but I don't perish. *Isn't this how someone drowns?* But my thoughts sharpen. Fresh oxygen filters back into my brain. *Is this happening? Yes.* My chest expands, and then contracts. I'm not dead—and yes, I can breathe underwater. How?

Doesn't matter. I have to head off the spy. Anyone who went through inordinate lengths to overhear my parents must have an enormous payoff. With renewed confidence, I tear through the water.

A rounded chamber, thirty feet tall, opens before me. Beyond the surface, lamplight spreads the spy's shadow on the wall. When the lamp moves, I swim up and hoist myself onto a rocky rim. The light halts, so I freeze. Can I submerge back underwater without him seeing or hearing me? When his shuffling noise fades, I stand, allowing my lungs to clear the water filling them. I dart after him down the dark passage.

I squeeze out of a small cave opening surrounded by ranks

of ghostly trees. Cool mist clings to a sweet apple scent. *Greene's orchard?* Strange, we never found this entrance, but my chicken-hearted friend wants a safe life void of any adventures.

My senses home in on an odd clanking sound. The figure sneaks past the Hill family house and disappears into the darkness. Where the trees end, overgrown turf begins, which lines the eastern way from town. Street lamplight brightens an enormous pack draped over the spy's shoulder. In an instant, my quarry vanishes behind the old meetinghouse.

Before I place a toe on the road, I check for the constable or the king's men. *Clear.* I take a deep breath, let it out in metered bursts, and then scramble across it.

To my relief and dismay, nobody lurks to the rear of the decrepit building. Either I lost the trail, or this wasn't the spy's destination. I scamper to the far corner. Last year, on a dare, we searched for a way inside, so James and I found two loose foundation blocks, which he worked free. Now anyone can squeeze through it to the crawl space. Since then, I'd discovered it had settled off-kilter, which loosened the floorboards. The loosest ones make up the coat closet floor, the place where no one will think to fix them. This discovery should serve me well tonight.

CHAPTER 5

COUNSEL FROM LIVING PAGES

I play with the gap in the door to strike the best balance to see, to hear, and to keep my anonymity. Elders crowd around a long table. Margaret slides her chair across worn floorboards, which brings the room to order.

"Thank you for coming," she says, pushing spectacles up her small nose. She counts everyone with her finger. "Seven." Her gaze shoots to the runner. "Where's Sebastian? You should've summoned him first, because he has the longest distance to ride."

"I did," James says.

She frowns, making him shift in his seat.

Silence.

Within an uncomfortable ten minutes, a breeze pushes against the closet door, so I push it back where I had it. A man with copper-flecked hair, wearing an elegant riding coat, flits inside the meetinghouse. "I was eating a sundae, Maggie," Sebastian says, his eyes leveling on my dad. "This had better be good."

"And dripping with warm chocolate, pooling in the dish?" Cornelius interjects.

Distracted, he sits opposite Margaret, and says, "Loads, a work of art."

Cornelius licks his lips. "After my mail circuit, I turned around to ride here without supper or dessert."

Margaret slaps her hands on the table. "Stop with the food talk! William, you have the floor."

My dad clears his throat a few times and dabs his forehead with a handkerchief. After a false start, he finds meaningful words to say.

"There was a reason to call you, but where this leads may be too risky. Thirteen years ago, we sacrificed a great deal . . . I can't ask you to do it again. Sorry for wasting your time." He eases into his chair and scans the crowd through steepled fingers.

This won't end well, I think.

"Wait a minute," Winston says. "You had something important to say earlier tonight, so tell us now."

"He's right," Cornelius says. "*We* voted on the decision to leave the kingdom back then. I daresay most want to try again."

"Hear, hear," Anthony, Greene's dad says. His crimson vest and round belly give him the shape of a giant apple.

"I second it, Ant," Herky says. "Forces worked against us then. Why did you call this council?"

Sebastian plays with the buttons running along his middle. As I recall, he didn't vote the same as the others. Everyone talks at once to persuade my dad to tell his story. A clever tactic. He has them where he wants them.

Dad raises his hands, which ushers a quiet into the room. "Today, my son and I traveled to Dunbury. The day dragged on, uneventful . . ."

I snort and then cover my mouth, but no one notices.

"On our way home, over Miller's fields, the Evening Star burned bright, reminding me of the time we fled the kingdom. This light fell from the heavens and landed before us." My dad pauses for a second, building anticipation. "From it strode a noblewoman, a queen from the Olden Days. She wore a silver circlet with jewels reflecting her brightness. Golden locks rolled off her head, washing over her shoulders. She gave me this book." He fishes it from his coat pocket.

She'd given it to me. Strange how he remembers things. He hands it to Margaret, who, wide-eyed, flips through pages.

"Your story makes sense," Winston says. "I walked my rounds then, and when I saw a distant flash, I wasn't sure if my mind had played a trick on me. But then a yellow light streaked over the horizon and chased the first one away. Strange."

"William, this tale beats any you've told," Sebastian says. "Your phobias, government conspiracies, the decline of the kingdom, all point to you being delusional."

My dad chews his lip.

Anthony jumps up before he can react, his sloping eyebrows show an intense face. "A sarcastic tongue is brother to envy. You're green under the collar. Why do you hold a grudge against William?"

This will be good.

Sebastian taps his head. "Your problem lies right here, Anthony. Unreasoned faith is sister to a halfwit. Many plausible conclusions can explain what happened. For instance, he journeyed far to Dunbury, so it exhausted him."

"Why do you say his story can't be true? He has no reason to lie. I, for one, am not too full of myself to deny it."

"Fine, show the world your simplemindedness. I see where this conversation ends, because it's in your eyes. And I hear rumblings at the market. I'll have no part in your schemes to disobey the king."

My dad raises his hands to silence the argument. "It's the truth, my son can verify the story."

Sorry, Dad, you're on your own.

"William, you speak the truth as you understand it, but there could be another explanation. At night, the mind does strange things."

Winston rolls his eyes. "Does my testimony count for nothing?"

A light shines from the book, growing with intensity. As if on fire, my dad drops it. The others gather around him, but Sebastian stays in his seat.

"The cover looks different," Dad says. "There's an embossed tree on it." He opens it as if it were a door caging a wild animal. "The pages are blank . . . wait . . . I see handwritten script now, ancient Bormaġian. I can try to interpret the words."

Margaret prods him with her elbow. "Go ahead."

"Quiet, everyone, here it goes. 'Peace, friends; let not your hearts trouble you. I am Wisdom's Light. Sophia, they call me, an elder with the Council of Fire, and servant to their master. Take courage, for we hold Wheatlanders in high regard. We saw your plight these long years. By the Master's will, El'Darios the Great, we choose you as keepers of his very thoughts, inscribed in this book.'"

I recall the old cover and new pages. His ideas would be ancient yet fresh for today.

My dad continues reading. "'I wanted to meet with you face to face, but the Thinning between the worlds passed hours ago. Stalwart, you people weather the storms assailing this kingdom. Behold, another tide of adversity gathers like storm clouds. Take courage, for we will be your help and your strong confidence. Together, we shall forge a grand work no evil power can gainsay.'"

He lays the book on the table but leaves his finger between the pages. Margaret clears her throat in a "get on with it" manner. He casts her a thoughtful glance and continues his translation.

No time to overthink things, Dad.

"'Though prone to weakness, the heart will search for freedom.

When anyone responds to our revelation, their thoughts fill this book.'

"'In the wide world, the first enemy was Malgroth, although his right name passed out of memory. His so-called brother, Ishglof, dwells beyond the green veil. We understand little of Malgroth's origin, but he existed long before the Dark Years, before the creation of all you see. Among the celestial elves, the Council of Fire, there was none greater until his fall from our realm.'

"'Now he is another kind, a splintered shadow, but given over to its darkness. He rules from Eskelon's cold towers, far above this world. To him, men and women are pieces on a board, which he manipulates and uses to his nefarious ends. His servants issue from his mind, taking shape as black mists, which poison the unwary. With overthrown understanding, they fill his army's ranks and desire power for its own sake. These slaves do not know they fulfill their new master's bidding.'

"'Even though your king is not in league with the Dark Lord yet, I will send you to a faraway land away from endless war. In the West, a glorious sun shall rise; from the dregs of your decaying kingdom, I intend on birthing forth the greatest people the world has ever seen.'"

The elders jabber among themselves. They must share my questions, too, but their discussion pauses when a song rises from the pages.

"Deep into the West, a ship shall sail,

Liberty's chance shall soon prevail.

A land at rest, the people, blest,

Her heart and power they all avail.

Far across the mystical blue sea,
There forge a land both just and free.
The ocean foam, five score shall roam,
A journey wrought through adversity.

When they set sail, prosp'rous winds prevail,
Away to rill and flow'ring dale.
Their hopes and dreams, beneath moonbeams,
Friend wind gives way to strong, stormy gale.

A fierce tempest arose in the night,
Proud faces turn to sheets of white.
A howling gale with pounding hail,
Down one swell, up to lofty wave height.

Far away from the fair homeland shore,
A little ship, the faithful bore.
Their chief desire a burning fire,
Labors and life dawn the first-year sore.

The river by the haven shall flow,
On the fair banks, a seed will grow.
Tall tree of life, drum, flag, and fife,
Out of the East, a chilling wind blows.

Dearest life and hope begin to pine,
In dark, my glory then to shine.
The sting of death and final breath,
They will rise above on wings of mine.

These people who dwell across the sea,
Lifting their voice for liberty.
Many shall come toward the sun,
A beacon of light for all to see."

At her last word, the glow within the book dies away, but stillness blankets the hall. Dad closes the cover, leans back in the chair, and drums his fingertips together. David and I'd been little when my parents had attempted to leave the kingdom. Deep in my heart, I knew they'd try again someday.

"What part do we play in her plans?" my dad says. "Do we ignore them?"

"For months, this idea has been growing in my mind," Margaret says. "George and I have spent sleepless nights discussing it. We believe the Lady has been whispering to us, but the last time we tried to leave meant a jail sentence for many Wheatlanders. Life without my husband was difficult, and his health declined.

"Today, our people carry heavy debt because of rampant crop failures. Land grants to new settlers appeal to everyone. Our young sons and daughters won't fear the king's endless war with T'Anak, and we won't worry about the midnight knock on the door." She pushes spectacles up the bridge of her nose, and lamp flame reflects in her eyes. She leans forward, both palms pressed on the tabletop. "We've lost our library, half our freedoms, and live under a watchful eye, but the journey west will be dangerous, giving us much to consider."

Everyone talks at once, making it difficult to understand their words. Anthony and Sebastian continue their argument with their wild, gesticulating hands, Margaret and George whisper alone, and Herky, Cornelius, Winston, and my dad share their joy.

"I can tell where this conversation will end," Sebastian says with a raised voice. His eyes level on Anthony. "Has the stench of the king's dungeons washed out of your clothes? Have the wounds from the chains healed?"

"What do you mean? Speak plain," Greene's dad says.

"I'll explain it so even you can understand it. You've stayed in there before, now you're ready for another visit? I'm sure His Majesty's whips will welcome you again." Sebastian shakes his head. "I pity your forgetful minds and your bruised backs. What you did years ago brought his judgment. The banishment from Heathfell carries to the Wheatland elders, forever. You know how our law works. The political climate hasn't changed, so the same laws are in force. Do you think he'll relax his emigration policy for us, the dregs of the kingdom?"

Margaret rolls her eyes and heaves a noticeable sigh. "You focus on *one* con with no solution to offer."

Sebastian shrugs. "What could be worse than jail time?"

"I'm undecided," the chief says, weighing one hand against the other. "Wheatlanders who disappear at midnight when King Alfonse's thugs call or our children drafted into his armies. Anyone who thinks for themselves may just *vanish*." She flutters her fingers in the air for effect.

"Disappearances?" Sebastian says. "The rabble-rouser Dirk Hubberthorne got what he deserved. He was always looking for a fight, so the king's men took him to Heathfell for questioning."

Margaret points a narrow finger at him. "Never to come back. The neighbors heard them bash in the front door during the night. No one has seen him since then. What crime did he commit?"

"Many people return, Bill and Clare Hoggins, for example. Although he didn't work out at my market, he's doing well now. Again, the king's guards will catch you, beat you, and your second stay in the dungeons he'll make worse than the first. The king believes we sympathize with our kingdom's enemies."

My throat tightens, because I'd helped a T'Anakim man. I may disappear on a stormy night, and nobody will find me again.

"Besides," Sebastian says, "there's no need to steer our families into harm's way. We have a good life here. The king's men leave us alone for the most part and people earn a respectable living."

"Respectable living?" Anthony says. "I tightened my belt another notch today."

"And that's a bad thing?"

"You've done more for yourself than eke out a livelihood, Moneybags. Most Wheatlanders stand in line, dangling on the edge of bankruptcy. And there we'll wait, never getting ahead. Something new could be better. Our connections here aren't so . . ." Anthony snaps his thick fingers a few times.

"Lucrative?" Herky says.

Anthony points at his best friend. "Yes."

". . . and dubious?"

"Yes, again, one hundred percent shady."

Sebastian's deep frown doesn't last long. "I'll concede the point and assume you escape the kingdom."

A wide smile spreads across Anthony's face. Herky shakes his head and rolls his eyes.

The market owner paces. "The Bormagian settlement in the west will offer resources and protection. Did you ever hear news from those lands?" No one faces him. "I'll enlighten you. Settlers report a wildland, dangerous, and its soil yields thorns and briars. The native people torture outsiders as part of their barbaric customs. Count on late supply shipments. The Mystic Sea growls as if a hungry beast, devouring ships, swallowing land, and leaving wives destitute and children fatherless. Remember, the mothers teach the young ones the old rhymes. 'Frothing, foaming, the Mystic Sea moaning. Churning, turning, the Mystic Sea burning. Storming, hailing, the Mystic Sea assailing. Weeping, wailing, the Mystic Sea prevailing.' Is sailing across it worth any price?"

Cornelius drums his fingers together. "I appreciate your point of view, but you're still new to Wheatland. We have more ill history to remember. A wise man once said, 'If you lightly esteem your freedom, your freedom will lightly esteem you.' Life has risks, but with Lady Sophia on our side, the balance tips in our favor."

"Hear, hear," Anthony says.

"Test these words you hear as the mouth tastes food," Cornelius says. "Many tall tales surround the western lands."

"Tall tales, indeed," Sebastian says, rolling his eyes and wagging his head.

"Merchants fabricate endless myths. That way, they can scare off rivals. We want to preserve our lives from systems hostile to it. Years before the time you remember, Wheatlanders lived among the T'Anakim."

The market owner steeples his fingers, flexing them ever so slightly.

"But their children wandered too far from their roots. There, foreigners can't own property or hold good-paying jobs. On the verge of starvation, they returned. Since then, what did they find? The king wages war, sends spies, the Collector drains our wallets, and crops fail year after year.

"This will be different, for the Council of Fire wants to help us. Lady Sophia visited William, an event we believe. They see every end, for their power knows no bounds. How can we pass up a powerful friendship?

"The natives may be barbaric, but the Lady is aware of this. They might come under her illuminating influence. Tell me, what important effort ever came without difficulties?"

Sebastian shakes his head. "Your fortunes have changed in one respect, but not in another. Who'll bankroll this journey, or buy your homes? You need a financier, or the voyage is going nowhere. No magic book hocus-pocus can do this for you. Friends, be honest with yourselves . . . you're not brave sailors, but farmers, laborers, craftsmen, and country gentlemen. Try to build the best life here."

"I've thought long and hard," Herky says. "Selma and I knew this day would come, so we made plans regarding our things. My brother from Garlow will take over the ranch. He'll combine his herds with mine. When more trade comes west, he'll send heifers and bulls."

Sebastian lets his hands drop on the table.

"Stop fussing," Anthony says. "Herky shared his idea with me years ago. It caused Ferne and I to think along the same lines. My nephews will work the orchard, which buys us time if we need to return."

My dad snaps his fingers. "After settling in the new world, we can come back and finish our business affairs. I'll rent Fairview instead, because many people would give their right arm to live there."

Everyone talks at once.

Margaret raises her hands to quiet the crowd. "We've heard both sides. Does anyone else have something to say?"

Anthony's hand shoots up and waves. "I second the motion Cornelius made."

"Let's vote, gentlemen. Should we sail west? In favor, say, aye."

One by one, the ayes ring out with Sebastian casting the lone dissenting vote.

She nods with satisfaction, careful to avoid his sour stare. "Ayes have it, so the motion carries. Now the tough part—find a ship and crew."

My dreams vanish when faint clanking seeps in from outside the meetinghouse. *Familiar . . . can't place it.* If the elders didn't chatter, they'd notice it, too.

Orange light flashes. Without warning, a lit jug flies through the window and crashes onto the floor. Shattered pieces land everywhere. I jump back. Flames grow, sprinting to a small puddle before the closet. Fear roots me to the spot. Before I can react, a fire blazes before me.

"Fire!" Winston shouts.

Jugs crash here and there. The hall brightens with a hellish glow. Elders swat at the unyielding flames with their coats. With all windows curtained in fire, the door proves to be the best chance of getting out alive.

My dad tries the doorknob. "Locked or barricaded from the other side."

Hungry flames lick the ceiling rafters while billowing smoke pushes its way toward the floor. For me, the way out lies beneath my feet.

CHAPTER 6

THROUGH FIRE AND WATER

Anthony thunders toward the door. It doesn't stand a chance. His bulk barrels through, splintering it off the frame. To my relief, they have their escape route—now for mine.

I drop through the hole in the floorboards and then crawl to the opening in the foundation, avoiding smoke wisps, which squeeze between spaces in the wood above me. Timbers creak and answer one another in a haunting song.

The building burns fast, igniting my own fears that it will collapse. Better scoot before it crashes. At the crawl space corner, I breathe easier, but my relief is short-lived. Where's the hole? Best I can tell in the faint orange light, someone stuck the blocks back into their place.

Time stretches on for an eternity. Still, the conflagration laughs at my pitiful yells for help and useless kicks at wedged foundation bricks. I've read people trapped in a fire also die of smoke inhalation, a lung problem caused by breathing in gases and soot. Death

by asphyxiation doesn't seem a painful way to go, but I don't want to die—not yet—not this way. Hopeless, I curse my hard luck. I survived drowning, but now fire and a collapsing building will kill me.

Muffled shouts filter through the foundation blocks, but spooky moans creak over them. A series of cracks cascade to a rumble. *This is it.* Timbers crash to the floor overhead, stabbing into the crawl space. Fiery embers cover my body and sparks swirl in the air. Through the gap, a half-eaten roof burns with leaping flames.

I flick ash off my eyelashes and pat out little fires dotting my clothes. They smoke with burn holes, but the coals didn't scorch my flesh. I grab a smoking orange coal. Warm, but nothing else. For the second time today, I've stared death in the face, but escaped. Rebecca had said the lamp handle was hot, I recall. Water and fire are my friends. Still eager to get out, the timbers smashed a rift in the foundation, so I crawl through it and dash away.

Distant shouts build in front of the meetinghouse. In my haste to hide, I stub my toe on something heavy. A ceramic jug. Curious, I pull free the cork and sniff the open mouth. Acrid fumes force a dry heave from me. The orange firelight illuminates it enough to make out a wolf's head on the label, but I can't read any words. I toss the evidence in plain sight, then crawl into nearby bushes. Among the tangled branches, as expected, I find the arsonist's sack. After a few moments, my dad rounds the corner, water bucket in hand. He heaves it onto the fire, but the angry flames just laugh.

An adrenaline surge keeps my eyes wide throughout the night. Hours melt midnight into early morning when insatiable flames had reduced the meetinghouse to ash. As the gray dawn bleeds into the sky, the chance arrives to learn the crime scene's first clue. The bucket brigade—James, the elders, and close-by neighbors, stand, sit, or lie on the ground in exhaustion. I sneak to a cluster of bushes, closer to where everyone rests.

A weary clip-clop ambles toward the exhausted fire fighters. Sebastian halts his red mare for a second. "Martha will miss me," he says, tipping his hat. He urges his horse onward, a dust plume rising as he canters north.

"Nothing more we can do," Margaret says. "Let's go home."

The crowd disperses in every direction, but the elders stay.

My dad holds up the jug. "Before we leave, I found evidence I want to study."

Winston snatches it from his hand, turns it around, and frowns. "As I expected, the wolf's-head label. 'Wolfie's Finest Moonshine. Just one sip and you'll be howling for more.' No wonder the meetinghouse burned fast. Have to ride far away to find any, because it's illegal in this borough. I'll bet the assailant drank from this jug instead of destroying it."

Anthony snatches it from his hands. "Impossible, I don't see his drunken carcass on the ground. Do you?"

Winston frowns. "What if not, who cares? He still could've fled the scene."

"You're not following me, Winnie, it's potent. Take it from a guy who knows. A casual drink will put you on your backside for a week, and a whole jug could kill ten men."

"You don't say."

"I'm sure he didn't have the chance to burn this one. He must have vanished when I smashed the door. When I used to drink this stuff, only the Childers Market sold it."

The constable rubs his beard. "You drank—"

Anthony's bushy eyebrows pull together into a frown. "Everyone regrets things they've done in their past."

"There's much profit in bootlegged goods."

Margaret grabs the constable's shoulder. "But he doesn't sell it anymore. He gave us his word. I believe him, because I *never* see it there."

Herky dashes to the elders and holds up a sack. "Look what I found. The arsonist can't carry four jugs with two hands. He must have carried them in this." He flips it over and points. "A Childers Market symbol stitched on the back, which means it's new." Winston tries to snatch it. "Not so fast, Winnie. Whoever hid it didn't want it discovered. The inside could hold a clue." Face alight with wonder, Herky's arm sinks deep into the bag. "Nothing."

Anthony's mood darkens. "I believed Sebastian had the wits of a fox, but with half the scruples. The rotter played us for fools."

"Are you implicating him in risking our lives and burning down the meetinghouse?" Margaret says.

"At least he sold the means to commit the arson."

"Which makes him an accomplice," Winston says.

"He may have a co-conspirator. You saw how he doesn't want us to leave the kingdom," Anthony says. "He'd lose his customers. Far be it from Mr. Moneybags to throw a lousy half cub our way in charity."

"Sebastian gives to those in need, half lions notwithstanding. You don't know the money he gives to others, but I do."

"Name one."

"I won't. His dealings, his business. Not yours, not mine."

Anthony folds his arms in disgust.

"Conspirator, pah! Don't be ridiculous," George says, eyes boring into him.

"To be sure, conspiracies have existed from early recorded history," my dad says, "intricate or simple, but always with the mastermind at its center."

Dad means well, but sometimes he doesn't think before he speaks.

Margaret shoots him a dark glance. "This evidence could be months old. Besides, he didn't have time to organize the arson."

James wrings his hands. We've been friends and pranking conspirators forever, so I can tell when he wants to say something important.

"What, James?" Margaret says. She knows him better than I

do because she raised him ever since his parents died when he was young. Even though he's a few years older than me, a love for books, the tales told at the fireside, and curiosity over the wide world bind us together. And he always wanted a younger brother, which he got in the finest quality.

"He didn't want to come, so I explained to him what William told me."

"What did you say?"

He counts on his fingers. "The Lady's visitation and an urgent meeting with the elders. He must have connected all other details."

"And he was the last to arrive at the council, even though he has a fast horse," Anthony says. "Did just his dessert make him late?"

Herky studies the jug, spinning it in his hands. "They have valid points, Margaret. It didn't claim his life, but with us around, we stood an excellent chance of getting out alive. He could have had a trick up his sleeve to get us out or at least get himself out."

A tingle slithers along my spine as ideas flood my mind. Sebastian must know these floorboards and foundation blocks are loose. He could hide in here, stash a wet handkerchief nearby so he can breathe, and then escape. Did his accomplice replace them to trap me? Or even betray him? Interesting idea.

Margaret slaps her hands on her sides. "This is only guesswork!" she says. "Go home and gather your wits, then we'll talk more." She storms away with George in tow.

James whistles a mournful tone. I can't risk trying to get his attention. No one dares a word. Their sheepish expressions confess they went too far this time. Would someone put their life in jeopardy to gain an evil outcome?

My dad follows Cornelius, so a sudden panic grips me. Our neighbor will give him a ride home. More chores if he finds my bed empty. *Go!*

I steal from bush to bush, tree to tree, with the gray morning cloaking my whereabouts. At the square, I dart off the road to a shortcut across James's property.

When I near Fairview, my dad, after saying goodbye to Cornelius, plods heavy-footed for the front door.

No time to catch my breath. I hustle to my bedroom window, which should be open enough for me to slip into my room.

I lift my foot to the sill, then hoist my body. When I wriggle through, I drop to the floor and creep toward the junky side. This couldn't be easier.

Halfway to bed, my foot presses a creaky floorboard, which freezes me to the spot.

"Now what's the troublemaker doing?" David says groggily. A flint strike pierces the gloom, then lamplight fills my bedroom. "Do I smell smoke on you? You're *so busted*, you irresponsible little dolt."

"You couldn't even imagine the things I've seen and done. And if I didn't go after . . ." *Stop, can't bring a first-class clod into this situation.*

"Try me."

"If it's the same to you, I'll tell you the new big secret in exchange for your loquacious tendencies to be more, shall we say, taciturn?"

Confusion and anger fight for dominance on his face. "What? Speak plain."

Halfwit. "Meaning your complete silence."

David thinks for a moment. It looks as if it hurts him. "Deal."

CHAPTER 7

THE GREAT CHORE SENTENCE

David's faraway look tells me the arson and leaving Wheatland sinks deep into his thick skull. Grayness lifts with sunlight peeping through the shutters. I want to go, provided my friends do, too. For the time being, my powers and calling as first warden—whatever that means—must stay incognito. Until I know more. How do I have these abilities? Who wants to kill the elders, and why? Many questions with zero answers—best to sleep on it.

As I drift off, random images spin in my mind: Jonah, my dad, and the Two Gems. Grandma and Grandpa. When they fade, a rectangle forms into a dark door. When it opens, an onyx with obsidian stone fortress peaked with six towers looms in the distance. Anguished sobs, quiet at first, build in desperation.

"No . . . no," a gasping voice pleads. "Jonathan, David, only you can save me." The crying diminishes to silence. My little trembles grow into violent shakes.

"Wake up, dear," my mom says, startling me awake.

Eyes flickering to life, my hand shields the brightness. She always snaps open the shutters. She sits on my bed, nose pinched. Mom's silvery-blue eyes study my face with concern. She pulled her chestnut hair back, but a few fallen strands frame her round cheeks.

A busy spider, dangling overhead, descends a silk thread anchored to the ceiling.

Mom offers a tentative smile and smooths my bushy hair. "Are you well?"

Would anyone in my circumstances? Happy as a fish underwater, can bask in flames, but I am powerless to help a woman in mortal peril. The same person's voice from the waterfall pool nightmare. Grandma, who's alive, locked in the most terrible place imaginable—Eskelon, the fortress of the most evil entity even my mind can conjure. I can't go . . . I'm no fighter.

"Fine," I say, my expression trying to dismiss her for asking. Mom's eyes search mine. She doesn't believe me and can ferret out a lie before you know she's onto you.

"Then rise and shine, time to begin the jobs I assigned you." She starts for the door.

My heart deflates. I forgot—the inevitable day one in my week-long chore sentence. Their punishments are like the annoying distant cousin you don't see often but wish it was even less. It's late summer, and I can't squander any days before back-to-school time. Besides, I have watchmen to prank, cows to tip, and a self-righteous brother to humble.

She stops and turns toward me. "Dress, then come to the kitchen." When she disappears into the hallway, I punch my pillow.

David's awake and working. His smoothed bedcovers could bounce a coin high into the air, I'm sure. He always sleeps on top of them, the weirdo. A rotting egg in his pillowcase will mix things up a bit.

His tidy belongings fit on a nightstand, but mine, buried in mountains of books and trash, emit a strange odor. If I could find that banana from last week, the air quality may improve. Mom wants me to clean it up for sure.

I reach up, and with thumb and forefinger squish the multi-legged nuisance. *I hate spiders. Too many creepy legs.* I roll out of bed and wipe its guts on my brother's perfect bedspread.

From a heap, I pull on khaki trousers and a faded navy-blue shirt. I grab my quill, and near my headboard, etch a line in the wood paneling. Day one of unjust punishment. Finger-combing my hair, I stumble out the door, ready for what she throws at me. My bed, I leave a mess.

At the kitchen table, David shoves an egg-and-sausage sandwich into his wide mouth. "Yours," he says, pointing to buttered toast on a plate.

I'd love to shove it in his face, but who wants even more chores? Mom's kitchen is spotless, and she intends to keep it that way.

"The early bird gets the worm." He drops the last tasty morsel into his gaping trap.

"You can have the slimy dirt-eaters to yourself. Who knows what goes into sausage, anyway? Parts, I hear."

David's jaw contorts. With that word picture in his mind, his breakfast must sicken his stomach.

He exits the kitchen in a hurry, leaving my mom to stare at his greening cheeks. She squeezes my shoulders. "When you get back, clean your father's library first. Pep keeps missing under the credenza, so give it extra attention. And don't forget to scrub the privy, dust the living room, sweep and wax the wood floors, take out the trash, and muck out the stall you call your 'domain'—it's atrocious. Here's your list."

"When I get back?"

"Your father will tell you. He's in the library."

As if summoned, my dad rushes into the kitchen. "Awake?

Good, you'll come with me." He stirs a heaping spoonful of cocoa into his coffee, then takes a long draw. "At last night's council, the elders voted to leave Wheatland again. Trouble is, Sebastian cast the lone dissenting vote. He'll make things hard for us if he puts his mind to it. He's crazy to miss this golden opportunity."

"It's the chance of *our* lifetime," my mom says, "but not *his*. He has a different outlook on life."

"Regardless, we need his influence. He hinted his wife is sick—"

"Again?"

Dad nods. "I want to help with any chores they may have. Spread goodwill and rebuild trust." He turns to Mom. "We'll be back in a couple hours so you can put *your* son to work."

She rolls her eyes and offers a wry grin. "As you say."

"Oh, the meetinghouse. Fill in David, and I'll fill in Jonathan."

Good, my brother didn't snitch on me. I fake a perplexed stare. No one but my Auntie Fanny could act more theatrical.

"Let's go," Dad says.

Along Green Hollow Way, birds speed overhead. As we travel northbound, apple scent drifts from the orchard's leafy arms. In town, we zigzag through traffic and pass the king's men picking through the meetinghouse ashes. Dad says their reports to Heathfell portray us as defiant people. One could have been the spy outside our window and the other the arsonist. Are they searching for evidence, or planting it?

Beyond the North Wheatland Road and Fairfield Road intersection, tall rooflines interrupt the landscape. An oversized barn and several smaller buildings make up the Childers Empire. Crowds throng wagon workers, who unload crates, boxes, and barrels stenciled "Made in Heathfell."

"Come on," my dad says after scanning the grounds. "He's still home."

When we rejoin the road from town, I recall most people don't venture this way. Legend scars the borough's northern region—the

Haunted Moors. Child disappearances, strange creatures, and dangerous thugs dominate the stories Greene tells me. Could they be right?

Oaken arms reach from overhead as if to snatch me. A granite bridge with black-oak timbers spans the swift Wheatland River's east fork. In another mile, my dad assures me, we'll come to the Childers' farmhouse.

The route meanders westward and opens to a vast emerald meadow where the Wheatland River splits into its west and east branches. The west branch runs southwest by the hollow where I live, while the east fork bends toward Heathervale at the Forest of Heth. Nasty place, so I also hear from my friend.

Ahead, the Childers' farmhouse stands among a wide-canopied elm grove. Not what I expected from the richest man in town, for it's humble, and not a palace.

Trees at a bend obscure the turnoff to the avenue leading to their property. A low rumble growls in the earth, so we halt. My dad's eyes suggest he feels it, too. At its peak, a horse speeds around the curve. I dive off the road before impact and land facedown in the weeds. With a swift jerk, a dark hand hoists me to my feet. Familiar coffee-brown eyes flicker underneath a hat curling black hair.

"Sorry," James says.

"What on earth are you doing?" I say, dusting off my trousers.

"Fifteen minutes ago, this stretch was empty. You hurt?"

"No, let's check on my dad."

"Yes."

I sprint to the other side, following my dad's pathetic groans to where he lays sprawled among tall weeds. "Dad, you all right?"

"Landed on a log," he says through gritted teeth. We each grab an arm to help him. He smooths his coat. "Thank you, boys, I'm okay, just a little shaken."

The runner manages a tentative smile. I pat him on the back, which puffs a dust cloud into the air.

Mud caked on his boots suggests he's ridden for days. His work never ends. "Where are you going?"

He glances at the ground. "Council business, you know I can't tell you anything." His glance flits to my dad.

While James helps him, I sidle to his sandy-colored thoroughbred, Dust Storm. He brays and sidesteps away. I hold up my hand, palm outward, because he can act temperamental. Ears twitch, and soft amber eyes say sorry.

"You didn't do it on purpose," I say, stroking his velvety muzzle.

"Why are you riding so fast, James?" my dad says.

"Urgent elder business. You know, from last night. Had I stayed longer, I could have learned straight from them and not needed their letter. If there's nothing further, I have a tiring ride ahead."

"Let me see it."

He fishes it from his coat pocket and hands it to him. I lead Dust Storm to a place where I can peer over his shoulder, and to my surprise, he pretends not to notice.

To Mr. J. Howe,

When you're back, come to my house. The elders want to send you east as soon as may be. I'll give you more particulars upon your arrival.

Sincerely,

Mr. S. Childers

P.S. Pack for the weekend, just in case.

P.P.S. Pass along your expenses to me when you return.

P.P.P.S. Hurry.

My dad can't hide a betrayed expression, because they didn't authorize a communication to Heathfell, and he must know only Sebastian is behind it.

James taps the parchment. "I couldn't keep council business waiting, so I readied Dusty and raced away."

My dad's reticence eases in a few awkward seconds. "I don't recall any—"

I stick my pointy elbow into his side. "Late night for you, Dad, but I'm sure you remember," I say to help him recognize this excellent opportunity to find out what he's doing.

He scowls, but then understands my intention. "You were saying, James?"

"Sebastian said to deliver this letter to Heathfell. With a secondary contact, Mr. Vespasian Walsh. Nothing can jar his instructions from my mind . . . to Mr. Oliver Iskander, Heathfell town, East Borough. A dodgy place, but I won't complain. I'll go wherever the council sends me."

"Good man."

"And you're feeling okay? Sorry. Time for me to get going."

My dad extends his hand. "Thank you, I'll manage."

James mounts Dust Storm but pauses.

"What?" I say.

"A couple months ago, I met a young lady in Heathfell."

My throat tightens. "And . . ."

"And . . . this week, I'll ask her to marry me."

What? How could he do this? An unsure expression replaces his hopeful one. How could I prepare for this news? I grunt weakly.

"Made up my mind this morning. I haven't even told George and Margaret yet."

At least he let me know first. "But they've raised you since you were seven. They're the closest thing you have to family."

"Except for one."

"Thanks for the vote of confidence."

"But I don't see them much, being on business everywhere."

He saw them at the meetinghouse, but I won't dare allude to that. "If this woman makes you happy, then I'm for it."

"Great, wait until you meet her. She's wonderful, and we're a perfect match."

"Does this mystery girl have a name?"

"Siany. She works for her dad, the chief healer. I met her at the Three Oaks Tavern after an unfortunate accident Dusty and I had. A story for another time. Wish me luck."

"Tell me how it goes."

"Count on it. And I'll need a best man, so help me find one, okay?" A wry grin spreads across his face.

"Don't say anymore. I will."

His smile flattens, and he nods, tipping his hat. With a jerk of the reins, horse hooves dig into the dirt, and they burn a path away from us. What is Sebastian doing by sending a secretive letter? I have to find out before someone gets killed.

Within my mind, I debate every cynical permutation of Sebastian's motives, not realizing hoofbeats draw closer. My dad steps off the road, so I do the same.

Around the bend rushes a pristine mare dressed in a silver-studded harness, pulling an elegant wagon. Sebastian wears a long black riding coat. The horse obeys a tug on the reins to stop.

"Hello William and Jonathan. What brings you this way?"

"Came to visit you and Martha and see if you need help with your house chores," my dad says. "We met James, who was rushing along the road. He had *interesting* things to say."

Sebastian's countenance falls. "Sure, he did. Martha is fine and I'll see her at lunchtime. Climb up next to me, and I'll take you back to town."

We both slide onto the bench. Dad turns to him, saying, "He said you sent him on council business. We never commissioned a letter to Heathfell, so what's happening?"

Body straightening, he raises a palm upward. "It's my business," he says in a firm voice. "I'm not doing anything wrong, or seditious.

All I can say right now is he's doing me a big favor. Can't help that he thinks we sent him." His eyes break their contact with ours.

I know what the letter said, so he's up to something.

"If the king's men find out you sent our runner to Heathfell unbidden, there'll come reprisals. To them, we'll always be T'Anakim sympathizers."

"Don't worry, I'll handle them."

Before we could hear how he might influence them, the wagon turns into the market driveway. Any chance to learn of James's errand must wait.

"Trust me, in time you'll understand everything. I'm late for work, so please excuse me, I can bring you this far."

"Fine," my dad says, "appreciate the ride."

Sebastian extends his hand to us. I hesitate before shaking it, because I can't help thinking he's up to no good. If I find Wolfie's at the market, we'd have him for sure, but when will I break away from this chore prison sentence?

We trudge through Fairview's courtyard. From the backyard, my brothers' wild play punches the air. Lucky brats.

"My library first," Dad says in a sharp tone. "Do you remember how I want the books arranged?"

Meticulous to a fault. "Yes."

"Back so soon?" my mom says, trailing my scurrying littlest brother.

"I'll meet you in the parlor, Eliza."

"And Jonathan, don't forget the list your mother made for you."

How can I forget, it's a mile long.

CHAPTER 8

HIDDEN HISTORY

In the library, the old book leather scent mixes with a hint of tobacco. Pipe smoking, a relic of my grandpa's bygone era, adds class to the room. A panorama of books stretches from wall to wall. Years of collection worth a small fortune. I sink into Dad's plush chair, rock back and forth, and fidget with the desk's brass handles. Chores can wait a few more minutes.

Noises as if someone is working next door echo toward my house. *Linus?* I set my hands on the window frame and lean out. "Hey, get over here, you loathsome churl!"

The work sounds stop.

Gunnar, then Rebecca, round the corner.

I try to hide, but it fails to happen.

"Hey, yourself! And what did you call me?"

Heat rushes to my face. "Winsome girl." I motion her over with my hand.

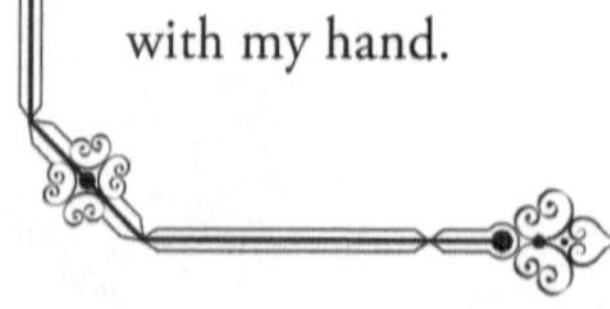

"Sweetheart, your cocoa's ready," her mom, Leigh, calls from the front yard.

"Be right there," she says, turning in her direction.

"Sorry, thought you were Linus," I say. "Is he still sleeping in your backyard tent?"

"Him? No, he awoke early and went for a hike. My brother belongs to the woods. He likes his adventures. So what did you want?"

"I have bad news."

"Oh?"

"When my dad and I looked for Ulgar yesterday morning, he wasn't there."

"You're kidding."

I stare at her with shocked incredulity and spread my hands apart, palms upward.

"Where do you think he went?"

"The forest, no doubt."

"Nothing we can do for him at this point. I hope his wounds don't kill him."

"Does your dad believe you?"

"Nope."

Her blue eyes widen with excitement. "Did you hear the meetinghouse burned to ash last night? Constable Beasley will investigate it as an arson."

"Not much surprises me anymore."

"What else do you know?"

Now I've done it. I gulp, searching for words to say. "No one knows, but I was there."

Her arching eyebrows slide into a deep frown.

"Listen before you judge me."

"Okay, spill it."

"After dinner, I took the trash to the corral and outside our kitchen window was someone spying on my parents' conversation.

I followed the spy to the meetinghouse, and while the elders held the meeting, I saw him or her light the place on fire."

She nods a few seconds. "At least your story makes sense. I couldn't control Gunnar last night, because he caught a scent or a strange noise. I didn't let him off the leash for fear I'd never see him again. Did you tell your dad or even Constable Beasley?"

Glancing downward, I say, "If the king's men find out I broke curfew, they will beat me to a pulp in the town square to make me an example to others. Besides, it was dark, so there's no chance I can recognize anyone but someone who walks on two legs."

"You'll solve it alone?"

I shrug. "That's my plan."

"Always the lone wolf. Let me help."

She'd get in the way, but I can't say that. "I won't allow you to get into trouble. And I don't want any more of it. Think I want chores for an eternity?"

She leans in the window, hair brushing my cheek, and cranes her neck from side to side. "Shouldn't take you long."

Never been this close . . . A spark flashes in me, heat rushes to my face. Her cheeks flush, piercing eyes see through me. My mind tells me to give her room, but my feet don't want to move. My heart will burst out of its ribbed cage.

"Rebecca!" her mom says.

Startled, I step away, head smacking the window jamb.

"I called you twice," she says, red hair glistening in the sun.

"Be right there."

Curiosity crosses her face.

"Hello, Jonathan."

"Mrs. Avery."

She hesitates for a second before heading for the front yard.

Rebecca offers a shy smile, but then it flattens. "I want in . . . to team up with you. This person could've killed my dad. Imagine what that would've done to my family. Who's next? Do you think a king's man or even our T'Anakim friend did it?"

How can she step from our moment so fast? I take in a nervous breath and let it out, annoyed. "I'd believe one of them over Ulgar, but what do they gain by doing it?"

"They hate us. Pathetic, showing up late at a crime scene."

"Yes, I saw them."

"My dad says they've been looking for witnesses, but for sure it's a pretense."

"Reminds me, chores. Another prime day wasted."

Rebecca rolls her eyes. "You don't like work, do you?"

"With so many things on my list, this isn't near the top."

"I have plenty, too. Bye." And as if nothing happened between us, she flicks her fingers in a subtle wave. She glides toward the front yard, her dress complimenting curves missing last year. My thoughts drift away with her.

Books and clutter dot the room, the biggest one on the desk. Strewn parchments lay across something long. I move them aside to uncover the hilt. Fine craftsmanship adorns a firefly's body with head, thorax, and abdomen. Etched rune letters spell words from an unknown language. A comfortable fit in my hand extending a few inches beyond my palm. And sturdy protrusions—antennae—bend outward at the tip. Must be the quillons, hand protection should an enemy blade slide down its length.

I set it on the desk and face the bookcases. If I hurry, I'll have time to search for references to the Two Gems, the Two Combining, or even my abilities.

My dad's meticulous order, starting from the bottom: thick history and encyclopedia books, then lexicons and dictionaries beside my mom's precious little space for school materials. Next, poetry, fiction, and fantasy, then the top two shelves, great thinkers, philosophers, biographies, and even a few romance novels. *Romance, yuck.*

I pull open a famous philosopher's complete works. By its

cracking spine, I believe my dad never opened it. My eyes scan the first chapter . . . *Dull.* I slip my fingers along a middle page. May as well be guilty of his allegations. I tear it top to bottom, replace it backward, and shelve it.

To my joy and relief, the Lady's book catches my eye, so I grab it. Good to see he rescued it from the flames. One thing Malgroth and Ishglof want to destroy, but I won't let them. I slide down the ladder and drop into the chair.

As I flip through pages, I pass by sections of text until I find the first blank page. I expect ornate script to appear, the same way she spoke to the elders. Nothing. Why not? I slam the cover.

A sudden worry drops upon me that Dad will catch me shirking my chores, so I grab the broomstick and force it under the credenza. I pull out a colony of multiplying dust bunnies. After several tries, a clean floor emerges from the mess. Baseboard grime stands out even more. *Yuck.* I wet a rag and, with elbow grease, wipe away the years. A knot spins in place and, loose, it slips onto the floor. I scour it with my thumbnail. Someone stamped a circle with two short lines forming a *V.*

Familiar . . . I snap my fingers—the hilt. *A key.* I snatch it from the desk, fit the end into the hole, and twist to the left. A rumble bleeds into wood scraping on wood, mechanical gears turning, and an odd clunking noise. I step away when the credenza top rises toward the window, folding the floorboards into a stack. When the cycle finishes, the gray outline of stairs descends below the ground. I dart to the library door, lock it, and shove the key into my pocket. *No one can see this before me.*

My jaw drops when I peer over the edge into a secret entrance. To what? I ignore the warning shiver snaking along my spine. One way to find out.

I take a deep breath and force spiders and other creepy crawlies from my mind. Inspired by fragile courage, my left foot takes a brave step downward. The stairs creak until I reach a tiled floor. Tree roots poke through cracks in a timber-braced earthen ceiling. A musty smell masks an acrid tinge, hanging in the air.

When my eyes adjust to the darkness, the gray outline of a room twenty by twenty opens before me. On the far side, something sparkles silvery-gold. I meander through furniture and different sized objects to shelves filled with many weird things. The glow belongs to a powder swirling in a glass jar.

I pick it up, so its magical light can help me find a lamp. But when I turn, it illuminates a figure wielding a blade. Fear paralyzes me for a second, but then I realize it's a suit of armor outfitting a mannequin. A two-handed sword points tip upward in a weapon rack.

The gray sunshine falling from the library outlines a lamp near the stairs, which I grab, and with a flint, strike a dark-piercing spark onto its wick. A growing flame brightens an unfamiliar world. More than a library, the room hints at something beyond my experiences. Shelves hold jars, flasks, and beakers of strange substances and luminescent plants, shying at the illumination, crowd a table. This is a workshop.

I set the lamp on a desk and take the sword off the rack. Magical light curves along an intricate pattern etched into the blade. When my arms dip under its weight, I place it back on the stand.

The breast piece, designed with a firefly's two-plate chest in mind, has gold filigree accents. From there, horizontal plates merge into the fauld and tasset, which offer waist protection. The first three are black, the last two are pale yellow and match chain-mail leggings and greaves. From ornate shoulder pauldrons hangs a split cloak. *Narrow wings?* I rub the material between my fingers. Not metal, but a flexible kind I've never seen or felt.

Another mannequin displays a suit of armor. In contrast to David and me, one is akin to the other, but smaller and with other slight differences. Crafted in the same motif, the first set looks bold, muscular, and aggressive; the second graceful, stealthy, and agile. Instead, this suit's weapon is a longbow, but the adjacent slot is empty. I lift the bow from the rack and run my fingers along its length. The imprinted design matches the two-hander. The signature of the same craftsman? I hold the grip with my right hand and the bowstring with my left—and pull. My arm turns to jelly under its heavy draw weight.

I place the helm on my head. The brim drops lower than my eyes. Whoever put it here didn't have me in mind. It'd work for Hazo. When I fasten the chin strap, it shrinks on its own. I struggle to yank it off, but it won't let me. The resizing stops at a perfect fit. In an adjacent mirror, my reflection shocks me. It transforms my bland self into that of a fierce warrior. If David could see me now . . . I look tough.

Paintings and diagrams bordered by carved frames cover the walls. Among them, a map showing who-knows-where, another displays firefly anatomy, but one catches my eye even more. In it, two knights stand before a black void, fearless, armor resembling the sets in this room. One wields a fire sword and the other, a two-hander. I make a muscle, but there's no comparison with them in the painting. It can't portray us, can it? We're *not* fierce warriors.

A gloomy castle with fortified bulwarks, a long-fanged portcullis, and six towers sharp as spears looms in the backdrop. My breath catches in my throat. Eskelon. Lady Sophia says I must go there with my brother. Unless I find and hide the Two Gems. *Easy . . . who am I kidding?*

An image of my dad pops into my mind. Yesterday, at the dinner table, his eyebrows looked singed. I race upstairs, snatch the hilt, and then rush back downstairs.

The fine etchings and attention to detail stand out as master craftsman workmanship. But who teaches this trade? No one, not here. I flip it over, spin it around, poke, prod, and bite it. I don't have a clue how to turn it on. My dad figured it out and got an enormous surprise . . . I snap my fingers. It didn't *want* to be held by him. *On . . . please.* I'm not ready when the firefly's abdomen glows bright yellow, the mouth opens, and out shoots a flame, which grows a yard. A close-range weapon to complement the long-range bow. And it appreciates manners, same as Rebecca.

Tip pointed up, the blade gleams pure and radiant. Electricity races into my arm and then throughout my body. I stare deep into the light, but I sense it's doing the same with me, searching my soul. We have an understanding—a partnership.

In an open place, I swing it with forehand and backhand slashes. Rigid as steel, yet it doesn't appear to be steel. Magic fire. I've heard of such things, but in tall tales, Greene tells. If there's good and bad magic, how can I tell them apart? The picture with the two warriors catches my eye. The armor is the same, so they must be Hôzai knights, too, although I'm stuck doing humdrum chores, not storming a castle. I force out a frustrated sigh. *Turn off, please.* I set it on the desk.

A flower-shaped brazier with straight legs curling up at the feet stands nearby. Its sooty firepan means someone has been using it. No wonder I had to scrub the library baseboard. I dip my fingers into the little mound and find it silky smooth between them, unlike tobacco soot.

I scan a room full of interesting choices. Strange things lie on the desk. Two open books and a well-worn haversack, which I slide beside a spent pipe. Next to it lies a ring, which should be Grandpa's wedding band shown in the portrait. He'd been studying here before he ran to save Grandma. Warm pride builds within me. I pocket it for a keepsake.

Nothing beats a good reading chair. It must have enough padding, so your muscles don't cramp. This one's perfect. A quill stands in a dry inkwell. The open pages are blank and gold leaf accents the cover, the spine, and the title: *A Faerie History and Their World* by Conrad Jackson. *Grandpa?*

Faeries, who are they? As I flip through, many passages catch my eye. "Faeries and their lesser kindred, pixies, called the Good

People or Wee Folk, are magical winged beings. They dwell in the Other World they name Tuatha Dé Danann. Usually short, they stand only a yard high, and are mischievous, owing to the pranks they play on mortals."

My kind of people.

"Many faerie types live there, those of the earth, moon, fire, and water. At the Thinning, the time we see the green veil in the evening sky when day and night are weakest, they pass through doors into the mortal lands called earth." I muse over the word "Thinning," twilight, in this world.

"A faerie's wings produce a silvery-gold dust, a magical substance with many uses." I glance at the jar with the dancing sparkles.

"Faeries use their doors to enter the mortal world. Most take pride in their clever concealment. Earth faerie doors, found on cave walls or on the ground, are the easiest for humans to find. Moon faerie doors are the most ubiquitous during the evening hours but elude their sight because they don't look for them. Water faerie doors, made in streams or lakes, and fire faerie doors, created in magical flames, are the most dangerous to them. Seldom do they live to tell they discovered one. Even if mortals find a door, only the Wee Folk can pass through them because their wing dust holds the magic of Tuatha Dé Danann."

I flip ahead a few more pages. My gaze falls upon an unfamiliar word: *Pyro-transmotion.* According to Grandpa, the term means "The technique fire faeries apply to 'puff over' to the Other World. The practice involves burning their dust in a brazier which creates the door." Was he a fire faerie? He didn't have wings.

Entries such as "Abductions," "Appeasements," "Circles," "Kingdoms," and "Thinningologist" pique my interest, yet, I stop flipping at a small section titled "Halfer."

"A slang term for faeriekind and mankind offspring. They do not have wings, so they cannot produce dust. To enter the immortal world, they must apply it to themselves from the faeriekind matching the door. They keep base abilities and the life-spark, which manifests as an alternate hue to the eyes. Visible at an angle, it can be any color of the rainbow, except green, which the Creator saved for faeries." *Amethyst in Dad's eyes. Does he know?*

I set the book on the desk, contemplating what I read. My grandpa and grandma were "halfers." So am I.

Fidgety, I shift in the seat, then thumb though to a section called: Prophecies. Near the top, I read Prophecy Wars. He wrote a few full pages on this subject.

"The Dark Lord's hope rests on the foretold Two Combining. Since he destroyed prophetic writings during the Prophecy Wars, he believes no written foretelling remains to challenge his ascendancy. In his deception, he has forgotten El'Darios the Great, Lord of the Worlds, who has hidden the Prophecy of the Two underground. There to rest until the proper time."

A chill races throughout my spine, and I snap the book shut. A foreboding sense washes over me as if a cosmic will unfolds before my eyes.

I stick my finger between the pages and reach for the other one titled, *Writ of the Hôzai*. At the open spot, I find lines that cause heat to rush into my face.

"When moon is ill, and sun is dark,

Hillock bare without faerie spark.

Ring in want of joyful dance,

Merriment dead from dagger's lance.

Naked tree ails in winter's bite,

Dawn e'er jailed by eternal night.

When hope is barren and waxes stark,

Come they bearing two worlds' mark.

By a great will, they are brought forth,

Mortal and eternal inborn worth.
Second shall be greater than the first,
A hidden enemy, he accursed.
Rising above their humble means,
One clad of earth with silver moonbeams.
The other fierce foes fire and water can bend,
Creation's Lord and Master shall send.
Two lands, the twins will mend,
Until the time appointed at the end of ends.
The dark door opens in the West,
Lying beyond their greatest test.
To the darkest realm straight it leads,
Them driven on by dire need.
There they will seek what was lost,
The two worlds joined at high cost."

They must call this the Prophecy of the Two, the very words Malgroth wanted to destroy ever since the Prophecy Wars. But he didn't, because it's true, El'Darios hid them underground.

There's more, but I close the book on my finger. According to what the Lady Sophia said, the dark door leads to his realm. The reference to bending fire and water must refer to me, but how do the earth and the moon relate to my brother?

Nothing happens by accident. She meant for me to find this prophecy. I glance at the painting. David and me? How? If Malgroth and Ishglof discover the Two Gems, they'll wreak chaos and cause mass death. People may die whether I do anything. How can I avoid doing this? Faces pass through my mind, family members, Rebecca, Linus, and James. I hop up and step to the picture. It tells a story—mine.

Once I decide, there's no turning back to my boring but safe life here. Everything I love is at risk. But I could locate the Two Gems and hide them. No need to search for Eskelon. *Another great Jonathan Jackson idea!*

Jonah could have one and no doubt he'd help me look for the other. If that doesn't work, how can I find the door leading to Malgroth's domain?

David and I were born more than twins. We share the same uncertain future, and it's time he knows this, too. Our destiny lies beyond Wheatland. I force out a deep breath, my resolve steeling. My search starts with Jonah Winslow.

CHAPTER 9

THE DUNBURY DETECTIVE

Dawn arrives on Wednesday with my hands tucked under my head and eyes boring holes into the ceiling. With the Two Gems rattling around my brain the whole night, who could sleep? I thought through a plan to slip away to Dunbury, but it's a long trip and I may get murdered by a highwayman, or torn to shreds by a wild animal.

Commotion grows in the hallway. My parents must be awake, so there's a chance I can have a real breakfast today. I shuffle past David's bed, still accommodating my brother. A first.

My dad enters the kitchen, drains his coffee, pecks my mom on the cheek, and brushes by me.

"Goodbye?" I say, annoyed.

"Sorry," he says, "I have loads on my mind. Be back tonight to inspect your chores."

I ignore what he said at the end. "Where are you going?"

"Dunbury, to speak with Jonah."

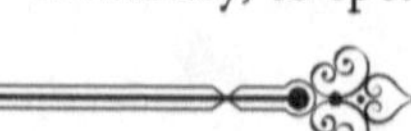

"Again?"

"He'll travel to Heathfell by the weekend to do his research, so he can also listen for any political rumblings."

"Wait here."

"Why?"

"Because I'm coming with you."

Dad narrows his eyes. "Why? What—"

"Nothing, just a chance to see my master and learn from him."

He seems to accept the lame excuse. "Hurry up, then."

Walking will give me time to plan to steal Jonah's gem.

When my dad and I reach Dunbury, the sun peeks over the tree line. Along the road, my yawns stopped, but my muscles ache from yesterday's chores. One day has gone, three or four more, depending on my parents' mood. Can't forget to add today's tick mark on my bedroom wall.

In the town square, crowds build, chatter crescendos, and merchants ready their wagons for another busy marketplace. Jewelry vendors and fancy confectionaries contrast with feed sellers and farming tool brokers. Dunbury is Wheatland in many ways, but larger and more cosmopolitan.

Jonah lives on the far-west side. After several blocks, Dad points to a two-story brick house with gray shutters and dull brass coach lamps. "There." We pass children playing ball in the street to a wrought-iron gate.

I shove my hands deeper into my pockets and turn my face away from the blustery wind. We step along the slate sidewalk, which leads to the front door. The walk didn't spark any creativity more than one idea to grab it and run.

Overgrown bushes crowd the house, weed-choked flowerbeds display spent springtime annuals, and an odd sense nags my mind. When Dad raises his fist to knock, he stops mid-swing.

Silence.

No road traffic and no ballgame.

From the gate, curious eyes study our every move. Their blank faces suggest something may be wrong. His knuckles rap against the door twice, but there's no answer. Before he can call again, footsteps halt the swing. With a soft creak, it inches open, bringing a red-rimmed eye into view.

"Yes, what is it?"

"Hello, Mrs. Winslow, I'm William Jackson." He points to me. "My son, Jonathan."

Her eye narrows for a moment but then widens in recognition. "I remember you." She slides the chain off the door and opens it wide. She rushes knobby fingers through unkempt hair. Gray circles frame her baggy eyes and a black dress stretches to her bare feet.

She extends her hand to us. "Please, call me Gwen."

At my turn, I shake what feels like a dead fish—clammy and limp.

"Pleased to meet you again," Dad says. "May we speak with Jonah?"

Her palm cups her mouth. "He isn't here."

"Something wrong?"

"Come inside, gentlemen."

We shuffle into the foyer. The deadbolt clicks into place. Nobody in Wheatland locks their doors, or even leaves a lit lamp throughout the night. Walnut-paneled walls with framed paintings adorn the vestibule. One displays a green coat of arms with two crossed swords. She leads us to a parlor overlooking the front yard.

Sculptures of people, dragons, and winged men dot the room. A sun-faded piano sits near the window. Floor-to-ceiling bookcases span the far side. The place could be a mini library and museum combined into one.

My dad takes an armchair opposite Gwen, which leaves me the seat by the piano. He shifts in his chair, crossing and re-crossing his legs.

He cranes his neck everywhere. "Impressive collection, bigger than the last time."

Tears well in her bloodshot eyes. "He collected everything you see here. The mythological objects he believed represented actual people or beasts. In many ways, he was childlike, a side I loved the day I met him. He respected our history, no matter the mistakes or achievements, knowing human progress comes through effort and risk." She steps to a part of his collection near me. "This globe dates to the Olden Days. It served as an educational tool in the royal mastery school. During this period, great explorers traveled throughout the world."

"We respect him, too. 'Loved,' 'believed,' what do you mean?"

She dabs her eyes in earnest. "I haven't seen my husband in two days. No one has. The last time was Monday morning when he visited someone at the library but never returned. He didn't say who he wanted to meet. You know how Jonah can be."

My dad's face flushes red as his gaze drops to the floor.

She bites her lower lip. "He met with you, William? What's happening?"

"Nothing out of the ordinary. I brought Jonathan, too, so he could learn the ropes. He wants to follow in my footsteps." He clears his throat. "He asked us to help him research . . ."

She lowers her glance. "I see. Jonah always discovered secrets and intrigue. I was afraid this day might come. Who can stay unsnarled by this business? After he left for the library, I cleaned his study. This time, he tracked mud and grass into it. The backyard stable door was ajar, so I wonder where he rode to at that hour. Also, I found this scrap of paper on his desk. His handwriting never looks *this* rushed."

She hands it to my dad, which he reads, "'I. M. and the Thinning.' What does it mean? These initials could belong to hundreds in the kingdom."

"Maybe it's a town?"

He muses on the idea.

"I won't be any help. We left work out of our conversations."

"He's protecting you. People believe the librarian job is as stale as two-week-old bread. But there's no telling what crimes, improprieties, or scandals you'll uncover. Things you unearth could cost you . . ." Dad blushes because he said too much. "He often spoke of strange dealings with stranger folk."

Quit while you're behind, I think. The Thinning is twilight when faeries and pixies can enter our world, but I. M. will be hard to figure out.

Gwen rubs her forehead. "I'm a broken old woman. What could I have done to protect him? Many things lie beyond my reach. Since June, he's been so busy he couldn't spare a moment for chores, sleep, or even me. He'd work late and as each day passed, my optimistic husband became paranoid."

My dad looks downward. "Sorry, Gwen."

"I contacted Constable Quesinberry, an officer who loves justice, the night Jonah didn't return. Passersby saw him talking with a man and a boy outside the library. They said both you and he left in different directions, but then the trail goes cold."

Dad fingers the slip of paper. "Do you mind if I keep this?"

"I hope you find it helpful." She dries her tears with a handkerchief. "Oh dear, in this fuss, I've lost my manners. Care for tea? It's the finest the market has to offer—orange peel with cloves."

I flash a quick smile. "Yes, please."

"I'll bring it straightaway. I put a pot on the fire before you came and now I hear it singing."

When she disappears into the kitchen, I poke around the parlor. The place reminds me of the workshop under my dad's study, but the display pieces are historical, not magical. The stand nicks my finger when I give the globe a careless spin. No lands appear west of Bormágo, but the words *Unexplored Regions* mark empty areas. *Old,* I think.

Gwen carries in three teacups, a teapot, and assorted buttered scones on a silver tray. As she pours the tea, an orange tang diffuses into the room. Before I sip any of it, a loud rap thunders on the door.

My dad sets his teacup in the saucer. "Expecting anyone this morning?"

"No." She scurries into the foyer. "Hello, please come inside."

A garbled, deep voice answers her. "Thank you, ma'am. Visitors?"

"Yes, this way." The deadbolt snaps into its place. A bulky man covered to his boots with a black coat, barrels into the room. His silver lapel badge catches light streaming through the window.

"Constable Quesinberry, I'd like to introduce Mr. William Jackson and his son Jonathan. They're from Wheatland Town."

"Two persons fitting your descriptions saw Jonah last," he says in a gruff tone. His flaring nostrils under a bushy mustache implicate us further. A sword hilt peeks out when his hands slide to his hips.

My dad chokes on his words, so I take over his part. "Sir, no doubt you have to follow every lead, but it makes little sense for a long-time associate and his *young* son to have a motive to harm Mr. Winslow." The word *young* annoys me, but it's necessary to prove a point. "Besides, those same eyewitnesses saw him leave a different way. Here's the question: Who else wants to hurt him?"

Quesinberry muses over my logic. "True. Where did you go?"

"Home—nowhere near here."

The constable stuffs his hat under his arm, then jerks sketches from his long coat. "Familiar?" One shows a porky-faced man, and the other's size dwarfs a mountain. The resemblance to Rej and Hazo is unmistakable. "Monday afternoon during my library rounds, a loud noise grabbed my attention. At the scene, two miscreants were searching the back stacks. They couldn't be the book-reading kind. The bigger man tried to stare me down, but I meant business. They left peaceful enough, but cursing 'Wheatlanders.'"

"I overheard them planning to kill us," I say, not caring if Dad thinks I'm lying.

"Oh?"

"Never seen them before," Gwen says. "And thank heaven."

"They must have watched us enter the library," my dad says. "We call this one the Collector, but his right name is Reginald. He records the debt and tax payments from the Wheatlanders." He points to the other picture. "His muscle. I hear him called 'lunkhead,' 'halfwit,' or 'fathead' by his employer, but he's known as Hazo. I understand they live somewhere to the north. They come south the last Monday each month."

Constable Quesinberry offers a flat smile. "I'll search the countryside for them and will be in your village at the next collection. Questions demand answers, and stories need testing. Excuse me, good day."

"After you, sir. Time for us to go home, too." My dad taps him on the arm. "And, when you come to Wheatland Town, bring backup."

"Thank you, Mr. Jackson." The forceful man pumps my dad's hand for longer than he enjoys. When his viselike grip releases, he rubs sore knuckles behind his back. The constable doesn't know his own strength and will mash it as if it were a boiled potato. I glance away until any handshake offer vanishes.

"I'll be in touch as soon as there's a development." He tips his hat, then hurries along the sidewalk.

My dad presses her hand between his own. "If you need anything, please send for us. Mail comes every weekday in Wheatland."

"I will. And thank you."

A fragile hope Jonah is alive diverts my thoughts the entire way home. Was he crafty enough to elude the two devils, so I can hear his heroic story when we meet again? When we pass by my dad's well-manicured flower beds, a testament to a labor of love, my pace slows to a crawl. Chores.

I wish I could spend my time in the Workshop, but with chores piling up like excuses to avoid them, I don't have a choice. The town rumor mill might be grinding my excellent reputation into mushy grist, so it will stay my secret. With my dad, you never can tell. Besides, the place is fascinating, and I haven't discovered all its mysteries.

After an hour, the library has a shine to it. Time for a break below ground. I turn the firefly hilt in the keyhole, which fires off turning wheels and moaning wood, opening the secret entranceway. Lost in thought, I descend the steps into its grayness. The abbreviation I. M. could stand for "Ishglof and Malgroth," but my hunch tells me it's something else. It may relate to the Two Gems and the Two Combining.

A rap on the library door startles me. The knob tries to turn. "Jonathan!" David says. "Why did you lock it?"

I leap up the stairs. "One moment." The entrance to the Workshop takes forever to finish its close cycle. *Hurry!*

"What are you doing in there? Open up, now."

"You haven't afforded the requisite time."

"What? Will you speak plain, weirdo?"

"Study books for longer than a second, ignoramus."

He pounds the door, sending a shock through my body. Glad it wasn't my skull.

"Wait, you dimwit!"

Knuckles crack. "What did you call me?"

When the cycle finishes, I straighten my shirt and put on my best business manner. I open the door. "What? I'm working hard."

"You mean hardly working." He stretches to look around me. "Dimwit?" My brother shoves me back a few feet. "I heard strange noises."

"Nope, not in here, gastrointestinal or otherwise."

He wags his head. "The entire house shook. Happened yesterday, too."

"The sound of industry. Think I'm in here reading books? I

should say not. Our father deserves the cleanest library free labor can buy."

David rolls his eyes. "Whatever—Mom wants you. Your Great Chore Sentence, as you call it, got greater. Putting away fifty hay bales into the Avery barn falls to *you* and Linus. Lucky you, now I need to find another way to exercise today."

I frown, then say, "Doesn't that woman realize I'm tired of these chores?"

"She's your mother, so show her respect! Cheer up, it'll do those things you call *muscles* some good."

David smirks, triumphantly. I slam the door in his face and lock it before he can enjoy the feeling.

When I figure there's no risk of a punch in the arm, I sneak from the library. In the living room, Mom reads to Conrad Junior. Distracted, he sings to me, "Clean, clean, clean all the day long. Big brother Jonny, sing a chore song."

Little imp. She flushes and cups her hand over the toddler's big mouth. She'd made my punishment into a nursery rhyme and taught it to him. Anything to teach vocabulary.

When my flickering anger cools, I say, "Yes?"

"Be a dear and take two pies to Mrs. Avery. Wait for Mr. Holms to bring the hay bales."

"I heard, thank you. Why do I have to do Linus's chores, too?"

"I promised David would help them. This week the responsibility falls to you."

My jaw muscles throb as I stomp toward the kitchen. *I hate it when people promise away my free time.*

"Remember, they save us every time we use their wagon."

A guilty sense flashes over me, so I stop. Anger drains with my slowing breath. She's right.

"Mr. Hoggins bought chocolates from Caene & Beane's Confectionary."

"From Heathfell?"

She nods.

Expensive.

"He's such a dear. Have *one* before you go."

A large tin sits on the kitchen table. I glance over my shoulder, fish out *two* pieces, and shove them into my mouth. Sumptuous flavor eases away my dreadful day. Gourmet chocolate can make the worst days the best.

Apple pies cool on clean towels, so I wrap them in a loose shroud. Songbirds cheer my arrival when I step out the front door. The sun, past its highest point, paints white cotton balls on a blue canvas.

I inch up their porch stairs, careful to not drop my mom's artwork. "Could use help," I say through the open window. Rebecca holds Gunnar back, because he could trample me.

"Give me those, please," she says, holding the door wide with her hip. "Tell your mom thanks."

Linus slides around her. "Can you handle this job?"

Before I mention I'll be fine, a wagon stops in front of the house.

"Hello, Mr. Holms."

"Greetings, Linus. Brought it back and better than when you lent it to me." The rancher nods, but his tawny eyes cast me a perplexed look. ". . . Jonathan? Where's David?"

Sick of these comments. "Home. I heard you need a real man for the job."

A smile plays on his lips. "I'm in a hurry. A late heifer's calving today. Tell your parents I say hi."

"Will do," Linus says. "And thank you."

"May I come and help with the calf, Mr. Holms?" Rebecca says.

"Sure."

She disappears into the house, but within a few minutes, she darts back out wearing an old dress and carrying her satchel.

Herky urges his bay horse onward and they disappear around the bend.

We traipse through the backyard to the barn. I've seen them do this before and the part each worker plays. One attaches a bale to a pulley and hoists it to a small door. The other releases the hook and stacks it inside the hayloft. Neither job looks fun—either swelter in the dusty hayloft or the rope turns your arms to jelly. I'll try my luck on the ground.

We're halfway done when my muscles give out mid-hoist. Linus reaches for the bale, but it's beyond his reach. It crashes, just missing me, and smashes into pieces.

"I need a breather. Come down."

"Make this one quick, because I have other chores today. Want to switch jobs again?"

Not going by that rotting skunk anymore. It has burned my nose hairs along with my sense of smell. If I tell him where to find it, he'll know I dumped it there. "I'll stay outside, you're better up there."

"Don't blame you." He pinches his nose and waves his hand over it.

I press my lips together, saying nothing.

"If David were here, we'd be done."

"But he's not."

Linus leaves the barn, rescuing hay bits from the tangles of his flame-red hair. He pours water for me, then tops off his own.

I study lemon chunks swirling in the glass. "Rebecca doesn't miss any yummy detail."

"Your extra chores . . ." He plays with the sweat running down the pitcher.

I wait for him to finish, so he can rub it in.

". . . they'll end in no time." He chugs his water and I wonder if he even tasted it.

"Such wisdom, Linus, but not soon enough."

He looks away then back. "Rebecca told me you heard the meetinghouse burned."

"I'm sure you know I was there."

He nods. "Any theories?"

"None." I rest my head on my knees.

He shakes his head. "You were there, tell me more. What's up with you today?"

I massage my aching arms. "Not much to say when my dad ruins my summer. Besides, I can't stop thinking of poor Mrs. Winslow. What if her husband met with foul play? Some apprenticeship I'll have."

He rolls his eyes.

"What?"

"You're *so* insensitive. Do you ever think of others?"

I raise my hands, palms up.

"Skip it. What if Jonah's out of town?"

I shake my head. "And forgot to tell his wife?"

"You told me everything you know about the Two Combining, so maybe he's investigating more clues."

I frown. "Or he met with foul play and he lies dead in a shallow grave somewhere."

Linus shrugs. "Doubtful." He pours another half glass and downs it in a couple gulps. "Work won't get done by itself."

"A pity, isn't it?" When I spring up, a kink stabs my back. He doesn't notice—or doesn't want to notice—my groans. More to do at home. Hope I make it.

By late afternoon, I finish the hay bales. Through the library door, I hobble down the stairs into the Workshop, stretching achy muscles along the way. I step forward a few paces but then halt, because something feels wrong. A black spot hovers by the desk. A book thuds onto it and skips to the floor. I ease backward, knock into the brazier, and it crashes on the tile. I fumble for the lamp. The first flint strike doesn't spark. *Calm yourself, Jonathan.* The next one sparks and sets the wick aflame. Golden lamplight fills the room, but an opaque void kills any light coming near it.

The black mist sails toward me, freezing my blood. Did Lady Sophia say how to defeat them?

Ten feet, closing fast. What are they?

Six feet. *Think!* Roots seem to grow through the floor, ensnaring my legs.

Four feet. A thought sparks in my brain . . . The meeting-house—the Lady's words surface. Malgroth's servants issue from his shadowed mind, so evil thoughts will overthrow mine.

Three feet. A defense must be good thoughts.

Two, one . . . bitter cold sweeps over me. Darkness fights its way into my inner sanctum and takes no prisoners. My parents— unfair—David, their favorite. Stronger and more likeable than me. Mastery school, what a joke. I'm less than nothing when Despair's talons sink into me. The sword from the rack . . . I should end my life.

Golden lights pierce the room and then disappear into my mind. Peace floods my being as I consider my parents and my brother do love me. My worth lies in who I am, not in what others think.

Between the opposing sides, what's right? Darkness or light? Malgroth, or Lady Sophia? My choice is the light, so I resist the attack with all the will I can muster.

My vision clears as I stagger to the desk and flop in the chair. The last tremors from a nervous shake exit my fingertips. It's gone. I won . . . for now. Deep inside, I know it couldn't have been the ultimate showdown between a boy from Wheatland and the Dark Lord Malgroth. I'm not stupid.

Shuffling feet echo behind me, causing a gulp to stick in my throat. Another black mist? Maybe worse. I swing the chair around to face the inevitable.

Worse. David stands at the foot of the stairs, his countenance ashen gray as if he's seen a ghost.

"What—"

"We need to talk."

CHAPTER 10

FANNING THE FLAMES

The next morning, my eyes flicker open, but to my surprise, my brother stares down at me.

I roll to my other side. "Leave."

"Mom has another assignment for you, so go see her."

He's not being rude, because the things I told him yesterday—the Thinning, faeries, black mists, Malgroth and Ishglof, the Two Combining—would jolt anyone. I've had time to take it in, but he hasn't.

I stumble into the kitchen deep in the sleep fog that arrests me every morning. My parents drain the last drops from their coffee mugs. Dad points to the chair across from where he sits.

I sit.

"We asked Auntie Fanny if she needs help around her house," he says.

Warmth drains from my face. *No . . .*

"She agreed, so report there after you eat breakfast."

My jaw muscles throb as I stare him down, heat kindling in my cheeks. I don't care if I earn another week for doing it. Great

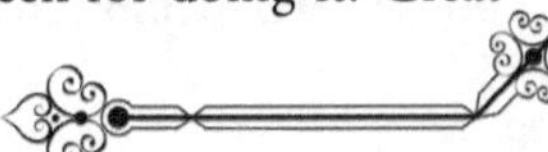

Aunt Frances Higginbottom is the rumor mill behind this crush on Rebecca, and other notable tall tales. What new shred of information can she extract and use against me?

Mom looks away, and Dad shifts in his chair.

A volcano of angry lava builds within me. I might blow.

"Linus will drive you there on his way to the market, but since we won't know when you'll be done, find a ride back. Mr. Holms may come to the hollow, so check with him."

My head drops to the table. Can't take much more.

She massages my shoulders and kisses my cheek. "Cheer up. I can cook for you roast turkey, mashed potatoes, and stuffing for dinner tonight. Will this make things better?"

"With gravy?" I mumble into my arm.

"Heaps."

I one-arm hug her neck. Good food always sets my mood right.

When I realize my lateness becomes more silk for Auntie Fanny to weave into her next gossip web, I stuff the crust in my mouth and dash out the door.

Linus stands in the wagon seat with reins taut in his hands. Bruno won't budge, so he jumps out, grabs the harness, and yanks. He has no chance of making him stand.

"He needs his carrots."

"The dumb donkey had them. Any more and he'll turn orange. My sister is busy."

"You'll never convince him he's had enough. I've seen how she does it." I croon while rubbing his rough face, and when he stands, Linus's eyes widen.

I shrug. "Rebecca's way, not mine. He likes her."

Too soon for my liking, Linus pulls the reins by a yellow ranch with red shutters and front door. A wide porch spans the width of the house. Two rocking chairs creak a consistent rhythm. My aunt feeds a steady stream of yarn into busy needles. Her fingers look stiff, but they can still go through two skeins a day. The speed picks up with the conversation pace. Beside her sits a childhood friend, Prudence Yackley. To them, life in Wheatland revolves around knitting circles, socials, and small-town news. A white tabby cat named Queenie purrs between them. If I had a quarter lion for the times the beast scratched me, I'd have a mattress full.

Auntie Fanny peers at the road over half-moon spectacles.

"You'll get run over, child. Come here."

No doubt she's been staring that direction since my dad left earlier this morning. My leaden feet refuse to budge. Any investigations I planned in town will have to wait. I sidle across the street, up the three steps, and into her outstretched arms. She plants a pruned kiss on my cheek.

"Look, Prudy, he's tall and handsome. Not as towering as his twin, mind you, and scrawnier, but there may be hope."

I ignore the slight. My best years are ahead, and hers behind. "Hello, Auntie Fanny and Aunt Prudy. Doing all right?"

"Fine," my great aunt says. "To business. What mischief brings you here?"

For a moment, my mouth dries as words escape me. "Dad believed you might need an outstanding worker around the house."

Unconvinced, the old woman glares at me. "Poppycock, boy! If Willie thought we needed one as you say, he would've sent David." My face flushes warm. "There may be another reason they've given us my niece's mischievous twin. I'm good at finding out secrets." Her glower lightens. "But, I prefer brains over brawn. Glad to have *you*." She hugs me again with a grip that'd squeeze sugar from beets. My arms don't connect around her girth. "Come with me, honey, and I'll tell you what to do."

Inside, decorative plates adorn the kitchen wall, jars and spice bottles stand in neat rows, and no dust dares to show on the counters. The lemon cake she baked earlier cools on the shelf.

"I have a few minor jobs, and if you actually work, there's a shiny silver lion in it for you." I offer a spontaneous smile. Money will make this torture worth it. How can I get Mom to fall in line, too? She scribbles a quick chore list: rearrange hard-to-reach boxes, bring up last year's jars from the cellar, and chop firewood.

"You have what you need, so it's back to my knitting. A chilled lemonade each in a half hour, please. Don't make it too sour."

"Will do."

I return with what she ordered, when she wanted it. Auntie Fanny sets down her work when a man with dirt-streaked socks rising to his knickers halts in the street. The rider cranes his neck in our direction, but they pretend he isn't there. My great aunt monitors his whereabouts with quick flits of her skeptical eyes.

He doffs a felt hat and runs fingers through his salt-and-pepper hair. "Excuse me, ladies, I'm new to the countryside. Is this Wheatland Town?"

Aunt Prudy's eyes dart to her companion but never rise above her smallish nose.

"My name is Oliver Iskander, and I rode from Heathfell. Do you know Sebastian Childers, who lives somewhere on this side of the forest?"

Auntie Fanny's fingers pause. "Mr. Islander, it's not our habit to engage with the sort from the East Borough and those looking for a reputable gentleman."

Aunt Prudy manages a quick smile.

"The name is Iskander, ma'am, and I have honorable intentions, for I've known Mr. Childers a long time."

"These years wore away his hometown from your frail memory?"

Her lifelong friend snickers at her disrespectful attitude.

Taken aback, the man raises his index finger and his jaw slackens. "Our mutual trade has kept me from enjoying this countryside. If you'd point me in the right direction, I'd be grateful."

"What business did you say you have with Master Childers, Mr. Olander?"

"It's *Iskander*. We're associates, and I have urgent news for him, regarding our most important client. And other pressing matters. I pray you, please tell me where I may find him."

My aunt's mouth drops into a contemplative frown telling me she's hunting for gossip.

"He lives and works in the North Wheatland country. Take that road until you run into his market," she says pointing. "If he isn't there, take the same way further until it bends west. There on the left, you'll see his cottage among the overspreading elms."

"Thank you, you've been most helpful."

My aunt dips her head in a slight bow but says no more. Iskander disappears along the northern road so I head back to work.

I finish the work in good time, so I pour myself another well-deserved drink and then go outside to negotiate my dismissal. They bandy a topic back and forth in hushed voices.

As I step onto the veranda, Queenie launches a surprise attack. Claws bared, she leaps to my shoulder, head, then scampers into the house and disappears. Another quarter lion for the mattress.

"I can't be silent any longer, my dear," Auntie Fanny says. "Iskander is an odd-looking fellow. Wouldn't you agree, Prudence?"

She's prodding for agreement.

Aunt Prudy drops her knitting. "I should say so," she declares in her nasally voice, "and he's in partnership with *our* Mr. Childers. Can you imagine?"

My great aunt leans forward in her rocking chair. "Our reputable market owner consorts with dodgy Heathfellers, so decent folk may speculate about his scruples."

I catch my lemonade before it sprays everywhere. *She should talk.*

"No wonder, with business blowing this tumbleweed here and

there. His poor ill wife, fending for herself. A son would've done her good, but none ever came. Heaven didn't smile on their union."

I take another long pull on my pulpy drink.

"We see why, Prudy, because the mischievous earn their comeuppance." Narrow eyes flit to me and her shriveled finger presses upon her turtle-like lips. "Right away, I believed the stranger lived in the capital city, because his bumptious accent gives him away. A government fellow, judging by his signet ring and fine riding clothes. A secret agent for the king?"

A secret agent who asks for directions? Laughable.

"Fanny, you're keen to notice."

"Not everything on me is falling apart, my dear." She taps her noggin. "Still have my sharp mind. At my age, that's saying something. Now, where was I?"

Aunt Prudy says nothing. She hasn't a clue.

"Iskander, the stranger," I say.

"Oh yes, thank you. He reminds me of that disgusting Collector fellow, only not so rotund. The one who drains the Wheatland pocketbook each month."

"Do you think Mr. Childers has gambling debts, and this man came to collect?"

What a reach.

"Possible. His vast wealth reeks of mischief."

"I wonder what the other girls have to say, Fanny."

"Let's find out. Jonathan, be a dear and help us." She presses two silver lions in my hand. "Your tuppence for today. Hitch up Old Willa to my carriage and bring her around front. Then you may leave with my blessing. We want to call on a couple friends. Come, Prudy, you don't make important calls dressed for housework. The weekend's fast approaching, and I wish to have news for Gathering Day."

I guide her spotted Percheron to the gate where her walkway meets the road. Passersby offer me uncertain smiles, rushing by to avoid the town busybody's wide net.

They strut to the carriage, ready for serious business. I help them in, careful to free their dresses from the step, or Auntie Fanny's prominent hat feather from the roof. When they're tucked in, I hand her the reins.

Slow hoofbeats approach behind me until the constable and the two king's men pass by us. I bite my lip, because Sebastian, head bowed and wrists bound in shackles, shuffles between them.

"Pray tell, what's the hubbub, Winnie?" Auntie Fanny says.

Our lawman reins in his horse, so the others follow suit. "We caught a man red-handed trying to buy Wolfie's at the market. Mr. Childers claims he doesn't keep any on the premises, but we found it. He knows it's contraband in this borough. Now we have a link to the meetinghouse arson."

Sebastian shakes his head. "You have it wrong, Win. Told you, I discovered the jugs stashed in the barn under a blanket. I didn't put them there."

"Who did?"

"How should I know?"

"You can recount all the merchandise on your shelves and their sales each month, except for this? Your friend from Heathfell rode off as a thunderbolt when we tried to detain him. When we ascertain his name, and the runner comes back, I'll extradite him for trial. For now, you're the number one suspect in the meetinghouse arson."

"But I'm innocent."

"Excuse me, Constable, I can help," Auntie Fanny says with importance. "The person you describe is Oliver Iskander from the East Borough. Judging by his clothes, he's at least a prominent businessman in the capital city. Earlier today, we gave him directions where he might find Mr. Childers. Now we understand he's the shifty, beady-eyed sort, no doubt guilty of many vices."

Winston nods. "Thank you, Mrs. Higginbottom, you've been helpful in the cause for justice."

As their carriage rolls east and the men disappear into the jail, I head home. Dad will want to hear this.

"I'm back," I say when I charge into the foyer. I sit and pull off my shoes. Muffled voices spill into the hallway, so I edge into the living room archway. My parents stand close together, my dad holding a letter.

He taps the parchment with his finger. "This is from the Wheatland-Dunbury Library Council. I'll read what they say . . . 'As to the vacated District Chief position, you shall hereby exercise the full duties and privileges therewith.'"

"Wonderful, you deserve a promotion."

Dad shakes his head. "Hmph, more headaches from nasty patrons, and limitless responsibility." He pushes the letter into his pocket.

"How are your aunts?" my mom asks.

"Fine. I finished the work, so they let me off early."

"More time for chores here," my dad says.

Figures. "But first, I should tell you what happened."

My parents cast each other a tentative glance.

When I finish explaining Sebastian's arrest, shock has spread across their faces. Silent at the beginning, my dad then paces the floor, cycling his fingers into fists.

"William, dear," my mom says, "there's nothing you can do."

"I doubt it. Winston's quick to jail anyone. With him on the job, finding Iskander could take weeks. What's Martha to do?"

My mom's eyes brighten, and she snaps her fingers. "We could go see her tomorrow, bring food, and lend a hand around the house. I haven't visited with her in a long time."

I straighten my arms and clench my fists. *Brilliant!* Chores keep getting in the way. I'll never find the Two Gems.

TROUBLE ON THE MOORS

Friday dawns with an air of hope—my last chore day! Fingers crossed. I fade in and out of sleep. Water droplets race down the window until a bright sun breaks through the gray morning. David's wrinkle-free bed lies empty. Chatter cascades from the hallway.

I start when my dad pops into my room. "Ready to go?"

Stretching, my leg brushes against crumpled paper under the covers. "Where?"

"To Mrs. Childers's place. Didn't anybody tell you?" He shakes his head and then leaves, muttering.

In my sleep fog, I muse over it. Not sure if anyone did. Don't know. Don't care. Most times, David gives me one golden opportunity to wake up, and if I miss it, there'll be no other warning. From my covers, I fish out a crumpled bag, and unwrapping it, discover my sandwich from last week. *That's where it went.* Excited for a decent breakfast, I tear it open. Acrid rottenness infuses into the air. I crumple it again and throw it toward the trashcan on David's clean side. Dead accurate—right in, no rim. My roommate won't tolerate garbage anywhere but in my domain.

I dress, finger-comb my hair, do a breath test into my hand, and scratch another tally mark on the wall. Ready for the day. When I sidle into the kitchen, I see my dad wasn't kidding. No one here, not even a breakfast. I dash out the door to find Linus and Rebecca climbing into the wagon with my family. Seven Jacksons, two Averys with Gunnar, sacks, and boxes crowd me off it. Mired in the mud, the donkey will have a strenuous journey, but I'll be trudging beside him in it, too.

Mrs. Avery hands them each a goody bag. They rummage through theirs and share what they got. I wish for a handout, but maybe they don't notice me. Bruno lurches ahead. Someone must have lit a fire under him, for his spirited canter leaves me well behind the wagon. At this distance, Linus's whittling shavings won't hit me in the face.

An apple flies toward me, which I catch midflight. Somebody knows I didn't have breakfast. How nice . . . wait. One side has a large bite in it and slobber hanging off it. Bruno refused it, and so it comes to me next. Gross. I toss it over my shoulder.

Beyond James's house, the stiff-necked donkey decides he can't take any more labor, so he sits. The wagon jostles to a halt. Grabbing the harness, Linus pulls, Bruno resists, and so the fruitless tug-of-war goes on forever. "Stupid, mule-headed . . ."

Rebecca taps him on the arm. "You're making it worse. I have this." She strokes the donkey's face, crooning with a gentle voice. In no time, life returns to his legs and he staggers upward. She pats his neck. "Good boy." Hiking up her dress, she climbs back onto the bench next to her brother. "See, nothing to it." Spirited, he catches fire again, and so the chase continues.

With the town miles behind, we venture into the little-known but often-feared North Wheatland countryside. At the westward bend in the road, the Childers farmhouse nestles in green pastures, bordered by the glistening river. Along the lane, trees spread overhead, forming a living tent but not even a songbird welcomes anyone. The home, smaller up close than I had guessed, has brick walls, a slate roof, and matches the adjoining carriage house and stable.

Linus reins in Bruno near a hitching post. One by one, the passengers unfold from their cramped quarters. Conrad Junior's pouty face goes unnoticed by my mom. After dusting off their long dresses, adjusting their outfits, and stringing goody baskets to their arms, Mom and Rebecca are ready to call. Two white rocking chairs sit silent on the veranda beside a door adorned with a bittersweet vine wreath.

She hesitates, takes in a deep breath, lets it out in metered bursts, and then knocks. At first, there's no reply, so she raps on it again. Inside, curtains sway back and forth. A moment later, the door creaks open and a scowling woman waits in the doorway. Gray-streaked brown hair fastens into a tight bun. Her frail body could blow away in a stiff wind.

She narrows her eyes and nods. "Morning, Elizabeth."

"Hello, Martha." My mom holds up the baskets. "Dinner and a few other things you may need."

The peace offering doesn't wipe the scowl off her pallid face. "The constable arrested my husband yesterday."

"Which is the reason we're here. Brought food and we can help around the house."

Her frown straightens.

Chitchat continues, but a distant rumble draws my attention to the road. Galloping hoofbeats near, then Rej and Hazo rush by, but the elms and lane bushes hide me. The North Wheatland Road climbs higher toward a region many people call the Haunted Moors. At its height, they turn off somewhere. When I last saw them, they planned to kill Jonah, but my dad and I would've been innocent victims.

"Jonathan," says my dad's distant voice, "time for work, not daydreaming."

A pang of annoyance rises in me, but I believe Mrs. Childers needs me, too. After today, the chore sentence should end. Unless they pull a fast one. "Coming."

David leads us marching ants to the backyard. My leg muscles strain and my knees knock together when Linus lowers a small bag onto my shoulder.

"Want Thomas to help you?"

My little brother has a huge sack draped over his back. "Another word for comedian is fool," I say. "Don't be either." He spreads his hands apart in innocence, but I turn tail and plod after the line.

Rebecca props open the door with one hand while pointing inside with the other. "She wants the big things in the cellar."

I peer down the narrow, steep staircase. *Of course she does.*

David navigates it first. No problem for him. I wrestle a new grip before I follow, unsure of my steps. Momentum carries me faster than my legs want, but I reach the bottom before they buckle. My twin and I must hunch so our skulls don't crack on the overhead beams. He dumps his sack on the floor, which blusters musty air into my face. I drop mine, unconcerned if it splits. My stiff arms extend straight only after much effort. Tidy filled jars line shelves throughout the cellar. Now they have enough food to last a long siege.

Rebecca leads us to the living room. One portrait hangs on the wall—their wedding day. Mrs. Childers was beautiful back then, but sickness has stolen her best years, abandoning her at frail old age. My dad struggles to keep a conversation going, so Mom helps him. Linus's warm breath puffs on my neck. He carried a large sack on each shoulder, but David hefted three.

"What else can they do for you?" my mom says. Junior tugs on her arm, so she tries to escape his grip.

"Another thing is," Martha says, "I can't manage the dogs. If I don't feed them, the big one may eat the other." She flashes a quick smile.

"Boys . . ." my dad says, pointing random directions as if I understand what he wants.

"Where do you keep food and water?" Linus says.

"The well is outside the kitchen door and further back from there, the shed." She points to David. "This boy can draw multiple gallons. You may need that much."

"Not a problem," David says.

"When they get to know you, they'll be your best friends. Don't be afraid. The black one I named Coal, a nickname for Charcoal, and the other one is Max, short for Maximus. You'll see why."

David and Linus scamper away, but my exhausted legs won't let me chase them. I push open the back door and a cool wind brushes across my face. Fairview House has acreage behind it, but this back-yard meadow, dotted with groves and a nearby coppice, stretches a mile to the shimmering Wheatland River.

They halt by the outbuildings, and when I catch them, faint growls come from the shed.

David hesitates. "What's that sound?"

Linus passes him. "The dogs, silly."

We ease open the door, step in, and skirt past racks of tools to a fenced corner. Linus pulls open a gate and steps into their gray domain. I follow at a distance and slide around two water bowls that lie upside down, one the size of a sink. Farther in, a shadow looms big, but the other much bigger. Coal ambles from the gloomy corner. His whiny greeting suits a tail wagging low to the floor. Linus soaks up all the slobber the dog's tongue can muster.

A shaggy-haired face pokes into the light, teeth bared. Max must weigh three hundred pounds, his paw spanning twice any dog's paw. Ecru fur covers a wide body.

His gaze fixes on me. *Will he attack?* I might be one or two bites for his jaws.

The great dog glances at the new friends Coal and Linus. Lengthy drool threads hang from long fangs. He takes a few steps toward me. But his growl turns to panting, and his tail thumps like a battle club. Intelligent eyes stare into mine.

"I think we understand each other," I say. Max's wide tongue slides across my face, leaving it slick with slobber.

"You're right," Linus says with a chuckle.

"Water," David says. "Be back."

Rej and Hazo's ride north consumes my thoughts. What if they're holding Jonah captive? A shiver races along my spine when I consider the Haunted Moors and the legends surrounding it.

David returns with a full bucket and dumps it into Coal's bowl. Both dogs push their faces into it, so the lapping contest begins. Max stops every so often to allow his friend to have an equal part.

Linus looks on with interest. "Gunnar will get along with them great."

My brother steps away from us. "This'll take many trips."

Now is my chance. "While you finish here," I say jerking my thumb, "I'll see if anyone else needs me."

They shoot each other a furtive glance and shrug. "Okay, I guess," David says.

I step aside, careful to make it look natural. When I round the house, the trees lining the lane lead to the road, stretching to the horizon. Jonah could struggle for life in a dank pit somewhere. My walk kicks into a jog as I turn north.

Sweaty hair sticks to my forehead. Far behind this hilly terrain, the Childers farmhouse glistens as a small jewel on a green velvet pillow.

Cool mist clings to the high moorland air, popping goosebumps across my arms. I unroll my shirt sleeves, but it doesn't help much. Beyond a bend in the road, a lane splits to the right. They must have come this way.

I reach a blackened iron gate, with a script letter *M* split between the halves, flanked by two stone edifices. Uneven dirt blends to flat brick. Scarred maples and beeches edge the avenue. *Lightning strikes?* Black oaks crowd them and between their gnarled arms stretch vines of woven nets. Shadows play tricks on my mind. *Did one move?* Trees can't shift or walk, can they? Moist moss blankets the ground, creating mildewed air.

My feet ache from the long trek, but an expansive courtyard rewards my curiosity. In the center stands a dead fountain with human figures twisted to form a tree similar to Rowen. A mansion with high-peaked roofs, stone walls, and dark windows looms through the mist. The place looks abandoned, but fresh hoof tracks disturbing leafy debris tells me otherwise. The front door rises tall and ominous beneath a deep-set overhang. Cobwebs crisscross it from corner to corner.

You must do this.

Curiosity and cautiousness fight for dominance with each step toward a door more akin to a mausoleum entrance than to someone's house. *Knock or go home? Neither, I just need a peek through the side windows.*

My second step underneath the overhang catches on a loose brick. Before I can react, a snare grabs me, and my world goes topsy-turvy. A net digs into my head and back, pinning my arms backward. No hope reaching the sword.

I spit spider webbing from my mouth. A muffled thud interrupts my struggle. Again . . . and again. Someone is coming. Inside, click-clacking footfalls echo on a hard floor. They pick up pace to match my racing heart. I bite on a cord, but its abrasiveness feels as if I bit into a pinecone. No way can I chew through them. The door creaks open. With a violent jerk, I spin around to meet murky-black eyes, too close together. Hazo's evil grin fills my vision.

"Hey, Rej, look what the trap caught." A rotten meat and bile stench wisps from his crooked teeth.

"Who, Hazo, a trespasser?"

"A dirty Wheatland rat, or I'm sore mistook."

"Cut the vermin down, you lunkhead, and let's bring our little guest in to see the boss."

CHAPTER 12

THE BOSS

After Hazo's swift knife swipe to the rope, my body crashes to the ground. The greedy giant tears open the net like a spoiled boy would a mountain of birthday presents. "Hey, this one was at the li-barry."

Rej grabs my jaw and twists my head side to side. "If I'm not mistaken, this brat's daddy owns nice property in the Wheatland green hollow."

"The land the boss wants?"

"Quiet, halfwit, don't tell his business. Kid, you're in a pickle, because no one's here to save you."

"Who's his dad?"

"Assistant to the meddlesome former chief librarian."

Hazo taps his head with a finger. "Oh yeah, Jonah. We nabbed him—"

Rej presses his hand to his mouth. "Shut up, fool!"

The big man blinks a few times, then frowns.

"Why are you here, kid? You rats should stay away from the *Haunted* Moors."

I say nothing.

"He's a quiet mouse."

"You'll talk to the boss. He has his ways."

They march me through a vast entry hall, past a mahogany grand staircase, through a hallway lined with suits of armor, and into a dim library. A tree stump trophy with lichen for a beard hangs on the wall. *Weird.* A dying orange glow flickers on a gray head above a high-back chair. Over the mantle hangs a woman's portrait. Her pointed ears poke through auburn hair cascading over a white gown.

"Isn't she exquisite?" a raspy voice says, turning to face me. The old man's hollow eyes cause a racing chill along my spine. He points his bony finger at me. "Who's our guest, Reginald?"

"Sir, I found him hanging around our front porch. Won't talk, but I recognize him as William Jackson's son."

"Conrad's grandson."

The fat man yanks my chin upward. "Looks like him."

The man's eyes bore into mine. "After a manner."

"Boss, he and his father visited Winslow at the library."

"When the constable came by," Hazo says, "we needed to 'liminate them another way."

The Collector drives his riding boot heel into his toe. "Such a kidder you are, stupid."

A murderous scowl grows on the big man's face.

"Not to worry about petty trespasses," the man says, "it's a reunion with old friends when you mention Conrad Jackson and Jonah Winslow. Where did my manners go? Come by me, lad, and have a seat by the fire. Reginald, stoke it before the moor mist chills my guest to the bone, and when you're done, fetch him jasmine tea."

Orange peel is better, but I don't complain. I fall into a velvet chair.

Rej drops the poker and lumbers away, muttering curses at his butler duties.

"What's your name, son?"

"Jonathan—and you know my last name—Jackson."

"True, you're quick. Please excuse the way I greet those who call. I didn't think anyone might come by today. With so much riffraff wandering the moors, one can't be too careful."

"I *am* uninvited, sir."

A smile stretches across his face. "My name is Mr. Miller, but you can use my first name—Ichabod." He spreads his hands outward. "Welcome to my home, High Moor Manor. What's the reason for your visit?"

I snap my fingers. "I remember . . . You're I. M. from the note." Heat rushes into my cheeks when my mouth spews the words.

"Note? I'm sure I don't understand." An awkward silence thickens between us. "I suppose borough folk still regard me up here."

I start when Reginald hands me steaming tea, which I place on an end table.

"No need to be jumpy, because you're my guest. Tell me what it said." Miller strokes a well-trimmed but patchy beard.

"I told you—I. M. No more. What makes you think there's more?"

"Not much to go on, but my initials do spell I. M. Your dad's looking for me?"

"No."

His forced smile flattens to a thin line. "Experience protects me from a deceitful novice like you. I believe a curious person will write cryptic notes while they're investigating someone."

This novice can outwit you any day. "And I think villains at heart see even doodling as clandestine. The innocent rise above any suspicion."

"The boy speaks in proverbs, gentlemen." His countenance falls. "Maybe so, but why does your dad believe the I. M. trail ends here?"

"Not sure what you mean."

Miller no longer tries to smother his anger with polite manners. He leans in, stale breath puffing across my face. "Keep your secrets then, but I'll let you in on one. You pathetic peasants don't see a storm building on the horizon, which will cost you everything. My plans served me well, for most in town owe me their entire worth."

"So *you* are—"

"Most Wheatlanders think Reginald makes the money off your people, but he's my bookkeeper and butler."

"Hmph," Rej snorts.

Miller points to a well-dressed man in a painting, surrounded by grain mounds. "My forefathers settled this land long ago through a grant from the king. When prosperity came our way, we ended up owning half the town and our namesake fields. Everyone owes me something, except the market owner and you people in the hollow. I foresee this changing. The Golden Archie wheat disease will spread until it affects all in Wheatland. When I own everything, there'll be one boss with no elders."

"Rotten beast! Many suffer because they can't make a decent living off the land, and your high rent is the sucker punch."

"Which is the plan, lad. But I prefer the term *businessman*." Miller spreads his hands in an open gesture. "Who can resist what destiny plans for him?"

"You've told me your plan, so what's keeping me from telling it to everyone?"

An evil grin stretches across his face. "Go ahead, if you think they'll believe you. I'm not blind, for I have eyes and ears everywhere. No one will listen to a boy with your reputation."

I slam my fists on the chair arms. "I've heard enough. Thanks for the tea." *Rebecca's manners are rubbing off on me.* Before I can jump up, porky hands force me back into the chair. Miller snaps his fingers, which cause a snaky vine to grow from it. In an instant, they wrap around my body.

"Stay. There's a good boy."

"Let me go, you fiend."

"Or what?"

I struggle, but the thick cords won't allow me to break free.

"Trespassers beware." His face nears mine again. "Nice chair? Amazing what magical beasts live in these parts. Compliments from a faraway place. Tell me everything on the note, and I'll allow you to leave. News from Wheatland Town is my greatest interest."

My eyes widen in fear when the vine snakes around my throat. "Call this thing off me, and I will."

Miller snaps his fingers. In turn, it uncoils and disappears into the chair. "I've released you, so you had better uphold your side of the bargain."

I rub my neck, weighing my escape options. "It said 'I. M. and the Thinning.' But my father didn't write it. Mrs. Winslow gave it to him when we came to call. She found it on Mr. Winslow's desk the day he disappeared."

Miller's frown eases. "Funny you express it that way. I suppose all troublemakers simply need to vanish."

Blinking several times, I say, "You mean . . . you killed him?"

His eyes dart away from mine. "Jonah, your grandfather, and I knew each other since we were young. You may add we were once friends. Over the years, they became idealistic, so we parted company. Conrad and I didn't see eye to eye for other reasons. Winslow's penchant for ancient things proved to benefit me. I thank him. Well, his memory."

In a rage, I ball my hands into fists and struggle to loosen the cords.

"He had something I needed." Miller pulls two necklaces from his shirt, each holding a pale-green gem. They magnify the dim light, as I recall Jonah's did at the library. One has the chain he wore, silver twisted around gold. *The Two Gems from the Prophecy.*

I squeeze the chair arms. "How could you take his life and steal his necklace? You're a common thief."

"Thief, true, but not *common*. With me, there's nothing ordinary. Both weren't hard to acquire, I just needed to be patient. Destiny always makes room for the talented. Consider your grandfather, for instance. He was the noble one, and look where it got him. In the end, no magic could save Bernice, a woman who should've been mine."

Violent thoughts stream through my mind. I want to make his nose more crooked with my fist. "Leave out my grandpa and grandma, you prune."

Miller grits his teeth. "In case you haven't put two and two together, it's all about them. Your grandfather is the reason I am what I am." He caresses the gems beneath his collar. "In time, I learned to thank him. For his part in my inevitable rise to power. After he stole Bernice, I vowed I'd come out stronger, wealthier, and more powerful than anyone before me. Before long, I met a lady who replaced my affection for her." He gestures to the wall.

"The stump? Tell me, does a beard made of lichen scratch when you kiss it?"

"The woman, foolish lad!"

"No self-respecting girl could go for a mess like you. I doubt she ever loved you."

Miller's face turns red with rage but then it passes. He fingers the necklaces. "At long last, the pieces come together. I can return to my true love, a chance nobody has the power to take away from me."

"You may have Wheatland under your thumb, but you're not half the man my grandpa was. His bravery drove him to save my grandma from drowning."

"Ah yes, he tried and failed, because he wasn't a good swimmer. One must understand his own limits and who his foes are, but to know your foe's limits is the real task. Your grandfather caused his own death the second he jumped into the water. As for boldness, when they recovered his body, everyone saw terror etched into his face. The fool."

"Believe what you want, because the opposite is true. My dad was an eyewitness and tells us the story every year. When he arrived at the pool, she went under, never to return. A man wielding a mace fought with Grandpa. After struggling, they fell into the water. Dad stared for minutes at the bubbling blackness, but soon his dad floated feet up and without shoes. The strange part was his facial expression."

Miller's forehead creases with amusement. "What a tangled web you weave, lad."

"Grandpa's face was expressionless."

"Don't tell lies. You expect me to agree with your contradiction to the official record, most of which comes from your father?"

I roll my eyes. "Official? The investigators only knew weak evidence and came up with their lame theories. My dad obviously had covered up the parts he knew people wouldn't believe. Fine, old geezer, don't believe me since you think I make up such preposterous notions."

Miller raises his frail hand to strike me . . . but his frown eases into thoughtfulness. Why the thought distracts him doesn't matter.

My finger slips into the teacup handle, but he misses my intentions. I fling the steaming tea at his face. *Direct hit!* I leap toward him, tear the pendants from his neck—and a bit of his shirt collar—and sprint for the door. Beyond Hazo's reach, I must beat the slow-as-molasses Collector and grab my sword. His jiggly arms snatch at air when I fake one way to go the other.

"Kill him!" Miller screams.

I skid into the hallway.

Heavy breathing means Hazo follows me in hot pursuit. While sprinting, I manage a quick glance back, but I wish I hadn't. Hungry for another murder, the henchman closes in fast. He'll nab me.

The big man throws something. Halfway down the corridor, it

wraps around my ankles. I sprawl face-first as the gems sail into the air. Helpless to catch them, they hit the wall, clatter onto the floor, and skip several feet away.

He thunders towards me, killer eyes fixed on his prey. I unwrap the tricky vine tendrils, hop up, and dart for them. My unsteady legs cause a clumsy misstep—my hand snatches air. Momentum carries me the wrong way, but him straight to them.

Distracted by triumph, he caresses the glimmering stones, grinning with glee. I push a suit of display armor with all my might. A hundred pounds of polished steel and leather lands on his head. The clashing echo resounds throughout the marble hallway. The Two Gems fall from his greedy clutches.

"I'll take those," I say, rescuing them from the floor. "Thank you . . . twit." I step on his hand as I dash away, sparing no time listening to his cursing and death threats. I halt at the lead armor display, a modern piece, and push it into its neighbor. They tumble in succession toward my hapless enemy.

I finger wave at his floundering mass, turn and sprint through the foyer, dart through the door, and bolt across the courtyard. Lungs burning, I bend over to catch my breath.

"Jonathan?" a familiar voice says.

Startled, I peer into the gray mist. Gunnar pulls Rebecca from it. David, Linus, and the dogs follow.

"Wonderful hike up here," Linus says, eyes lifting to the manor. "Who spoiled it by sticking a haunted mansion there?"

"Why do you expect him to say anything?" my brother says. "He just lies and abandons everyone."

When my panting eases enough, I say, "Long story. Let's go before they murder us."

Fear fills his eyes. His lips form an "m" sound, but they venture no further.

Linus fidgets with his hands.

"Stop," Miller says. He and Rej leer at us from the porch.

"There's no way you're leaving my property with those gems. Give them to me, now."

"What's he saying?" Rebecca says. "Did you steal something?"

"I'll explain later. He's the thief. A *common* thief."

Miller and Rej advance on us, so we take a few steps back.

"Isn't there always a mountainous man tagging along with the Collector?" David says.

"He won't bother anyone," I say. "Took care of him. Gramps and his well-fed doughboy can't catch air—"

A harsh whine and a stifled scream interrupt me. Gunnar lands feet from where I saw him last, sprawling on the pavement. Hazo, blood streaming down his forehead, grapples with Rebecca. He wins the quick struggle and forces his arm around her neck.

"Surprise, side door. Didn't see me coming, pipsqueak?"

I grab my sword and will it to burn. Eager yellow flame blazes a yard long. Point up, I slash the air downward. "Let her go, you spawn of a demon."

A triumphant glint grows in his eyes as he wraps serpentine arms around Rebecca's body. "I don't think so. One step and I'll crush her into sweet marmalade."

I halt, but keep the blade burning.

Linus holds his hands palms outward. "Easy, now, don't hurt her."

"Hand 'em over, rat."

Miller and Rej advance toward us.

I point the sword their direction, rooting their feet. I advance on them.

"Two choices, lad," the old man says, spreading his hands. "One more step, and I'll order him to end her life. Want that on your conscience?"

I halt. *Is he bluffing?* I cast a withering look at Hazo. His determined expression doesn't falter. He will kill her, no question. The Two Gems . . . Hiding or destroying those means saving the mortal and immortal worlds. Many people I've never met would live. But one I've known my whole life would die. I lower my blade and will it to turn off. "Stop, you win. I'll give them to you." I fish them from my pocket and hold them between my fingers. Green light shimmers within them. *I was so close.*

"Good lad," Miller says. "Toss them to me. No tricks, then Hazo lets the girl go."

When I do, he snatches them with a nimble grab. A malicious grin spreads across his face. "You did the right thing."

If he was going to share an amazing monologue of his bright future, he doesn't. A shock wave reverberates through the earth, welling fear in his eyes as they train upward. *Thunder?* No, heavy footsteps pound the ground.

Miller and Rej hurry to the manor. I spin around to face a massive tree ogre. Lichen whiskers stretch from a severe countenance, and dark pits for eyes pock woody skin. His canopy fans in warning. Enormous fists threaten pulverization, and his sharpened roots promise to skewer the nearest people, Rebecca and Hazo. She throws her head back into his face, causing a small snap, thrashes for her life, and breaks free. Blood flowing, Hazo holds his nose, howling in pain.

Enraged, the ogre raises a heavy foot high overhead and forces it onto the big man. A sickening crunch turns my stomach. He shakes, then moves no more. *What a mess.*

With two quick leaps, Rebecca eludes a stomp and races to my side. Barking and growling tear the air. Max and Coal attack. Roots, forming a portcullis, shoot from the ground, barring our escape toward the house. I will my sword to ignite, but too late. The ogre swipes at me with his fist, pinwheeling me through the air. I crash, roll a few times, and land in a heap. The world spins. *Where's the hilt? . . . And my balance?*

Dark vines grab David and Linus. With a swift jerk, their bodies fly into the air. He shakes them as if they were rag dolls.

Vines entangle my neck and ankles. Spine taut, the monster pulls. I flail and fight . . . no use. No more energy in me.

This is it.

Without warning, they loosen, so I fall to the ground and roll to my belly. Rebecca, wielding a thick branch, swings at them with hefty blows. The dogs tear woody chunks from before, behind, and at his flank.

Roots burst through the cobblestone pavement to form a wall Max can't penetrate. In a one-two combination, jab to the muzzle, cross to the head, the monster finishes Coal with a glancing kick to the ribs. The black dog slumps to the ground.

"No!" she shouts. "Get the evil beast, Max. Come on, Gunnar!" She sidesteps a pounding blow and a clever vine attack.

With a cunning counter-move, the ogre separates them. Spear-shaped roots aim at each defender, which may mean their end. I sprint to my sword.

"Behind his whiskers—do you see it, Max?" Rebecca says. "No woody hide protecting it."

The great hound cocks his head to listen. Does he understand her? He lunges for the throat, but the ogre sweeps him away.

It's his one weakness.

Fiery point forward, I charge the monster. He blasts roots through the earth, heaving me into the air. With a reflex motion, he snatches me with his hand. My sword plummets to the ground and the blade retracts. I squirm to loosen his grip.

Nothing works.

The tree ogre stares at me with a curious gaze, but his wonder doesn't last long. He opens his mouth wide, bearing his square teeth.

"Jonathan, catch," Rebecca says.

I snatch the hilt midflight, will it to flame, and with a reflex motion not entirely mine, stab the monster's throat. In its death throes, the monster crashes to the earth.

Tattered vines, wood chunks, and tumbled soil and stone litter the battlefield. A surreal nightmare. In its midst lies the broken tree ogre carcass. Linus and David flank Rebecca, who tends to Coal, under which spreads a red puddle. Max stands guard nearby in case anyone else should try to harm us.

She presses her hand on his wound to staunch the blood flow. "Quick, Linus, tear a strip from my dress hem."

"What . . . but why?"

"Do it!"

He tears a lengthy piece and hands it to her. She doubles it to form a tight bandage around the dog's middle. When she's satisfied the bleeding has stopped, she sits back on her heels.

"At home, I have a poultice to reduce swelling." With care, she cycles each limb. "I can't tell if he has broken bones. I'll ask Mrs. Childers if she'll allow me to observe him at home. After all, she'll still have Max to guard her, and he's worth more than two dogs."

"We should move Coal to the wagon," Linus says.

"And we better hurry," I say pointing into the woods. "Our friend Woodrow here had a family." Tree ogres stream from the shadowy woods.

"You and David do it," Linus says. He picks through the debris until he works free a straight piece of wood. "I could make a strong spear from this hardened root."

My brother and I transport the injured dog to the wagon. There, we find Bruno munching on a carrot. Underneath his slobbery mouth, a green pile fills a bushel basket. He doesn't care for the tops.

"Got here just in time," David says as we set our wounded friend onto the flatbed. "He'll want more carrots."

"How do we explain his injuries?" I say.

David fingers his tattered shirt sleeves. "And our clothes."

Rebecca holds her hands palms outward. "I'll handle it. They'll believe my story, more than what you three tell them. I have some time to conjure something from thin air."

She shoots me a wrathful glance. "Why did you come up here alone, anyway?"

My hands slide to my hips. "Suspects in Jonah's disappearance rode by, so I had to investigate. Besides, I found out more than my master's fate. Miller has the prophesied Two Gems, and he wants to leave for the Other World. After many years, he's still in love with a faerie princess. The fool has no clue what awaits him there."

Rebecca's warm eyes meet mine, she takes my hands, and pulls me into a hug.

"For a few minutes, I had them . . ."

"You saved me, instead. Thank you."

"Didn't give it a second thought."

"Save it for later," David says pointing down the driveway. "Unless you want to fight Woodrow's relatives."

CHAPTER 13

THE PORTAL IN THE POOL

Fairview House sleeps under a gray blanket against the Thinning's pale-green backdrop. David knows of the faerie world from me, because I told him important details when he found the Workshop. But James, Linus, and Rebecca don't know an immortal realm even exists. I'm sure they'll say, "Why didn't you tell us sooner?" The longer I wait, the harder it will be to appease their wrath. I considered telling James when we passed his place, but everyone looked eager to come home. His engagement also contributed to my hesitation. So begins the slow decay of our friendship.

Everybody unpacks themselves from the wagon. Whiny brothers, a demanding Conrad Junior, and my dad's shortening fuse, provide the needed distractions. David hoists Coal out and sets him on the ground. To this point, my parents think his wounds are slight. In our conspiracy, I help Rebecca with Coal while David and Linus run interference with Gunnar. We cleaned ourselves up at the well the best we could, but under scrutiny with decent light, our tattered clothes will raise questions.

I had to coach her with lying, because it became obvious fast she's no good at it. A seasoned professional—me—has a remote chance to slip it past my mom. Still, I wonder if she bought that we, and the dog, fell on sharp bramble while playing. Rebecca went along with it, even offering her health services for the week.

Coal follows us into the barn with a pathetic hobble. I guide him to a corner padded with deep hay. Bruno's stall is near it, so the patient will have droll company. Good thing the donkey doesn't talk, otherwise everyone could learn my skunk carcass prank. The putrid scent still lingers here.

"I'm going on a supply run," Rebecca says. "Wait here with him and watch for any worsening in his condition."

"Sure."

She peeks from the barn door and then steps into the yard. When I rub Coal's ears, a relaxing wave spreads throughout his body. "You were brave today, buddy. Nobody can hurt you here." He leans his face into my fingers until a distant voice causes his ears to perk up at attention. "I hear it, too."

Coal whines, wide eyes on full alert.

"Stay, boy."

"Jonathan," Rebecca says in an urgent tone. I rush to the barn door and push it open. A few paces from where I stand, she points into the gloom. I scan my backyard. Nothing . . . wait, I see it, too. A dark figure at Fairview's back door. Not sure who.

We step toward the intruder. Maybe Ulgar? No, too small. Arching flower trellises and low-hanging tree branches, colorless in the waning light, give the house a haunted look. When I glance down to watch my steps, he dashes into the gray evening.

I sprint across the yard, zigzag around bushes and trees, and leap over flowerpots. He rushes straight for the waterfall pool, leaps onto the rim, and then dives in with a headlong splash.

I halt, then Rebecca slams into me. "Go!"

"One second, what I have to say is important. I know where this chase will end." I fish a glass vial from my pocket. Silvery-gold powder dances in a cool glow. "Haven't had the time to tell you the strange things I've learned."

She gestures toward the pool. "Your timing stinks, he's getting away."

I show her the vial. "This dust will help us get through a faerie door."

Rebecca points a cautious finger. "What is . . .?"

I pop the cork, sprinkle the powder on myself, and then I blow a pinch full onto her. It clings everywhere.

"It's in my eyes."

"Sorry. Whatever happens, trust me. Hold your breath until we make it to the other side."

Her fingers interlock with mine. "You better explain this later. Let's go." Hand in hand, we jump into the water.

The waterfall's rumble deepens with each yard we swim. Rebecca is a natural swimmer, though I never see her practice. Deeper we dive, until a green light pierces through the gloom. The intruder struggles beneath the powerful undertow. *We have him now.*

Twenty feet, then fifteen. As we race to the murky bottom, he strives to an illuminated rectangle etched on the wall. It reminds me of the one in the cave's pool. Rebecca yanks on my arm, shaking her head and jerking her thumb upward as bubbles jet from her mouth. I shake my head. Again, she jerks her thumb toward the surface.

"We can make it, trust me. Hold what breath you have." She tries to talk as I did, but loses more precious air. She breaks upward, so I drag her back. Horror replaces the shock in her eyes. She thrashes and strikes me many times, but they're powerless thuds in the heavy water. When she tires, I grip her head, plant my mouth on her mouth, and blow the air I have into her lungs. Her horrified gaze ebbs to incredulity.

"Trust me, you won't drown."

Her okay signal motivates us to continue the chase. We fight through the swirling current. With a last-ditch push to catch our quarry, we claw our way forward. The intruder reaches for the door as we each grab an ankle.

Passing through a water faerie door differs from what I expected. A powerful rolling wave—gurgling bubbles—the scent after a thundershower might do it justice. We tumble with him and then sprawl onto a tiled floor.

We land in a room the same size as the Workshop, but without tree roots poking through the ceiling. Luminescent fungi grow on the walls at even intervals, which emit light akin to daylight. A single lime-green torch glows by the door.

Rebecca hacks up half the pool in violent spasms. She slaps my arm, and panting asks, "How can you breathe underwater?"

Before I answer, water expels from my lungs and nostrils, the conversion process from one breathing medium to another.

With a guttural wretch, the intruder coughs up water onto the floor. When he collects himself, his angry glance eases into confusion, then recognition.

I've seen this man, too, but I can't place him. Faces scroll through my brain—friends, enemies, acquaintances, neighbors, and relatives.

Relatives. Long-seated fear gives way to a fragile hope with unexpected joy. In my mind, a fuzzy Monday-morning image materializes. *Those clever green eyes!* I point at him. "You're the man in the portrait outside my bedroom."

"Oh?" he says.

"Grandpa?"

"I believe so."

CHAPTER 14

THE TWINS AND
THE TWAIN

"You're in my son's family painting," he says. "What's your name?"

I hesitate, but in my heart I know he is my grandpa. Bright green eyes, square jaw, vest with formal coat—all these features match the man in the wedding portrait. I help him to his feet. "Jonathan. My twin is David." The missing years hit him and me like a flood. Tears stream down our cheeks, and we hug away the deep-seated pain. "I always wondered how great it'd be to have a grandparent in my life."

"Me as well. They stole so much from us that day."

"Why did you come back?"

"Long ago everything happened so fast with your grandmother, I wasn't wearing my wedding band. Left it in my sanctuary while I was reading. Someone destroyed my brazier, so I had to try another door."

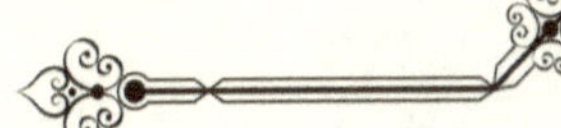

Oops. I riffle through my pockets, and upon finding the ring, hand it to him. "Looking for this?"

He takes it from me. "Thank you, it means everything to me."

Rebecca pulls me away from him. "Fool, you must have oxygen deprivation. Don't let him bewitch you."

"Not true, I'm part water faerie."

"Part *what*?"

"Remember what I told you about the spy?"

She nods.

"Found out the hard way I can breathe underwater. Same night I learned flames can't harm me either, which means I'm half fire faerie, too."

"Which explains the hot lamp."

"You're the son of *two* kinds?" my grandpa says.

"Yes, it's rare."

"Rare? Try never in history."

Rebecca frowns, grabbing my shoulder. "Whatever. Still, it's impossible, because your grandparents died. Everyone knows they drowned. Don't be fooled, stupid."

My jaw drops. *Harsh, what happened to her manners?*

"Not possible, young lady?" Grandpa says.

"Her name is Rebecca Avery, and she's my neighbor."

She shakes her head, hands perching on her hips. "A case of mistaken identity, or you're a ghost. Maybe a sprite, because you love water? Everyone in the borough knows you died."

He takes off his wet coat and gives it to her. "This hides what could complicate life in simple Wheatland Town." Two membranous wings unfold from slits in his vest.

Rebecca gawks at him and rubs her eyes. "Not seeing this . . . it's a weird dream."

Grandpa flaps them, which puffs air onto her face. "Believe now, young lady?"

She offers a tentative nod—reaches out to a wing—but takes back her hand.

"Full-blood faeries have them and even some have pointed ears. Halfers—part faerie, part human—don't have either. But a halfer is always half faerie, hence the name. Magic makes it so. And magic does what magic wants. Sometimes an entire family line has magic, while others may not have it in generations. Accept it as the natural order between the worlds."

"How can you prove it exists except by sound reasoning?" Rebecca says.

Grandpa takes in a deep breath and lets it out in slow frustration. "It's a pity how attitudes have changed in mortals. In the Olden Days, folk used to believe our stories and teach them to their children. They believed without seeing. Elder testimony and tradition handed down to the next generation were the only proofs needed. My dear, in this wide world there are many fantastic things to consider, which you may never see or make logical understanding of them. Don't rely on just one of your senses."

She bites her lip and nods.

"Since we established I *am* alive, I can answer your question. Grandma and I didn't die. I haven't ever been dead in my life. Most humans never learned faeries fake mortals' deaths and abduct them."

"Why?" I say.

"For sport. But in our case, for a different reason."

"Meaning?"

"You must want the long version, lad." He spreads his arms outward, palms up. "People don't believe the old legends anymore, but their ancients called this place the Other World. A trite name if you ask me, but in faerie speak, we call it Tuatha Dé Danann. It's the blessed realm belonging to faeries and their kith and kin, pixies. But home to other magical beings such as sprites, leprechauns, clurichauns, brownies, pookas, korrigans, and so forth. Banshees, the portents of death, being the worst."

He points to the wall. "One day through this door, I happened upon Bern washing her family's laundry. Her beauty and innocence enraptured me."

"You fell in love with Grandma while she did . . . her chores?"

A perplexed look passes over Grandpa's face. "From then on, I wanted to live among the mortals. Later, I learned my folk abducted a hermit from the East Borough named Conrad Jackson. To fit in better here, I took his identity. In time, Bern and I married, so the rest is history. My true name is Conri II, born to King Brádach and Queen Aveleen. If that isn't motivation enough for evil faeries, I'm the captain sent to find and secure the Two Gems. To end a threat, Malgroth and his thugs seized your grandma and me. So much for keeping a low profile in Wheatland. They tried to lock us in the Eskelon dungeons, but I escaped before they brought me there. During my escape, they stole through a door I couldn't enter, so I lost her."

"How could this faked death fool my dad?" I say. "He saw you die."

"An abduction happens this way: First, the victim goes missing; then someone finds a corpse. Water faeries 'drown' their victims before they kidnap them; fire faeries show theirs burned but leave enough to identify the body. Moon and earth faeries tend to be honorable, so they don't abduct mortals. Sometimes abductees become slaves in the immortal world, but most times they're returned here with a strange nightmare memory.

"The key to figuring out an actual death versus an abduction is they stink at copying the victim's physical traits. They leave out teeth, use the wrong hair color—you get the idea. For instance, I heard a family died in a fire. When the constable investigated the tragedy, even though charred, he found their faces wearing smiles. The little devils stand close by giggling, while the loved ones grieve. When the funeral is over, the imposter finds his way back to Tuatha Dé Danann."

"Why do they hold so much power?" Rebecca says. "Can't anyone stop them?"

"Yes and no. The ancient magic of the mortal realm wanes, but the faerie realm has become stronger. They're not in balance anymore."

"How has this happened, Grandpa?"

"Not long after its founding, the mortal creation suffered a cataclysmic deluge caused by breaking up the great deeps and rending the skies. This, in turn, made its magic wane. Today, faeries control the time between the worlds. A couple conditions restrain the faerie realm from dominating the human one. First, the separation of the Two Gems."

"You mentioned those," Rebecca says, shaking her head. "What are they?"

"Ancient history most don't care for now."

"And what is the other, Grandpa?"

She spreads her hands in frustration. "Rude. My question before his."

"The other reason is more complicated. It's El'Darios the Great himself, Lord and Master of the Worlds. Darkness fears him most. No one has seen him for a long time, but many believe the old prophecies saying he'll return, take back his own, and heal the mortal world."

"Your book tells the entire story. I read it in the workshop, what I call the secret laboratory below the library. I had you pegged as a halfer, too."

"How did you access my sanctuary?"

"I found the knothole in the baseboard. The firefly weapon Lady Sophia gave me acts as a key, too."

Grandpa gives his head a slight shake. "*She* gave you?"

I tell him the details of the Fairfield Road visitation and the book, then I pull out the sword hilt and place it in his hand.

He studies its craftsmanship with a keen eye. "She doesn't visit just anyone, for she is El'Darios's daughter, who does his bidding."

Breath sticks in my throat, and I find no words to say.

"You're my grandson and my brother." He fishes something from his coat pocket, wills a sword to burn, and with an artistic display, flourishes it, ending with the point held up. The magical glow transforms his kind face into a warrior's determination. "It's plain she chose you two, like me, to guard the eternal and mortal realms in the Order of the Hôzai."

"What did you say?"

"Prophet warriors. Most knights speak prophecies, but all defend those spoken by El'Darios."

I glance downward. "She spoke of this, but a mysterious light interrupted our conversation."

"Ishglof, the one who hounds my hunt for Bernice at every turn. He was at the pool, too, on that fateful day."

I nod. "Later in the night, she said many things to our elders through the book. They're in her plans, too."

"The Lady's enemies watch for the prophecy's fulfillment." Grandpa beckons me to come closer. "Let me see the faerie spark hue in your eyes." He positions my face until the light shines at the right angle. After a moment, his fingers slacken.

He doesn't look straight at me.

"What?"

"They are . . . you have the two worlds' mark, brown, a mortal world color mixed with green, an eternal world color. The Prophecy of the Two speaks of . . . my grandson? Let me guess, your twin brother's eyes are the same."

Goose bumps pop all over my arms. "Yes."

"Two faerie kinds makes sense. You're from both realms—the Elected Ones."

"Lady Sophia said the same thing."

"David's time must come. She gave me a two-hander for more than just safekeeping. Folktales call you Brothers' Bane, saviors of the worlds. Near the end times, they will enter Eshbanáchbor and defeat Malgroth and his brother Ishglof." My grandpa paces the room. "These years I've searched only to find they belong to my family."

"The dark door leads to the wicked realm. I saw it in a nightmare."

He nods thoughtfully. "Then El'Darios knows you."

"For sure," Rebecca says, "everyone knows dreams and their interpretation come from him."

I gape at her, not knowing how to respond.

Her hands slide to her hips. "It's common knowledge in Wheatland. Not saying I believe it."

"Malgroth is aware, too," I say. "He spoke to me in a nightmare."

Grandpa's kelly-green eyes flash. "What happens?"

"I see a dark door leading to a fortress with six towers looming in the backdrop."

"Eskelon."

I nod.

"Have you told your brother?"

"He's been to the workshop. I let him know everything I knew at the time."

"Does he have the nightmares?"

"No, I don't think so. Grandpa, you mentioned the lost gems coming together. We call this the Two Combining." My gaze drifts aside. *How can I tell him I failed?*

"At last, you'll answer *my* question," Rebecca says, interrupting.

"You've learned about it, Jonathan? Our meeting is no mere chance event. A greater will works here, beyond what we may guess. I'll explain to you the whole truth. It has a double meaning referring to the brothers Malgroth and Ishglof. The former being dark lord over the mortal world and the latter over the faerie world. You see, El'Darios separated them, and under normal circumstances, never to reunite.

"The other significance finds its roots in ancient dwarf craft. I'm no expert in it. Long ago, greater dwarves mined them from the heart of the Sacred Hill in Tuatha Dé Danann. Creation imbued their wills with extraordinary power. The prophecy foretold by Lord El'Darios says there must come a period when the two worlds will align as one. These gems can bridge them anytime, so the barrier between the realms has no real significance. As master of time, the person who holds them owns the future. Words from the Two Combining Prophecy are:

> "Twin gems from the Danann World mined,
>
> Heart and Soul of the Faerie King.
>
> Their power World to World bind,
>
> War with desolation shall bring.
>
> Twain lords their power combined,
>
> One lord their influence will scatter.
>
> To darkness, the Twain rule will bind,
>
> For One, the dark power will shatter.
>
> Black mists issue from shadowed mind,
>
> Men's wills to capture.
>
> Clear mists the lost will find,
>
> Deep longing to enrapture."

"Whoever reunites these gems, masters the Thinning. I sought them named in the Greater Dwarf tongue Barázvazaad, or Heart and Mind, but haven't discovered them yet. If they unite, the brothers will combine their power and overwhelm the worlds with evil thought and darkness."

I grab his arm. "I found them."

"You—how?"

"Had them in my grasp . . . long story, but an old acquaintance of yours, Ichabod Miller, has them now. If I didn't hand them over, he would've killed Rebecca. Had no choice." She caresses my shoulder. "He's going back there for a faerie girl."

"Don't blame yourself," Grandpa says. "Miller is wily. A heart set upon intense love will stop at nothing—no matter how dangerous the road. Love may quicken the senses, but it also can make one blind. His is a sad tale. Years ago, he met Princess Fia at a pool in his namesake field."

"The one by Rowen?"

"Yes. He fell for her, but not she for him. Now the mound lies barren since the faeries and pixies began fighting five years hence. But he never forgot the door."

My eyebrows rise. "The Golden Archie crop failures happened because of Other World infighting?"

"Happens all the time. The high blessings of the Good People go with them."

I start when the lime-green torchlight flickers.

"What is happening, Mr. Jackson?" Rebecca says.

"Drat it! You both must go back before it turns red, otherwise it will not be today in your world."

"Please help me find the dark door, Grandpa."

"I might have what can aid you, so I'll find you again. Until then, look for creative ways to fulfill the prophecy. And expect their evil servants to oppose you at every step."

I nod.

He rests his hand on my shoulder. "I'll search for Miller, but chances are he's long gone or in hiding until he's ready to act."

I throw my arms around him. "Thank you."

He doesn't answer but seems to dwell on a deep hurt. Must be Grandma. Or parting ways. *Will Dad believe any of this?*

"I'm glad you're not dead, sir," Rebecca says with a smile.

"As am I, child. Hurry, go."

I push open the door and we dive to the other side. She closes it and we follow the bubbles to the surface. On the pool's rim, I consider what happened. Now I understand more than ever, David and I must travel to the dark door before it's too late. How? By running away from home? I won't get far through the forest. Maybe an opportunity will present itself?

CHAPTER 15

WILLIAM'S FOLLY

The next morning, the savory scent of eggs with smoked bacon lures me out of bed. Then what happened yesterday seeps into my cloudy thoughts. I shuffle into the kitchen, the scraping of pans abrasive in my ears, and drop into a chair beside Pep and Thomas.

I wonder if Dad knows his father is alive. How will he believe my story, since it seemed no time passed when Rebecca and I returned?

"Dear, stop picking at your breakfast," Mom says, her eyes searching for answers written on my face. Such traumatic events can quell even the most voracious appetite.

My ears register a knock at the door, but my mind swims in thoughts and emotions.

She leaves to answer it. I hear it open and she calls out, "Jonathan, James is here."

I freeze in the kitchen archway. My mom's arms wrap around

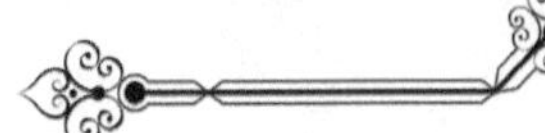

him like ribbons on a wedding present. All signs point to the inevitability of his engagement. Marriage ruins everything.

Cycling through ums and ahs, he finds meaningful words. "I've something to tell you."

Now comes the wet blanket on our friendship.

"I asked Siany to marry me and she said yes."

My mom nudges me with her elbow. "Isn't the news wonderful?" She extends to her tiptoes, holds his face in her little hands, and kisses both whiskered cheeks.

After some days' notice, I'm not ready with an answer. "Great, when will I meet her?" *Does my expression betray my words?*

"Two weeks, the day before the wedding."

Heat rushes into my cheeks. "Not much time."

"It'll be in Wheatland because we want to live here." He rests his hand on my shoulder. "We'll always be close friends, even during this new chapter in my life. Besides, you're my best man."

His lightheartedness lifts my mood. "Do you have a few minutes?" I ask.

"I'm between jobs."

"Mom, we're going out for a walk."

"Be back in time to finish your chores."

Indescribable relief washes over me because I have only mine to do.

Dad stomps into the foyer. He drops beside me on the bench as I pull on my shoes, tears off his own, and then throws them to the floor. "Still nothing."

"What do you mean?" my mom says.

"Winston said the king's men will handle Sebastian's problem, but they're not in a hurry. Martha needs him, and we're too busy to ride up there every day. Wish I could do more."

A haunting suspicion gnaws at me. Dad's desperate moment may translate into more chores for me. And just when I broke free of my punishment. *Can't have that.* My quick fingers work to finish tying them. Nothing must put time with my best friend at risk. With luck, I can extend a walk into a day of good old-fashioned mischief.

Bars of moonlight stripe my bedcovers as I reflect on my day with James. Today was tame by our standards, but I recall the old days when he and I used to roam the town into the wee hours, tip over cows, or hide in the graveyard after playing tricks on whoever had night watch. Never got caught. "David? Did Dad act weird earlier today?"

"Huh," he grunts, half-asleep. "Maybe."

"No one caring for Mrs. Childers bothered him."

Silence.

David's rhythmic breathing ends the conversation.

My mind races throughout the night, keeping me awake. Early in the morning, soft commotion and dark-roast coffee fragrance seep into my bedroom. By the time my eyes flicker open, the gray dawn leaks through the shutters. I roll out of bed, shuffle through the hallway, and drop into my chair at the kitchen table. Wasn't my imagination, somebody did make coffee, so I pour a mug for myself. My first pull jolts my eyelids wide. *Dad made it.*

A note in his scrawl leans against the flower vase, but this life-giving nectar is more important than it. Footsteps approach, and in trundles my mom. She tousles my hair but is more interested in the letter than why I'm awake now. Saves me a white lie. Mom's tired eyes perk up with each sentence they consume. Tears well there and then stream down her rosy cheeks.

"You okay?" Her faraway stare won't look at me. I lift the note from her fingers.

My dearest Eliza,
I can't sit idle while Sebastian rots in jail. I believe the only
person who can clear his name is the man from Heathfell, Oliver
Iskander. Going will be risky, but it's a chance I must take. My
heart tells me he is innocent, and strange things are happening
here. I'll rent a hearty pony from Sanderson, so don't worry. Back
in a few days. Please accept my humble apologies for my actions.
My love to you.
Yours affectionately,
William

Likewise plagued by insomnia, David stands in the archway, so I toss him the letter. As he reads, his expression turns to stone. He sets it on the table and cradles Mom to absorb her sobs.

"He'll be okay."

No he won't. What was he thinking? We could've cared for her for a couple weeks.

I find a spot on the living room floor and lift my legs onto the couch. David stretches his limbs, pushing mine off it. *Brat.*

Sunlight grows along the ceiling then, over the hours, shrinks to nothing. Our sulking together benefits the soul, but only for so long. We must wait and hope. A knock on the door shocks us from our comfortable places.

My mom swings it open, and croaks a tentative greeting. "Hello . . . gentlemen."

We join her. Winston, flanked by the two king's men, fidgets with his hat. "Good day, Elizabeth. I'd ask for William, but a reliable source saw him ride east. Sanderson said your husband rented the horse for the entire week. Where did he go?"

"We'll take it from here," a soldier says, sidestepping in front.

They both wear leather breastplates bearing the royal insignia and a sword belted at the waist. One, whose broad noggin blends into massive shoulders, stands a head above the other. The squat person sticks his wide foot in the doorway and thick hand on the door jamb. His skull tattoo peeks beneath a mail shirt. I puff out my chest to look more impressive. Doesn't work—nothing to stick out compared to them. David could take out one, but impressive strength may not mean he's a skilled fighter.

"Not another toenail inside my house, mister," my mom says, vein bulging in her forehead.

The tall man smiles crossways pointing to himself then his comrade. "My name is Farzir. My associate, Alcred," he says in the swollen-tongued accent Auntie Fanny despises.

She refuses to offer her hand to them. Each man submits a slight bow.

"My husband isn't home. Come back another time."

"Where did he go, ma'am?"

"Personal business is just that." She glares at Winston. "At least it used to be."

Farzir spreads his hands, palms upward. "I want to keep law and order."

"But instead, you achieve the opposite."

"You know as well as anyone why Sebastian sits in jail."

"Excuse me, Martha has no nursemaid. Unclog my doorway, so I can attend to the aftermath of your *law and order*."

"We're not looking for trouble, but if William violated the Order of Banishment, then there'll be some. Everyone knows what the king does to offenders."

Alcred moves his hand from the doorjamb. "Tell us when he comes back."

My mom's scowl doesn't ease with the request.

"I see," Farzir says. Each soldier offers a slight bow, turns on their heels, and retreats through the courtyard. Winston, pale from the drama, glances at Mom with concern, but she meets it with contempt.

The afternoon breeze sweeps the sky clean when Linus, David, and I reach town to run errands. Customers at the Childers Market glance at us but then their eyes dart somewhere else. Same thing the next day, but this time we're at Hill's fruit stand. Greene pretends we're not there and lets his mother wait on us. *Brat.*

By Friday, I've learned people aren't shy with their grumblings, because the winds have fanned the gossip flames across the borough. Tall tales are growing, and their thread of truth stretches as if it were spider silk on the wind.

On the gathering day before the wedding, a rooster crows, dogs bark, and worry settles upon Wheatland along with a thick fog. Everybody heard the king's men received new orders so they'll ship out early. Weird . . . Today my family will face the whole town at once. No update on my dad, so they must believe the worst.

A chill breeze blows across the festival grounds, as do the glares Auntie Fannie and her posse give my mom. We settle in our usual seats, with the Averys sitting in our row. Even surrounded by many people waiting for George Roberts to speak, the empty feeling in my stomach isn't from hunger. David's uncertain look says he feels it, too. Anthony's portliness eclipses Greene's slight frame, but at one point, he catches my eye and offers a weak smile.

Wheatlanders listen to our elder statesman wade through a long-forgotten history. His voice, easy on the ears, in time turns eyes drowsy, necks rubbery, and my mind to lunch.

James invited the entire borough to the wedding. My fingers still ache from sealing and stamping countless envelopes. George, the de facto justice of the peace and his surrogate father, will preside over the event. Since the meetinghouse burned, the next best place to have it is here. Weather prognosticators, Herky Holms and others, say no rain on Saturday, but we believe they're half-right most times. Good thing no one pays for their guesses.

Rebecca weighs George's every word. While she's thoughtful over what he says, for this reason, I find it hard to concentrate. Except on her. Golden hair cascades in ringlets down a crimson dress that hugs her curves. Stray wisps flit across her soft facial features in the playful breeze. If I peel my eyes away, it'll ease the annoyed frown growing on Mom's face. Next to impossible today. They drift toward George, but roam back to her when Mom, satisfied, returns to listening to the lesson.

On Monday, wagons stream into town carrying decorations, tables, chairs, barrels, salted meats, greens, and desserts. Even fireworks—everyone's favorite—slip past Beasley's nose. Most weddings have had more food, so it's plain the privation dog has bitten most folk.

The week passes as if it were a single night. Friday morning at James's cottage, Linus, David, Rebecca, and I witness two wagons pull into his driveway, one loaded with crates to make up for the food shortfall.

James shifts his weight from his left foot to his right and back again. I rest my arm on his shoulder. "Remember, the wedding party will stay at your place. Whoever needs a room can spend the night at the Roberts' home, or at mine and—" He scuttles to the wagon, leaving me midsentence. He offers his hand to a lady wearing a feathered hat and an emerald dress with puffed sleeves. After her comes a youthful woman dressed to match. When the younger one steps to the ground, she springs to her toes and throws her arms around his neck.

"Missed you, love," she says, staring into his eyes.

Time to break up this lovey-dovey stuff. "Ahem."

Her wholesome face, framed by nut-brown hair, pops from behind James's dark head. She extends her hand. "You must be Jonathan, I'm Siany." Her eyes smile as warm as her rosy cheeks.

"Pleased to meet you."

"My best friend talks about you every day."

"Only good things," he says with a hitch in his voice.

A balding man laureled with curly gray hair shakes James's hand.

"My father, Rombart Merriman."

"Pleased as well, Jonathan," he says.

James pokes me in the ribs with his elbow. "He's *the* famous royal healer."

"I see. You must meet my neighbor. For sure she's a fan." I wave over the others.

After quick introductions and light chitchat, an uncomfortable silence grows between us. To break it, I say the first thing coming to mind, "Is Siany a family name? I've never heard of it."

David slides his foot over to step on mine and Rebecca shoots me a caution.

"Glad you asked. Long story, but I'll give you the quick version," she says.

I cast my detractors a sideways glance.

"My parents had me late in life, so to honor the blessing bestowed from above, they named me Healing in ancient Bormaġian. They kept the traditional spelling, even though She-on-ee would help most people pronounce it right."

"I trust your trip went well, Mr. and Mrs. Merriman?" James says.

"Tired," she says. "We pushed through the dreadful forest to spend the night in Heathervale. Enough chitchat, how are the wedding plans? I wasn't given much time to plan anything, let alone journey here. Flowers and decorations must say creative perfection, the food a culinary masterpiece."

Does she know this isn't Heathfell?

Siany grips James's arm tight. "Mama, please . . ."

"How can I help? Goodness knows we brought anything and everything."

"The whole borough pitched in," James says. "Since my parents died, Wheatlanders care for me whenever I have a need. Our wedding's no different."

"My sister and her friends picked the wildflowers," I say.

"Wildflowers? How . . . quaint," Mrs. Merriman says, her smile flattening.

Rombart offers a nervous chortle.

The groom clears his throat and nods. "After you settle into my cottage, we can watch the preparations progress."

"Watch?" she says.

Other relatives and I stay with James on the wedding eve. Around the Roberts's kitchen table, our repartee turns to banter and to rehashing old stories. No covert adventure makes it to light. I learn differing opinions about Heathfell, the monarchy, and the brewing conflict with the T'Anakim kingdom. Many in the capital city believe our borough still sympathizes with our enemies to the south. My mind drifts back to my midnight visitor who disappeared the next day. Forgot to tell James about him.

The first chance comes when we get ready for bed. I share with him my nightmare and tell him about the enemy defector, but leave out details on my grandpa and my lineage. For now.

Deep in thought, my friend fiddles with the bedcovers. "Not sure what to say."

I fluff the feather bed with my fists.

He shoots me an astonished stare. "Easy, calm yourself."

"Sorry, I wish my dad had met him to prove I wasn't lying."

"He will think what he wants. Let your good character defend you."

"Hilarious."

"I'm serious. Big of you to help the man, especially since he's T'Anakim. You and Rebecca did what you could. Let's pick this up later so I can get sleep." He blows out the lamp.

I stare at the moonlight shapes the window lattice makes on the ceiling. What happened to my dad? Did he find Oliver Iskander and is on his way home? Wishful thinking. He alone sought to defend Sebastian and care for Martha. And no one will help him, except me.

James paces the gray hallway. Dawn chases low-lying clouds away, which dare to threaten the bride's perfect day. Birds singing cheerful songs dot the trees and the eaves. No doubt, Siany's transformation into a stunning princess bride will begin soon.

I wander into the Roberts' kitchen to find the pensive couple sipping their coffee.

"Good morning, Jonathan," Margaret says. "Did you sleep well?"

"Yes, ma'am, but James didn't. He's been pacing around for hours."

"The poor dear."

"Do you have any cucumbers?"

George offers a confused frown. "Why?"

"For the dark circles under his eyes. Need to hide the evidence the groom paced the halls all night."

We spend our final day together covering every missed conversation over the past few months. Whenever I mention Rebecca, a weird grin plays on his lips. He should resist the crazy drivel I "like" her.

Before two in the afternoon, we split up to separate dressing rooms. My bath last night lasted long enough. In no time, I'm ready to leave, having finger-combed my hair twice, straightened my tie, and passed the armpit sniff test.

James stares into a mirror, a faraway look suggesting uncertainty. I offer a slight smile and smooth out the coat wrinkles along his shoulders. "Let's put the finishing touches on you. You'll be fine."

He doesn't say a word but his tentative facial expression warms. Terrified, no doubt. With final adjustments—straightening his bow tie, picking off stray fuzz, and expunging small food stains—he's ready.

Dust Storm dignifies our grand entrance into the festival grounds. Crowds fill neat rows on both sides, but collect toward the back. No doubt, people see not a mere blessed event, but a free meal. James joins George on the stage, where Margaret adds the final touch of class—the carnation boutonniere.

At 3:00, everyone quiets in anticipation. From 3:05 to 3:15 the din rises, heads turn every which way, and knitting needles flit with energy. To Wheatlanders, five minutes is casually late, but fifteen minutes late borders on rudeness. I catch James's glance a few times but realize my raised eyebrows and half smile aren't helping his nervousness.

In the crowd, mothers chide antsy boys, girls play with their dolls, and a new conversation begins each minute. Clyde's family sits in the back. I didn't expect them to come. Mrs. Hoggins, along with her two daughters, Imogene and Iona, wear white gowns and a shimmering pearl necklace each. It's been so long, I don't recognize them. The older one is around Goldie's age, but they never visit each other. Mr. Hoggins and Clyde wear suits with a vest. I wonder at their opulence, yet I'm glad to see a prospering family in depressed Wheatland.

James and George exchange tense smiles, but in a few moments, faint nickering and clip-clopping hooves echo from the south. Siany's entourage races into the grove. They park cockeyed next to the Avery wagon, stream to their reserved front row, and dodge annoyed glares.

But the stares don't last.

Rombart, driving the bride in the second wagon, appears like a long-awaited friend. He parks and takes her hand to help her to the ground. Radiant in her flowing white dress, Siany's heartfelt smile melts the frosty mood that settled on the grove.

The head usher signals the strings to play. A screechy violin whirrs discordantly against the others. Mr. Atwood and the band begin the processional. Siany stands with her dad at the end of the aisle. She smooths any wrinkles from her gown, locks arms with him, and follows her niece at a generous distance. Father and daughter glide arm in arm, beaming left and right to forgiving smiles.

Nut-brown waves ripple down her back to reach a long dress train, which meanders through a rose petal stream strewn by the girl. At the end, he kisses her cheek, and offers her hand to James. His joy settles the battling emotions in me. Smile or frown, happiness wins the battle on my face. These two are *perfect* for each other.

My part in the ceremony—providing him the ring and making certain he doesn't faint or forget his lines—goes as I expected. I'm positive this wedding will make its mark on the Wheatlanders' minds for a long time.

Whoever came to get more than a happy memory enjoy the party afterward. Now and then, Rebecca's eyes catch mine, sending a warm feeling throughout me. Didn't realize I was looking at her.

Wheatland Borough parties are tame compared with other places in the kingdom, but all last until late in the night. This one, more toward the middle, doesn't feature the tumblers, fire breathers, log rollers, or illusionists I hear some do. Wheatlanders consider sword swallowers crazy, but not unknown in other places. I wish my dad were here, but I believe he's here in spirit.

Siany finishes the traditional bouquet toss to the eligible girls, then Herky, Anthony, Greene, and Rombart lift her in a chair. David, Linus, Clyde, and I push James into one, too, and follow the parade. I hoped to catch up more with Clyde, but I always have another best man duty getting in the way.

Dressed in full armor, Farzir and Alcred watch the festivities from a distance. I wonder how long they've been watching. How could they suspect any wrongdoing? It's a wedding!

The sun bathes the grove in a faint orange glow, announcing the thinning and signaling the servers to prepare dinner. An hour later, evening chill seeps in to turn a brothy fog into pea soup. I wait in the buffet line, plate in hand, when a curious jangling sound nags at me. It lures me east, away from the distracting people. The others join me under the mist-wreathed oaks.

"What is it?" Rebecca says.

Everyone else must hear it too, because their celebrating dies down.

"What do you think?" Linus says.

I strain my eyes to see anything. Clanking steel mixed with pounding on the earth grow in the festive air. Chills race down my spine. "I have an idea."

I point to a faint orange light. "There, look."

"Torchlight?" Rebecca says.

"You're right," David says.

Lights pop from the thickening white sheets. Heel strikes and hoofbeats ratchet louder up a nervous echelon. Phantasmal, grim metal faces issue from the gloom. On cue, plate-mail-clad dragoons flip shields sporting a fierce lion, stained crimson with the blood of experience, to their off-hands. They form an impenetrable wall, drawing sword tips upward.

CHAPTER 16

UNWELCOME COMPANY

The vanguard double-times it to encircle the grove. Behind them, infantrymen with tall spears rush to command the lead. Their captain, wearing a fish-scale steel hauberk, trots into the circle astride a white charger. To his flanks stand the famous haelan-magi—the healer wizards—whose faces hide in deep hoods. Their legendary exploits praise their long and mysterious history. Further back step the fleet-footed archers clad in leather armor. The cavalry, mounted upon midnight stallions with crimson and gold saddle blankets, form the rearguard. Ways to escape vanish. I've never seen or read about a more refined war machine. Farzir and Alcred, swords drawn, enter the tightening net.

Their captain thunders onto the stage, his glower paralyzing every movement, even the knitting needles. "Wheatland Town, I'm Tirás, commander of the regulars. His Majesty King Alfonse, may he live forever, sent me to summon your leaders. When I call your

name, join me here. The elder registry notes these people: George and Margaret Roberts, joint chief elders."

One by one, he calls everyone. The warlord takes a silent count. "Where is William Jackson?"

Winston steps forward, chest inflated more than usual. "Beg your pardon, sir, I'm the town constable. He left here last week. Nobody knows his whereabouts, but we're cooperating with the king's men to ascertain—"

"So I've learned. We got your detailed message sent from Officer Farzir distancing yourself from this conspiracy to violate the Order of Banishment. The king will hear your special case."

Winston blushes and drops his gaze to the floor. "T-thank you, sir, I followed protocol to the letter. Sebastian Childers is in jail, awaiting trial. I can fetch him."

The captain turns to his lieutenant, a youthful man with a patchy beard. "Aráza, go with him. Jackson is the one we have in custody."

My eyes mist. Dad rots in the Heathfell dungeons while we wonder what happened to him. Deep within me, I can't deny the truth of it. David's blank stare tells me he feels the same way.

In a few moments, they return with the rogue elder shackled hands to feet.

Tirás considers the prisoner and says to Winston, "Childers?"
"Yes."

"Doesn't look as dangerous as you wrote, so unbind him."

Sheepish from the slight, he fishes out keys from his pocket and frees him.

The captain pulls a scroll from his satchel and sliding a finger along its opening, breaks the seal. "'His Majesty King Alfonse, may he live forever, knows one week past, the Wheatland Town elders sent unbidden a man to Heathfell, East Borough. An action which defies their banishment. The Wheatlanders sympathize with our sworn enemies, the T'Anakim. For these contrivances, I hereby place them under arrest. The royal court demands they answer charges connecting with this conspiracy. Those levied against them are violating and conspiring to violate the Order of Banishment, aiding the enemy, and sedition. Guards will extricate the remaining elders to the capital city. Signed, Charles Tarleton, Esquire, Chief Counselor.'"

Several strong-armed soldiers flank the accused. A collective Wheatland gasp chokes the grove, but an empty ache sets in my stomach. Family members embrace each other, looking into terrified eyes for comfort. They'll find none. My hands clench into fists as my stomachache turns into an angry jaw throb. Unfair . . . but the tension eases. Could use this to my advantage; after all, Heathfell lies on the straits leading to the Sea and to the West.

"Secure everyone to this grove," Tirás says to his men. "No one leaves or enters save by my command. Lieutenant Aráza, front and center."

The cavalry man snaps to attention, saluting. "Yes, sir."

"The T'Anakim defector may still hide somewhere here. Scour every inch until he's found, but don't forsake the surrounding environs. Raze the place to the ground if you must. Find him!"

"Sir, yes, sir." Aráza's hand flies back to his side.

A distant scuffle breaks out between soldiers and the Hoggins family. They've returned to the celebration at the wrong time. The stronger regulars subdue them in a moment and Captain Tirás orders them bound and led away. Will a second trip to Heathfell spell their deaths?

Their ransacking Wheatland Town lasts throughout the night. No one can sleep with the comings and goings of soldier detachments. Mud-caked riders gallop through town every hour. Sunday dawn makes no promises, because I wonder if they'll kill, beat, or enslave us to satisfy their tempers. Provisions arrive on a wagon, which gives me hope. Sebastian, they say, "donated" blankets, food, and water, but it wouldn't surprise me if he didn't know. Soldiers dig makeshift latrines on the far-eastern side, but the fickle winds carry its stench everywhere. James and Siany whisper while alone and hand in hand. Army invasion must rank as the worst disaster to hit a bride's day ever.

By Monday morning, the third consecutive day, I haven't had a bath since Friday. What smells worse, the latrines, or me? The sky brightens from its dull gray with a fuzzy sun rising over distant Heathervale. I feign sleep when Aráza, the officer I've caught eyeing Rebecca on a few occasions, speaks with Tirás in hushed voices.

"Sir, my men scoured every inch here and at the countryside hamlets. No T'Anakim spy. Perhaps our intelligence is old?"

"Maybe so. My magi have discovered no one, either. Sometimes I wonder what use they serve. A strong back and sword arm work more than their spirit-world conjuring."

"I agree, sir."

"Prepare the company to leave with the prisoners and take a few provision wagons. The remaining families can return to their hovels. See to it they don't cause trouble."

"At once, sir."

Perfect! My way to Heathfell. After I rescue dad—or die trying— I'll make sailing plans.

Linus and David scamper by, straightening their disheveled hair and messy clothes.

Up to something? I wave them to me. They change direction and head toward me.

"What?" my brother says.

Making sure no one overhears me, I say, "I have a plan to rescue Dad, but I'll go alone. Don't want you slowing me down or getting in the way." *Truth is, I have no plan.* I make up plans on the fly. David raises a finger, ready to speak, but I cut him off by saying, "You can't dissuade me. And don't tell Mom until I'm gone." I point to the wagons next to the latrines. "I'll hide away in a chuck wagon, but I need a diversion, first."

"Sure," they say together. Surprised, there's no time to dwell on their ability to see reason.

"We're good at making distractions," David says.

I arch a brow. *No matter.* "When I figure things out, I'll send for you."

The strengthening sun lifts a blue sky overhead. Tirás's general move-out order flutters through the camp, so we sneak near the wagons. Two guards stand watch.

"When we get started," David says, "look for the best time to duck into the wagon closest to the latrine. And don't mess this up, okay? We have one chance."

I slip to the starting point. My eyes water and my nose burns.

"Hey!" Linus says with an angry cry. "In line with everyone else."

"If I won't, who will make me?" David says.

Thuds and tearing clothes add to the realism. They couldn't do a better job.

A harsh voice cuts in, saying, "Break it up, boys."

Now or never.

"What's wrong with you two? I'll teach you a better lesson than the last time."

"My tapeworm is giving me fits again," Linus says.

"Nasty," David says, "every Wheatlander has them. Sometimes I'm in the privy for hours."

He's overdoing it, but it works. The other soldier inches away, so I scamper toward it.

A third guard.

I slam my back against the wagon wall, heart hammering at the near miss.

An untied canvas flap ruffles in the breeze. With two quick

steps, I dart in before he can suspect me, and inch forward as if on hot coals.

"Mikey, give me a hand with these boys," the first soldier says.

I freeze to the spot. When the jangling armor passes, I sneak around crates. Sacks line the wagon's front wall, when I shift one away, a shriek frays my last calm nerve. Stunning blue eyes stare into mine. When our moment of shocked incredulity fades, I whisper, "You shouldn't be here, Rebecca."

"We had the same idea. You're not the only person who'll lose their dad to the Heathfell dungeons."

"Move over."

She wags a warning finger. "Move over, what?"

"Please, the guards may search in here."

She disappears into the little compartment between the sacks and the wagon wall. I dive in and drop beside her. Thoughts of soldiers mistreating their prisoners crowd my mind. The innocence in her eyes disintegrates any tact in what I say. "Heathfell is not the city for a helpless girl. They'll catch you and . . . fill in the blanks."

Her countenance hardens, and her eyes kindle a blue flame. A nervous chill runs along my spine. *Now I've done it.*

"There are many measurements of strength. If the only way is by muscle size, then you don't qualify, either." I open my mouth to explain, but she covers it with her palm. Nose to nose, her gaze digs into mine. Never noticed she has freckles. "Have you thought of character depth, morality, and resolve? Cleverness and resourcefulness mean nothing to you? Remember who rescued *you* from the tree ogre."

"Rescued me? I had things under control. It died at *my* hand." *More or less.*

". . . because I threw you the sword."

As I devise a new argument, jangling armor nears us. She folds her arms, scowling. I keep watch through a gap in the sacks.

"Those boys are strong for dumb farmers," a soldier says.

"No doubt. I may get a black eye, and if I do, he'll regret it."

The canvas flap flies open, and two disheveled heads poke into view.

"Hitch this one to the team and I'll do the same for the other. Tie this shut. I want nothing falling out, or the lads getting at the grub before the captain calls for lunch."

CHAPTER 17

THE FOREST OF HETH

Light leaks through a knothole in the wallboards. Arms crossed, Rebecca won't look at me. Sometimes my mouth gets me into trouble. Fear bubbles from my stomach when the wagon wheels lurch forward. Going ahead without knowing what to do is a recipe for disaster. Rebecca's cold shoulder frosts the gap between us. She, at least, might have a plan, but I have no chance of learning it now. I press my eye to the knothole and see nothing but a horse's hindquarters. The smell might become unbearable. My comeuppance for the skunk prank. Calm melts into my nervousness, because I'm surrounded by a jangling steel wall. What forest terror can get at me? But I wonder what the *soldiers* will do if they catch me.

Rebecca crawls from the compartment and peers through a gap in the crates. Her frown eases, which permits me a turn, too. The space aligns with a hole where the two canvas pieces tie together. I

move two of them over to give me a better view ahead. Between the drivers' shoulders, the world roils with a sea of well-ordered men.

The wagon hits a chuckhole; I wobble, unbalanced, and fall into Rebecca's quick arms. For an uneasy, yet exciting moment, our eyes meet, causing heart flutters. Her icy wall melts, the air warms between us. Everything becomes better now . . .

Then she drops me, I hit a crate, and it falls on me. *Guess not.*

By midmorning the Eastham hamlet lies behind, so we descend into Heathervale, where late-season wild roses sweeten the breeze. Ahead, the countryside marches upward to the looming Forest of Heth, or Hethwood, as Wheatlanders know it. This place weaves creepy legends in the looms of Wheatland's gossip circles.

At the forest's narrow entrance, twisted burr oaks form a living gate which glowers at us. The company re-forms into two abreast, so we end up at the rear, but alongside the elders' wagon. A horn blast signals the columns to move.

Close trees squeeze the air, making it heavy in my lungs. We jounce with each chuckhole we hit on the serpentine path. Moss and bracken ferns edge it below, and dense tree crowns block out the blue sky. Sparse sunbeams break through to reach the light-starved floor. Now and again, I catch a glance from Rebecca. Not icy. She must be thawing.

The column outdistances our dawdling pace, but I sense their watchfulness won't let us slip too far back. Peacefulness settles here, but the occasional wagon creak or horse nicker breaks the monotony. *Perfect time to escape? How will I get to the capital city unscathed? Best to stay here.*

Light chitchat from the elders blossoms into a conversation. "It's strange," George says, "I live near here, but have been through the forest only on the way back from the Heathfell prison. Here we go again."

I sit on a crate to hear what I can through the canvas.

"Been here long ago on a dare," Herky says. "Right, Ant?"

"Childhood dares keep us young, my friend."

"Pappy and Granny told frightening fireside tales, giving their grandkids nightmares for years. An odd bunch they were. I'm trying to remember the one that took place in the Wild Hills."

"What do you recall?" George says.

"A tale of wicked men, an ancient king, lots of action, warfare, and death. Sound familiar?"

"Sure. Long ago, six brothers fled the mainland and settled east of here. Folk were wary of strangers, so they were unwelcome. In time, the people drove them away, but the outcasts found refuge deep in the Wild Hills, an inhospitable region in eastern Hethwood.

"Within the year, they sought revenge. They ransacked the village, kidnapped young ladies, and slinked back into the gloom.

"A fortnight later, the royal army arrived. Lore-masters say he was looking for a chance to prove himself. Thus, the king's pride was his downfall. He vowed to mete out retribution, so his son led an elite force to crush them. He didn't find birds in a cage, but cornered wolverines.

"Intrepid soldiers marched through a narrow passage between two steep cliffs. The brothers dropped a huge rock to halt their advance and then rained heavy stones on them. Young ladies, bent to their captors' wills, shot arrow volleys from trapdoor hideaways.

"A brother lost an eye when a spearman struck him with the shaft. They impaled the prince's head upon the same spear, but his body, no one recovered. In a rage, the king commanded his troops to attack at dawn. When he awoke, he discovered his army's utter ruination. It's unclear how they defeated the powerful force in their sleep, but most believe dark sorcery rumored to originate within the Wild Hills empowered them.

"The brothers left him alive, so he will always remember the defeat. He mounted his charger and surveyed the camp's desolation, but his foes lurked among the trees. Dauntless, he held aloft his sword, Gamólig the Ancient Fire, and uttered judgment. 'Spirits of kings, the just rulers of Bormágo, curse them in the name of Cempa Brædan, eldest and wisest. As these enemies have been, so you shall be henceforth in a twisted form.'

"White fire burst forth from the blade, pursued, and caught them. Falling on all fours, in madness, they passed into legend. Barren, the hilt then split in two."

"Did you take lessons from my pappy and granny?" Herky says. "You have their evil gift for nightmare storytelling. I remember the king slaughtered them."

"No, William and Jonah spent tireless hours questioning the forest lore-masters. After the king's death, the royal family changed hands because he had no heir. Many believe the brothers never died."

"That's crazy," the apple farmer says with a chortle.

"You laugh? Then it shouldn't bother you when we pass straight through their lands."

Silence.

"This road is old, Anthony."

"Why would the king spread a different story?" Herky says.

"Those who hold to generational rule will hide weaknesses. They're worried a stronger family might take the throne by force. It wasn't so among the Orligs, who predated the Bormagians."

"Orlig barbarians allowed their once-cultured societies to crumble," Anthony says. "What can we learn from them?"

"Yet it was their custom to vote for their rulers. The elected men protected every citizen's rights by upholding the law."

"Not everyone could elect leaders," Margaret says. "This power only belonged to men of good families, because they thought others were too dumb."

"The long decay of time corrupted them," George says. "As a result, chieftains couldn't control their desire for power. Complacent families allowed corruption to spread, unchecked. They could have demanded reform, removed the old leaders, and even elected new ones, but they grew satisfied with trivialities."

"A rare person serves for the people's good," Anthony says.

"An inspiring example is an Orlig commoner named Valstan who worked his fields in peace until barbarians invaded his country. The chieftains called him into service, and there he distinguished himself by his wisdom and valor. In time, he became their greatest general. After defeating the savages, he stood at the height of his popularity."

"And then he seized power," Anthony says, "and his appetite grew for more."

"But the story doesn't end that way," George says. "When the elders offered him the kingship, he refused them *twice*. The land was safe, his duty to country ended, and so he returned home in peace. He gave up all authority and went back to plowing his fields."

Wonder fills Rebecca's eyes.

I shrug. "Rulers don't act that way anymore."

A scant breeze flutters against the canvas but high winds sway the tree crowns. I dab my forehead with a handkerchief, Rebecca fans herself with a plate. When I find bread, I offer it to her, but she eats jerky she found instead.

Hours fortify the quiet wall between her and me. I chew my bottom lip and consider how to break through this silent treatment. But if anyone hears us . . .

Our horse team stutters, which causes back pressure on the harness. I brace myself because the path drops off at a precarious angle. The sure-footed horses navigate the downward slope well. Pounding water thunders when we approach a pool fed by waterfalls. Soldiers break ranks, and the drivers unhitch our team and lead them to drink.

I offer a full jug to Rebecca, who snatches it without a glance. She offers a cool smile. When she is midway through a deep gulp, a branch snaps and a weak shadow lengthens on the canvas. Her eyes widen. One tie is undone. I motion for her to dive into our hiding place, but we were comfortable for too long. A second and a third one dangles untied. No chance to duck for cover.

A raspy voice causes breath to choke in my throat. "Oi, what do you think you're doing?"

Silence.

How can he not hear my thumping heart?

"I ain't doing nothing, Sarge," another person says.

Tension eases in Rebecca's face, and I breathe again.

"Tirás will tan your miserable hide. His whip hasn't seen action today. No one touches this wagon until the first one's empty. Now fall in, you scum." Heavy footfalls trail away.

"We're in luck, the flap's open," I whisper.

"Darkness covers our escape the best. How far are we from the border?"

I shrug. "Good question. I don't want to leave here when we could still have miles until we reach the forest's edge."

Minutes bleed into more hours while we wind through endless trees and over rolling hills. Wheels skitter upon roots springing from gnarled oaks edging a gorge. With each passing foot of altitude lost, the darkness suffocates the light.

"Are those catkins or stringy moss dangling from the branches?" Herky says.

Winston points overhead. "They're everywhere."

I struggle with unkind thoughts toward the constable, but I can't deny he's right. A faint horn blast grows above the baggage train clatter.

"What in the world . . ." Herky says.

"The all-clear signal," George says. "Whenever troops enter untenable ground, they scout it, secure it, and sound a horn so the column can advance. We're safe."

"A fool's hope."

"We'll be fine, because these are career soldiers, not mindless rabble," Anthony says.

A charger canters to our wagon. "Halt, driver," Tirás says.

Aráza's horse trots into view. The young officer salutes. "Sir?"

The captain studies his surroundings. "I don't recall passing through this gorge."

"Nor do I, sir. How did we arrive here?"

"I checked the map, but we must have left the main road unawares. Since the scouts have blown the signal, we should advance."

"By your command, sir. I'll get them moving." Before he urges his horse, the captain seizes his arm.

"No, order your men to be on their guard. I have no love for this place. I'll lead the columns forward. You stay rearward and make sure we have safe passage back."

"Yes, sir."

Tirás speeds toward the front, and Aráza to his horsemen.

The trailing hoofbeats blend into an unfamiliar sound. "Horses?" I say.

"Sounds if—" Rebecca says.

"The teams pulling the wagons."

"Something is spooking them. Let's leave before they bolt."

She secures a small vial in her dress pocket. I grab my satchel and fling open the canvas flap. We throw ourselves from the wagon into uncertain surroundings.

Preoccupied cavalrymen point at threads hanging from top tree branches. At their ends, dollops of black goo hang overhead. Pale sparkles swirl around them. As they stream to the gorge floor, they burgeon into man-sized spiders. Some spider-kind, some half-human walk upright upon two legs, and others carry babies on their backs, which leap at the soldiers. Many more sprout from the ground as if they were disgusting red, green, and yellow weeds.

"Trapdoors," I say. "Look out!"

"Attack! Kill the usurpers," they croak. "Kill, kill!"

Our wagon speeds away, but we don't stay to watch the outcome. "Follow me, Rebecca."

We hug the gorge wall to escape the battle. Cavalrymen hack at or trample their enemies, but black-bearded spiders snap their jaws or wield makeshift weapons.

She dashes forward with me close in tow. "Keep moving toward the column head."

At the column's middle, the carnage is most severe.

"Went from bad to worse," I say.

Spearmen impale their foes while archers cut down others at range. Haelan-magi show their true worth by casting terrible spells that melt their victims inside their bodies.

Even with massive casualties, nothing can quell the enemy breakers smashing against the soldiers. A spearman drops dead in front of me. His killer—evil delight growing in his eyes—turns his wrath toward us. I sidestep between Rebecca and him, reaching for my satchel. Before I undo the flap, a severed spider arm wallops me across the middle. I soar several feet before crashing to the ground.

A heavy boot presses on my chest. A warrior, half man, half spider, clutches a large rock over his head. Pitiless eyes gloat at me. "Nobody's gonna save you now, eastern wretch." In a second, he'll drop crushing death upon me.

"You—over here," Rebecca says. "I'm the better catch."

As the fighter turns his attention from me to her, misty fire streams through the air, and its yellow glow erases the shadow across her face, illuminating her eyes. We watch in horror as the magic bleeds through the warrior's chest, arm sockets, mouth, and nostrils. His hands release the rock, but gravity can't surpass the pace it consumes its prey. The earthen weapon slams into an ash pile. The haelan-mage nods to us, and job finished, takes on other foes.

I roll to my knees and struggle to my feet. "Thanks for distracting the warrior, allowing the mage to work his magic. Thought I was a goner."

"You're welcome. Quick, follow me to the wall. Should be safer there."

My bruised ribs complain when I cough, but I do as she says.

At the column head, a humongous rock and a relentless spider line block the vanguard. Who's on the other side is anyone's guess.

Rebecca feels along the cliff face. "A cleft, over here." I follow her to a hole and into an up-sloping tunnel which opens to a shelf a few yards above the floor.

I point beyond the battlefield. "Look, Captain Tirás is fighting with an enormous black-and-green spider."

Aráza leads a cavalry charge into the line, but his opponents struggle to keep the two captains separated. Tirás's flashing sword finds its mark on many occasions. With a quick reflex, the spider lord spits venom and hits his charger in the eye. In agony, the maddened horse spins like a wild bronco. Tirás sails through the air and lands hard.

The captain wobbles to his feet, but his opponent takes time to recover from the blademaster's well-placed strikes. Tirás shakes off a daze, and emboldened, grips the gleaming sword afresh. Point forward, he charges his foe. Ready for him, the wicked opponent shoots venom, but he evades the attack, spins then plunges his blade through the spider's leg. Black liquid oozes from the wound. He retracts the vengeful sword and follows with a backhand slash to a bulbous eye. Poison flies, hitting Tirás in the eyes. He clears the green slime from his face, collects himself, and heaves an overhand strike. It lands wide, wedging between two rocks. The spider lord sidesteps his prey, who pulls in vain to free his weapon.

Lieutenant Aráza spurs his stallion for a redoubling charge against the wall of warriors.

Bodies crash to either side—he's through the line!

The young military man closes the distance, but too late, for the spider lord's mandibles sever Tirás's head from his shoulders. He strikes the enemy, slicing him wide, and a fresh fountain gushes from the lord's abdomen. His horse skids to a halt then speeds toward him. With a blade thirsty for blood, he swoops in for another attack.

The spider lord shoots a silk thread high into the branches and bursts up the line. Aráza, not accepting his escape, leans forward in the saddle, wringing every ounce of speed from his mount. He raises the sword.

The enemy lurches upward.

When his blade passes underneath him, it clears the abdomen by the smallest measure.

Spiders sound a general retreat. Obedient to the call, warriors skitter up lines to the cliff's high rise. Aráza dismounts and kneels beside the fallen captain, head in hands.

We backtrack from our hiding place. Human and enemy body parts mingle together throughout the battlefield. Clingy webs impair our movement. "Should let the lieutenant know we're here, because then he can set a guard . . ." I say, but Rebecca no longer strides alongside me. I turn back. She's caught in a trap, and close by, a spider emerges from a trapdoor lair. I rummage through my satchel, find the sword, will it on, and dash toward the villain.

"Let—her—go, filth!"

My initial blow flies out of pure adrenaline, not skill, and so it falls wide. The ambusher counters with a swift venom attack, but my errant swing pulls me out of harm's way. I recover and heave an overhand strike, which sparks the ground.

We circle again and again. *Make the first move and you're dead.* I toss the hilt between my hands, trying to force him to commit to a fatal movement. *Keep your footing and your focus.* As I sweep the blade in circular motions, he lunges after its downswing. I sidestep, swing, and chop off his leg.

Forelegs up, defeat growing in his bulbous eyes, he croaks, "I surrender."

"Filth, I bested you. Step away from her."

"As you wish, swordsman." He lowers a bristled head in obeisance.

I dip the blade, reflecting on my swordplay in the Workshop. The lesson books had prepared me well but being a magic sword, how can I explain the miss?

Rebecca's eyes grow wide. "Look out!"

Too late.

A stinger stabs into my back. At first, it goes numb, but then it burns. A conflagration courses throughout my body as if it were dry bramble on a summer day. Wicked gloating spreads across his face.

Warm breath brushes my neck. "Fool," another raspy voice says.

My legs turn to jelly. Before my eyes darken, Rebecca turns over and over between the spider's hairy appendages like a spool being wound with gross thread. My cloudy vision spins in circles. Cords entomb me head to toe. The spider hangs me over his back, and I lose my stomach in our quick ascent up an escape line. Aráza's hazy face burns with rage. He swings his sword through the air beneath me. Poison drives thoughts from my conscious mind, but the young lieutenant yells, "Volley!" before I lose them completely.

CHAPTER 18

A BROTHERHOOD OF A DIFFERENT KIND

Poison seeps into my bones, my brain swims. *Must fight this.* I still feel my toes, so, good.

Arrows whirr past my face and sink barb, shaft, and feather into the warrior. He loses his grip, so we slide three yards down the line. The force isn't enough to work the stickiness loose. I dangle above the archers, my swelling head ready to pop. With a final energy burst, the spider climbs it and leaps over the cliff edge. Tipsy, he sputters, I hit the ground, and he no longer moves.

Colored spots pepper my vision, breathing deadens. A spinning sensation muddles my brain as if I'm rolling down Bigsby's Hill back home. *Home . . .*

In poisoned dreams, I jerk upward, because someone or something picked me up and threw me over its shoulder. Disembodied, I fly, halt, and then go again. For how long, I can't say. At last, I drop hard and land contorted. Deadened hearing awakens first, then my sight. A gate slams, and multiple footfalls trail away.

My heavy eyes flicker open, but I wonder if they did. Pitch dark, except for a red light struggling to break through, spawns in me deep dread. When I blow spider webbing from my nostrils, breathing comes easy. So does my sense of smell. The air reeks of barf and excrement. I wiggle . . . and then wiggle more. The silk casket loosens. If I could only rotate my arm . . . There, I did it. Now I can move my hand upward, tear the web off my face, and pull each side to a shoulder. In a few moments, I free my body from the mummifying wrap, and with much effort, stand. Every muscle in me stretches as if I've been asleep for years. I lean for support on a sticky stone wall. *Gross, more spiders.*

Red light flickers from a torch outside a barred door. *A prison cell, great.* Two worlds will suffer Malgroth's wrath if I don't stop him. I may rot here until my last day. Wish I brought David. He'd be helpful in a pinch. Maybe Rebecca—

"Most aren't so fortunate," a nearby voice says.

"Who's there?" I reach for my satchel, but it's gone.

"Your constitution must be strong to overcome the poison. Do you hail from Wheatland?"

"Who are you?"

A swarthy face dressed with a black beard pokes into the light.

"You're one, too. Get away."

"Yes, a spider living under the king's eternal curse, and as you see, I'm in jail, same as you."

I nod.

He extends his hand. "My name is Helon. And you are?"

I let it hang there. "Someone."

"All right, Someone. You were out cold for hours, but it's hard to tell exact time inside this cave."

"Why did they imprison you?"

"I'm a dissenter, a rebel they call me, among other names. The

Establishment doesn't tolerate anyone who questions their decisions or how they treat our people. They're masters at spinning deceitful webs until wife, children, friends, and town turn against you. Once, I was captain of the guard."

"My name is Jonathan."

Helon nods. "Better than someone."

"Did they capture a girl, too? She's blonde, blue eyed . . . and, you know, pretty."

"I heard other noises after they brought you in, but it's difficult to know for sure."

"What way did you dissent?"

"I believe a wise monarch should rule instead of this brotherhood, what I call the ruling Establishment. They wouldn't hear me, except for the elder brother Ablushek, who'd become king. The most rabid opponent was the second born, Sarsekim.

"In addition, we should give this region back to the folk we overthrew. When the Bormaġian king cursed my people, we withdrew into the forest. There, we found peaceful spirits who ruled here with benevolence. We met trust with domination. After we subdued them, they retreated into the natural world. I used to hear their hearts beating in the trees. If we left, they'd return. We could buy land in the Wild Hills, but what's enough when you deal with rascals?"

"You're a kind man . . . uh, creature, not like the others."

"'Man'? There's little mankind in us anymore. The Bormaġian king can release my people from this curse."

"I hope he does someday."

Helon gazes at me with a curious expression.

"What?"

"You remind me of a good-hearted fellow from Wheatland who was an insect lore-master. He saved my life, but it's a long story to tell."

"I guess my grandpa, Conrad Jackson. He read and traveled much."

"Yes, he's the man. A strange fate has brought us together, my friend."

"He left for the Other World."

"Never heard of the place."

"Tuatha Dé Danann."

Shrugging he says, "Doesn't help. Is it far?"

Distant footfalls echo from the corridor. Light grows until it leaks into this dank hole. Evil eyes peer through the door slat. "Hello, Helon, I've come to check on *him*." The guard points. "Awake, my little guest?"

"You're observant," I say.

The iron lock screeches open, allowing a big-armed thug to rush into the cell. He pokes me in the chest. "I'm your jailer, morsel. Show respect if you expect to make it until morning." He jerks his thumb sideways. "My captain is sleeping beyond that door, and his orders are to keep you alive until the Brothers inspect you. But if you had an 'accident'—guests die every month—either natural or unnatural." He grabs my face then pinches my arm. "Meat is scarce these days. We used to have abundant birds and stag, or the occasional man flesh."

"We have no food because the Establishment takes war spoils for their families, Ochran," Helon says.

"Not mine to say." He slaps me across the head. "Nothing but skin with bones you are. You should plump up and become tender if I hung you for a while."

"Everyone knows Wheatlanders grow bitter with the hanging," I say. "Let me and the girl you captured go so I can spare you the misery."

Ochran spreads his hands. "Think there's another delectable morsel here?" He steps closer to me, his stale breath puffs on my face. "An acquaintance of yours is she, oh, maybe a girlfriend?"

"A friend, yes, for my part."

The jailer studies me. I struggle to hide any emotion, but it's no use. "Morsel, your girlfriend is dead."

"Impossible." My cracking voice doesn't sound convincing.

Grim news sparks a glint in his eyes. "She died on the way here. Maybe a lad had his fill?"

Words choke my throat. "Liar!" I scream, or try, but almost nothing comes out.

A grin spreads across his face.

"You've had your fun," Helon says. "Leave the boy be. Your boss must want a report on the prisoner's progress."

Ochran studies my fellow prisoner. "Yes, Captain, you're right. I'll wake up the old villain."

Darkness seeps into the cell when the light drains out. A concussive wave echoes throughout the hallway after a heavy door slams.

Guilt wracks my mind. The horrible man-spider sees what I didn't want to see. Deep inside I care for her, but now it doesn't matter.

She's gone.

I say little for hours. A few times, Helon tries to make conversation, but I'm not in the mood. Muffled shouts grow down the hall. Footfalls race to our door, it flies open, and Ochran springs into our cell.

"Go, my brother, you're free."

"What do you mean?" he says with shocked incredulity.

"Ablushek is dead, killed by the intruders' sword wounds. The others are fighting for his power. Quick, rush to Sarsekim's aid. He'll show favor to a deposed captain."

He thinks for a moment. "Whether he will or won't, who can say? Maybe you're right, but I'll spend my freedom away from this place."

He leaves the cell, but Ochran blocks my way. An evil glint grows in his eyes. "As for this one, I promised myself I'd hang him until he's tender. I'll meet up with you, Captain. My advice, take up the position you once had."

Helon grabs him by the neck. "Do *not* harm the boy, who's done nothing to deserve this treatment. Our quarrel is with the Bormagian line, not with Wheatland."

The jailer frees himself from the grip. "Protecting this rat? We can share him fifty-fifty."

"I'm thankful you freed me, but I can't let you hurt my new friend."

"After all we've been through, don't be a fool. Noble ideals found you this home, and the same will be your grave."

Ochran pushes him further inside, slams the door, and darts to the left.

An uneasy feeling overtakes me. "I don't trust him."

Through the slat, Helon fidgets with the handle. "He told me it was faulty, in case I needed to break out. If I can . . . there." He swings it open. "Go!"

I dash the way he ran. The last cell door stands ajar, so I peer inside it. Ochran, in red spider form, has Rebecca pinned to the floor.

"Lying scum!"

"Jonathan, help!"

The spider jabs his stinger into her middle and wrenches it out. A blood trickle turns into a stream.

"You don't scare me, pipsqueak." Quick as lightning, he wallops me with a sideswipe, sending me crashing into the wall. Two blurry images come at me, but a yellow one jumps him.

Ochran spits venom, which hits Helon in the face. He reels in pain, but I can't move to aid him.

"Fool, the only sense you'll see will burn your eyes."

Although blinded, Helon demonstrates a dance of war hinting at a valiant past life. Jaws and stingers snap, thrust, and tear flesh, but it's over in a few moments. Ochran lies defeated in his own blood, and Helon is quick to follow.

The former captain morphs to man form, wincing with each labored breath. "Tell your grandpa I repaid the debt. Farewell . . . my friend."

Black spider blood mixes in a pool with Rebecca's red blood. My thoughts turn to her.

"No—" Her skin is ashen, her eyes, slits. I press her clammy hand to my lips. "Stay with me, please."

Weak words form on her mouth. "Too late for me." She continues to bleed from the stinger-sized wound. Her jaw falls slack, her eyes roll back.

"Don't . . . How do I save you? You're the healer, not me."

Her chest struggles to rise and fall. All my fault. Why didn't I leave her in Wheatland? Too strong-willed to listen to me. I remember the battlefield. If not for her, it would've been my grave. Great tears leap from my eyes. Random images flicker through my mind. We're in my backyard again with Ulgar bleeding. What did she do for him? Pressed his leg wound with her hand to stop the flow. Same with Coal. The next image to flash is before we leaped from the wagon. Her medicine, the same stuff she used on them.

I press my palm to her abdomen, pushing harder until her blood stops welling through my fingers. With my other hand, I search her pockets for the vial. When I'm satisfied the bleeding has stopped, I tear a hole in the dress, pop the cork, and slather the orange paste on her wound.

Color seeps into her cheeks. I blink, once, twice, but it's true, the stuff works. After a few moments, her eyelids flicker open. Warmth brightens her face, so I believe she'll make it.

An hour passes before her pulse is strong and lethargy disappears from her eyes. We need provisions. "I'll come back with water."

"Vial, please."

After everything she's been through, manners are still important. She sticks her pinky in the opening, measures the dollop size with her eyes, adds more, and then smears it on her tongue.

"Gross."

She keeps her mouth sealed, but the corners turn up a bit.

I pull the door shut to hide her. Alert to danger, I inch down the rough-cut corridor toward the exit.

"Sir."

My ears perk up, hairs rise on my neck. It's coming from a nearby cell. I slide open the slat and find warm eyes staring at me.

"Please let us out."

A small crowd gathers behind the man. It never occurred to me prisoners filled the other cells. "My friend comes first then I'll be back for you. In a few moments."

"You're kind, good sir."

A heavy door that could survive a riot stands between me and freedom. Where's the jail captain?

I peer through the space under it. Can't see him, because it's too narrow. Inch by inch, I push it open, the faint creak fraying my nerves. It takes a few inches for a gigantic spider sleeping at a table to appear. How he could sleep through the civil war outside astounds me. Food scraps, half-empty goblets, a keyring, and my satchel litter the table.

I step closer, weighing whether I should grab the satchel or the keys first. Eight steps separate me from freedom or death. Seven . . . six . . . five . . . four. He could close this distance in an instant. Two away, I reach out my hand but take my eyes off the prize. Black liquid pools in front of the hairy captain and onto the floor. A jagged slice stretches from one side of his neck to the other. Stone dead. Ochran's last job, no doubt.

I rummage through the satchel, pulling out my sword. No book. What'll happen if it lands in the wrong hands? Before panic can grip me, I tear the room apart only to find it laying on the fire-wood pile. I let out a slow breath.

I stuff it inside, grab the keys, a water skin, and dash down the hallway. Rebecca sits with her back to the wall, eyes closed. I stoop to examine her. Full color, pink in the cheeks. She's pale to begin with, but at least not ashen. When I tap her shoulder, her eyelids flicker to life, and a smile spreads across her small face. She throws her arms around me, warmth flooding my body. I could stay here forever.

After a long moment, I pull away. "Take water." I ease the skin to her mouth and tip it. Little sips turn into raging gulps. When she comes up for air, the skin's empty.

"So good," she says. "Thank you for everything."

"Don't thank me yet. When you recover your strength, we need to escape this civil war."

Her jaw drops open in question.

"You'll see. Wait here. I must set more prisoners free, too."

I return to the man's cell. Red torchlight falls upon three men, whose clothes were fine once.

"Dear boy, how can we thank you?" one says, pumping my hand.

The others pat me on the back. "We've waited two weeks for this day," a man with a bushy mustache says.

"Hope those vile demons get what's coming to them," says the third.

"Run, while you have the chance, but don't wait for us."

The men flee and disappear behind the thick steel door.

That leaves two more unchecked cells. One turns out to be empty; the other, a decayed corpse's tomb.

When I return to Rebecca's cell, she's leaning on the wall for support. She staggers toward me, wraps her arms around my waist, and lays her head on my shoulder. My first hint of what's coming next is her breath brushing across my ear. Her warm lips press to my cheek, which electrifies me. This is all the thanks I want.

"Can you walk?" I ask, still caught under the sway of her kiss.

"I think so. This salve is powerful. Figured we may need it."

"Good thinking. Ready to go?"

CHAPTER 19

CALAMITIES AND CONFESSIONS

Spider, man, and half man, half spider bodies litter the street. Long-burned huts smolder, and overturned wagons lie empty. Sick trees overshadow the evil village, which is the blight on the forest. The reek and gloom testify to the Establishment's indifference to their people.

The sun dips below the horizon, dragging the unwilling day with it. I had hoped to leave with more light in the sky. Rebecca hobbles to my hiding spot across the street from the jail.

"Brought a second water skin. Another drink before we move out?"

"No thanks, I'm fine. I think the stinger missed anything vital."

"The main gate must be at the end of this road," I say, pointing away from the dying sun.

"And when we get there, what's your play?"

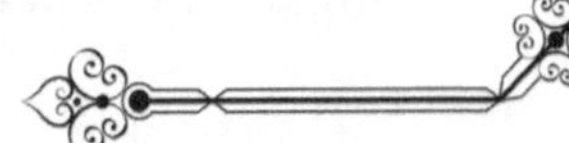

"A nine-step plan to elude our captors, including several complicated maneuvers I learned from famous generals."

A quizzical look crosses her face.

I give her a wry glance. "No, it's much simpler—find the gate, create a diversion, and leave."

She rolls her eyes and chuckles. "It'll work. Let's go."

We dash from cover and dodge random sentry patrols and rogue citizens. Around a corner, we jump back to avoid a mob beating someone. We slink to the opposite side of the street, sneak past them, and dart to the end. I crane my neck rearward.

"What?" Rebecca says.

"He's a man I released from the jail."

She strokes my shoulder. "Sorry, nothing we can do now."

I chew my lower lip. The thick ring of thugs obscures him from view. My conscience nags at me to help him.

A guard standing near them points in our direction. "Hey, you there!"

She yanks my arm before I react, whisking me through one alley, over a couple streets, and beyond another road. Gasping for breath, we halt at a hill. Tall palisades surround the rise, fortified heavier than the jail compound. Loud yelling surges then dies out.

"What is this place?" I say.

Rebecca holds her abdomen. "First, I need to breathe. Dizzy. Lost too much blood to hold a sustained run."

After a long rest, we follow the wall to a small gate guarded by two soldiers. We find a spot where we can peer through it. Fine houses juxtapose against the ramshackle commoner dwellings we passed. Cheers break from a tall rise, drawing the guards away from us.

"Now's our chance," I say. We inch nearer to get a better view.

A fist-pumping crowd encircles a yellow-and-black spider. At his feet, four corpses lay hewn to pieces. The victor changes into a swarthy man. His followers erupt into wild applause and chant,

"Sarsekim, Sarsekim, hail King Sarsekim!" He raises a bloody hand to accept their praise, and attendants bring a golden litter. He reclines in it, and they parade him through the mob.

"Let's leave before they find us," I say.

"Over there," Rebecca says, pointing. "The main road."

We dash from one light-starved alley to another and encounter no place immune from the gruesome civil war. Good fortune favors our flight when the street widens before the exit. High palisades, a stockade gate divided in two, and canvas guard huts stand in our way. We duck behind barrels to hide from vigilant sentries.

Rebecca locks her arm in mine. "Now what?"

"The diversion. With luck, no one will be home."

We disappear into a big hut. Faint lamplight flickers on dead bats, birds, and other small animals, which hang like garments on a clothesline. She grabs the lamp and presents it to me.

I refuse it, holding my palms outward. "You may have the honors."

A grin spreads across her face. At once, she smashes it on the ground. Her satisfied look turns to worry when the flames sprint along the splattered oil and shoot up the walls.

"Let's go," I say.

I need not tell her twice. We dart away, find shelter near the gate, and settle behind boxes with a superb view of freedom. Smoke billows from the tent, spewing a rancid odor our way.

"Uh, Glob-lob, do you sees what I sees?" one guard says to the other.

"Sure do, Raknidd. Put it out before the chief suspects us, 'cause them huts belong to Sarsekim's men. Don't want them nasty lads getting ahold of me."

When they rush to the tents, we sneak from the gate, dash along the path, and dive into thick bushes.

"Couldn't be easier," I say. "Which way?"

"Doesn't matter, tomorrow morning we'll find our bearings."

I point to an overgrown trail leading into the crowded forest. "There, not used by anyone." As I spring toward it, Rebecca pulls me back and cups a hand over my mouth. No chance to protest. An immense creature skitters in front of the bush.

A harsh voice tears the evening air. "Quiet, Glob-lob," says Raknidd. "Can't hear nothin' over your clumsy feet. Go human, so I won't hear so many of 'em."

"Don't care. We should be at our posts. What if—"

"Stop yer tongue flappin'. When we took off after those burning huts, something dropped off the road. I aim to flush it out." The man-spider licks his lips. "Remember, you no good lout, *I* saw it first."

"We're here against orders. What we gonna say if the captain comes to the gate? Even worse, what if the Goody Two-shoes Helon gets his job back? Suppose he wants revenge on his accusers. He will report us for sure."

My fists ball and I clench my teeth together until they hurt. Rebecca pulls me in closer and shakes her head. I want them to pay for destroying Helon's reputation.

"Never mind either captain. They can blow dust for all I care. Besides, I know how to work them."

"The hut is burned to a crisp. Suppose it spreads to the others. We'll be blamed for sure."

"Then go back, ya lily-livered sissy. I said somebody came this way. Could be a spy, or something yummier. Or both."

The quavering spider drops behind his partner. "D-do ya think it's an eastern soldier here to avenge blood? W-what if they attack the village in the night? With everything out of sorts, we'll be slain for sure. Sarsekim's men will party tonight and leave us to shoulder the guarding."

"Why don't you shut up! Help me find this thing, ya no good daddy longlegs. Come on this way. I got an idea how to catch the puny rabbit. And when the dawn comes, he'll wish he was never born."

The brutes head up the embankment where, between two trees, they spin translucent webbing. Rebecca releases me.

"Nice reflexes," I mouth. "Thank you."

She offers an uncertain smile and motions with her eyes we need to leave.

We inch away from the guards until we make enough distance to hide our flight. She hikes up her dress and shoots past me. I follow the jackrabbit the best I can. Over mossy turf, decaying logs, and leafy trails, we dash until her legs give out.

Rebecca stumbles and sprawls on the ground.

"Keep going," I say, puffing.

"Not . . . another . . . step." Her chest shudders as it rises and falls.

"We need a full mile between us and them."

In between breaths, she takes long pulls on the water skin. The normal color in her face came back, but I can tell her rubbery muscles lack oxygen. I pull her up, drape her arms over my shoulders, and carry her piggyback. She lays her head on my shoulder, melting into my body.

Slogging through the brush with a person on your back—no matter how wiry—saps my energy. Balance unsteady, weight uneven, I step with as much care as my wobbling legs allow. The forest plays tricks on my mind. Long vine tendrils or branch hands stretch as if to grab me. Near a dark pond, the fractured bullfrog chorus, wind piping eerily through broken reeds, and the onset of night pick at my nerves. Through the trees, tattered clouds dress a pallid moon. *Must push farther.*

We trudge onward until reaching a glade with a single arching tree in its middle. The sapphire sky bleeds into peridot, but a glimmering star stands as a sentinel over it. With much effort, I lower Rebecca to the ground because my arms stick in a bent shape.

She refuses my hand. "I can stand because I have more energy."

"Good." I crane my neck in many directions. "What is this place?"

"Beats me."

"What's the stone arc over there?" I say, pointing.

"Same answer." She bends to have a closer look.

Someone put them in order. In curiosity, I tap one with my foot. A gray cloud sprays from its top. Coughing, I fan it away. A talcum powder odor mixed with mustard wafts in the air. "What the devil?"

"Spores. They're mushrooms or toadstools, not rocks. It's hard to tell in this light." She arcs her arm. "And see they form a vast ring. The two arcs meet over there."

"Gross, I hate all fungi."

"Are you crazy? They're tasty when you fry them in butter and serve them alone or with beef. My mom cooks them for us every week. She knows how much we love them."

"May be poisonous."

"No."

"How can you tell?"

"Bormaġian flora and fauna can challenge even the brightest student. I've been studying it for years, so I know if handled with care, these will have tremendous medicinal properties."

"Play your cards right, and I'll set you up with the best teacher."

A mischievous grin grows on her face. "Too late, I've talked to Siany. Lessons with my new master begin after her honeymoon."

My hands perch on my hips and I shake my head. Our circle of friends intertwines even more.

I flinch when waist-high grass rustles in the dead calm. "The tree," I say, pointing.

We sprint away and stop at its wide trunk. Reminds me of Rowen with the height and crevasses scoring ancient bark. Rebecca hikes up her dress, knots it in place, and scoots up before I can offer her a boost. I grab a hold but find climbing a tree different from a cave wall. I scrape my forearms all the way back to the ground. The rustling grass noise grows, but I don't see what causes it. A predator would still be hungry after eating me. A shiver races along my spine. Or worse, a spider who tracked us.

I try again with better luck. When I reach the first major branch, I throw my leg over and hug it tight. After a short breather, I climb into the canopy to meet Rebecca. Below, treetops ripple as waves on a dark green sea. Mushrooms, tracing a path, ring us as if they were borders of a surreal city.

"You're stronger," I say.

"Orange muskwort is the quickest-acting herb to heal wounds. The blue variety has a different effect. And mixing them can, as the masters claim, unlock death's shackles."

I nod with admiration. "You know more than I ever imagined."

She lowers her gaze but doesn't answer a word.

A narrow moonbeam falls through the canopy and paints the grass silver. Several others follow until the air, the tree, and the turf glow.

"Hear a flute?" I say.

Her eyebrows dip in thought. "And a lyre."

Hundreds of white sparkles dance along the moonbeams.

Rebecca passes her hand through one. "They're exquisite. What are they?"

"Moon faeries, or pixies, and just how I pictured them."

"I've seen fire, water, and now these."

"The last kind is earth."

"Earth? How are they made? With dirt?"

"No idea. Can't deny the rustling grass and bright rays. The Good People will visit us tonight."

"Good People?"

"The name they prefer even though 'good' doesn't always describe their behavior. You need to make them feel that way."

She casts me a sideways glance. "Hmm, I understand."

"Earth and moon behave better than fire and water. They'll tolerate others within their ring."

"Nice to see a sunny side to Tuatha Dé Danann."

Cradled among the branches, moonbeams brighten her delicate facial features. "Rebecca, I want to rescue my dad, same as you, but these dreams . . ."

"The Dark Door?"

"I believe Miller tried the Two Gems. Hard to explain why, I just know it."

"What'll you do?"

"After we release our dads, I'll hire a captain and crew. Then David and I can sail west. It won't take much to persuade him to join me. Mom will have Dad again."

She looks away, lower lip pushed out in thought.

I hold her soft hand. Warm eyes search the recesses of my soul, nudging my deepest emotions. Her expression longs to hear more. "Been hard, but I've come to grips with my feelings," I say. "In the chuck wagon, I said hurtful, stupid words. Didn't mean them. You're not weak, and sometimes I think you can do anything. It's just I don't want bad things happening to you in Heathfell."

Acceptance with a hint of playfulness fills her eyes. "Where's Jonathan and what have you done with him?" A wry smile darts across her face.

"This is hard for me."

"Sorry to interrupt, please continue."

"I care for you, more than a neighbor. I want to be more than your friend."

She leans toward me, as far as the branches will allow. "I sense it, too. After I dropped you, I felt awful. I forgave what you said. Our relationship can withstand much more."

"I'm sorry for them."

She winks. "Your manners are getting better."

My eyes drink the love in her eyes. What does she see in mine, maybe acceptance or uncertainty? I want to slide next to her, to reassure her, but close-knit branches allow room for one person. I lean with my back to the trunk, kiss her hand, and press it to my chest.

Soft music and playful lights nurture these feelings in me. Minutes melt into hours of mesmerizing dance within the mushroom ring, although the only faeries or pixies we see are moon. Comfort beams through the thin overcast from the pale Evening Star. I wonder if I'll ever meet Lady Sophia again.

Rebecca's grip slackens until her breathing becomes slow and rhythmic. She couldn't fall, but I could. I tether myself to a branch, so I don't break my neck.

Sleep tendrils entwine me, a restless dream catches me. In it, a long table fills a grand hall. At its head sits a white-haired man. His flowing beard grows on a perfect face. Clear mists issue from his mind, which materialize into seven translucent figures. When each takes a seat, they burst into flames touched with gold.

Darkness floods my mind, blood freezing. Far above me emerges a dais, and an enthroned being like a fractured shadow. Obsidian hair, beardless, but his eyes, dark as a moonless, rain-drenched night, pierces my soul. From his mind issue black mists who steal forth into the wide world. War ensues between them, and it rages across time. In the West, the clear mists, shining as myriads of stars, overcome them.

CHAPTER 20

FAREWELL TO FRIENDS

My stomach reminds me it's the second day without food. A blue-and-green bug skitters across the branch above me but has enough manners to avoid Rebecca. Can't believe the gross thought of eating it would ever cross my mind. It finds a hidey-hole beneath the thick bark. Wildlife will find no better home than amid the Good People.

Coolness clings to the gray morning, forming fog into hovering ghosts. Breath steams from my mouth and nostrils. The forest wakes with rustling here, indistinct calls there. Rebecca stretches awake.

"Sleep well?"

"Yes," she says through a yawn. "And you?"

I look away. "No."

"Another nightmare?"

I nod. "In it, I saw Malgroth, El'Darios, and their warring thoughts. How do we overcome the darkness? May be impossible, but the dream shows the Dark Lord fails."

She chews her lower lip.

"And why do I never see Ishglof? As if something has happened to him."

"You'll understand everything when the time comes. We should move on, because there's no telling how many miles to the forest's eastern edge."

Rebecca navigates catlike to the ground. She wipes herself clean and smirks at my apprehension. "I can catch you."

"Not necessary."

I clamber downward, doing my best to keep myself from embarrassment. When I land, she pats her hands together in mock applause.

Matted grasses lie everywhere. She stoops for a closer look. "Moon and earth faeries had a party."

"They're too busy enjoying life to bother with mischievousness. People placate their water and fire cousins with milk to coax them to behave. Doesn't always work."

"What brats."

"Hey now, don't make fun of my ancestry."

She offers a wry grin.

I point toward the marching sun, which sends its shining vanguard over the eastern tree line. "Let's take advantage of the daylight."

The bright timekeeper climbs cloudy steps to its noontime height. Without a compass or map, it's difficult to discern the way east. By midafternoon, we find a glade where cruel vines slithered around their prey and choked their life away. What remains are hollow-hearted oaks, a shell of their former majesty. In the distance, a ridge overlooks a flat wasteland.

"I've heard of this place," I say, scanning the wide devastation. "People call it The Withers. Nothing good happens here."

"What do Wheatlanders know? Most have never left their yards, let alone seen the far countryside."

Amid the waist-high grass, we search for a way down the

precipice. In time, Rebecca calls out, "Over here." Switchbacks, carved into the sheer cliff face, meander to the forest floor.

"Good eye."

"Good enough."

With each foot of altitude drop, the air dries to lip-cracking levels. Eerie vapors distort a vast wasteland of tortured basalt rock. Even tufts of grass grow no farther than the path, but odd-shaped cacti find adequate nourishment to survive.

Rebecca scrunches up her nose. "Awful sulfur smell."

"The forest must have gastrointestinal problems."

Her eyes fasten to mine. "Smells worse than the skunk that died in our barn."

I glance away from her, hoping she doesn't stay on the topic. "Oh?" I kick at nothing in particular on the ground.

"Know anything about it?"

"A skunk died in your barn."

"Something other than the obvious?"

"Who, me?"

Her hands slide to her hips and a thin eyebrow arches high. "Especially you."

Don't blow it, not now. Just got on her good side.

"Maybe revenge for someone overfeeding an oven fire?"

I'd schemed for days on how to get back at Goldie for her tattling ways. Overbaking it will humiliate her. But it burned hotter than I wanted, I recall. Rebecca's brother, my lookout man, I left in the kitchen for a moment. *Long enough, the dirty sneak . . .*

"You mean Linus—"

She nods. "—caused your week of chores? Yes. He feels awful, but you gave him a brilliant chance to get back at you."

I shake my head in disbelief. "Him?" A wry smile crosses my face. "My pupil makes me proud. With the skunk, we're even." In my mind, "even" means I'm still slightly ahead.

At the last switchback, the trail opens to a wide plain. Hard pan soil stretches forever, each step releasing stinky fumes. Minutes creep into hours, hours into weariness. The land undulates into loose, tumbled rock mounds flanked by bare cliff faces.

Around a bend in the path, I halt with my hand outstretched to prevent Rebecca from pressing forward. "Do you hear it?"

"What is it?"

"Voices." I point at the cliffs. "Hard to tell from where, though." As we follow, indistinct words become a conversation.

"Give them to us, give them to us," a croaking voice says. "We want them, yes we do, we want them."

Cawing erupts in agreement. When the chatter subsides, a different person speaks. "Stand aside, they don't belong to you."

"Bandits," I say.

Rebecca chews her bottom lip.

We climb a large mound that curves with an amphitheater's rounded shape, and in the middle, a hundred crows encircle two golden eagles. Each is russet capped and several times my size. The stuff of Greene's legends. With each attempted escape, the ruffians swarm and ground them. They feint an attack from the front so others can snatch a feather. Each time, they avoid a beak snap or talon slash by a hairsbreadth.

Cheers and taunts erupt with each successful melee. "We will have them, you hear, we will," a crow with a conspicuous beak and mottled feathers says. Loud agreement breaks out among the bird ranks.

"Be back."

Rebecca frowns. "These aren't natural birds. They'll peck you to death."

"The eagles can't fly or maneuver without their feathers. Don't worry, I have a plan. These crows sit at the bottom of the intelligence pool."

"Careful, please." She presses her lips together and reaches for my hands.

Our fingers interlock. Her eyes fall deep into mine, igniting a spark which fans to a chest-thumping flame. I pull her in, hands sliding along her back . . .

A loud screech breaks apart our moment. The eagles.

I skid down the loose rock mound, following its perimeter to a breach. *Breathe, Jonathan, breathe.* Cawing dies off when the ruffians notice me passing into the arena.

"Lookee there, a man-creature," their chief says, hopping toward me. Wild agreement stirs the crowd.

"Let them go," I say in a tough-guy voice, but its youthful crack doesn't help sell it. I can best them with better reasoning than their own. And a little deception.

The crow leader glances back to his flock. "Why oh why should I listen to you, fledgling? We could peck out your eyes—yes, we could—and rake your face before you see me."

"I'm no ordinary boy, as you guess, for folk know me as Fire Friend and Water Wizard."

I pull out my sword, will it to burn, and so the brand's yellow flame shoots from the hilt. Challenges and threats erupt from the flock. I grasp the flaming blade with my bare right hand. Wonder crosses the leader's face. When I touch it to the ground, sparks fly, charring the rock.

It parts the air with a hiss when I snap it toward the sky. "I'm Star Reacher, The Bearer of Many Labors, Brand Winner . . ." With this title, I sweep the sword from side to side for effect. ". . . Ogre Slayer, Black Death Eluder, and Viscount of the Veil."

And First Warden.

"I've crossed hundreds of leagues bearing tidings."

The leader hesitates, then bows. "Long Bill they call me, chief of the woodland flock. I'm your humble servant, oh great one who walks among the stars of heaven."

I frown and dip the blade. "What's going on here?"

The crow raises his wings. "We claim our prize, we do."

"And why are eagle feathers a trophy?"

"Because the easterners buy them for corn and meat scraps—a beakful each, they will. Who can gainsay such a reward?" Wild caws swell.

"The *simple* may think them great, but to the *wise* they're trifles."

"It's not *simple* to pluck the feathers from the Lord of Skies. But what's the greatest prize, News Bearer? Tell us you must, oh Viscount of the Veil."

"Yes, tell us, you must," caw the others.

"If you solve my riddle, receive their gift, then worthy you shall be to learn my oracle."

"We want to hear you, Eluder from the Black Death," Long Bill says.

"Listen to my words: Fly toward the dying red sun, even when the day is done. Deep in the forest still, six nests atop a round hill. To the reward you call, sweet melody without gall. Hidden your honor shall be between tall leafy tree. Search among the shadows gray even though cloudless day. Black eyes meet kindred fowl, reward paid from swarthy jowl."

Chief Long Bill convenes with his lieutenants. They hop in a dance as if the ground is hot. When they exhaust themselves, he faces his flock and holds up his wings.

"A sign which speaks to great rewards." The crowd hops around, forgetting the eagles. "It does, it does, my people. Hurry, find these nests. Our prize, we must have." Fervor ripples through the cawing swarm. "We must have our reward, we must." A black whirlwind spirals into the sky.

A dull crunch nears until Rebecca stands beside me. She loops her arm in mine and whispers in my ear. "Amazing."

Her breath tickles it, sprouting goosebumps upon my arms. I turn to the eagles, pointing between the two of us. "I'm Jonathan, and my friend, Rebecca."

She extends her hand in friendship but blushes as she realizes her error. "Sorry, my mistake. You don't have hands."

"My name is Fléogan," the bigger eagle says, "and my mate Soarián, Lord and Lady of Skies, from the western mountains to the Great Forest. Please excuse her want of replies, for she has not learned man speech."

"Pleased to meet you," I say.

"Me too."

"Are you okay? Can you fly?"

"I believe so yes," Fléogan says. "Lost primary feathers will make flight difficult, but not impossible. You have saved our lives, friend, traveler." The two eagles bow low. "And our way, young ones, is to bow because the Great Creator did not give us hands."

Rebecca curtsies and I bow in the same manner.

"We're traveling to the East Borough, but have lost our caravan." She casts me a furtive glance, but I hint at a shrug.

"I see," Fléogan says. "Since the sun sleeps longer each day, we have journeyed from the summer aeries in the west to winter in the east. Wicked slack jaws waylaid my flock near the border. They honor no man or beast, for they refused to face me in single combat."

Rebecca shakes her head. "Tsk-tsk, what horrible pests."

The eagles bow low again. "It is our custom to bow twice," Fléogan says, "once for respect, once for friendship."

She curtsies once more as I bow to our new friends.

"I am impressed with your keen mind, Jonathan, for I know those same nests." The great bird spreads his wings, gives a quick flap, and surveys our surroundings. "This *inhospitable* place marks the edge of the Brothers' dark lands."

"I'm glad they're behind us," I say.

"We have seen no other eagles," Rebecca says.

"As I feared, but I hope to rejoin them as soon as may be. My kin dwell in the mountain aeries fencing the forest's northern border, near to here. They master sky and land, so man and bird coexist in harmony. The Brothers' dark arm does not reach into those lands. There we can gather our strength to hunt the crows. Where do you hail from, my friends?"

"We live in a small hollow in Wheatland Town," I say. "Rebecca is my neighbor. My ancestors have been there for generations, on my mother's side."

"I knew a remarkable man from there, who was an avian and arthropod lore-master."

"You mean birds and insects?" Rebecca says.

"Right," Fléogan says.

"Was his name Conrad Jackson?" I say.

The great bird frowns, eyes widening. "Indeed, it was but how—"

"I'm his grandson, Jonathan."

"Well, bless me! I am pleased to meet you. Any kin of Conrad, I regard as my dear friend."

"While in the Brothers' prison, I met someone who knew him, too."

"This does not surprise me, although it surprises me you escaped. Your grandfather ranged far afield. I venture to say his business is his alone."

"Yes, his father sends him on important errands."

"Does he fare well?"

"He does . . ." I sense Rebecca's eyes on me.

"Jonathan means he's alive but is searching for his kidnapped wife."

My clenched jaw throbs. "Evil faeries did it and Grandpa traveled to the Other World to save her."

The eagle lord's expression turns grave. "Sad news caused by little devils who don't belong in this world. They do not know compassion."

"Couldn't agree more."

"Tell me, what is your caravan's purpose? Are you traveling to Heathfell?"

"We are," Rebecca says. "They arrested our fathers on a senseless charge. We hope to have them released."

"A pity. I've been to the borough of men, but I do not venture there often. Their bowmen are cunning and see my kind as trophies for their halls. We shall bear you to the Wold beyond the Wild Hills. Your caravan may recover their strength in this region before venturing on for Heathfell. The noble-minded proprietor, Mr. Greenstock, keeps a full larder. My sentry will watch for your return."

My gaze drops to the ground, I take a deep breath, and let it out in bursts. "I won't be coming back."

"Why ever not?"

"My quest. Rebecca will fetch my brother while I search for a captain and crew."

The eagle's golden eyes kindle a flame. "A quest?"

"My first idea failed, so I have to find the dark door in the West."

"The one leading to the black void, Eshbanáchbor?"

"And to the lord of Eskelon, Malgroth."

"Have you gone mad, child? They say the dungeon's cell doors open for nobody save by their command. But once inside, the captive cannot escape. Goodness knows neither shall give the word to release you."

"I don't plan on getting caught. Besides, it's my quest to prevent the Two Combining as part of the Prophecy of the Two."

"Yes, I know too, for my people teach them to our fledglings. El'Darios, the person I call Goodness, will make the creation new, but first comes war with desolation."

My stomach churns as I glance at Rebecca, whose eyes round with fear. I puff out my chest. "No other choice for me, sir. If the Two Combining takes place, Malgroth and Ishglof will run riot." The air thickens between us.

"Then I am afraid I cannot help you. To aid you is to kill you. In this brief time space, I have grown fond of you."

Rebecca kicks at something random on the ground.

"Then we'll trek on without you."

I start away when Soarián screeches an ear-splitting cry.

The eagle lord searches the skies. "We tarried here overlong. My lady spies a fast-approaching black cloud."

"Crows?" I say, gulping.

"Afraid so. Quick, we have no time to lose. We shall aid you this once. I will bear you, and Soarián will bear Rebecca."

Fléogan bows his shoulders low so I can climb onto his back. It's trickier than mounting a horse, but with his help, I straddle his neck. The great eagles kick off the ground and speed up to blazing speed. Evergreen branches slap my feet.

"Grab my feathers, pinch in your knees, and don't let go no matter what happens." My stomach stays behind, but everything else shoots toward the clouds at an eye-watering pace.

The thrill of flight drives mortal peril from my mind. At home, songbirds undulate from tree to bush. Often, I'd imagine I was one. But no songbird could match this intense climb. A bird's body is designed for flight—crafted wings, hollow bones, body in perfect balance—many parts working together in a symphony of motion.

The forest fades with each powerful flap of his wide wingspan. They're suitable for soaring, but speed is another thing. A chaotic cloud dapples the setting sunlight, and a cacophonous threat bleeds into the air. I lean forward to help his sleekness.

"Fléogan, the crows are gaining."

"I hear them. Forty yards back."

In a minute, our lead melts to ten.

"Hold on."

As he performs sharp maneuvers, I dig my knees into his muscular neck to keep my balance. Riding Dust Storm was perfect training for this because the thoroughbred won't allow just anyone to ride him.

"Caught some of us, they did," Long Bill screeches, "but not all, no. Six nests, we've heard of the black terror, we have. Your joke will be your sorrow, it will."

My triumph lasts a clipped five seconds as the dark cloud overtakes us like a rainstorm does an unprepared traveler. One attacker swoops and nicks my head. Another dives and misses my shoulder. Fléogan breaks his momentum to allow one to buzz underneath him.

Distracted by left-flank attacks, I'm pummeled by two crows from the right. Unsteady, I fumble to regain my balance. Strike three knocks the wind out of me. My body lifts into the air.

Time stands still . . .

Blackness swarms around me. I crash through the thick cloud of crows. As I pick up free-fall speed, watering eyes blur my tumbling vision. I try to yell, but the heart in my throat blocks any words. At this rate, a mile high will give me only seconds to live. Can I dodge fate this time, immune to the crushing force of impact? I'm not a cat with nine lives. *This is my end.*

The wide forest converges to a single spot I will hit. At four thousand feet, three killers vie for the sport of my death. My satchel strap thinks it's a hangman's noose, trees hope to skewer fresh meat, and the ground will break my body apart. Three blurs into two in a couple quick seconds. Nobody can save me. One thousand feet. I haven't found my voice. Five hundred feet. Pinecones taunt me from the treetops. Another second and I'm dead. "Goodbye, Rebecca."

Something pinches my torso and yanks me from free fall. Crows crash into the forest. I do not. The Lord of Skies caught me—mostly—but my stomach feels as if it kept hurtling toward the ground. Splat!

When Fléogan performs a barrel roll, he flings me into the air and by the time he rolls out of the maneuver, I land square on his back. I grab his feathers before he zooms upward again.

We level out high above the tangled black mass. "Wah-hoo!" I shout, pumping the air with a fist.

Soarián finishes off a few enemies, then joins our ascent. Long Bill struggles to catch us, but the sky masters fly beyond his reach.

"Amazing," Rebecca says. "He doesn't have a chance."

"They have not learned to soar atop warm air pockets," Fléogan says. "Eagles have mastered it."

"Nothing is warm up here," I say. "Maybe we could drop a thousand feet?"

"When the crows break chase."

The evening's dark blanket covers the forest floor, stars poke their heads through an inky curtain, and crisp wind drives through my muscles like nails in lumber. Rebecca's teeth clatter, but with thick feathers, the birds could continue for hours. Numbness spreads to my lips, my jaw judders, and my fingers tingle.

We drop two thousand feet into a tepid air layer. Rebecca's hair, caught in the pleasant breeze, streams behind her. Arms out, eyes closed, she drinks in freedom. I want to move closer to her, but one Wheatlander per eagle is the weight limit.

Purplish-gray humps grow out of the horizon. When the last ounce of fear drains out of me, our friends descend into the shadowed forest.

"Shouldn't we keep going, Fléogan?" I say, pointing.

"Indeed, the Wild Hills lie in the distance," he says, "but too far for today. Below is an aerie where we will sleep tonight. We make for eastern Hethwood tomorrow morning, but we shall not stay overlong in those lands."

Dense foliage camouflages his target. Rolling from the last turn, we head straight for a verdant wall stained with gray night. At the last second, he pulls up, we veer sideways, and we crash into a small landing zone. I fly off and tumble a few times across floorboards.

When my vision settles, I sit.

The great eagle staggers to his feet. "Sorry, I lost more feathers than I thought."

Soarián flares just in time and lands on the rail with perfect control.

High walls meet a roof lush with vegetation dangling over the sides. Stylized tree designs, etched in the gables, hint at an artistic flare beyond eagle ability. A thin chimney pokes into the night sky.

"Fléogan," I say, "did your people make this place?"

He unfolds his wings. "My kin cannot build such as you see here. Long ago, the eagles and the woodland folk formed a league bound by friendship. They crafted this aerie. A hidden staircase winds around the tree's trunk, ending at this trapdoor. They use the fireplace, but I do not think it wise to start a fire. I sense those vultures are out there."

We exchange tales deep into the night, but I find his more interesting. He agrees to propose my quest to his chiefs. Their council could offer the wisdom and the allies I need to stop Malgroth's evil plans.

Silvery fog shrouds the forest when we turn in for bed. The wide area reminds me of my spacious living room back home. Fléogan and I lie on one side, Soarián and Rebecca, the other.

My sleep pattern undulates until I awake during the late watches. No moon. blackness curtains the wooden walls and thick raftered ceiling. A storm rumbles in the distance, sending a tremor and foreboding prognostication through the aerie.

A soggy morning dawns with a torrent battering the safe house. By midmorning, the gale continues, but Fléogan prepares to leave.

"This is the best weather we will have today," the eagle lord says. "No sign of the crows, but they are a sneaky lot. Be on guard. If fortunate, we shall soar above this storm."

"Let's hope the luck holds," Rebecca says, offering an uncertain smile.

My friend lowers his shoulder, so I mount, and he kicks off into the turbulent sky. Gray rain sheets limit my sight to a few yards, trying to smother the excitement pumping through my body. Far below, the tallest trees hold up a fog layer, tenting the forest with a roof. I turn up my collar with one free hand in hopes it will keep me warm and dry. Droplets pelt my eyes when I force a glance toward Rebecca, whose dress is a flapping flag beneath Soarián's sleek frame.

"Friends," Fléogan says with excitement, "the clouds will lift a mile ahead."

And put an end to this bronco ride, so my stomach can rest.

As he promised, the air warms, the ceiling lifts, and the rain halts, but my teeth chatter. Breaks in the overcast allows the timid sun to caress my face.

Vulgar caws jolt the peace calming the skies.

"Little devils won't catch me," Fléogan says.

I'm not sure he's correct. We must be carrying several pounds of water weight alone, not to mention passengers. He pitches upward to make for the patchy cloud layer. Long Bill's mob gains on us, but our lead is far enough. We disappear into the clouds first. Vapor curls off the wing tip, pointing toward Rebecca, a phantom image to my right. I grip the feathers tight as vertigo befuddles in me a rising or falling sense.

Caws call out in the thick gloom. If I'm knocked off here, there's no way he can save me. Within a few tense moments, we rise above the cloud layer into the piercing sun.

"Arrow or not," Fléogan says, "we must speed to the Hethwood Inn, or perish trying."

Threatening curses erupt when the black cloud emerges from puffy cotton clouds. The dull forest edge sharpens on the horizon. The fittest birds will win the race to the East Borough, but the ones we ride have threadbare feathers, heavy with water.

"I see you, boy," Chief Long Bill screeches. "Wait 'til I catch you, for your eyes have seen me for the last time, yes, they have."

"Pay him no mind, Jonathan," Fléogan says. "The Hethwood Inn lies this side of the horizon, and nearby, an encamped host. By my life, no harm will befall you." His sudden rush widens the gap between the two flocks. Soarián earns a narrow lead as her wings flap in a perfect rhythm with Fléogan's.

Tumbled gray rock streaks by for miles. It gives way to lush meadows, leading us to glide over a slate-roofed inn. Beyond its walled courtyard, the Heathfell host camps in sleepy peace.

Surprised sentries fumble to draw swords when we touch the ground. Random voices call here and there throughout the camp. Half-dressed Lieutenant Aráza darts from his tent. Maddening caws add to the confusion. I leap from Fléogan and sprint to the young cavalryman.

"Sir," I say breathlessly, "the crows are the enemy, so protect us and the eagles."

The lieutenant assesses the scene and draws his sword. "To arms, men. Drive back the crows."

Black streaks swoop upon the archers, but a quick arrow volley pierces their numbers with swift death. Several birds fall, but the rest redouble their attack. Waves dive at the soldiers, trying to rake their eyes or peck their faces. Aráza's blade finds Chief Long Bill's head, splitting it in two. In the end, the king's army overpowers them, and the decimated flock retreats.

"Close call," Rebecca says.

I crane my neck everywhere. "Where did Fléogan and Soarián go?"

"They were just here."

I point at two infinitesimal specks in the sky. Before they vanish, calls echo back.

"It must mean farewell," I say.

CHAPTER 21

THE WHEATLAND CONSPIRACY

Our ragged caravan trades rolling meadows for lowland bulrushes and salt fens, the hallmark of the southeastern lands. Aráza told Rebecca and me, by law, stowaways become his prisoners. Still, I believe he has mixed motives for bringing a beautiful girl south with him. We march on foot, surrounded by a picket fence made of spears, having lost both wagons in the battle. I've read of Heathfell, the seat of Bormagian power, but to see it rising glorious beside the sea steals my breath. Many palace towers, golden in the setting sunlight, lift the night canopy high overhead.

Aráza's company queues behind townspeople jamming the gate. Door wardens scrutinize credentials, but we pass unchecked. Two hundred heels pound over creaking bridge timbers, through the tunnel dotted with murder holes, and into a wide yard where a wagon waits for us.

The moon and sun trade places in the darkening sky. Through dismal streets we ride, halting outside a gray-stone fortress, the top of which I can't see because fog lays in sheets. Guards jerk everyone except Rebecca out, clasp us in irons, and lead the chain gang toward the keep.

She hangs her head in frustration. Her dad tenses his jaw muscles. No doubt his hurtful words to her turn over in his mind: "You shouldn't have come" and "I can take care of myself." Fear of losing his only daughter shows in a weird manner. In time, he'll realize her love for him will climb any mountain but unresolved hurt will plunge her into the deepest sea.

Aráza must have other plans for her. I trust him with her welfare, owing to his honor. Maybe she'll end up in the royal kitchens, but I'm an accomplice with the elders, not a young girl with an innocent smile.

Guards herd their prisoners inside, but the reek draws us deeper, through dank hallways and descending narrow stairways, to the abyss of decay, our cell. They shove me inside with them, and skidding on the floor, grime smears across my hands and clothes. Cut stone interlocks the floor, walls, and ceiling. Tight seams will keep even a thin parchment from fitting there. The door bolt slides shut, locking out the free world.

Moonlight falls onto another prisoner sleeping on scattered hay. Standard-issue robes engulf his unassuming form. Still, I'm glad to have the elders with me. He may be crazy. I'll never forget Helon, the man-spider who died defending me against the evil jailer. My throat constricts and my eyes mist. How can we contact my dad? Did these dungeons crush his strong will?

I join them in a circle where no one dares a word. Back home, the harvest party starts tomorrow, I recall. I'd give my left ear to hear the squeaks from Mr. Atwood's fiddle or enter the Bigsby's Hill tumbling race. Rebecca always chides us, declaring we'll break our necks. She doesn't understand boys. If it's dangerous, I'll try it once, maybe twice.

Apples so large you half drown trying to get a bite on one will fill tubs. If I'd known last year I could breathe underwater, I could've won the contest for sure.

The other inmate's head, shaved to deter fleas, rolls into the moonlight. His emaciated form resembles . . . I scamper to him and turn his face upward. Gray circles mar his puffy eyes, which flicker to life.

"Dad! Dad, can you hear me? It's Jonathan." The amethyst flash outlines the brown in his irises.

"S-son? Been so long."

In a vulnerable moment, I forget our petty squabbles. This is my dad. Tears blur the shaky hand he raises to my cheek. "Missed you, Dad."

"Me, too. Help me sit."

Minor cuts and faint bruises cover his face, so he recoils when I touch it.

"Who did this to you?"

Fear stains his eyes, but he says nothing. My words must bring back frightening images.

The others gather around, each unsure whether to act happy or sad.

Sebastian steps through the crowd. "Why risk everything to clear my name?"

Dad balances his weight on his hands. "A fair trial is your right, because you're a free Bormagian. I had a plan to help, but it failed."

Stares level on the Wheatland constable. Anthony sticks his finger in his chest. "Each cut and bruise on William's face is your fault, Winnie."

"How many times do I need to apologize?"

His thick fingers now grab his shirt. "Once more."

"Sorry, William."

Nose to nose, Anthony's stare bores into Winston's eyes. "Doesn't cut it, friend. You crossed the line, never to return."

He prepares for the worst.

Anthony's fist opens and closes. "Did this place figure into your plans when you wrote to the king?"

Dad stumbles between them. Instead of beating him to a pulp, he lets go to support my dad.

Margaret jumps to her feet. "All elders are culpable when one breaks the Ban."

Dad nods. "The chief is right. I took a risk and lost. I forgive him. Forgive me, too."

Winston offers his hand to Anthony, who after a moment, shakes it. Judging by the constable's wince, too hard.

"The Lady is a powerful friend," my dad says, "but what's her play?"

"What do you mean?" Margaret says.

"We won't have a fair trial, if we even get one."

Their faces turn to stone, but Anthony's turns red with anger. "Why, we've done nothing wrong. The Ban is ridiculous."

My dad sits straighter and everyone gathers around him. "Visitors were just hushed voices outside this door, but I learned a few things. Our banishment is a tool, but I'm not sure of its purpose. It was the chief counselor, Charles Tarleton's brainchild. He prosecuted us as the chief inquisitor when we tried to leave the kingdom thirteen years ago. Since then, there's been a constant information feed to here from Wheatland, through the two king's men. His guards knew I was coming, so it didn't take long for them to throw me in jail."

"What does he want?" George says. "We're nothing to him."

Cornelius shakes his head. "We aren't fighting people."

"I'm with Corny," Herky says. "Makes little sense."

"Perhaps," I say during a lull in the mumbling, "they inculpate us not because we're miscreants, but felicitous scapegoats."

Eyes level on me. Margaret and George nod, Anthony turns red with frustration, Cornelius, Herky, and Sebastian rub their fingers on their chins, and Winston is a blank sheet. But my dad beams with acceptance. Wish I could save this moment in a bottle.

"Sorry, I love big words."

Dad winks at me.

"People are useful in many ways. Tarleton may pin blame on us, but the question is, how will we become his scapegoat?"

"It makes sense, son. Throughout our history, political conspiracies involved individuals of humble circumstances. The puppet master pulls their strings, and when the crowd swims in their fervor, he drowns them in it. What outcome *does* the architect wish to accomplish?"

"The obvious answer is the kingdom. Those in power need more."

"We're going to die," Anthony says, slapping his hands on his sides. "We—are—doomed."

Margaret rolls her eyes. "Calm yourself."

Sebastian paces with his arms folded behind his back. "I can't deny my blame. As they say, 'Truth is the antidote to misunderstanding's poison.' You deserve a good dose. After mulling over the past injustices done to you, I changed my mind about you sailing west. I hatched a plan but needed James to pull it off, so I wrote a letter for him to deliver to my friend."

"Can you see why most elders distrusted you?"

"Did I misuse the office, Maggie? I admit it, but time was against you. My intentions looked mischievous, even though I had good intentions. I own a stake in a prosperous shipping business, The Eastern Lands Trading Company. We own a pair of fine sailing vessels, the *Express* and the *Spring Herald*. Partners Oliver Iskander and Captain Horatio Jones agreed to carry you west, but I never told the chief investor, Ves Walsh. Iskander's visit was a company meeting that spiraled off course."

"You won't join our journey, Sebastian?" George says.

"My road doesn't lead that way. Martha's frail health means we had better stay in Wheatland. Besides, this plan has come to naught."

"Never know what *could* happen," Herky says. "We're alive, so there's hope even in this dungeon."

"Beg your pardon, but Tarleton will see us hang," Anthony says.

"I'd cling to a fool's hope rather than to none. We need a cheerful song."

Anthony blurts out a nervous chuckle and rubs his hands together. "Since I'm the *gloomy* one, I'll start the singing. Nothing beats an old favorite written by our dearest rancher. Join me." He clears his throat. Herky narrows his eyes in skepticism.

"Down, down ye go to cheery Wheatland Town.

A river runs through it, swift and blue.

Wheat fields border it ripe and golden brown.

Rumbustious little ones, mommies shew.

Dear 'uns caught in meadow's lure,

Dancing among the thistle and clover.

Deep in the night, their steps endure.

Someone even brought his dog named Rover."

Herky smiles but waves it off as unimportant. "Kid's stuff, wait until you hear this one, Ant. You, after all, are its inspiration."

Shock spreads across Anthony's face as he begins.

"Tho' heavy arms be ripe with yield,

Their master's gone through woody field.

Betimes the bright sun's warmth to feel.

For biting fish brought rod and reel.

Instead of work a nap to steal."

Greene's dad blushes as deep as a late autumn apple, but his friend continues to roast him.

"Skeeters, 'n flies find fresh meat to bite,
Snoring away through moonlit night.
Good wife beckons her husband home.
Will he e'er leave that blessed loam?"

Anthony wags a warning finger. "Your words are nonsense, not poetry."

"Thank you, Herky," Cornelius says. "You've entertained us long enough. Here's a good one from the Wheatland archives. You know it, so join in where you can."

"Green pastures bless the hilly north,
Clanking cowbells wag back and forth.
Lush grass fatten the heifers red,
White milk, the countryside is fed.

Wooded southland, the orchard's home,
Tangled roots dig into rich loam.
There the green hollow's beauty rests,
Beneath mother bird, a safe nest.

Eastward the grove hosts laughing fun,
Ribboned trophies the sporting won.
Potato sacks hop, three legs stand,
Music wafts from a summer band.

Westward the golden wheat fields grow,
Ol' Archie the choice grain to sow.
The sun sets on our blessed land,
Yielding fruit from the thresher's hand.

Dawn to dusk the golden sun runs,
Across the skies till day is done.
Dusk to dawn, the silver moon flies,
Sentinels, Wheatland, e'er to prize.
Fair Wheatland Town in the Wheatland Borough,
Plowing long rows of loam in the place we call home."

Eyes water, noses sniff, and the dreary mood changes. "Here's a song every Wheatlander knows," my dad says.

"Fair of face and framed with gold,
Wisdom speaks from days untold.
Beginning of beginnings,
Until the end of endings.
Great, her works from age to age,
Shadowed foes against her rage.
From streets call to make souls wise,
Hearts of men, her greatest prize."

Far into the night, we sing of our land, our town, our families, and the Lady Sophia until we can't keep our eyelids open. Hours before dawn, I dangle between sleep and wakefulness. The Lady's voice echoes in my mind. "Awaken, First Warden, for evil stirs in the late watches."

Footsteps stop at the door, startling me.

"Why does Tarleton want to meet us here, Ozbern?" a squeaky voice says.

"We miss each other, because I'm on duty and you're not. Do you think we need the details for the job we're doing this week, fool? By the gods, Zek, I can't believe you and I are related. Shut your trap and unclog your ears, because he's coming."

I feign sleep, but squint to see what happens next. When the window slat slides open, devilish eyes count his prisoners. When they turn an evil shade of delight, the slat slams closed.

"All here and you've thrown in a young boy for good measure," Tarleton says. "Now my plan moves into the final phase. At last, thirteen laborious years will bear fruit. Nobody can see us together again. Understand?"

"Yes, sir," Ozbern says in a low purr.

"Let's go over the job one more time, men. I told King Alfonse the Council of Lords moved to this week, because of my favorite excuse—the T'Anakim resurgence. I'll make sure he and I are alone in the council hall. On my signal, you knife him."

"If only you two are there," Zek says, "how can we kill him?"

"Dunderhead! You'll be hiding there."

"How do these Wheatland elders fit into your plan?"

"I'll explain so even you can understand. My plot to remove him has been a long time coming. But the best laid plans take seasons to flower. Years ago, I linked these Wheatlanders with the T'Anakim, so the king banished them from Heathfell. Perfect motive for revenge. The guards he set to watch them, I control. Earlier this year, my tireless work to secure votes came to fruition. At last, most lords will affirm the kingdom's transfer into the International League of Kingdoms. The unwilling few must follow or fall in this political cataclysm.

"With this in the works, I activated my new Wheatland contact, the one who replaced Hubberthorne. You remember him as too sentimental for the spy job. Next thing I hear, their meetinghouse burned to the ground, and they arrested a town elder for the crime. Perfect motivation. I gambled on someone breaking the Order of Banishment, and it came true. The trap has sprung.

"Jackson sprouted a conscience, so he sought Oliver Iskander to testify on Sebastian Childers's behalf. A few people know we caught him before he connected with him. For the newspapers, I'll fabricate a story that he's the king's killer. The others are his co-conspirators, so they'll hang, too. Holding the Council after this tragedy will guarantee a positive vote.

"You men stand before something great. Forces work to reshape this kingdom to eclipse the old order. Anyone who hinders its progress will succumb to its might. It matters not if you're a peasant or a king."

"But, sir," Zek interrupts, "I know the law says even they deserve a fair trial."

"Your brother thinks he's a budding attorney, Ozbern, but he doesn't realize those in power are a law unto themselves. This maxim and the Wheatlanders stand in opposition. A trial is an inconvenience *the people* won't allow them to enjoy. You'll see. The broom of public fervor shall sweep them away in the funeral procession of their dead king."

Silence.

"I've said enough. My banker will pay you beforehand, but make sure you do the job well. Quick death, no noise, as your reputation says. My man will take care of you at the extraction point." Spirited footfalls clap against the stone floor and then fade to nothing.

"High strung, that one, Zek. When the job's done, we're takin' our loot and getting outta this dump. Maybe the T'Anakim would welcome us with open arms? We know useful things."

"I don't want to do it."

"Muttonhead! We ain't talking here. Just 'cause the boss is careless doesn't mean I'll be. Move along the corridor."

I stick my ear near the gap under the door but freeze when the slat slides. If he opens the service door, too, we'll meet face to face. Time hangs in dead space for an eternity. I prop on one shoulder, ready to roll away, but it snaps back, and the men leave.

"What's this nonsense you're cooking up before our biggest-paying job, Zek? You must admit, the chief's outdone himself. Trumped-up T'Anakim threat and a fake Council of Lords? A stroke of genius. Don't forget, he's willing to pass over our 'indercretions,' as you call 'em. Can't spend half my life behind these doors."

"The word is '*indiscretions*,' Ozbern."

"Them, too. No matter."

"Wheatlanders haven't done wrong except come back to Heath-fell. Jail time should straighten them out, but this lawyer wants to pin an assassination on them. True, we don't care one bit for the king, but how many innocent people will Tarleton ruin with this plot? It won't stop with these here."

"They're just useful suckers."

"My point, brother. How can you live with yourself?"

"Tomfool! You picked a fine time to sprout a conscience. You leave me no choice." A sword unsheathes; there's a brief scuffle and a thud.

"You decide whose side you're on, Mr. Goody Two-shoes. The plan doesn't work without another, and you agreed. Unless you want this steel stuck in your gizzard, you'll fall in line quickly."

"No need to get crazy, man. We'll do this your way. Put that thing away." The sword scrapes back into its scabbard.

"Glad you see sense. It's your turn to watch these Wheatland rats. I'll bring an extra knife, in case you grow jelly legs and lose your nerve."

"Do you still have the map?"

"Don't worry, I can walk those catacombs with my eyes shut. This parchment is just a precaution. When we get out at the secret exit, we go our separate ways. Can't have this pettifogger taking care of me. As I said before, don't follow me, because then there'll be trouble for sure. We'll meet up at the Serpent's Head Tavern in T'Anak City. If you're late, I'll find you." Footfalls echo throughout the corridor.

Our predicament is worse than I imagined. I roll over and stare into the darkness. *Mr. Hill's right, we're doomed.*

My eyes flicker open from a troubled sleep. Dawn stabs through the ceiling vent. Others shift in their places. I awake each elder and motion to the corner. With a hushed voice, I tell them the conspiracy details.

Margaret casts Anthony a sideways glance. "Before I hear every way we will die, it's fortunate that Jonathan awoke in time to overhear it. Lady Sophia could save us."

Anthony's scowl threatens to douse her fragile hope. His lips separate as if to speak, but he doesn't.

Clamoring foot traffic builds in the hallway. Hooded eyes and a pudgy face framed by brown hair cut with a dull knife pops into the service opening. Inside slides nine bowls. Stuff they claim to be breakfast.

"Oi, Wheatlanders, I'll give you Zek's specialty, which I call *gruel surprise*. It ain't a casserole, nor is it a surprise, but at least I'm not giving you *just* a bowl of dirt. There you are, enjoy."

The brownish-orange porridge with yellow chunks floating in it turns my stomach, but knowing Zek didn't want to sell us out gives me confidence it's edible. We eat in silence and when finished, push the bowls through the service opening.

During my last week, sand in the proverbial hourglass falls from life to death. A western journey to find the Dark Door fades to the background. Who will save me from the evil elven lords in control of malefactors? Prophecies? Nonsense.

After Wednesday's breakfast, muffled voices speak with the guard outside our door.

"Never seen you before, young lady," Zek says.

"Never been here," a thin voice says.

"No one can go into this cell. Strict orders from Chief Counselor Charles Tarleton."

"Maybe so, but my authority comes from King Alfonse, may he live forever. He wants to show a small kindness to the condemned traitors."

"None of those in here—"

"Stand aside unless you want me to fetch him. Then we'll see if he's in a mood to add one more name to the executioner's docket. Look again at my credentials. Notice the authentic royal signature and seal."

A key turns, the deadbolt scrapes, and our door creaks ajar. Life in the cell stirs. Torchlight glints off a circlet, wreathing golden hair. Her velvet court dress lays over vine-decorated white brocade. A basket sways beneath an open hanging sleeve. Her piercing baby-blue eyes are unmistakable—the young lady is *Rebecca*.

Behind her stands a primped attendant in a crimson-edged black doublet, a short sword dangling at his hip.

She raises her hand for silence. "Guard, leave us."

"I must stay," Zek says.

A slight smile flashes when her glance meets mine. "The king's champion, Aráza, will protect me. He earned his appointment as captain of the royal attaché and citadel commander. I don't want your services."

"My lady—"

"Go!"

Her protector blocks the window slat so no one can see inside the cell. I nod with recognition.

Rebecca herds us toward the back. "His Royal Majesty, the King, wishes to show kindness to the Wheatland traitors. He's the high and powerful monarch of Bormágo, who minds even the condemned."

Silence.

She looks over her shoulder and nods.

Aráza kicks the door. "Leave," he threatens.

Confused steps scurry on the other side.

Rebecca passes around a basket, so we stuff our mouths with cakes, scones, and bread. She hides her face in her hands until heavy breathing calms into a regular rhythm. When she gathers composure, she acknowledges her dad, but maintains a frosty distance.

Hands flit in urgency, but her voice softens to a whisper. "I have terrible news. We think something wicked involves you, the king, and the chief counselor."

"We?" Cornelius says.

"The king's daughters and I. Long story. We planned this meeting, created the royal orders, borrowed his seal, and forged his signature. Aráza said he'd help us."

"I overheard the entire plot," I say, jerking my thumb toward the door. "I eavesdropped as Tarleton spoke with this guard and his brother. We're scapegoats in their attempt on the king's life."

Rebecca's face twists. "Makes sense."

I convey to her what I know. When I finish, she says nothing, but pokes out her bottom lip.

Aráza steps into the light. "Much rings true, but to prove any accusation against Charles will be difficult and dangerous. King Alfonse, may he live forever, trusts him without question. This means Prince Albert's life is in danger, too, but he's out of the country. I'll write a secret communiqué to warn him."

"As to Tarleton's plans, we must talk to a trusted noble," I say.

"But if he has been poisoning their minds for years, how can you know who's loyal to the king?" Rebecca says.

Aráza waves a finger. "There's one."

"Who?"

"The Earl of Castle Inverness, Arek, is my brother. He'll *always* be true to the royal family, so I can ask him. If he believes the council starts *next* week, then your story has merit. It proves Tarleton lied, so it warrants an investigation."

"But it lies far to the north," Rebecca says. "The king will be dead before you return."

"I'll use errand steeds. I'm a fast rider, my lady, because we cavalrymen can even sleep in the saddle. My king's life is at stake, so I won't rest until I return with my brother before the evil deed takes place."

CHAPTER 22

A LUCKY BREAK

Two days later, Friday dawns bright through the ceiling vent, but it doesn't brighten my mood. Today Tarleton will execute his master plan unless Aráza and Arek can stop it.

Hasty footsteps near our cell. A rough conversation drums through the solid steel. At its end, the deadbolt screeches and the door bursts open.

Ozbern doesn't hide his contempt when he points at me. "There's the little rat." His dark hair curls underneath his helmet, and his gray eyes match the dreary prison walls. "Don't keep him long."

Two guards jerk me from the cell. In passing, one glowers at Tarleton's accomplice. "Your will means nothing compared to the king. I showed you my orders stamped with the royal seal, now stand aside." I enjoy a smirk, but Ozbern seethes in a cauldron of tight-fisted rage.

They shackle my wrists and whisk me along the dank hallway to a door. Nervousness rushes out and joy floods into my being. One guard works the key in the lock, but the other grips my arm tighter. A squirt of warm liquid splatters across my face. What the heck? Red. Blood? The guard's grip slackens, his eyes roll into his head, and he slumps to the floor. Life drains from a long slice in his neck.

I leap aside as Ozbern's knife misses me and lunges for the guard working the lock. He senses trouble in time and sidesteps to avoid a direct hit. With one hand, he staunches the blood flow from his side, and with the other, he draws a similar blade in an icepick grip.

Two street fighters circle me as carrion vultures over a kill. I duck and spring toward the door to miss the first slash from the guard. He's bleeding, but he continues to fight with ferocity. Ozbern slashes a backhand, missing the guard's face by an inch. The big man sidesteps the attack and counters with an overhand strike. The blade bears down on Ozbern's off hand and opens a spurting gash.

Trembling, I try a key in the lock, but fumble it. With a tinny crash, ten keys sprawl on the floor. I snatch the keyring and jam the first one in again—no. Now the second—nope; the third—not so lucky. On the seventh attempt, the rusty mechanism works free as the only person who can save me falls dead. I force the door open, dart to the other side, and shove it shut. The deadbolt slides into place in time to absorb a thundering charge. Loud obscenities and threats stab through the steel.

I rush from the guardroom, dash up dark steps, and burst through an archway which opens into a wide prison yard. Guards march or keep watch everywhere, but with luck, no one sees me. They won't find out what happened in the dungeon until lunchtime.

A small building stands thirty feet from me. If I can make it there, I'll hide, devise a plan, and figure out how to remove these shackles. No time to second-guess if they locked the door. When the posted guard leaves, I dash for it, throw it wide, and duck behind a barrel. Empty, except for weapons.

Minutes stretch into an hour with no prospects to improve my condition. Every noise, loud voice, or guffaw sets my nerves on edge, because I'm wracking my brain for an escape plan before lunch arrives.

I crack open the door. Gatehouse, stables, guardhouse, and sentries make up the compound, with one guard at the top of the stairs. Lucky for me he returned after I charged by his post. Two gatekeepers work the pulleys to raise the heavy portcullis. "Put your backs into it, men. We're hungry," their gray-bearded captain says.

Lunchtime has come and my chance for a plan has gone.

A wagon driver urges his horse team into the yard. Indistinct yelling blurts from the street. Soldiers draw their weapons and dash toward the ruckus. They subdue a rowdy townsman who, between stifled curses, declares the innocence of his locked-up brother.

Through the chaos rides Rebecca, blue court dress forcing her to ride sidesaddle. A mounted guard shields her from the crowd. Her protector isn't Aráza, who couldn't have returned this early.

She hands the officer a letter, which he examines with care.

"Captain, you must know Kyrus belonging to Aráza's men," she says.

"I do, my lady."

"I'm here to meet two of your troops who'll escort a prisoner to the king."

"Captain Ploriz, my lady," he says with a bow, "was expecting you an hour ago. The detail arrived early. Can't imagine what is keeping them."

Maybe death?

"Sorry, time got away from me."

"Should I check on them?"

"Please do, I'm in a hurry to return to the palace."

"I'll rush the transfer paperwork, then go downstairs. Kyrus, come with me."

I edge open the door. Rebecca, back towards me, pats and strokes her palomino horse. "I'm Fire Friend and Water Wizard," I say in a tone above the background noise. Alerted, she scans the yard. "Star Reacher, Brand Winner . . ." Her eyes land on my position, lower lip pushed out in wonder. With each audible clue, she nears the weapon storehouse. ". . . the Bearer of Many Labors, Ogre Slayer, Black Death Eluder." No one else notices me calling to her.

Her finger eases the door wider. "And you are Viscount of the Veil." With a sharp glance over her shoulder, she slips into the depot and closes it behind her. "Jonathan?"

"I'll explain later."

"Can't wait to hear this."

"Quick, get me out of here. But first . . ." I hold up the fetters. "And I need my satchel."

Rebecca folds her arms and shakes her head.

"Please."

"Better. I swear you were born in a barn. Your prison robes won't do, either. Be right back."

After a few long moments, she returns with my stuff, the keys, and new clothes.

"How did you get those?"

"The guard thinks I'm instructing the stable hand while I wait. He'll soon find out his key ring is missing." She unlocks and I escape from my shackles.

"Nice work. You're full of surprises."

"Hurry." She pushes them into my chest and turns her back to me.

I bury my nervousness, because the perfect lady wouldn't dare glance at me in my skivvies. Would she?

I tear off the robes, happy to leave the gross things behind me. But these new clothes—a loose white blouse with a ruffled collar, tight khaki pants, and black knee-high riding boots make me look dumb.

"You did this on purpose."

"It's what I could find, so be thankful." Her stern frown blends into a wry smile. "You look adorable."

Adorable? Oh boy.

I wait outside the guardhouse door for her to come back.

Guards unload the wagon and stream through the dark archway. In moments, Ozbern will sound the alarm, and he'll get me.

"Captain Ploriz," Rebecca says, "I have to leave on an urgent errand. I'll return to collect the Wheatland prisoner. Raise the portcullis so this stable boy can lead out my horse."

Kyrus spreads his hands. "I must join you."

"Wait here for him and before you miss me, I'll come back. After the lunch chaos settles, they'll bring out the boy."

"Then let me help you, my lady."

"But . . ."

"I insist."

Before they leave the guardhouse, I hurry to the stables and find a stable boy currycombing Kyrus's chestnut stallion. Rebecca's palomino mare shines in the light streaming from the windows. I approach her mount from the side, but she shakes her head twice and grunts. With an easy touch, I stroke her face. When she calms, I open the stall gate and lead her away.

"The snob called for her steed?" a voice says.

My face flushes at the insult. A young man, far too old for this work, wipes sweat from his brow.

"Yes. I see her coming."

He extends his hand in greeting. "Name's Borgus. You're new?"

"Jonathan. Been a week."

"Funny, never noticed you. Must have the night shift?"

"That's right. Tough hours."

"When you return, help me muck out these stalls."

A long row stretches to the far end of the building. These are chores I won't be doing. "Sure, I'll be straight back." I guide the palomino into the yard where Rebecca waits with her escort.

Kyrus helps her mount the horse sidesaddle, so with rein in

hand, I lead her to the gate. Guards work the pulleys to raise the portcullis, long inch by long inch.

Hurry!

Ploriz stomps toward me. His deep frown melts any confidence making it this far had given me. "Boy, who are you?" he says, pointing.

I could fit under it now, but Rebecca couldn't. There's no way I'm leaving behind the one who can protect me.

"I'm Borgus's brother," I say. "He wanted help."

The captain eyes me from top to bottom.

He isn't buying it. Sweat coats my palms.

"Told him to confirm visitors with me. The ninny will never graduate beyond stable boy. Wait here."

The portcullis inches upward. *Can't they put their backs into it more?* Rebecca doesn't move a muscle. How can she? In seconds they'll see through my disguise. When it reaches the top, she nods for me to lead her into the bustling street.

Ozbern hurries through the archway with other soldiers. Wicked eyes scan the yard. He sees me.

He rushes my way, hand on his knife.

I'm dead!

"My lady," Kyrus says, "he said to wait."

"Take me out, stable boy."

I yank the harness.

He steps between the horse and the gate. "I wasn't told, and who else can protect you?"

"Stay here, okay?"

He bows. "As you wish, my lady."

Throngs of commoners, wagons, and work animals jam the street. Captain Ploriz, with Borgus in tow, points in my direction. Ozbern hurries by him. We try to force through the thickening mob. And Rebecca can't appear as my accomplice. He reaches the portcullis, bloody knife drawn.

Ploriz yells, "Stop the boy." The stream of people carries me away from the prison.

Rebecca's horse struggles to keep calm. The mare may bolt.

"Jonathan, help me."

I stroke the horse's muzzle. "Easy girl, you're okay."

The same boisterous townsman from hours ago rushes the gate. "Oi, you no good louts, release my brother!" Several friends rush to his side. Chaotic fighting ensues, enveloping guards, Ploriz, and Borgus into the fray.

The crowd pulls away from us like oil and water.

"Get on," Rebecca says. I climb up and wrap my arms around her middle. She urges the horse forward.

Ozbern raises his knife for a throw, but the people press him. He drowns in an angry human sea.

After several turns, she guides the mare into a dim alley a comfortable distance from the prison.

We dismount and I draw in a few calming breaths. She wraps her arms around my chest and pulls me into hers. Her braid drapes across my shoulder. For a moment, I cradle her head with my hand and take in her flowery scent. I pull away, curiosity besting my need for her hug. "Why did you go to the prison?"

"Before he left for Castle Inverness, Aráza arranged for his men to come for you today."

"Won't happen, because they're dead. Ozbern, Zek's brother, made sure. I escaped with my life, then hid in the weapon storehouse."

Rebecca shakes her head. "They were to bring you to the king. Now, I must do it."

"You . . . know him?"

"No, just his daughters, Princesses Catherine and Edalein. We found it difficult to get on their dad's calendar. Besides, Tarleton always hovers nearby, the venomous wasp."

"Slow down." I touch the branching circlet woven into her hair.

"Earlier this week, I couldn't believe you walked into my cell, and now look at yourself."

She pulls at her dress waist. "I'm a lady-in-waiting for the princesses, and their good friend."

"Thought they'd stick you in the kitchens. How does a prisoner earn a position reserved for nobility?"

Rebecca's smile falls to puzzlement. "You're right, how *did* I get this job?" She tallies the steps on her fingers. "Left the prison, stopped at the servant's quarters, and Aráza introduced me to the head maidservant. She bathed me, dressed me in this exquisite gown," she twirls once, "and brought me into the palace. Then she assigned me to the princesses. Their last attendant, Lady Penelope of Brackensford, they didn't care for much. They never knew of her, because she's so far removed."

"Aráza's your answer."

"But why?"

"Because he likes you. He was goggling at you the whole way from the Hethwood Inn."

"Nonsense."

"How many times did he ride back to check on you?"

"He checked on *us*."

"I was an afterthought."

She sticks out her bottom lip in a pause. "He doesn't know me."

"Rebecca, a well-used mirror will have a tough time letting your pretty face go."

She stares at the floor, cheeks reddening by the second. "My turn. How did you break out?"

"After Aráza's men came for me, Ozbern jumped them. He's a skilled knife fighter, and with surprise on his side, the guards had no chance. Busy with his death dance, I locked him in the dungeon and escaped to the yard. I waited forever and wondered if I should give myself up."

"Good you didn't, because Ploriz would have sent you back there."

"So, what's our next move? The assassination will happen tonight, setting in motion Malgroth's grand plan for this side of the veil."

"The princesses are my allies. They must tell their father or delay him."

"We have until five o'clock."

"It's noon now. They expect me at the meeting place."

"Wish I was back in my secret workshop. If I knew how things would turn out, I'd have brought everything with me."

CHAPTER 23

PLANS AND COUNTERPLANS

We ride across the Heathfell River bridge to the eastern island, avoiding guards and errand riders along the way. Can't believe we made it this far with these birds of prey circling everywhere. Rebecca brims with street smarts, timing dashes around sentinels and concealing us in cover. Where did she learn this stuff?

We halt at a line of open-air shops with merchandise ordered in neat piles. She holds up a bright tunic to herself. "Cute?"

I shrug.

She rolls her eyes and continues digging through more outfits. Jewelry, handbags, and gowns don't escape her trained eye. Most passersby ignore us. I rock back and forth on my heels, wringing my hands. *Doesn't she realize the king's life is at stake? Can't she shop with her girlfriends and save me the boredom?*

She whisks me away from the booth. "Put on this hooded robe, please."

"All this wasted effort shopping for just this?"

She stands with her hands on her hips, wagging her head. "Boys never learn. By now they'll have circulated your full description, so a cleric disguise will help. If I only had time to shave your head."

"Um . . . no, thanks, I like my hair."

The white-stone palace gleams in the high sun. Seated atop a sheer cliff, it commands a wide view over the vast sea. Ghostly Eskelon stands in stark contrast to it, but both are hostile to me.

Rebecca's cheery smile is our passport farther inside, but I push away the idea she knows the guards by name. She has been busy since we arrived in the capital, and today it serves us well.

We halt outside a lengthy building built in the same motif as the palace. Small merrow statues—mermaids—dot the tiled roofline, and a life-size one welcomes riders dashing in and out every minute. I turn my face downward when guards and couriers rush by me. When will they discover two of their own died while a conspiracy blossoms against him they swore to protect? If Ozbern plays it right, he won't stick around when they do.

"Come, Brother Abelard," Rebecca says with her nose in the air. "The royal chapel awaits."

"At once, my lady," I say. *Hope she doesn't enjoy this too much.*

She hands the reins to a stable boy who bows and leads the horse inside the stable.

We glide up a smooth stone stairway, along lavish hallways, and through a spacious courtyard to a tower. Crumbling masonry rises four stories and peaks at a pointed roof.

A fragment breaks free, hurtles to the ground, and skips to my feet. "Is this place safe?"

She chuckles. "Not a chance. No one comes here, because the king condemned it years ago."

I kick the piece so it skitters across the pavement. "I see why."

At the top, an archway opens into a dusty attic filled with old furniture. Sunlight streams through spaces in the roof tiles. I lean against the wall, catching my breath and giving the fire time to burn out of my legs.

"You're late," a voice says. A dark-brown-haired girl, around my age, strides from the shadows. She stands with arms akimbo and leans to one delicate foot.

"Princess Edalein, am I glad to see you."

Mahogany eyes rimmed with thick lashes dart from Rebecca and fasten to mine. She looks me up, down, and then eases into my personal space. My pulse rockets to an infatuation level.

Footsteps echo nearer until another girl strides into the room. Blonde with ivory skin, she contrasts with the first, but manicured features highlight both. Her annoyed stare flits to the tiny gap between Edalein and me. I step backward to diffuse the tension.

"Live forever Your Royal Highnesses, Princesses Catherine and Edalein of Bormágo, this is Jonathan Jackson, the boy who overheard the plot against your father."

I bow.

"We cannot thank you enough . . ." the blonde princess says, while her sister closes the distance between us with a romantic gleam in her eyes. She pulls her away and locks arms to keep her out of my orbit.

I stare at my toes. "Pleased to meet you, Your Royal Highnesses."

"As I was saying, good work, Lady Rebecca and our new friend, Jonathan."

"Will anyone find us up here?" I say, glancing around the room. "And it appears a bit . . . run down."

"No, even our schoolmaster and governess don't discover their wayward pupil if she hides here."

"Not until I'm ready for them," Princess Edalein admits. "And enough with the titles. We're family . . . per se, and Jonathan is a new friend. 'Lady' and 'princess' are too formal."

Catherine glowers, blue eyes piercing through her sister's insecure defense. "What do you mean, 'per se'?"

"Um, I should tell you the finer details."

She folds her arms, gnawing at her lip.

Edalein glances at the floor. "Rebecca isn't our distant cousin. In fact, she's not related."

"What did you do?"

"But I told Aráza I won't say a word." Her eyes widen and she covers her mouth with a hand.

"He's behind this?"

She unfolds her arms, fingers splayed. "Don't be mad at him. He knew we were . . . uh . . . between ladies-in-waiting. I trust his judgment. The man's much too dreamy to hurt us."

Catherine shakes her head. "A lie is a lie."

Edalein stands with her arms akimbo. "So what if I didn't tell you the finer details? Get over it, you prude."

"You and father are alike, but principles guide him. Your bleeding heart guides you."

"We should talk business," Rebecca says. "Time is short."

"Jonathan, we believe your story," Catherine says.

"Tarleton is crooked," Edalein blurts out. "He has tried to corrupt our brother, Albert."

"Edi means we have a good reason to think this."

"This evening, they want to go through with their plan," Rebecca says. "We can't wait for Aráza, so we must do something now."

"This is dreadful," Edalein says. "We've sought twice to meet alone with Daddy. Each time someone cancels the appointment. I spoke with our teacher, Morris Popplewell, but he thought I made up the story. Who could joke about such a thing?"

"Can't blame him, Edi. You always make up stories about why you don't do your schoolwork. Or why you're late to school."

She raises her hands, palms upward.

Catherine glides her dainty fingers along her chin. "Birds carrying away your last paper comes to mind. Crazy."

Edalein glowers at her sister. "Everyone knows they build nests."

"In autumn?"

She pouts, arms folded.

"You earning a passing score on your end-of-term exam is possible, but not probable."

Rebecca taps her foot. "We're wasting time with this bickering."

Catherine raises an index finger. "Right. We should interrupt his counsels. If we demand a guard always attend him, he won't refuse."

"Make it three," I say. "But pick wisely because we don't know how deep this conspiracy goes. Tarleton's word against yours, remember?"

Faint footsteps echo in the stairwell, growing louder and sparking panic in the princesses' eyes. I gesture at the furniture in the back, so we hide behind a weather-beaten wardrobe.

From our safe place, I recognize one of the two people who enter the room.

"Is this tower secret, Tarleton?" Ozbern says.

"Don't worry," he sneers. "I come here often whenever I need solitude. What happened at the jail?"

"A couple guards came for the Wheatland kid. I couldn't be too cautious, so I killed them and hid the bodies, but the boy escaped the dungeon."

"How could you let him?"

"You try knife fighting Aráza's men."

The chief counselor slides his fingers along his narrow jawline. "It's fortunate he left town, but he didn't tell me or King Alfonse his errand."

"The Wheatlander must be miles from Heathfell."

"Don't be too sure. Guards will stop him at the gates. Use your crone network to find him. Something doesn't add up here. The new blonde girl at the jail, Aráza leaves the castle . . . I smell a counter-plan. Make her disappear in what looks like an accident."

Rebecca bites her bottom lip. Edalein rests her hand on her shoulder.

"On it, sir." The guard starts for the stairwell, but Tarleton grabs his arm.

"No, focus on the main job. The council chambers. Be there by 4:30 sharp. I'll watch the king until then. Been hard keeping the annoying princesses away from him."

"Think they suspect us?"

"They're too dumb to figure out my plans, especially the good-looking one. She's a blank sheet."

Edalein's face twists with rage. Rebecca puts a finger to her lips.

"If the plan changes, I'll tell you."

"Don't worry, we'll be there."

"If your brother gets cold feet, make sure they become permanently cold."

Ozbern nods. "Right, boss."

"The pay for your trouble will be more than you've ever seen."

When the last footstep fades, I poke my head into the open. A chill snakes along my spine. I imagine the Heathfell underbelly hunting for me.

Edalein, arms folded, grits her teeth. Tarleton's words must bother her.

"We need to act fast," I say.

"Agreed," Catherine says. "We'll find my father and corner him no matter what."

"It'd be safest for you to stay here, Jonathan," Rebecca adds. "Once we warn the king, we can come back for you."

"And you? You heard the threats."

"He can't touch me, at least not in the open. Too many guards know me. Besides, the princesses need me."

"We have a few hours to save Daddy, so we better go," Edalein says. She caresses my hands. "Thank you."

Catherine grabs her sister, and the girls disappear down the stairs.

I tear off the robe disguise and throw it on the floor. *Brother Abelard, hmph.*

Couriers, nobility, and palace staff pass through the courtyard. A few stay. On the far side stands a stone clock tower showing three o'clock. I prop my head in my hand with my other fingers drumming on the windowsill. No one ever looks up to this towering death trap. The clock's hands inch along with the sauntering nobles.

The girls owe me a blow-by-blow retelling of their mission. If Catherine didn't whisk Edalein away, she might have dragged me with, too. *She's so . . . wow.* A pang of guilt bothers me. How can my infatuation with her tug at my feelings for Rebecca? Can't I like both?

As the long hand labors to reach four o'clock, three men stride across the courtyard. The one wearing a black robe motions with his hands while talking to another dressed in a crimson-edged white robe—Tarleton and King Alfonse. Zek trails them a few paces. I rub my eyes, but the image is real.

They disappear through a door at the far end. What happened to 4:30? My chest tightens, my breaths shorten. The king is a dead man unless I do something. I no longer care what he did to us long ago. No one deserves to fall into Tarleton's net, and the princesses don't deserve to become orphans.

Nerves steeling, I dash down the crumbling staircase and halt in the archway. I need a plan. But what? I can't come up short when he needs me most.

A servant boy sets a tray on an empty table. Hands fidgeting in a parade-rest stance, he scans the courtyard, biting his lip.

I dart to him. "Lost again?"

He gasps, hand checking for a heartbeat. "You scared me. Who are—"

"You're clueless. The duke's allergies are acting up, so he and the duchess will take refreshments inside his chambers." Pulp fans from the lemon wedges floating in the glasses. "Where are the scones? Smithers didn't tell you?"

"Eh, sir?"

I exaggerate an eye roll. "You ninnies mucked this one up, so I'll shuttle them there and *try* to smooth things over for you." Arm around his shoulder, I lead him out the way he came into the courtyard. "Maybe I can stay his whip, but no promises." Great tears form in his eyes. "Run along to the kitchen. I'll find you two later."

"Bless you, guv'nuh," he says, pumping my hand. "Won't happen again."

"Better not."

He forces an awkward smile.

I shoo him away with my fingers. "You still here? Go."

When he scampers from sight, I scoop up the tray and hustle after the trio. A wanted fugitive who can't wield a sword well pursues dangerous men. What am I thinking? At the door, I draw in a few quick breaths, ignore warning chills, and push it open.

No one. I follow the hallway farther into the palace's west wing, passing a servant. *Ask for directions? Do it,* I think. "Did the king pass this way?" My voice cracks with immaturity.

"Yes, he and the chief counselor went to the council chambers."

He jerks his thumb rearward. My clueless expression must have been his trigger. "Take this hallway to the first right turn, then follow to its end."

I start in that direction, but he grabs me by the shoulder.

With a beckoning gesture, he says, "Let me see your credentials."

"Even better than them, I'll tell Smithers to give you a weekend pass to the city for your efforts. My treat, so I'll take care of everything." Incredulity on his face turns to delight. The chance to visit the outside world sinks into his thick mind.

"Mighty righteous of you, sir."

Brainless staff. "Meet you back at the kitchen."

His instructions are good, because I find the long hallway. I peer around the corner. Zek stands guard.

Breathe in, breathe out. I belong here. "I belong here," I echo with my thoughts.

Zek's simpleton features sharpen into focus. A side door flanks him, which I figure as Plan B.

"Servant boy, this place is off limits."

I raise the tray to obscure my face. "Chief Counselor Tarleton ordered them for himself and the king. Are they here?"

"Yes . . . no they ain't, leave."

"Which is it? Your boss must have his refreshments."

His eyelids crease. "Wait, who are you?"

I fling one drink in his eyes.

He curses. "It stings!"

Good thing the duke likes his lemonade more akin to lemon juice. I smash the other glass on his head and crush the tray into his potato-shaped nose. Solid silver conforms to his face. He drops into a heap. The main entrance is too noticeable, so I go to Plan B. I shoot to the side door, fling it open, and dash up the stairs.

I hustle toward the railing overlooking a spacious hall. Golden chandeliers dangle over a long table with the king sitting at one end and the chief counselor at the other.

"Trust me," Tarleton says. "They understand the urgency of this council."

I dismiss jumping to the floor as it's too far. Has to be another way. The early rising moon shines through a skylight along rows of chairs. *Few options.* No Zek. Out cold for sure.

"Charles, explain why Lord Arek isn't here."

"Must have an incorrect notation in my book, but everything will go ahead as planned. My plan."

The king frowns. "Whatever do you mean?"

The chandeliers may hold my weight if I timed a jump to them. Ozbern will have no choice to give up if I grabbed the counselor in a chokehold. But if Zek awakes, he'll become a problem.

Tarleton paces, hands behind his back. "A three-act tragedy took thirteen years to unfold, where Act One sets up the scapegoats, Wheatland and the T'Anakim. Act Two, the Wheatlanders imprisoned. Act Three plays out today."

A quizzical look crosses the king's face.

"The last scene where the brilliant attorney murders the narrow-minded king, pins the blame on someone else, and a new monarch rises in his place. Your son is next."

King Alfonse grips the chair arms.

"A different leader will usher in a glorious age of enlightenment as Bormágo joins the International League of Kingdoms."

"Fool. You'll trade faithful service for treasonous words? Who are your conspirators?"

"Tsk, tsk, don't you want to know? Your narrow-minded patriotism shall burn in the sunrise of a new day. On a wide political horizon, a storm builds ever hungry, too powerful for anyone to withstand."

A floorboard creaks behind me. I dodge the king's glance in my direction. Close call.

I pop back up, but something impacts my head, my vision spins, and I fall facedown on the floor. Warm liquid seeps into my hair; my nose, broken. I stagger to my feet.

Zek's blurry images rush toward me. His porky face grins from ear to ear. "I could've sunk the blade into your dumb skull, but I like to play with caught mice first. I locked the doors, so you don't get out alive."

With all my power, I ignore the searing pain and throw a

haymaker punch. But I aim at the wrong image. The strike flies wild and sets me off balance. I regroup, throwing up my fists in a defensive position, but he pounds me in the solar plexus. Air shoots from my lungs and causes me to double over.

Can't breathe. Help.

He strikes my head with the blunt end of another dagger, where blossoms a fresh wound. Blood streams into my eyes. I fall backward, and Zek's big boot rises over my face. Lemon essence wafts in the air. *This is it.*

But the worst never comes.

An arrow pierces through his head. He falls, his lifeless gaze staring into mine. Woozy, I bumble to my feet. Across the balcony, moonlight glints off an archer's black-and-yellow armor. I shake my head, but I can't deny the figure is real.

Wood splintering into a thousand pieces thunders below me. Aráza, Rebecca, the princesses, and another man stream through the demolished doors.

Captain Aráza points. "Tarleton, you're under arrest!" The chief counselor draws a knife and sprints for the king. Near me, the stranger's dull-yellow armor brightens before rapid twangs send two arrows into Tarleton's back. He flies forward from the impact.

The girls run to the far side of the table. A warning shout never finds its way to my mouth. Instead, I retch, because my head won't stop throbbing. My nose aches.

The princesses embrace their father, but the others scan the balcony.

Rebecca stifles a scream with her hand. "Jonathan!"

"Aráza, secure the gallery," Lord Arek says in his northern accent. "I'll guard the king."

"Look out," I squeak, but too late.

The distraction up here gave Ozbern his chance. His arm wraps around Rebecca's chest, and he presses a knife to her throat. "Everyone stays put, or the girl dies."

Lord Arek and Captain Aráza slide their hands from their sword hilts.

He sneers. "I mean business, Cap."

"Let her go. Take me instead."

"Don't think so, boss. I chose this one because she keeps you tame as mice. Can get sticky if I ransom a princess or captain, so I don't want to look over my shoulder forever." He sniffs her hair. "Besides, she'd fetch a fair price from the slavers."

"You harm even one golden strand on her head, and I promise to *always* hunt you," Aráza says, spittle launching from his mouth.

"Well, the hunt begins now, my friend. Time to go, honey."

When the rogue guard slides away from the others, Rebecca lurches forward to break his grip. In a second, the archer sends another arrow whirring and hits Ozbern in the forehead. The impact forces him to the floor, where he doesn't move again.

Blood pools next to me, weakening my legs and making my skin clammy. Time stands still, while my whole body feels like a thumping heartbeat. Someone eases me downward. The archer's blurry face fills my vision. His eyes glint with green light, his helmet the same as mine back home. His skin is silver?

Heavy footfalls race up the stairs, and the door flies open. "Who are you?" Aráza says. "Do *not* harm him!" He unsheathes his sword.

The archer wipes blood-soaked hair from my cheek, rests his hand on my head, and says:

"Jon Jackson! Jon Jackson!

Tho' sickly and waxen,

Seer's words to fasten.

Death's hand go a passin',

Spark's kiss alight 'un,

Bind life to thy Chosen."

He waves a glowing hand across Aráza's stern countenance, mumbling a few words. As if dazed, the captain blinks rapidly. The archer lowers my head to the floor. To his feet, he then passes into a nearby moonbeam. Befuddled, Aráza stoops to my side. "Rebecca, hurry, I need help up here. We'll lose him." My fingers and toes stick with imaginary pins and needles. Light replaces the dark edges crowding my vision. Death isn't so awful . . .

THE KING'S COMMAND

Gentle fingers rub sweet salve on my forehead. Warmth seeping deep into my spirit refreshes the life within me.

"Father, he's not ready," a familiar woman's voice says. "He lost much blood from the head wounds, and I can't abate his high fever."

"Should be dead," a man whispers.

"A greater power works here."

"This magic is the work of El'Darios."

"It may."

Her words give me the willpower to force my eyes open, first as slits, then widening to a blurry stare. Two fuzzy images sharpen into Siany and Rombart.

"Can you hear me, Jonathan?" she says.

I nod but wince when excruciating pain shoots throughout my neck.

She looks different in her healer's garb. Her hair falls divided across each shoulder, flowing from her tall chapeau and along her crimson robe. She offers a vague smile and pats my hand, the only part on me that doesn't hurt. "We turned up to see the hero."

"You mean the archer."

Siany gives her dad a furtive glance. "The arrows were unlike any we've seen. But we didn't find him or her at the scene. If it wasn't for the corpses—"

"He vanished into the moonlight."

They trade incredulous glances and shrugs.

"You took two knocks on the head, so you need rest. Your memory will return."

"Memory's fine."

"The royal family, especially the youngest, never stop asking if you're awake," Rombart says.

"Don't rush it, father."

"I won't. We've done everything for him, so now time must work her magic. Mavis, check on him every hour and make sure no one disturbs him. I'll inform King Alfonse, may he live forever, that he needs a few more days."

A bonneted servant woman steps to his side. "Right, sir. The poor dear. Been a week."

"Can I stay?" my dad says, drawing up beside Siany.

She nods. "Yes, but not over long."

"Thank you for everything."

Everybody leaves the room, but Dad. He eases onto the bed. "Proud of you, son, for your courage and . . ." He bites his lip. ". . . example in forgiving the king. After years, it's still hard for me."

I offer a small smile. "Did what was right."

He rubs the stubble on his head. "We look alike."

I touch mine, running my fingers through nothing. "Gone?"

"You were in abysmal shape. They shaved it, because they had to fix you."

Rebecca got her wish. "Oh?" A wry grin crosses my face. "We have more in common than our hair—or lack of it."

He squeezes my hand with care.

"So, how are you, Dad? You've suffered."

"The dungeons live up to their reputation. But I'm much better, thanks to Rombart's skill."

"I have loads to tell you."

"Don't rush it, son."

"Terrifying things have happened to me since Dunbury."

He must think a hug will hurt because he only touches my hand. "Sometimes fear of loss is the worst thing." His eyes widen. "Which reminds me, Captain Aráza gave me this parchment. Says it's yours."

Scrawled on it are three handwritten numbers, arranged in a series and separated by dashes.

"His brother . . . what's his name again?"

"Lord Arek."

Dad snaps his fingers. "Yes, he said it was yours. Strange scribblings, what is it?"

I study it on both sides. "Can't remember."

"It'll come back."

The rest of the day, we catch up on events from the past two weeks. I describe the workshop, Grandpa—this takes much convincing—the portal in the backyard pool, and the faerie world. Dad's eyes look dejected, but I make him understand he never had the chance to explain everything. When he accepts it with his usual "Just the way things are" comment, I tell him he has an amethyst hue to his eye color. The life spark of the Wee Folk. He muses on the idea, seeming to wade through a river of bizarre ideas.

By the time sun rays fade into the Thinning, my ravenous stomach growls. Dad comes back with our affable servant Mavis, who wheels in a dinner cart fit for a king.

"How are you, love?" she says, straightening her pinafore. A gray hair strand, loose from her cap, flaws her near perfect appearance.

"Fine."

She narrows her eyes. "You look better. Let's get food in you." She hoists me to a sitting position, fluffs pillows against my back, and sets up a bed table. "I'll return at bedtime, sir, and ask the elder Mr. Jackson to leave."

"Will do," he says. Mavis bustles out the door, and her heavy steps trail away.

"Who's here from Wheatland?" I say with buttered garlic bread in my mouth.

"Our family and the elders' families, as expected." My dad drops his gaze. "Sebastian returned home. Martha died while we were in prison." He lets the words sink into my ears.

My eyes mist. "Mrs. Childers is gone?"

He nods. "The entire town buried her, which was hard on your mom. I expect he'll come back here after sorting through his business affairs. Meanwhile, the king has plans and will make a special announcement when you're well. You should see the city square, the place hosting the celebration in your honor. He's cleaned out the riffraff, so folk say it has never looked this good. Wheatland didn't have a festival this year."

"No?"

"Couldn't find anyone with the heart to organize one."

I reflect on the many things that have happened in the last several weeks, but I'm still far away from confronting Malgroth, the enemy of both worlds.

As promised, in the late evening, the grandmotherly servant whirls into my chambers. She finds me gazing over the city. While she tidies the room, my dad catches her "get out of here" glare.

"See you tomorrow, son."

"When?"

"Early, if approved by you, Mavis."

"Should be fine," she says in her clipped Heathfell accent, "because our little master looks better. He left it to me, so I'm clearing you."

"For what?"

"A big day, for you'll stand before the king, sir. After a special ceremony, he's invited the city to a festival. There's talk he'll make your birthday a national celebration each year."

My mouth drops open.

"A holiday coming once every four years," my dad says with a wry smile. "Imagine it."

Mavis ushers me to bed. "Tomorrow morning, I'll draw your bath, sir, before the royal tailors come for the fitting."

"The what?"

"You can't go before the king in these rags, love. Honestly! Don't worry over anything." She shoos Dad out the door and blows out the lamps.

The next morning, curtains snap open, the sun pours in, and I shuffle to the warm tub Mavis promised. White foam caresses my aching body. I never want to leave.

She pokes her bonneted head into the lavatory. "Time's up, sir. I left a towel on the changing screen. Please dry off, put on your skivvies, and wrap up in the robe. Three minutes until they come."

My mom rushes in ahead of them. She smothers me with kisses, but then her watery eyes fix on me.

"What are these little cuts?"

I break her grip and glance at the floor. "Shaving nicks."

She straightens up, and a wide smile spreads across her face. "My boy is growing into a man."

Tailors measure me from head to toe. Within an hour, a blue robe trimmed with gold and a crimson hat hang on the changing screen. I duck behind it to transform into a royal dignitary. Mavis guides me to a full-length mirror.

"Bend down, dear, I want to hide the bandage," Mom says. "Half your head doesn't show. You boys have grown so much this year. There, perfect."

Door wardens labor to open carved wooden doors, revealing a majestic throne room adorned with statues and tapestries. At its farthest end stands a humongous statue of Braeden, the first in our monarchy. Sunshine from windows changes polished white marble floors into a frozen lake. My footsteps echo throughout the hall, clapping against the far walls. Guards hold swords aloft to form a steel archway to King Alfonse. Everyone in my life gathers below the dais.

I bend to one knee and bow my head low.

His golden scepter dips into my vision. "Arise, friend." A bejeweled crown graces his hair, touching a robe trimmed with snow leopard fur. Warm eyes, reminding me of Edalein's, beam at me.

"Jonathan, a week ago, you uncovered a plot to take my life. I'm forever grateful." His serious face eases to friendliness. "You may speak."

Nothing my parents taught me saw forward to this moment. In their defense, a commoner standing before the king is rare. I recall Rebecca's manners when addressing royalty. "Live forever, Your Majesty. Tarleton said we haven't uncovered the entire plot."

He pulls at his snowy beard. "Later I'll tear out the plot by the roots. But I need to know—" He searches for words. "Why were you my friend when I wasn't yours? For years, the Crown and Wheatland have been at odds, but yours aren't the actions of a T'Anakim sympathizer."

Many things circle in my mind, but then I latch onto the right one. "You're my king, ruler of this honored people. To let you die will be to let evil win."

A slanted smile crosses his face, and he nods. "Your bravery has earned you my favor, and your humility, my friendship. I name you king's friend forever. The same to everyone in your town." He claps his hands twice. A smallish man with sparse gray hair rimming a bald head steps next to me. He bows and takes a seat at a nearby desk.

"Recorder, make a notation. I declare eternal good will between the Crown and Wheatland." The quill slides along the page. "Regarding the Order of Banishment, I command the Wheatlanders to ignore it henceforth and forever."

I muse over our strange way to rescind infallible jurisprudence. After he signs the parchment, he presses a large-bodied ring into a wax dollop. It's official.

With a clap, he summons a page who carries a long sword on a velvet pillow. He kneels, and so the king takes up the weapon.

A split hilt. Gamólig the Ancient Fire, the king's heirloom!

"Approach the throne and kneel, Jonathan."

My nervous knees melt, letting me drop to the floor. Point upward, he lowers the sword's flat side onto each shoulder. The blade glimmers white with each gentle touch.

"Your fidelity to king and country, humility, and bravery against all odds won the day. I knight you in the name of King Braedan, eldest and wisest." I glance up at the statue to a face who seems to approve my knighthood. "Henceforth, the kingdom shall call you Sir Jonathan of the Wheatland Borough. Rise before me."

I wobble to my feet and smooth my robe.

"You're the youngest knighted by this court. As to your reward, name it, and I won't refuse you up to half my domain."

My eyes wander to my friends and to Edalein, whose stare shoots through me. She offers a playful smile and an innocent giggle. Rebecca casts her a dark glare. David gives me a thumbs up, Linus nods approvingly, and my mom and dad find it difficult to stay in their places. How can my mind blank out now? I must look foolish.

Time stretches into an eternal line.

Perplexity crosses the king's face, so my heart thumps with irregularity. "Take in a deep breath, Sir Jonathan."

To everyone, the answer may be easy. Ideas tangle together in my brain. Marrying well pushes its way forward over fame, fortune, or position. But to become a prince, brother-in-law to the kingdom's darling, Albert, gains all at the same time. My fingers tingle at the thought of having such an accomplished brother. Reality overtakes this fantasy. Duty, tradition, and responsibility—my life will never be my own again. Their idea of adventure is a fox hunt. *The poor fox.*

What of my people? The Wheatlanders can start anew in the West. If Miller doesn't use the Two Gems—I'm dreaming—I'd sail to the dark door. I don't need a dull existence with a finished apprenticeship and letters after my name.

"Your Majesty," I say in my most dignified way, "knighthood is any boy's dream. I have a request, though. Long ago, my people traveled beyond the forest. We settled a pleasant land, blessed by the Creator of this good earth with swift-flowing rivers, green pasturelands, and fertile fields. While I grew up, we honored his wisdom, who is our matriarch, Lady Sophia.

"In the last few years, weeds choked what little bounty the ground brought forth, so we've become near beggars. My people have put up with hardships and despair. We're Bormagians and will always serve as your loyal subjects, but many are sensing a call away from here. A fresh start is what I beg for them. The far western lands call to us."

Taken aback, the king muses on my words.

Edalein resembles him, but Catherine, not so much. No one ever mentioned what happened to their mother.

"Can't help my amazement, Sir Jonathan. You're young, yet mature, rustic, yet dignified. Even the way you speak suggests a brilliant intellect. You don't ask for your enemies' deaths; though, suffice it to say you have none. Neither do you seek riches, power, or a place in the royal family. The latter, I'd prefer."

Heat rushes to my face. *Keep your eyes forward.*

"The welfare of your people is a noble request, my friend. So be it according to your wishes. Wheatlanders shall sail west and become mighty Bormaġians. But I believe the hardships there will drive you back home. Furthermore, I assign Captain Aráza as Knight Protectorate to you. May he guard you with the same rigor and fealty he has shown to me."

The king rests his scepter across his lap and raises his hand. "I dismiss this gathering in peace. Until you embark, every Wheatlander is my honored guest. For now, it's festival time, in honor of my special friend."

A marble staircase flows from the third to the second floor and into the palace foyer. Sculptures and other artwork adorn countless alcoves. Whinnies echo through the open breezeway, announcing our carriage. Footmen leap off to prepare it for us.

The Wheatlanders crowd outside the great doors where an occasional puffy cloud sails through the ocean sky. Edalein throws her arms around my shoulders and kisses my cheek. Her soft lips and minty breath send electrified chills throughout my body.

"Edi, stop it," Catherine says. "He's turning pink."

"A well-deserved kiss for saving Daddy's life."

Catherine's hand cups the side of her mouth. "Father calls her an extrovert and me an introvert. I call her a coquette."

Edalein's head whips back. "I heard that."

"Good to know you're not ignoring me."

"You have a penchant for odd words, and so does *Sir* Jonathan," Rebecca says.

"Etymology is an apprentice librarian's hobby," I say.

Edalein's face turns blank.

Catherine forces her eyes closed and exhales with a burst. "Studies, dear, keep to your studies."

"A comprehensive and voluminous diction marks one's intellectual prowess," I say, chest puffing out.

Rebecca nods. "True, for sesquipedals like you use magniloquence to disguise their deep-seated demureness."

Heat rushes into my face, sprouting a smirk. She had the last word. A big one.

Edalein ducks behind me. "Morris and Ida! Hide me."

Catherine's gaze bores into her sister. "Act like a lady."

"They can't spot me."

"She can see over anyone and would direct him where to find us in this crowd. Finish your schoolwork, and you don't have to hide."

Edalein mouths disrespectful words at her.

"Homework over the summer is worse than a week of chores," I say.

"Rigor and tradition mark the royal life," Catherine says, "with never-ending subjects to cover, whether it be etiquette, diplomacy, or even mathematics."

Edalein sticks her finger in her mouth as if to vomit.

Catherine glares at her.

The crowd parts for an arm-in-arm man and woman who stroll toward us.

Catherine points at Edalein and using a hushed voice, says, "We should call our schoolmaster and governess Mr. and Miss Popplewell."

Edalein's arm links with mine. "Don't assume they're married, oh no. Brother and sister. He's a committed bachelor, she's a spinster." Edalein pulls me close, so her sweet breath plays on my face, eyes delving into mine.

I gulp, heart breaking through my chest.

She says, "Marriage is wonderful. I think you agree."

"They'll not be happy with your fraternization," Catherine chides in a low voice.

"Ahem." Morris doffs his tall hat, and his deep bow betrays a receding hairline. "Your Royal Highnesses, we have been searching for you." On the upswing, the schoolmaster squares his black frock coat, which covers a lanky frame. "Absence from your late lessons will cause the schedule to slip further. And with this festival, we shall lose more time."

"A simple mistake, sir."

"Not referring to you, my lady Catherine. Princess Edalein, studies wait for no one. Your father tasked me with molding you into cultured royalty."

"What Cate says is true, didn't Daddy—"

Ida coughs, her tight bun stretching back the years on her face. She straightens her lace collar and smooths her dress a few times. "You mean to say *Papa*, and accent on the *second* syllable, please," she declares as if through lemon-soured lips. "Remember, a final letter *A* is said 'ah,' *not* a dreadful 'ar' sound. And your sister's name is Catherine, not Cate. Diminutive thinking befits sailors, not princesses. Morris, tell them."

He licks his wet lips. "Yes, dear sister. In due time."

"But didn't Papa," Edalein enunciates, "inform you we'd be with our friends today?"

One of Morris's watery eyes spasms. "They have their minute place in life," he says querulously. "You must remember your station. Consider your governess and me. We have sacrificed much to mold the noble offspring into ladies fit for the rigors of royal life."

I stifle a chuckle when he rolls the last two *R* words.

He continues. "Years ago, when you were but wee lasses, the king hand selected us to shine our wisdom on an ignorant brood."

Edalein wags her head, but this time, Ida shoots her a dark glance.

"The staff alerted us that our charges wreak mayhem in the palace. These hallowed halls exude tradition, as shown in the many tapestries and paintings. Do not treat them as common galleries in a school of jackanapes."

The princesses stare at each other, eyes wide.

Morris continues his diatribe. "As I hear from the staff, you're running through the hallways, sliding down banisters, and racing through the kitchens. This conduct does not suit royalty. Add to this embarrassment tardy homework assignments, and we cook a recipe for a hapless upbringing. Understand?"

Both princesses reply in unison, "Yes, sir."

Ida's sour face eases into pursed satisfaction. "Made your point, brother. We expect you to complete your lessons after this festival."

"Yes, ma'am," Edalein says.

Morris bows. "Good day, Your Royal Highnesses." The punctilious siblings march toward the crowd.

"That didn't go well, Edi. He'll tell father."

"Don't you mean *Papa?*" I say. "Accent on the second syllable, please."

The king emerges from the masses and squeezes my shoulder. "My favorite person. Is everything perfect?"

"Your Majesty is the premier host."

"Good, good. I have a surprise for you." He pats his hands and leads me into the driveway. Through the gathering throng passes a stable boy, leading a snowy horse.

"My prize mare, for my honored friend."

Catherine stifles a gasp.

Muscular and proud, the horse nickers with an accepting nod.

"Your Majesty, how can I reply?"

"Say nothing. The joy on your face says enough. Today, you'll ride in my dignitary's carriage, second to mine. Come, my daughters, the festival must begin on time." King Alfonse trails away.

"The mare belonged to my brother," Catherine whispers.

"I didn't—"

"Don't worry, this proves a falling out between father and Albert happened. My flighty sister needs to pay attention to such things."

Edalein's stare bores into her. "If true, why does he do Daddy's bidding? Diplomacy with foreign kingdoms keeps him busy, and he negotiates good agreements. Everyone loves him for it. The trade guilds became richer under his administration. But you'd have him stay home so you both can be royal lumps."

Harold, the chief butler, marshals my parents, David, and I to the second carriage in a long line, but the other Jacksons march with Morris and Ida toward the rear. I see the schoolmaster and governess will supervise my younger siblings today. Morris's stork-like gait, even with the aid of a cane, tracks askew, but his dutiful sister course corrects him with her shoulder.

A whip crack urges our horse team forward. As the palace grounds fade behind us, crowds line the streets along our way to King Braedan's Square. Along the way, their loud cheers overwhelm the rumbling carriage.

Around the last corner, the first king statue rises from a crowd. The driver guides us to its foot, where a decorated wooden stage awaits.

"Look at the sun," Rebecca says. A thin black layer shrouds the sky.

"Chimney soot," Catherine offers. "When it mixes with fog, death follows."

"The rest is a brilliant blue."

She shrugs. "Father will introduce Jonathan soon, so be quiet everyone."

Rebecca interlocks her hand with my free one. Edalein won't let the other hand go.

King Alfonse raises his hands for silence. "Today, I honor a brave young man who models the spirit of Bormágo."

He drones on with a flattering monologue but my eyes wander. Edalein's doll face and smart fashion accenting a curvy figure are a natural eye trap. Catherine and Rebecca will disapprove of me looking at her, but for different reasons. A breeze whips through my loose clothing. Darkness over the city couldn't be from chimney soot. What then?

Dried bird dung streaks the statue's head, but my eyes narrow with disbelief. A man, not above three feet tall, wearing a green coat and a red cap, sits atop it. Can't tell if he notices me.

"Heathfell," the king says, "give a loud round of applause for my hero and yours, the kingdom's savior, Jonathan Jackson." The crowd erupts with clapping, cheering, and wild hoots.

Captivated by the little man, I'm snapped from the distraction by Rebecca's hand squeeze. I stumble up the steps, shake the king's hand, and face the thundering sea of people. I force my eyes forward.

The king asks a few simple questions to ease my stage fright. He guides our interaction with the crowd, and they laugh, clap, and cheer me into their hearts. When he closes the introductions, he announces there'll be food and games aplenty. Loud cheering marks the end of their attention to the speech and the beginning of the fun.

When I have the next chance to glance up, the little man has vanished. My eyes search everywhere for this needle in a haystack, even crazy places like the ridgepole of the nearby Three Oaks Tavern, a small farm's pigpen, a snake oil merchant's wagon, and an immense sycamore tree. Instead, I find someone I didn't expect. Mrs. Clare Hoggins stands in the crowd with a man, not her husband. She waves, but offers an uncertain smile. I wonder why she's not among the Wheatlanders and what happened to her family at the wedding celebration.

Edalein grabs my arm. "Let's go to the apple-bobbing barrels. Rebecca and I have a lady's bet I can beat you. What Morris and Ida don't know won't hurt them."

Rebecca's gaze drops to the ground, and a trace grin crosses her face.

CHAPTER 25

THE CIRCLE OF VALSTAN

By the uncertain stares from onlookers, I've smashed any apple-bobbing records anyone held. My barrel was the fullest, and at the end, none remained. I bite into a bright-red one and so the flavor tingles my tongue. *Apple perfection.* Edalein, who looks like a drowned rat, conceded after completing only half hers.

"How did you do that?" she says through intermittent guttural coughs.

"Just a talent I've developed."

Rebecca's smirk grows into a wry smile, ready to break into laughter. She covers it with her fingers.

The soaked princess seems to sense her "distant cousin" withheld important facts. My lips are sealed.

The day whirls by with exhibitions: sword swallowing, fire breathing, juggling, dancing, and clown and mime acts. Mrs. Hoggins and the little man disappeared, because I never saw them again.

When the sun sinks below the sooty haze covering western Heathfell, carriages whisk us back to the palace. The king shows me to a seat among his family—a subtle hint—at a dinner table adorned with fine place settings, real silverware, and crystal chalices that could make sweet music if given the chance.

Waitstaff serve a sumptuous seven-course meal. I eat one-handed most of the evening because Edalein won't surrender the other hand. Rebecca's concerned glances shoot my way throughout the entire mealtime. After long hours and a bursting gut, conversation drops to a faint low, so the families break for the night.

"Don't leave yet," I say to David, Linus, and Rebecca. "We need to meet."

Catherine breaks Edalein's unwilling grip on my arm. "Come with me, Edi." The two princesses, trapped in the king's entourage, drift from the hall.

"Follow me, everyone." I lead them to a council room where spiders, high in the ceiling corners, witnessed the last time people used it. The palace does not lack for rooms. We gather around a long table.

They sit, but I stand behind my high-back chair, drumming my fingers on it. "Anyone notice a little man atop the king's statue?"

Puzzled faces stare back at me.

"You mean a statuette?" David says. "A gargoyle?"

"On another statue's head? Didn't think that through, did you? You're more of a mooncalf than a moon faerie."

Bewilderment spreads across his face, which I ignore. "Better than that, Mrs. Hoggins avoided the Wheatland crowd, while consorting with a man I've never seen."

"Nope again. I'll give you it's problematic for her, but she can go wherever she wants. The little fellow must be your overactive mind under stress."

"After everything you've seen, you still won't believe me?"

"Put yourself in our place," Linus says. "Sounds weird."

David counts on his fingers. "You hear voices in your head, the faerie world, our dead grandpa alive, a little person on a statue, and Mrs. Hoggins with a mysterious man. You're asking us to accept many strange things in a short time."

"Good thing you have ten of them to help you count."

"Funny, you brat."

"You saw a black mist, and I showed you the prophecies."

My brother glances to the floor, chewing his lip.

"I believe you," Rebecca says, lacing her fingers together. "The faerie world is real, because I met Mr. Jackson Senior there."

Linus spins his finger around his ear and points to her.

His sister leans forward. "Fine, don't agree with us. I saw weird things today, too. Did you see the shooting star across the pale moon? Never seen that in daylight. The sun was dim even though the distant sky was blue."

"Didn't you hear the suggestion soot was the cause?"

She shakes her head. "After Edalein kidnapped Jonathan and the boys went on their own, a toothless woman grabbed my arm, and pointing upward, said, 'When moon is ill and sun is dark, dearie.' I thought she was crazy but then noticed it appeared stranger than when we first arrived."

Rebecca casts me a sideways glance. Does she believe Edalein's flirtatiousness is my fault?

"She quoted the Prophecy of the Two," I say.

Fear sets in David's eyes. "You mean . . ."

"Told you, it speaks to you and me."

His mouth hangs open.

"The ancient writing suggests the world will get bad before it gets good. The battlefront could be anywhere: Wheatland, Heathfell, the western lands or Tuatha Dé Danann. We need to be ready for it by organizing and being surreptitious."

"Organize?" Linus says with a creased brow.

David shakes his head. "Surrep—yourwhathurts?"

"How is 'clandestine' for you, dolt?" Blank looks and wide eyes stare back at me. *Guess not.* "Crack open the dictionary from time to time, guys. 'Secretive' better?" David's dim face brightens.

"What do you have in mind?" Rebecca says.

I spread my hands apart. "Can't do this on my own."

They peer at each other and shrug.

My brother nods as the corners of his mouth turn downward in thought. "Okay, we're in."

"Our path will be dangerous. Whatever strange things happen, report them to the other members. Whenever we want to meet, use hand signals or handshakes. Like this." I make up a few.

Linus does the same. "Or this."

David nods. "Perfect."

"We need a name," I say. They trade furtive glances and shrugs. "Anyone who names a group joining like-minded people gives them identity and purpose. Then it becomes a living thing."

"Makes sense," Rebecca says. "to inspire us during the dark times."

"Do you remember the story Mr. Roberts told?"

"The Brothers?"

"I mean the one with General Valstan. At the Dunbury library, I read a book with him in it. He lived in the kingdom before it formed."

"When weren't we called Bormágo?" Linus says.

"Long ago, the clans built a tribal confederation. When need arose, such as war or famine, they helped each other. A plowman named Valstan ruled over his people and served as their emissary to the Great Council of Tribes in ancient Heathfell. The elders and military leaders knew he once led his tribe in victory against a raiding band. In time, a large barbarian force crossed the straits and pressed north as far as Dunkelbirgh. An emergency elder council elected him as commander in chief, leading the clan army."

David lifts his hands, palms upward. "Wonderful history lesson, but so what."

"Don't you see? We're his heirs, fighting for *our* peoples' liberty. Instead, we fight Malgroth and Ishglof with Miller and Tarleton as their unwitting generals. Legions of others, too."

"I need a scorecard to keep this straight."

"It's a conundrum of twos."

"Also, we've been a circle of friends, bound in a common purpose."

"We can call ourselves The Circle of Valstan."

"Has a ring to it," Rebecca says.

"Pun intended," Linus says, winking.

They snicker in agreement.

"We have an identity now," I say. "But we need a symbol for messages and such."

She grabs a nearby quill and parchment, scrawling, crossing out, and then drawing again. When done, she holds up a script letter *V* with a circle around it.

"Love it," Linus and David agree together.

"It's perfect, balancing simplicity and artwork," I say.

She clutches it to her chest, eyes glowing.

"If there is no more business, I adjourn the Circle's first council meeting."

CHAPTER 26

A WALK IN THE DARK

My yawns grow longer and more frequent when I stumble into my bedroom and flop onto the goose-down comforter. A long day's weariness seeps into it. I want to stay here, but sleep won't be sound without bed clothes. I slip into the standard issue: a linen gown with a tasseled cap as ridiculous as my set at home. When I shuffle toward the lavatory, a wispy breeze from the open terrace door brushes my face. I close it behind me, but recall I shut it this morning, too.

Outer palace walls form a box around a neat courtyard beneath me. The black sky, pocked with stars, overlooks orange city lamp-lights mirroring them. Distant laughter ebbs and flows in a tide of fun with faint footsteps breaking up the serene moment. Passersby notice me, but don't greet me. No one else ignores me these days.

Room light misses the far side of the terrace, but it commands the best view. One by one, lamps go out across the vast capital. I should call it a night, too, but my thoughts drift to Rebecca and

Edalein, who present a problem I didn't have a week ago. Is it wrong to want both? I'm lost in my confused mind when a chance gust whips by, pushes the door shut, and leaves me in the dark. *Brilliant.*

Voices murmur beneath me. The two people I saw earlier step from the shadows. Spectral in the moonlight, they creep toward a tree. One keeps watch while the other kneels at its base.

Can't tell what they're doing. After a moment, they sidle away, building to a brisk walk. I reach for the ivy growing on the wall. Its trellis feels strong with thick support pegs sticking from the brick mortar. The royal gardeners must prune the long plants this way. I test it with one hand and foot before trusting it with my full weight, then inch to the courtyard floor.

I time my jump from the shadows when the patrol fades from the lamplight. Ninety seconds until the next one passes, so I scrabble to the tree trunk, and after patting around, I find a hole. My hand slips in with ease, and when it finds a parchment, I draw it back. I lay motionless as the second guard marches by my position. In the excitement, I miscounted his timing. When clear, I bound across the walkway to the trellis.

Note stuck between my teeth, I climb toward the balcony. I hop onto the terrace, scuttle to the door, and disappear into my room. When I sit at the table, I smooth out the wrinkles and find it's a document from Sebastian and Iskander's enterprise.

Eastern Lands Trading Company Bill of Sale

10 barrels olive oil

20 sacks barley, fine

10 casks molasses, blackstrap

5 sacks root of ginger, whole root

25 bushels dates

10 barrels pickles

1 crate linen pantaloons

20 bushels rutabagas

1 tub pork lard

1000 spools thread

1000 bales cotton

100 chickens

50 goats, speckled

50 head of hog

250 head of rabbit

10 crates loose tea

10 tubs cocoa, raw

100 casks Bormagian ale

100 barrels crude tar

Subtotal: 1,620 RL

Shipping Fee: 349 RL

Total: 1,969 RL

V. Walsh, Proprietor

Payment due in full upon delivery

I flop into the plush armchair, teeth clenching in frustration. Almost caught for no good reason. What would the king think if his newest knight was outdoors under suspicious circumstances? But why would anyone hide something unimportant? I snap my fingers and race to the nightstand, pull open the drawer, and fish out the handwritten paper my dad gave me. I smooth it out beside the bill of sale.

1-1-2	6-3-1	2-3-4	3-4-1	2-4-1
8-2-2	5-2-3	9-2-5	1-7-1	4-4-10
9-3-1	7-3-2	1-1-7	5-5-4	6-2-4
7-3-6	8-2-2	3-2-2	8-4-6	10-4-4
11-3-1	6-2-4	9-2-2	4-4-8	12-1-4
9-1-1	13-1-2	2-1-2	5-6-1	11-3-2
12-2-2	1-3-2	3-4-1	7-2-1	

Arranged in several rows, it may relate to the parchment numbers. A cipher? I've learned each letter in the secret message comes from the cipher's notation: line—word—character position in the word. Digits included. Should read it just like text. Determined to crack the code, I grab a quill, inkwell, and a blank paper. In a few moments, I decipher the hidden intelligence based on the key. It reads: *Adv force* Spring Herald *Thur 0200 wharf B.*

The *Spring Herald* belongs to Sebastian's company. Do they transport goods and soldiers? I have no proof to implicate anyone, although two brothers come to mind. Lord Arek and Captain Aráza command the king's elite troops. Why use a private ship instead of the royal navy? They have the means, but what motive? A deep yawn reminds me how little energy fills my body. Tomorrow, I can chase leads.

My eyes flicker open to morning sunshine filtering through an elegant lace curtain, brightening the mahogany bedposts. I sit up, stretching my muscles awake. My haversack from the workshop lies on the nightstand. *Who put it there?* I unclasp the flap to find my satchel, sword, and the Lady's book placed there with a note written in David's scrawl. *Open this part and stick in your arm. You're going to get quite a surprise.*

Halfwit—hand, not arm.

I unfasten the button, spread it wide, and discover a void. My fingertips disappear but don't touch a canvas back. Palm, wrist, forearm, arm, and shoulder sink into the compartment. It is enormous. Things flicker through my mind until I focus on one. An object lands in my hand, so I tug. The brazier's flower shape passes into the light. Someone reshaped the metal and replaced the pan. I push it inside, reaching for the faerie dust jar. Whatever I seek, I find. He remembered all my stuff.

A subtle knock raps on the door, but then it bursts open. My brother and neighbors stream inside, followed by my frazzled servant.

"Please, for the last time, you may not come into a knight's chambers unbidden!" she screeches.

Arm lost in the haversack, I turn away from her.

"Nonsense," Linus says, "we want to see Jonathan. He was a friend before a knight."

"He was a brother even before then," David says.

"Thank you, Mavis," I say, "but if you don't mind, I want breakfast in fifteen minutes."

"As you wish, sir. I'll tell the cook to raid the chicken coops." She bustles away.

David picks up his note and waves it. "You found this."

"Yes, I appreciate you thinking ahead, because I need my things."

"Thanks for leaving the workshop open. Although, I was lucky to sidetrack Pep before he discovered it."

"I didn't, but I've a good idea who did."

"Grandpa?"

"Must have a new brazier. He's a fire faerie. I wonder if he'll appear in the haversack. That'd be weird."

"The two-hander is perfect, and we had much fun together." He makes a sweeping motion with his arms.

My gaze flits to Rebecca, but her curve-hugging dress and

well-brushed hair don't capture my full attention. Instead, a pendant with an inset red gem hangs around her neck.

"Charming jewelry," I say. David and Linus drop their gazes to the floor. "Who gave it to you?"

Her eyes drift everywhere but to mine. "Aráza. It's a Heathfell custom to give gifts to friends. We're just friends."

An unavoidable long pause dangles in the air. I leave it there.

"Never guess what happened last night." I share every detail—silhouettes, the tree, the cipher, and the key.

Rebecca yanks the parchments from my hand. "Let me check." The others gather behind her. She deciphers the code quicker than I did, then compares our answers. "I found the same strange message. What does it mean?"

"Obviously, Aráza, the ranking royal guard, has access to any-where in the palace and he knows Arek gave me the cipher key. The silhouettes knew the patrol timetable." Nobody speaks a word. "Rebecca, next time you're cozy with him, ask if he has an ax to grind. I wonder if he'd stab me in the back when he's supposed to protect me."

She leaps to her feet. "Nonsense. Why would he give you the key? Arek is a perfect stranger."

"And what we know comes from his brother. Either planted the documents on me."

"Ridiculous."

"When did lover boy present you with this necklace?"

Silence.

"This morning, right?" Linus says. She shoots him a dark glance.

"Convenient," I say. "He's distracting you, by playing on your girlish emotions. Let's talk to Lord Arek."

Rebecca's eyes mist, her arms straighten, and her fists ball tight. "We can't."

"Why? Scared he'd indict his brother?"

Her voice chokes. "No, because he left on urgent business." She flings the parchments at me, stomps away, and slams the door.

Linus whistles a mournful tone.

I slam my fist on the table.

"Lose the attitude, you big baby. She's always been honest with you, but you're green with envy. Doesn't matter if a dashing, handsome, and brawny champion shows interest in her. You've got more going for you."

"Like what?"

Stony silence.

"You're . . . uh . . . her neighbor," David says.

I roll my eyes. "Drop it."

David, Linus, and I spend the day lounging in the courtyard. My parents pass by on a walk. Catherine guides Edalein on a course away from me, but toward Morris. And the servant I fooled cranes his neck for a look, but I hide behind my brother. Rebecca doesn't show. A couple times, I want to take them by the tree, but in daylight it's risky. Must be another drop-off tonight. If I can help the king root out the conspiracy, the entire kingdom will call me a hero. With that happening, she can't be mad at me for long.

Servants set up a dinner table, and the artful chef prepares a masterpiece. Linus and David inhale it, but I savor the food in my mouth. Sumptuous dinners won't last forever.

The celestial seesaw tips, now with the sun down and the moon up high. The Thinning promises a cloudless, early fall evening with Night's brush, painting starry pictures on the black canvas. I pull in my arms and dig my hands deeper into my pockets. Dim torches give as much heat as light.

Lady Sophia's book stirs my curiosity, and I say, "I'm ready to turn in for the night."

Our servant takes his cue to clean up our little camp. David and

Linus leave for their rooms on the opposite side of the courtyard from me. I step alongside the tree, careful to reconnoiter for information but not arouse attention.

When I reach the stairs leading to my room, a watchman greets me.

"Good night, Sir Jonathan."

"Good night."

He seems affable enough, but guards should never speak to their charges while on duty. Sometime, the king will hear he has this lackadaisical security. Both sentries, now in position, march opposite each other.

My feet step two at a time up the staircase to the second floor. Ruby-colored hallway carpet stretches to the end. A different guard stands watch at my door, his eyes fixed straight ahead. I bend into his field of view. I wave before his face. Nothing, not even a jitter. A hard-core professional soldier.

I fish the Lady's book from the haversack and soak into the chair. An author named Justus dominates the pages with writings on government, law, elections, and the military. His or her ideas sink deep into my brain.

Within a couple of hours, yawns become frequent, eyelids grow heavy, and the excuses for staying up die out. I toss the book into the haversack, slide the curtains closed, and change into my bed clothes. As I roll under the sheets, a strange noise freezes me in place.

Wings flap from different directions, making it hard to pin down the location. Fists tight in a defensive position, I inch toward the lavatory and kick the door. Nobody. Next, the terrace.

"Jonathan!" a voice says behind me.

I shriek, turning to face him. "Grandpa?"

"You didn't see me land over there?"

"No, because my suspicions lead me to the lavatory."

"Told you I'd be back." He retracts his wings, slips past me, and investigates the door I just kicked. "All clear."

The moon paints half his face phantasmal white with a green eye boring into mine. "How do you *know* I'm your grandpa?"

He steps nearer. A chill runs along my spine. I snap to a defensive stance.

Crazed with intensity, his gaze pierces through me. "Am I who you think I am?"

I shrug and step backward. "What do you mean?"

"Yes, I *am* Conrad, William is my son, and you are my grandson." Hands on hips, he shakes his head. "Can't take anything for granted. The Two Combining has happened with The Two Gems, now beyond our reach."

Images flash through my mind. "The little man I saw."

"A faerie among the first to enter before the Thinning."

I shake my head in frustration.

"Best I can determine, Miller tried to go back earlier this week, but Ishglof was waiting. Wasn't much left to bury."

"What'll we do? Today, the moon was pale, the sun dark. The prophecies are coming true."

"Now it's time for you to fulfill what the Ancient One has seen."

"I'm ready to take the faerie door to Eskelon and its lord, Malgroth. To end the suffering, for my family's sake, and for the sake of the two worlds. In Heathfell, I can find passage to the West."

He wags his head. "Sailing by ship won't be fast enough, so I'll work on another option." He sets his hand on my shoulder and offers a small smile. "First importance, don't trust anyone. My faked death was horrible, but now the barrier between the worlds has been torn. Hundreds, if not thousands may go missing tonight; of particular note, the lesser and greater dwarves from the Mountain Kingdom in the north."

I stare at the floor, biting my lip.

He lowers his hand and paces. "Uncertainty is the only certainty, but the truth will protect us. Test whoever wants to speak with you. If I say, 'To darkness the Twain rule will bind' you'll answer . . ." He motions with his hands.

"For One, the dark power will shatter."

"Perfect, not subtle, but it works."

"No doubt it'll take time for Malgroth and Ishglof to call evil beings to themselves. And who knows their first play?"

I step from the shadows. Moonlight washes afresh on me. "How do I find the Dark Door?"

"No one can say for sure."

"Seriously?"

He smiles and fishes a parchment from his vest pocket. "Except for this."

"What is it?"

"A map to help you on your way."

I unfold it and turn it over, then back again. "Blank." My shoulders slump and I hang my head.

Grandpa taps it with his finger. "This is no ordinary cartography. It shows every faerie door and where it leads."

I hold it close to my eyes but see nothing.

"One catch. Those who made it will exaggerate and lie to protect what's theirs."

"Then I shouldn't use it."

"You'll come across no greater map in both worlds, my boy. Even if its masters are smugglers."

"Pirates?"

"Indeed, the clurichauns are ale drinkers and rum runners. Those who bless the vine and the cane have banded together in recent years. But that isn't important now." He grabs it. "To read it, you say, 'By water, moon, fire, and earth, reveal your inward worth.'" As he speaks, a script *R* shows in the corner. "To keep the makers honest, I took precautions with my own enchantments. Speak any phrase combination after the first:

"'Show me water's way, no trick shall you play.'

"'Show the way of fire, be true and not a liar.'

"'Show the paths of the moon, only not by high noon.'

"'Show the trails of earth, be not stingy with wanting dearth.'"

I throw my arms around him. "Thank you, Grandpa, for everything."

"You're welcome." He peels away. "I must return to the Danann world."

"Will I see you again?"

"No guarantees." He takes me by the shoulders and stares into my eyes. "Jonathan, once one goes through his door, the black mere—a lake of nothingness—haunts the road to Eskelon. Tales say the moon and stars shine bright overhead, but it does not suffer their light. It's the first trap, a different evil servant, so be careful."

"Of what?"

"Not sure. But maybe your brother will know because he's of the moon. All for now, goodbye." Grandpa extends his translucent wings, leaps from the terrace railing, and flutters into the darkness.

The city slumbers beneath an uneasy blanket of night. Guards march in a precise route, ticking the hours like clock hands. At a point in my boredom, one sentry completes his rounds. Where did the other one go? I crouch in the darkest part of the terrace, eyes fixed on the courtyard. Silhouettes creep along the walkway and then disappear by the tree. *Another secret message.* After he leaves, they sneak off in the other direction.

Time to snatch this one. I'll crack this conspiracy wide open. I change into my clothes, ease past my distracted door guard, race down the stairs, and halt in the archway to the courtyard. I poke my head around it. When the patrol passes, I rush to the drop-off tree. My hand finds the hole and searches for a parchment. My arm disappears up to my shoulder. Still nothing.

Unless—

Twigs snap behind me. The patrolling sentry rounds the far corner. *Not him.* Muted footsteps quicken from another direction. *Better leave.* My arm slithers out, but when I try to stand, someone forces me back to the ground. My face hits the turf, and my eyes water. I roll over and kick something fleshy and solid. Bending double, the guard I met earlier groans with angry pain.

Strong arms and body weight pin me in place. I breathe in to yell for help, but a funny-smelling cloth gags me. Vapors flood into my mouth and nose. My hearing deadens, my eyelids droop, and my mouth goes slack. I can't control my extremities. Someone forces a rolled handkerchief between my jaws, shrouds my head with a burlap sack, wrenches my arms behind my back, and binds a thick cord around them.

"Air—"

"Shouldn't snoop around after dark, Sir Jonathan. Never know what could happen."

Female and familiar.

"Poor Wheatland rat," another voice spits.

"Shut up," a third person says. "We have a job to do. Let's get him to the Specter."

I recognize the last voice. I've heard the accent. My dreamy thoughts float away.

Memories of spider venom sprout in my mind. I lay as if my body has no bones. With a hefty jerk, I'm hung upside down, dangling free. My stomach churns. No stopping it now. I retch acidy dinner remains into the sack. The gag holds some back, so I force it back down my throat.

Up, down, fast, slow, so where will this agonizing journey end? My carrier drops me. A rough covering slides over me. A loud whip cracks and a horse team whinnies onward.

We speed along cobblestone streets damp with the night air, around hairpin turns, and through tunnels. At last, the crazy driver pulls the horses to a stop. "Whoa!"

Someone yanks my legs and throws me over a shoulder. Rusty hinges creak, a door slams, and hefty boots flog the floorboards. I drop into a chair.

Indistinct voices argue outside the room. "Hand me the rope." One kidnapper fumbles at untying the knot around my neck. Lamplight forces its way into the rough sack before being ripped off my head.

Whatever they poisoned me with leaves a headache in its wake. Fuzzy shapes, who loom behind intense light, sharpen into two distinct people.

"Gross, what's on his face?" the woman says. "Puke?"

I focus quizzically on her unwelcoming eyes framed by mousy-brown hair. Mrs. Clare Hoggins offers an indifferent smirk. She grabs my cheeks, staring at me with contempt. "Didn't expect to see me?"

I shake my head the best I can.

"Who else has the means to tell Heathfell of Wheatland's movements, and supply the Wolfie's liquid lightning to burn down the meetinghouse? Tsk, tsk, Clyde told me you're clever and will figure it out. Guess not."

The other guard shoots her an annoyed look. "You were careless. The king arrested the chief, so now we have a problem."

"We can strike a deal to get him back." She runs her fingers through my hair. "His Majesty loves his newest pet."

CHAPTER 27

RELATIVE REVELATIONS

Three kidnappers issue through the door, push through the guards, and loom over me. One in the center could be a younger King Alfonse. They're similar in appearance, but his eyes are very dark. To his right stands a gaunt man with deep-set eyes framed by black hair. To his left, a groomed nobleman towers over them, his face flawed by a scar across his brow—Lord Arek. The accent, too, I remember. No recognition or affability lives in his countenance, just indifference. My heartstrings play tug-of-war between disbelief and belief. At any moment, I could expect Aráza to join his brother, making the betrayal complete.

Their leader nods to my guard, who grabs Clare in a choke hold and covers her face with a cloth. After a brief struggle, her limp body falls into his arms.

"Well done, Ewil," he says. "Now execute my orders. Activate the two men in Wheatland and erase the entire ring there."

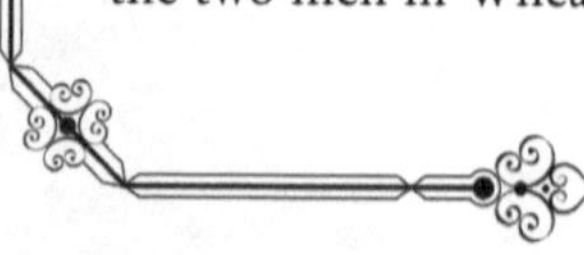

"As you wish, my Lord Prince." The brute hefts her over his shoulder and disappears from the room.

"Albert? They call *you* the Specter?"

Nodding, he smirks. "And you're Sir Jonathan, the kingdom's savior." He draws within inches of my face, then waves his wrist to fan away my stench. "But the kingdom doesn't need saving, but a violent razing. Nor should anyone protect my father. We will destroy him. True, Arek and Ves?" The two men nod.

"Why?" I say. "He is a good man."

Albert spreads his hands apart. "Simple answer—the International League of Kingdoms. My stubborn father opposes it. Charles Tarleton worked for years to countermand his aversion. But he proved a useful servant with his Wheatland spy ring. A casualty during this noble war, an end to which we sacrifice much, so others can push the objectives forward.

"I'm afraid you won't leave Bormágo as he promised, because I have a different plan for the Wheatlanders. Ves, it's time to draft the letter with the Specter's demands. The king will make an exchange, Sir Jonathan for the chief. Arek, stay with the prisoner. We have work to do."

Another burly guard joins the once true lord of Castle Inverness. My gaze drops to the floorboards, but as tension in my jaw eases, my sharp stare burns into the nobleman. "Disgusting pig, you set me up with the cipher key because you knew I'd figure it out and fall into your trap."

A cool smirk spreads across his face. "Clare saw an opportunity to nab you. And you have no reconnaissance instincts. You're a dumb mouse who can't resist cheese. Don't worry, you'll see the true plans for the kingdom come to pass."

"Spineless worm."

Arek's lips pull tight into a scowl, but he remains quiet. I've nothing more to say, too.

Over the miserable hours, the pieces of an escape plan fit together. "I have to go to the privy." Arek nods to the guard, who unties the ropes binding me to the chair. He leads me by the right hand, so I break his grip, punch the nobleman with my left, and dash to the door. *Locked.* Without warning, my body lifts, and I slam onto the floor. The guard's heavy boot presses into my neck. Arek, head cocked backward, staunches the blood flow from his nose.

The guard slams his foot into my side. And again. With silent screams, I writhe in excruciating agony. *Did a rib crack?*

"Enough," Arek says, "you may break him in half, and then we'll have no one to trade."

He drops me into the chair. A spasm rushes through my body. Rope cuts into my wrists and arms. They'll think twice when I need to use the privy.

Soon after, Ewil enters the room. I cringe thinking of Mrs. Hoggins's nasty fate. Was she deserving or just desperate? I reflect on her life and remember Clyde's mother as a kind person. She'd given him and me cookies whenever we came in from playing. Her family needed money, but at what cost?

"Is the prince's order done?" Arek says.

"Yes, my lord. And my men ride for Wheatland as we speak."

"Good, then you take my place, so I can attend to his business."

Ewil bows. "As you wish, sir."

Guard exchanges mark off the passing hours. Now they seem unconcerned with my biological needs. I miss the palace life with Mavis waiting on me hand and foot, attending to my every need. Will I have a chance to see Rebecca or enjoy time with my friends?

Around dinnertime, Ewil throws me hardened bread, which I finagle to my mouth with bound hands. Voices outside the door warn another retinue will follow. Albert and Ves issue inside the dim chamber.

"He accepts the terms," the prince says. "Clean him up before we leave. He looks nasty." Ewil leaves the room with them but returns with two full water buckets. He slices my bonds apart, careful to show me the long knife up close. "Hold up your arms." A frigid storm crashes upon my lanky frame. Teeth clattering, I've little time to prepare for the next barrage. It hits me harder than the first. Heavy clothes hang off my body as streams run from the cuffs.

He throws a new set at me. "Get into these. We move out tonight."

The dry ones smell better than my last outfit. He binds my hands, ushers me out the door, and lifts me into the crowded wagon. Arek's chance at revenge against me will come after the exchange. How can I be ready for it?

The driver urges on the team, and we trot through zigzagging alleys until we arrive somewhere on the far west side. Red torchlight flashes from the distant palace like demonic wolves in a dark forest. Do the princesses know their brother is a traitor? Catherine first noticed the change in him as strife between him and his father.

Ewil drags me from the wagon, pushes me low to the ground, and tugs me behind a parapet overlooking a road. Another one draws up next to ours and out jumps Albert, Ves, and several armed expendables. Archers fan out and disappear into shadowy cover, bows trained toward the far side.

We wait. And wait.

A light flashes in the distance.

"The signal for us to move," Albert says, pointing. "Arek, you lead the detail to the exchange site."

"I'll go alone with the prisoner, my prince," he says. "I must face my brother. Besides, our vulnerability will show good faith. Give the enemy no cause to shoot the chief."

"Make the transfer and come right back. We have other business tonight."

Arek yanks my hand, leading me toward the bridge. When we

step into the unknown, a chill races along my spine, leaving an ache in my stomach and a foreboding sense I won't survive. Each footfall on its cold stone seeps through my thin leather soles. Breath steams from my nostrils. Above the water, fog creeps like risen spirits. We halt midway. Arek's grip tightens, my arm starting to tingle. If this trade goes south, do the archers have orders to aim for me?

Had I not seen the signal, I would have believed no one came. I glance to my captor, his swollen nose purple in the faint light.

"Traitors never prosper," I say. "You'll get what's coming to you."

He digs his fingernails into my flesh, which is the only sign he heard me.

At last, when two figures appear, he pulls me forward. Each deliberate step sharpens them into focus. The guard, confident and athletic, is Aráza. His eyes flash with sober determination. The prisoner, standing a head taller than his escort, struggles with a limp. *Ulgar?*

He nods with recognition. "Little Wheatlander, we meet again."

My mouth, dry as cotton, hangs loose under a stony face. But the tobacco and fish smell is unmistakable. I throttle the air caught in my clenched fists. "Defector?" I spit. "More like, usurper."

The T'Anakim considers the slight with a contemplative frown. "You know nothing of the world, my young friend."

"Enough to keep me from becoming a liar." I yank my arm from Arek's grip, bile oozing from my glare at him. ". . . or a turncoat."

His face twists in rage.

I press an index finger to my cheek, then point it upward in contemplation. "Tarleton knew all along, didn't he? He ordered Tirás to search in vain for Ulgar, knowing the king already captured him. Brilliant plan to hide his identity and nurture the T'Anakim sympathizer seed in the public mind."

"Good sleuthing," Arek says. "But it's just a history lesson now. Give us our chief."

Aráza, jaw throbbing, pushes the enemy forward. "You're no brother of mine."

I rush toward safety, but my escort remains behind me. Knives unsheathe, so I dive for the floor.

"Death to the traitor of our house and king!" He parries a strike then lunges at the turncoat.

A few exchanges make it plain the captain knife fights better than the nobleman. A blow lands on the traitor's middle. Blood soaks through his shirt, and he slumps to the ground.

Bowstrings snap in rapid succession with missile deflections cracking all over the exchange site. I dash to the safe side, then doubling over, gasp for air. Aráza yanks me behind a bridge abutment before an arrow whizzes by my head.

"Thanks."

Eyes overcome with sorrow, the captain marshals me forward to the wagon. "Quick, Sir Jonathan."

The driver's whip cracks, so we speed along cobblestone streets, over stone bridges, and past dreary shops until he halts in the Three Oaks Tavern alley.

Aráza whisks me to the back door, rushing through the kitchen and into the dining hall. A small gathering chatters among themselves. My mom wins the race to me over my dad, so she wraps her arms around me. I may never work free.

"Stop kissing me, I'm fine." My ribs remind me they still ache. I wipe my eyes dry with the heel of my hands as the crowd closes in tight. Rebecca sits by herself in a corner. Our furtive glances meet for a second. Sebastian and Iskander, deep in conversation, sit at another table.

"What happened?" my dad asks.

I learned important things, so I struggle with where to begin.

The innkeeper's wife, sweating more than the ice water glasses she serves, sets a plate in front of me. A savory distraction won't help me tell my story. I tear roast duck off the bones and convey the kidnapping details between mouthfuls. When my tale of woe reaches the most dramatic part, Rebecca slips into the circle. I apologize for any stray food I spray.

"Aráza defeated his brother, so we left him bleeding on the bridge. Must be dead."

"Someone has to warn the king that his son and Arek are traitors," Margaret says.

"No time to investigate wharf B and also carry a warning message to him," I say.

"Unless we split up, Jonathan. George and I will see Alfonse. He knows us well enough to hear what we must tell him. Even at this late hour."

"Few guards would recognize you," Rebecca says. "I'll go with you."

"Aráza must, too," my dad offers.

"She'll be okay," he says. "Every palace worker is familiar with her. I'll take Sir Jonathan and another person."

"David, too," I say. "Rebecca's squad will have Mr. and Mrs. Roberts and Linus. The rest should stay here to keep watch for other dangers."

She gives me a small smile, which I return.

I sprint up creaky stairs to my parents' room. While I dig around for the haversack, Rebecca steps into the doorway. She pushes out her bottom lip and fidgets with her hands.

I inch toward her. "Sorry for what I said. I was a clod."

"Yes, you were." Her gaze drops to the floor. "Thank you for trusting me with this mission. It means the world to me. I want my life to matter."

"It does already. I'd go nowhere without you." We close the distance, ending in a warm hug. As we melt into each other, I cradle her head in my hand with her cheek resting on my shoulder. Flower aroma wafts off her hair. I could stay here forever. Me? I still smell of puke. But she doesn't care.

"Ahem!"

My eyes flicker open. We pull apart.

Linus stands in the doorway, finger ticking back and forth like a pendulum on a clock. "When you two finish wasting time, we have a job to do."

Aráza pulls out a knife or a throwing weapon from his coat pockets. The extras, he hands to the others. The man is a walking arsenal. I motion for everybody to gather in a tight circle. "Rebecca, your squad will contact the king. We have an hour, so be quick. Mine will collect intelligence at the wharf and frustrate Albert's plans, where able. Everyone meets back here by three o'clock. Got it?"

David's hands shake, but he tries to hide them from me.

"Don't worry, you may have a faerie trick up your sleeve tonight," I say. His sheepish expression changes to resolve. I can count on him. Aráza finishes securing his gear. His confidence reminds me of his fierce deeds in the forest battle. I couldn't ask for a better squad.

We step into the refreshing night air, but the dismal square leeches the excitement sparking through me. Aráza stops us at the eastern crossroad, a half mile from the inn.

"This is where we split and go separate ways. We turn south, but you continue straight east to the palace. Good luck."

Linus's confidence reassures me nothing will happen to Rebecca, so after a quick glance for a goodbye, our squads dart in different directions.

We sneak through dank alleys, ever meandering southeast.

When we reach a crossroad with a posted sentry, Aráza says, "Wait here."

Shocked at first, he beams with recognition at the captain's sudden presence. The two discuss something in hushed voices. After a few moments of Aráza's intense convincing, the guard snaps to attention, salutes, and dashes east.

We regroup when our guide waves us to him. "What did you tell him?" I say.

"He's a childhood friend, and one forever loyal to the crown. I activated a covert operation."

My brother's eyebrows bounce high, but he doesn't utter a word.

We follow him into the darkness. "The wharf is near, friends, so stay with me."

A salty breeze sends smelly fish and ocean scent our direction. When the last alley ends, a wide staging zone opens before the docks.

"If I'm not mistaken," Aráza says in a hushed tone, "B is southmost."

"The best place to hide a conspiracy," I say.

Old planks creaking underfoot set my teeth on edge.

"Deserted," David whispers.

"I think so, too."

Aráza presses his lips together and points the way.

Canyon walls of crates and barrels line the wharf. A three-mast ship with a maiden carved into the prow emerges from the thin fog. We scuttle behind nearby kegs. The ship's nameplate reads *Spring Herald*.

We slink from cover to cover, stopping near two men.

"Nasz Wrathbone oversaw the cargo load, Your Royal Highness," Ves says.

"His uses are few," Prince Albert says. "Everything better be in order."

"She carries enough supplies for a yearlong stay in the western lands."

This ship is my best chance to get there.

"Good, we'll land a hefty profit. You're the captain?"

"No, Horatio Jones. I just returned from sea. The merchants embark before dawn."

"Merchants?"

"Their operations will expand into these holdings. Sailing with us cost them a few gold lions each."

"Smart business sense."

"Is Lord Arek's injury severe?"

"He'll live. Aráza's knife wound didn't sever a vital organ. Lucky, the captain should've killed him. I tried to send a security detail with him, but he refused."

"He should pay for his disobedience."

"Anyone who opposes Arek must petition the League. But he's their favorite son. If I wasn't the natural heir to Bormágo, he'd gain the throne."

I can't read Aráza's face—conflicted, angry, and sad at the same time. I wonder how it must needle him to have a turncoat brother, one Alfonse trusts without question. And Arek's not dead, which will tarnish his reputation as the premiere blade champion.

"Rombart is overseeing his care. He believes an accident caused his wound. Best to keep him in the dark. I'd hate to stop using his services."

"I see what you mean." Ves points toward the palace. "It's time, my lord."

My eyes stare that direction until they tire. What am I looking for? After a few moments, an orange flash erupts, followed by a concussive boom, which spews fire high into the sky.

"A great rift severs the bridge to the eastern isle," Aráza whispers.

"The others!" David gasps. "We have to check on them."

"We should return to the inn."

I grip his shoulder. "Look."

Workers stir on deck as Ves and the prince disembark, passing nearby us. I stretch my neck to see something in the hold. Silhouettes stream after them. Cowls can't hide their unmistakable features. They're T'Anakim warriors, geared for rapid mobility. They disappear into the night, leaving the hardworking sailors to their tasks. With the enemy advance force moving into place, no doubt the full invasion troops are close at hand. We're out of time.

Smoke billows in the distance. I bite my lower lip. "Back to the inn," I say with a frayed hope Rebecca's squad will meet us there.

CHAPTER 28

WHERE ONE PATH ENDS, ANOTHER BEGINS

We step into the Three Oaks Tavern dining hall, where a crowd gathers around Rebecca's parents. Her squad hasn't come back. Mrs. Avery slaps her husband on the arm. "How could you let her go?"

He spreads his hands apart in innocence. "Give them more time. Besides, she made up her stubborn mind."

"She wouldn't have gone if you had said something, so enter her life and act as if you're her father. Everyone heard the explosion near the palace. Smoke still billows into the air. Our baby girl may be gone." She hangs her head in her hands.

Shocked incredulity burns into his facial features.

Every eye snaps our way. My parents hurry toward us.

"We saw the blast," I say, my gaze dropping to the floor. "All we can do is hope they weren't hurt."

"What did you learn at the wharf?" my dad says.

My eyes flit to Sebastian and Iskander, who stand in unison.

"Many things, most about the Eastern Lands Trading Company."

They trade quizzical glances with each other.

As my story unfolds, the two partners pace the floor, stopping to whisper to each other.

"Believe me," Sebastian says, "we didn't know Ves has treacherous plans."

"He's the principal partner," Iskander says, "but would run the whole business if unchecked."

My dad folds his arms. "Your lives may be in danger, because he might intend on making the partnership a sole proprietorship."

"Possible, because his ambition knows no bounds. But this—"

Footsteps halt our conversation. In stumbles Linus with George's arm draped over his shoulder. Rebecca likewise supports Margaret. Torn clothes hang off their frames.

We rush them to chairs, and a crowd swells around them.

Rebecca takes a long pull from a mug, then blots her mouth with a napkin. "We were crossing to the palace island when a blast erupted on the bridge, splitting it in two. We never saw the king. When I found a wagon, I drove us back here."

"Mr. and Mrs. Roberts have injuries, but they aren't serious," Linus says. "My sister field-dressed them the best she could."

George puffs out his chest. "Just a scratch."

Siany motions to the table with her hand. "Lie down here and I'll run for healing supplies."

Rebecca grasps her arm. "Wait." She picks up my haversack. "I stashed *everything* in here, even the rare stuff. Time to put it into my satchel and bags."

Siany counts on her fingers. "Do you have—"

"Oil of drake and gila monster saliva?" she says. "Yes, and aloe, too."

"Good, good."

The two healers dress the wounds with a stinking paste that bubbles when it coats their skin. When done, it soothes their pain and heals the damage.

"While the city sleeps, the signs of a full-scale invasion surround us," Aráza says. "With this nasty diversion, the advance force will head for the armory. The palace garrison is the largest and most fortified. Without a bridge, they must ferry soldiers in longboats to the mainland, which may cost hours. If the first ashore hold it until the landing parties arrive, Heathfell will fall. Next, the ships could pummel the island with cannon fire. If Prince Albert kills his father, he'll use the Wheatlanders, the T'Anakim 'sympathizers,' as the scapegoat. No one can save you from him. You must flee the kingdom while it's nightfall. Dawn will unveil our flight. Since I'm Sir Jonathan's protector, I'll join you. I'd say we have a half hour to pack up and set sail."

"I've seen the manifests this week," Iskander says. "The Spring Herald can handle this crowd. The hold will be full, but we have ways of fitting in passengers."

Sebastian unfolds his arms and spreads them wide. "But the merchants will take most of the space."

"It's worth a try."

Everyone speaks at once until Anthony whistles for quiet. "We voted to sail West."

"He's right," Cornelius says.

Margaret wobbles to her feet. "George and I can't go with you in this shape."

"But the prince—" my dad says.

She holds up her wrinkled hand to stay his argument. "We can contribute to this mission while in Wheatland. If Prince Albert ascends to the throne, he'll overlook us. His kingdom agenda won't focus on our borough. We'll leave the city in your borrowed wagon, then recover at the Hethwood Inn for a few weeks. Greenstock will hide us."

George raises his hand to interject. "We'll manage your properties."

"You interrupted me."

"I'll forget if I don't speak my mind, dear."

"He's right. When you settle in the West, return and work out your business affairs. Meanwhile, let us handle things for you."

As the offer sinks in, the families consider it. My parents need a moment to agree. "We're ready," Dad says.

Margaret scans the room, taking in the nods. "This is the quickest decision any elder or Wheatlander made. Everyone write instructions, including which bed mattress holds your life savings and legal papers, and then be on your way. We'll keep excellent records."

After a few moments, my dad collects their scribblings and gives them to her.

"There's one unresolved question," she says. "Since William showed the most leadership skill, I nominate him as the expedition leader."

Sebastian raises his hand. "I second it."

"In favor of electing him, say, aye."

"Aye," every elder speaks in unison.

"Nays?" I only hear crickets. "Abstentions? The ayes have it. What is your first decision?"

Dad stands, smoothing out his shirt. A determined strength settles on his countenance. "Pack up and be ready to move out in fifteen minutes. Captain Aráza, if you'd be so kind, gather your things and escort us to the wharf."

He bows. "My pleasure."

The dining hall clears in a matter of seconds with everyone scurrying to their rooms.

At the deadline, a sea of heads bobs like corks in the foyer. Well-known faces pop from the crowd: Avery, Beasley, Childers, Hill, Holms, Howe, and Jackson. Oliver Iskander shows last, pack in hand. He's right to dodge the coming invasion.

Footsteps and an offbeat clunking sound tread up the steps and onto the porch. The door swings open, letting in a curling fog. Dark figures stand in the weak light. Two in the front enter the foyer. They throw off their deep cowls, and the lamplight casts uneven shadows across their faces. One is the guard that Aráza sent on his covert operation. They offer snappy salutes which the captain returns, then make way for a cloaked man to step into our midst. He throws off his hood, too. A receding hairline sits atop a scarecrow's head and body. Morris Popplewell.

One by one the others join him, freeing long hair trapped by hoods. A husky guard closes the door behind them. Searching mahogany eyes flit to mine. Edalein chews the corner of her mouth, but then a playful smile spreads across her face. Catherine interlocks her arm in her sister's arm.

"Morris," Ida says, "do tell them why we're here."

Their schoolmaster licks his wet lips. "Yes, of course," he acknowledges. "Captain Aráza enacted Operation Ether—princess extraction. If I hadn't heard the palace bridge blowing up well behind us and passed by fretting guards dashing here and there, I would've wondered at his judgment."

"A hunch that paid off," the captain says.

"But I see the princesses must depart the city as a precaution."

"I'll lead this group to the wharf where a ship awaits, bound for the western lands."

"Very good, we'll sail with you to the Denby archipelago. We will ride out this storm there until the king sends for us. When do we leave?"

"Five minutes ago."

Indistinct voices and heavy footsteps rush by the tavern. When gone, James, Linus, and I dart to the stables to lead away Dust Storm, Bruno, and my white mare I call Aeronwen, Aero for short. Rebecca and David fetch the dogs, Gunnar, Coal, and Max. When Gunnar sees Dusty, he bares his teeth at him. Rebecca, too late to notice the dog's aggression, flies forward, but my brother rescues her from landing on her face.

"What's wrong with you?" she says, grabbing his muzzle and staring him in the eye.

Linus places his hand on her shoulder. "Nerves, I'm sure. His nose catches strange smells, and his ears hear weird sounds."

Distant shouts set me on edge. "True, let's go," I say.

Once we leave the square, Aráza leads us a different way to the docks. He speaks in private to every guard we meet, and when we pass, each of them doesn't hinder our movements. When we come to a crossroad, he raises his hand, and so we halt.

Impatience bubbles in me. "What's wrong?"

"This intersection should have a posted sentry, but I don't see a soul. Wait here."

I strain to peer through the gloom. A silhouette creeps along, disappearing into the night. Within moments, he emerges from a long shadow cast by a nearby streetlamp, cleaning a blade. With an imperceptible scrape, he returns a dagger into its scabbard.

"The T'Anakim soldier won't bother us anymore. We're close to the wharf, so follow me at a distance. Animals in the back. If I hold up my hand, stop the crowd. You must tell them: no noise until we board."

Distant voices pop in different directions. The city's defenses no longer sleep. Rushing along the straight road to the seaside, every stray sound could be a T'Anakim surprise attack. But it never happens. Stacked crates, barrels, and boxes line the docks. A wispy breeze stretches fog into long sheets, so the moon peeks through random breaks.

The *Spring Herald*'s faint outline looms in the distance.

I hold out my hand to stop Aráza. "Wait for everyone to catch up with us. I need a moment with my brother." I sign for him to come with me, so we slink behind crates.

His eyes may guess my purpose. "I've seen my abilities but not yours." I find the faerie dust in my satchel, uncork it, and sprinkle a pinch on him. It spreads over him. "Now wait."

"What's supposed to happen?"

I shrug and turn my head side to side. "We'll see." When the long silence between us becomes uncomfortable, I say, "Maybe nothing."

"Let's go back to the others."

The dawn hangs the first pale sheets of sunrays in the sky. Once haunted with creeping fog, the docks speak a breath of hope, which sparks soft giggling from children and whining from the dogs. Wharf B's faded sign squeaks a tune of freedom. The *Spring Herald,* my last chance to find the dark door, awaits. Sailors scurry along the deck, and boarders descend into the hold.

"Wait," Iskander says. "We need a word with the captain."

They speak with a man who could've been handsome in his younger years, but a hard life at sea has turned his face to leather. They shake hands and share a smile. Sebastian clasps his arm on the captain's shoulder, and they stroll along the wharf. Their negotiations continue until he spreads his hands in a sign of resignation.

They rush back to the crowd. "Horatio agrees to let us come for a gold half lion each."

"My distinguished partner promised to pick up the rest of the fee," Iskander says, elbowing him.

"Quiet, Oliver. No questions asked. Ves doesn't have to know. Grab your things and let's board. Once we get below deck, the ship will set sail."

Dad marshals everyone aboard, princesses with their escorts first, my family in the rear. He must think embarking last shows good leadership. A haphazard line snakes from the hatch door to the gangplank. Yellow smoke hangs in the fog. The cigar smoker, a sailor with a bedraggled beard and greasy hair tied back in a knot, leans on the helm, eyeing us suspiciously.

Nose pinched, David grimaces. "It's torture what people do to plants."

"His ill-favored look gives me the creeps," I say.

Contemptuous eyes suggest he's not happy with our arrangement.

"Nasz, report for orders," Captain Jones says.

The smoking man flicks his cigar butt overboard and saunters to him. His scowl shows crooked fangs, lacking care.

Bruno acts up by sitting on the deck, so the line's advance halts.

Linus yanks on the reins, but a thousand pounds refuses any movement. "Rebecca, help."

With the delay, my eyes drift back to the capital. This is the last time I'll see my kingdom. Its strength plain in the palace's thick walls. Its riches spring from hands working daily at the loom. Smoke from the bridge blast fans downwind. Do they realize these are nefarious machinations?

When carrots give the incentive for Bruno to leave the deck, it's our turn at last to follow. My mom shepherds my sister and little brothers aboard the dreary ship.

A bowshot twangs—

An orange glow streaks in front of my eyes, and the arrow embeds into the gangplank. Flame erupts, but I push my dad onto the ship in time. David and I leap back to the wharf.

Prince Albert nocks another arrow, fires, and the missile hums past my face. The shot, not intended for me, splits the ship's bowline in two. Ves unties the stern line, leaving the *Spring Herald* to float free from her moorings.

Yellow flame leaps from my sword. A second arrow slides in place, he draws the bowstring to his ear, and aims at me. At this short distance, it would pass straight through me.

"Not going anywhere, whelp," Albert says. "I can drop you where you stand."

Ulgar grabs the prince's drawn hand and jerks it downward. "Our quarrel is with King Alfonse, not with Wheatland. Let them go." Waning moonlight bathes the wharf planks.

The prince lowers his bow, nodding. "Better catch your ship, boys. And don't come back." The T'Anakim holds up his hand in a sign of peace. I do likewise, but could we ever have it?

Turning on their heels, they march away, and I put away my sword.

Albert stops. Ulgar angles toward him.

Darkness surrounds him, reminding me of the incident in the Workshop. A black mist, or maybe two, overtake him. He turns around, eyes darkening and contempt spreading across his youthful face.

Albert raises his bow and fires a rapid shot at David! Fear throttles my throat. Time stands still. No way can he survive a master bowman's precise shot. But only the vibrating arrow, embedded into a pile, remains where my brother once stood.

David—is gone.

The gangplank splashes into the water as the ship drifts away.

"Sir Jonathan, I'm coming for you," Aráza says. My dad, rope coil in hand, gives it to my protector.

"You can't get up here. I can handle this."

He continues to measure the lengths with his arm span.

"I order you to stay. Please."

Aráza stops measuring the rope and drops it. He dips his chin in a slight bow.

I turn to the central conspirator—Prince Albert. A man who'd destroy his father and the kingdom he holds dear. Indifference crowds his empty eyes. *How long has Malgroth poisoned his mind with dark thoughts?* "Come on, man to man," I say.

He looks me up and down. "Man to *man?*" He chuckles. "Okay." He hands the bow to Ulgar, then unsheathes a fine saber which he flourishes in an artistic movement.

I bite my lip. But no time to waste. I will my sword to ignite.

We circle twice to test one another's resolve. I lunge first, and he parries it easily. He counters with an overhead strike, which I sidestep. My blade pulsates, growing bright. Albert and I shy away from the brand's gleam. In those hours I practiced with it in the Workshop—even against the tree ogre—it's never done this. A surge of confidence electrifies me. I grip the hilt tight, ready for *its* next move.

The prince lunges, and I parry and riposte, nicking his arm. We circle. Blood drips from his elbow. His follow-up overhead blow flies wild and embeds itself into the planks. I step in with a pommel strike to the nose. Blood gushes onto the dock. He staggers back to regain his composure.

"Highness, let's go," Ves says. "They'll land, so we must be ready."

He considers his words by lowering his blade.

I lower mine, too.

Rage kindles in his eyes. He lunges for the kill—

The sword parries his strike—I can barely hang onto it—but my faster right hand stretches palm outward. Blue and yellow sparks spray all over my enemy. He leaps backward, brushing his singed beard with his sleeve. I can't say who's more shocked at my overt display of magic power, him or me.

Albert reaches into his cloak, grabs a vial, and smashes it on the planks. A thick cloud billows between us. Footfalls race away.

"This isn't over," he says, words trailing.

"David!" I cry, looking everywhere. "Where are you?"

"What do you mean?" his voice says.

Startled because of the disembodied voice, I say, "I don't see you."

"How's this?" My brother walks from the moonbeam shining at my feet. "This is how it works. It's as easy as taking a step. Faerie dust is amazing stuff."

"For sure."

My parents, Rebecca, and Linus gather at the railing, while the sailors hustle to their stations.

"Swim here," my dad says, "and we'll pull you to the deck."

When I hear a fluttering sound behind me, my dad's eyes widen and he points. Something drops on the floorboards.

"To darkness, the Twain rule to bind," my grandpa's voice says.

Unsure, I angle toward him. "For One, the dark power will shatter."

He smiles. "Jonathan, I found an earth faerie door nearby, which leads to the western lands. We must leave at once."

"Grandpa?" my brother says.

"You're David, right? I have much to share with you."

Their hug melts the years dividing them.

Grandpa rests his chin on David's head and peers toward the ship. He raises his hand. "Son."

My dad covers his mouth with a hand. "Dad?"

"I'll come back, William, and explain everything. I promise."

"Jonathan?" Rebecca calls. "You can't leave me!"

I shake my head. "Where one road ends, another begins, so we'll take our own paths. Two colliding worlds need caretakers. The Circle of Valstan has become the Wardens of the Worlds."

She covers her mouth, eyes wide with shock. Linus wraps his arm around her waist, pulling her close. They raise hands to say goodbye.

I offer an uncertain farewell wave.

CHAPTER 29

SHADOW AND DEATH

I wipe tears away.

"No time to cry," Grandpa says, tugging on my arm.

"An invasion force is out there," David says, pointing. "We may never see our family and friends again."

A stiff wind catches in the *Spring Herald*'s sails, driving it into the harbor.

I set my hand on my brother's shoulder. "He's right. Time is the Dark Lord's advantage."

David's eyes flit to him, then back. "Okay, let's go."

We chase him down the wharf, turn to sprint along the dock, and halt at a high cliff face.

Grandpa points and says, "We must climb over this rock outcropping to a ledge. Beyond it, a trail hugs the shoreline to a pirate cave outside the harbor."

David casts me an unsure glance.

"Follow me. I have experience scaling walls." But the part when

I fell into the pool back home, I keep to myself. Handholds grab firm. Satisfied, I swing my leg up for a foothold and bring up the second leg. They stay behind me at even intervals.

Slow foot after slow foot, we ascend the cliff. I can't stand to look at the wharf, getting smaller every minute. Last time I was up high, I fell off Fléogan's back, hurtled toward the ground, and almost lost my life. He's not here to save me. Arduous work ticks away the minutes. At last, I round the crest, roll onto the lumpy haversack, and relax for a moment. I cycle my hands a few times to relieve the muscle burn.

The sun just crosses over the eastern hill, burning a hole in fog layers. A new day will dawn on Bormágo—its destiny in the balance.

David pops up, turns, and sits next to me. "What fun! Now I see why Linus loves the outdoors so much."

"One more to go," I say, pointing to Grandpa.

He flutters up and over the edge and lands beside us. "You boys are strong," he says.

My brother grins at me.

"Chores," I say, returning a wry smile.

Grandpa points toward the shoreline. "The trail leads to the cave."

I can guess what he sees, but it's only a wear patch. One slip and I'd fall into the harbor, wasting precious time. We traverse the steep slope to the bottom as if we're goats. I labor along the shadowy path, but before a bend, distant voices root me to the spot.

I hold out my palm. "T'Anakim and too many for us three." We climb off the trail, but find nowhere to hide. The invaders will see us.

"What'll we do?" David says, turning to me. "There's no moon, so we're powerless against them."

"Not at all, you for sure. Halfers should understand how to activate their inborn abilities. Remember your ability with the moonbeams? How do generations of birds know where to migrate or fish find their birthplace?"

My brother chews his bottom lip. "El'Darios tells them?"

"Right."

"El'd—? Boys, myths are no good now. Some say he'll never come back."

David frowns. "Some say."

"Fog will hide us," I say. "This cool atmosphere has enough moisture."

"I wonder if earth faerie abilities include air?"

Grandpa nods. "It does. What do you have in mind?"

"Watch." When he takes a step, the air shimmers, and he disappears. "Look up there," David's disembodied voice says, noting the towering clouds above us. A whirlwind spins, sputters, and dies. The second try lasts a hair longer.

"We're waiting."

"Hold on, I'm learning this."

"No time for training exercises."

Without warning, violent updrafts race toward the huge thunderhead, coalescing into a vortex. Grandpa and I cling to each other for support. The cloud funnels to the earth and fills our locale with thick fog.

Indiscriminate voices pause at the bend. The pleasing T'Anakim language contrasts with what I remember about their foreboding features. Someone barks orders as jangling gear passes in the whiteout. Breath sticks in my throat.

The enemy squad leaves within a heart-stopping moment. I start when David steps from the air into the natural world.

"These powers are wonderful, because I'm able to move in close without them seeing me."

"Where did you go?"

"Up and down, in seconds."

"Lucky you, the exhilaration must amaze even the most audacious."

"Jealous?"

"No. Maybe I can disperse this fog with a little heat."

"Boys, hurry," Grandpa says, "the Thinning is fading fast."

From my inner being, I sense an energy stream to my extremities. Wispy flames emit from my fingertips then extinguish. I chew my lower lip.

"You must do better than that," he says with a chuckle. "Abilities link to your emotions. For instance, excitement, passion, revulsion, and anger go with fire. Water connects to serenity, boldness, and passion."

"Passion twice?"

"It's a potent emotion, found in both faerie kinds. You have a double portion."

"And me?" David says.

"What did you feel before you created the updrafts?"

"Desperation."

"The unbridled wind. Earth relates to shock and fear. Moon to trust, sadness, and hope."

"Ugh, sadness and hope."

"The two are always in tension."

I concentrate on my revulsion for the dark lords. Soon, I'll meet them and they'll pay. What they did to Grandma, Grandpa, and Dad long ago sets my jaw tight. A burning sensation wells from my stomach and brims into my hands. Tall flames leap from my fingers, but more concentration disciplines them into fire jets. David's eyes grow wide, but Grandpa's show fear.

Heat pulls the fog upward, clearing the shoreline in minutes. We scuttle along the path, eager to put distance between us and the invasion party.

"You boys need training, if you want to improve your skills," Grandpa says. "I can help you."

"Great," I say.

"But first, the cave lies around the far bend. Hurry! Only minutes left until we're stuck here another day."

My feet ache from pounding the tumbled rock. Behind me, longboats stream from the harbor to the shore.

"Watch your footing," I say.

Our path slopes to the shoreline where waves, over time, had carved a cave. I duck inside to find low tide left small puddles with shells dotting the floor. Algae coats the walls, and the fishy smell infuses into the air.

I start when T'Anakim shouts bellow from a longboat thirty yards from shore. How did we miss them?

"The fog didn't clear everywhere. Hurry, I'll hold them off, you boys find it at the back."

We duck inside while he blocks the cave mouth.

I fish out the vial of mixed faerie dust and sprinkle it on my brother, Grandpa, and me. David feels the wall for the door.

"I don't think you'll discover it that way," I say.

"Then how?"

I pull out the map. "Watch and learn. By water, moon, fire, and earth, reveal your inward worth. Show the trails of earth, be not stingy with wanting dearth." Green dots speckle the parchment. I slide my finger along the shoreline to the cave. No dot. "Where is it?"

David snatches it from my hand. "Let me see. Hmm, not showing on this piece of garbage."

Why doesn't it show this door? Unless it's a new one. Grandpa couldn't have created it, because he's of the fire kind.

"Earth faerie doors are the easiest to find. Can't you sense it, David?"

"What nonsense. Wait a minute, right there." A green dot shows on the map inside the cave.

"Temperamental," I say.

"Quick, go through it," Grandpa barks.

David wrenches the door open, spilling a blue glow on the floor, and jumps into a hallway.

Strange red light reflects off the puddles. Small flames flicker in Grandpa's palm.

"We can go," I say, "so leave them."

He glances my direction and the evil glint in his eye sends a shiver along my spine. Fires grow, twisting from his fingers. Two horrified men halt at the cave mouth. Palms out, Grandpa's hands shoot multicolored flame into their bodies. His magic reduces their corpses into a burning heap. The acrid smell stings my nose.

I grab David's arm. "Come on, the door's fading." We disappear through it into a long hallway. Puffy clouds race overhead through a turquoise sky. At the hallway's end, a grassy door sets into the sky. David pushes the hatch open and we enter a wide field bordered with trees. This daytime doesn't match the hallway. The perfect camouflage for a place no one should find. After sunset, the Thinning well at hand.

"Where are we?" David says, two birds fluttering between us.

"Not Tuatha Dé Danann, for sure," I say.

"How do you know?"

"Not weird enough." I uncork the vial and sprinkle dust on us. "In case it wore off you."

The hatch opens, and Grandpa struggles from the hallway and rolls onto the tall grass.

I step toward him. "Was killing those men necessary?"

He wags his head. "They were charging at me, so what else could I do? Sometimes the split-second decision is the right one."

David appears skeptical. "You can run."

Grandpa ignores his words. "Come on, boys, the Dark Door isn't far."

The hatch lies beneath a sprawling chestnut tree, which borders a wide meadow. Something shadowy black stands in the middle. As I step closer, the light breeze carries a pungent smell.

I pinch my nose. "Gross."

It is everything my dream showed me and more: shadowed, cold, and saps any joy.

"Ready?" I say to David.

His shock turns to resolve. "Yes."

"First, the armor Grandpa saved for us."

"Oh yes?" he says with obvious confusion.

I pull from the haversack piece after piece and lay them on the ground.

"Ah yes, the craftsmanship of the fire faerie lord, boys."

Must be forgetful.

We look masterful in well-sized Other World armor set with yellow tassets gleaming in the sun.

I hug my grandpa tight. Regret pangs my conscience. How could I doubt his judgment? "Thank you for everything."

He smiles, dropping his gaze. A tear forms in his eye.

I swallow hard. My fingers hover over the knob, dingy with untold years of disuse. I grip it. Coldness warms in a second.

"It accepts you," Grandpa says.

I twist and pull it open. Stale air clings to the ancient wood. Beyond lies profound darkness. When I step inside, I shield my face from a chilly bluster. David steps in, easing the sense of aloneness growing in me.

He closes it. We take in a deep breath. Together, we inch forward until light falls before us when the door opens again. Grandpa eases through it.

What the heck?

I didn't realize he wanted or *could* come with us. Confidence energizes me. Now three will stand united against the Dark Lord.

THE END

If you liked this novel, please consider leaving a review wherever you bought it.

APPENDIX: PRONUNCIATION KEY

Aráza	Uh-RAY-za	
Bormaǵian	Bor-MAY-zh-ian	Zh as in vision
Bormágo	Bor-MAY-go	
Edalein	ED-uh-line	
Eshbanáchbor	Esh-ben-AK-boar	
Fléogan	FLAY-o-gan	
Gamólig	Ga-MAH-lig	
Haelan-magi	HAY-lan-Ma-jai	
Hazo	HAY-zo	
Helon	HEE-lun	
Hôzai	Who-zai, or Hō-zai	
Nasz	Nă-z	
Ochran	Ok-rin	
Sarsekim	SAR-se-kim	
Siany	Shee-AH-nee	
Soarián	Soar-ee-AN	
T'Anak	TA-nak	
T'Anakim	TA-na-kim	
Tirás	TEAR-ahs	
Tuatha Dé Danann	Too-AH-THA Day Dăn-an	

The adventure continues in

WARDENS OF
THE WORLDS

BOOK II

THE LORD OF FORTRESSES